STRIKE
THE
SPARK

JEFFREY POOLE

Jeffrey Poole's Epic Fantasy Books
Bakkian Chronicles:
The Prophecy
Insurrection
Amulet of Aria
Disneyland Debacle (short story)
Winter Wonderland (short story)

Tales of Lentari
Lost City
Something Wyverian This Way Comes
A Portal for Your Thoughts
Thoughts for a Portal
Wizard in the Woods
Close Encounters of the Magical Kind
The Hunt for Red Oskorlisk (short story)
May the Fang be With You (Pirates trilogy #1)
The Hammer is Strong with This One (Pirates #2)
These are Not the Stones You're Looking For (Pirates #3)
Blast from the Past

Dragons of Andela
Harness the Fire
Strike the Spark
Crash the Thunder

Mysteries by J.M. Poole
The Corgi Case Files Series
18 delightful cozy mystery novels featuring corgi
sleuths, Sherlock and Watson

STRIKE
THE
SPARK

Dragons of Andela, Book 2

JEFFREY POOLE

Secret Staircase Books

Strike the Spark
Published by Secret Staircase Books, an imprint of
Columbine Publishing Group, LLC
PO Box 416, Angel Fire, NM 87710

Book layout and design by Secret Staircase Books
First Secret Staircase paperback edition: March, 2025
First Secret Staircase e-book edition: March, 2025

* * *

Publisher's Cataloging-in-Publication Data

Poole, Jeffrey
Strike the Spark / by Jeffrey Poole.
p. cm.
ISBN 978-1649142078 (paperback)
ISBN 978-1649142085 (e-book)

1. Andela (Fictitious location)—Fiction. 2. Epic fantasy fiction 3.
Dragons and mythical creatures—Fiction. I. Title

Dragons of Andela : Book 2.
Strike the Spark
Poole, Jeffrey, Dragons of Andela epic fantasy series.

BISAC : FICTION / Fantasy/Epic.

813/.54

For Giliane —

I'm really not too sure how I got so lucky. Thank you for being at my side! I'm the luckiest man on Earth!

ACKNOWLEDGMENTS

This time around, the story went a lot more smoothly for me. It might have something to do with the world and the character backstories already being in place. But, like with any book I write, a list of thanks are always needed.

First up is my wife, Giliane. She patiently listens as I spout ideas, and gives me her honest reaction on whether or not they should ever see the light of day. I'm also eternally grateful for my Posse, who beta reads my stories and lets me know where I've strayed, what sounds good (or bad) and so on. They are: Louise, Jason, Michelle, Yuliya, Wendy, Carol, Diane, Caryl, and others I'm probably forgetting from my Posse. Without them, I'd be a mess. :)

Finally, I'd like to extend my thanks to the readers, for giving my books a chance when there are literally hundreds of thousands to choose from. Thanks for being there, guys! It means the world!

J.

TABLE OF CONTENTS

Chapter 1 - Cael

Flying uncharacteristically low for their species, four sleek reptilian forms streaked above the sea, oftentimes coming so close to the surface that the splashing waves left seawater dripping from their abdomens. That might be because the fifth member of their gathering wasn't flying, but *swimming*. Many times, the winged dragons would notice their aquatic companion swimming in circles beneath them, demonstrating that she was more than capable of maintaining the speed their leader had set.

Green, slitted eyes shifted to the red dragon flying at the front of the formation. While he had known this particular cousin from Blaze for only a short time, he had been surprised to discover just how quickly he had given his trust to her. It might have something to do with the fact that Zeira had been able to break him out of the block of ice *he* had been imprisoned in.

"We'll meet again soon," the yellow Spark dragon quietly

vowed. "I don't care who you are, or where you go. You *will* answer for locking me in that slab."

"Did you say something?" a deep, rumbling voice asked.

Skellig looked left. There, less than twenty feet away, was a dragon even larger than himself. His new friend from the northern ice fields was looking at him with a questioning glance on his pale face. Gocri had said he was a Glacier dragon and that his home was comfortably beneath the ice.

Skellig grunted once. "Don't pay any attention to me. I'm just talking to myself."

"Discovered much?"

The Spark dragon let out an audible snort. "No. I was just thinking."

"Oh? About what?"

A heavily treed island suddenly loomed in front of them, forcing the companions to flap their wings to gain some altitude. Nuri simply veered around the land mass, as though it was no more inconvenient than discovering a twig had fallen across their path in the woods.

Skellig made a circular gesture with his claw. "This. This entire excursion. If someone had told me several weeks ago that I'd be accompanying four fellow dragons on a mission to unseat a maniacal biped who was intent on destroying our world, I would have accused you all of flying too close to the sun."

Gocri snorted. "I have been having similar thoughts."

"Do you think this will work?" Skellig asked, lowering his voice. "Flying to a human village?"

"If that is where Miss Jerica says we need to go, then *that* is where we need to go. Don't you agree?"

"I do, only ..."

"Never thought you'd be trusting a human this much?" Gocri answered, giving him a friendly smile. "That would make two of us."

Three, a voice said, in their heads.

Skellig looked down at the surface of the water. Nuri was there, looking up at the two of them.

"You, too?" the Spark dragon asked.

The water dragon nodded. "Aye. No regrets, though. I've

made some fine new friends, and have willingly fought side by side with you. If we are unsuccessful in our endeavors, and this is our last excursion together, then I will die a happy valthan."

"Your sentiment is returned," Gocri said.

"Thank you. Skellig?"

"Right there with you."

"Would the three of you like to be alone?" a new voice asked. The question could easily be construed as derision, but the mirth behind the voice said otherwise.

Turning, Skellig saw that their largest companion was now flying beside them. This dragon was unlike any species he had ever encountered in his extensive travels. Giant, gray wings easily dwarfed his own. Tendrils of wispy smoke seemingly trailed off their friend's wings after every stroke, and if he was not mistaken, he was certain if he stared long enough, then he'd be able to see *through* Sifula's body.

"What?" the vapor dragon wanted to know. "Why are you staring at me like that?"

Skellig shook his head. "No reason, Sif. I was just thinking that this is turning out to be a fabulous day."

"I'm not so sure about that," Sif confessed. "We're going to a human settlement. Jerica's home, I believe."

"Is that a problem?" Skellig wanted to know.

"I don't believe so, no."

"Then, why the concern?"

"Jerica's home is this settlement, so they'll welcome her with open arms," Sif answered.

"It'd be no different if we ended up going to any of our home regions," Skellig told their friend. "Speaking of which, where is yours? I don't recall you ever telling us."

"My home region?" Sifula asked. "Didn't I ever tell you?"

"You've never told it to me," Zeira's voice said, proving the fire dragon was eavesdropping on their conversation.

"We call it Rokke."

"Rock?" Skellig repeated. "Is that so?"

"Yes. Rokke is located on a small island near the southern tip of what I've heard you describe as the third continent. As you can imagine, there aren't many of us."

"Do you have a mother?" Zeira asked. "Father?"

"Of course I do," Sifula laughed. "How else do you think I came to be? Although, to be fair, I didn't really know either of them. I can't even tell you what their names are or whether or not they're still alive."

Surprised, Skellig shook his head. That certainly wasn't how it was in Gale. His mother was still in contact with him on a daily basis, and if Zeira hadn't been able to rescue him from the ice, he was certain his mother would have launched a full-fledged rescue attempt by now.

"My mother is like that, too," Nuri admitted, picking up his thoughts. "I don't think I'm in contact as frequently as you are, Skellig, and I know she lives nowhere close to me, but yet …"

"Yet … *what*?" Skellig asked, curious.

"I don't think she's far enough away," Nuri decided.

Gocri and Skellig both snorted with amusement.

"Do you not get along with your mother?" Zeira asked.

"Of course. She's pleasant enough to be around, only …"

"… she gets too involved in your life," Skellig finished for her.

Nuri nodded. "Yes, that's exactly right. Sometimes, I cannot help but think if she lived close enough, she'd be managing my life, right down to the smallest detail. What waters are safe, who I should be seeing, why haven't I laid my clutch yet, and on and on."

"Come now," Zeira scolded. "Having your mother care for you so strongly cannot be a bad thing."

"I certainly don't think so," Jerica's voice agreed.

The four flyers shifted their gaze to Nuri's back. A young human girl of fifteen sat there, completely at ease with the simple fact that she was in the presence of five dragons.

"How long do humans stay with their parents?" Skellig wanted to know.

Jerica sighed. "Oh, gosh, I don't know. Boys will typically leave to make their way in the world on their sixteenth birthday."

"And the females?" Zeira asked. "When we met, you insinuated your sire wished you to be mated with a suitable male?"

Jerica sighed again. "That was his wish, aye. It still is, as a matter of fact."

"But, it isn't your wish?" Nuri asked, confused.

"No, it isn't. Why are you confused?"

"Is it not the desire of all human girls to be paired off with a suitable male?" the valthan asked.

"There's more to life than cooking, having babies, and tending home," Jerica grumbled. "And now you're starting to sound like my father."

"I'm sorry, Jerica. I must confess, my knowledge of humans is limited. In fact, everything I thought I knew was wrong, and everything I now know to be true is because of you."

"Same," Skellig said, lifting a claw.

"That goes for me, too," Zeira added.

"I think we can all say we're learning from one another," Sifula said, earning nods from everyone present. "That's the beauty of our friendship. We ... Nuri, what is it? I can sense your alarm."

"Humans!"

Skellig felt their human's heartbeat increase. Jerica was interested!

"Of course I'm interested, Skellig. Wouldn't you be, if we encountered another Spark dragon? I ... Skellig, are you all right? Your pulse has quickened and I do believe you're close to hyperventilating."

"I most certainly am not."

"You are," Sifula insisted. "I can feel your alarm, too, and I can also sense you're fighting to suppress it. Was it something about another Spark dragon?"

"There it is again," Gocri announced. "I can feel it, too."

"Would you all please just drop it?" Skellig pleaded. "I'm sorry my thoughts were led astray. Better?"

"Are you?" Zeira challenged.

Skellig returned her imploring look. "Am I *what*?"

"Better, of course."

"Oh. Sure."

"You don't sound like it," Zeira accused.

"There is nothing to concern you," Skellig offered.

"You are my friend, Skellig. If there's something that's bothering you, especially about another Spark, then I share your concern."

"As do I," Sifula added.

Gocri grunted, by way of an answer.

"It's appreciated," Skellig said. "If something arises, I'll let you know. For now, let's just concentrate on what Nuri has seen."

"What *has* Nuri seen?" Gocri wanted to know. "Nuri, who do you see?"

"What."

"Hmm?"

"What," Nuri repeated. "I see a *what*, not a *who*."

Skellig snorted with amusement. "All right. What do you see?"

"One of the humans' floating vessels. Nets are being cast into the water, but they'll only collect the tiniest of fish. If you want the really large specimens, Jerica, then you need to tell your fellow humans to drop their nets considerably deeper."

Jerica stood up on Nuri's back and scanned the horizon. "Where are the boats? I don't see anything."

"You're looking in the wrong direction, Miss Jerica," Gocri said, from within her head. "You're looking west. You need to look northeast."

"We're heading west? How is that even possible? Nuri, are we going the wrong way?"

"Only because I have located your village and I am skirting around it. From a distance, of course."

"You said you saw some of our boats," Jerica insisted. "Where?"

"Look to your right. No, too far. There. Do you see them now?"

"No."

"You're a kairie," Zeira telepathically reminded her. "You can tap into our senses, as we can tap into yours. All five of us have spotted the vessels. And, for the record, there are two of them. Any one of us would be willing to share our sight, myself included. Remember, all you have to do is ... ah! I can feel your presence. You're sharing my eyesight. Do you see them now?"

"I do, yes. One of our larger galleons, and nearby, a fisherman's skiff. Oh, do you see the figurehead on the front of the galleon? You'll find it on the smaller boat, too, but near the stern. It's from Cael! We're here!"

"Why is there a wooden fish on the front of the boat?" Sifula asked, directing her question to their valthan friend. "I don't recognize the shape. What species is it?"

"It's one of the largest fish in our waters," Jerica explained, "and is very difficult to catch. It's a fast swimmer and somehow manages to avoid most of our nets. It's nowhere near as fast as you, Nuri, but it …"

"Does it have a long, curved snout?" Skellig interrupted. "Like a horn?"

"Yes."

"And a ridge of scales running the length of its back?" the Spark dragon continued.

"Yes."

"This symbol," the ice dragon began, "it represents your colony?"

Jerica nodded. "Yes. It's a picture of a sturgeon. It's what Cael is known for."

"How are they going to feel about the five of us appearing?" Zeira suddenly asked.

"They're humans," Jerica answered. "They're much smaller than you and they're always afraid of being eaten by something larger than themselves. How do you think they're going to respond? We have to handle this carefully. I don't want to cause any unnecessary panic."

Skellig shrugged. "That's a fair point. How should we do this? Zeira, do you have any thoughts?"

"Look at the north shore," Zeira instructed. "I see humans massing near the water. Because of us, perhaps? Very well. Jerica is right. We don't want to frighten anyone, so we'll split up. Nuri, you take the sea. Don't let the boats approach until it can be determined if they come in peace."

"Understood. Would someone take Jerica from my back, please?"

Skellig dipped low and gently snatched the human from

their aquatic friend's back. The instant she was gone, Nuri slipped beneath the surface and was gone. Skellig then turned possession of the human over to Zeira.

Jerica turned to give Skellig a scrutinizing look.

"Possession of the human? Really?"

"No offense is intended," Skellig insisted. "When you're with any of us, that particular dragon assumes responsibility for your safety. I was simply pointing out that responsibility has now been given to Zeira."

"Which I am fine with," the fire dragon added.

"Oh. I'm sorry for thinking otherwise, Skellig."

"No offense is taken, I assure you. Zeira, what would you have me do?"

Zeira pointed up. "Circle overhead. Stay out of sight. You're Jerica's backup, should she need it."

"Acknowledged."

"Sifula," Zeira continued. "Have you ever changed form while flying?"

"No, I've never tried. What would you like me to do?"

"You're accompanying Jerica. I don't want anything to befall her, and would feel much better if one of us was physically with her. So, with that in mind, would you care to assume human form again?"

"Of course. Skellig, stay there. I'm going to try changing to a human, while airborne. If things don't go my way, then I'm counting on you to keep me from falling."

"We'll do better than that, Sif," Gocri said. "Skellig, I'm dropping below you. Stay there. Zeira, below me, if you would."

"I see what you're doing," Sifula exclaimed. "You make me proud to be a part of this group. Thank you."

With the three flyers lined up over each other, in case one of them should fail to catch Sif if she fell, Skellig nodded his readiness. Sif moved her much larger body above Skellig's, and began to change. Her mass shrank, her wings decreased until they disappeared, and moments later, a clone of Jerica was falling through the air. Thankfully, she didn't have far to fall. Skellig and Jerica were less than ten feet away, and as soon as the Spark dragon noticed the transformation, he moved closer still.

"Hello again, Sif," Skellig heard Jerica say. "If we were visiting any other village, I'd say that would work fine. However, we're going to be visiting *my* home. I daresay people there would freak out if they saw two of me."

"Oh. That's a valid point. Very well, a moment, please. What about this form?"

By the time Skellig shifted his gaze from Jerica to Sif, the transformation was complete. She was definitely getting better at assuming new species! Gazing at the person Sif had chosen to emulate, he couldn't help but frown.

"What is it?" Sif asked, noticing her companion's expression. "Do you not approve?"

A very young human girl, sitting side-by-side next to Jerica, looked confused.

"Er, how old do you think that form is?" Skellig asked.

The little girl shrugged. "How old? I don't know. I'm not that familiar with human anatomy."

Jerica finally turned to see for herself what the person sitting behind her looked like. She stared, open-mouthed, for a few moments, before laughing out loud.

"Skellig called it. Sif, you might want to make yourself a little older. A girl aged seven will look out of place without her parents."

Sif pointed at Jerica. "What about you? Could you not be the girl's mother?"

"We'd have to look … related," Jerica decided.

"And we don't now?" Sif asked.

"Sif, your human form has green hair."

"Oh. I take it that's a color not typically found on humans? Are you sure?"

"When have you ever seen a human with green hair?" Zeira asked.

"I was just trying to switch forms as quickly as possible," Sif complained. "I wasn't thinking about specifics. Fine, you don't like green? What color should I make it?"

"Miss Jerica's hair is golden," Gocri pointed out. "I admittedly am no expert, but I would think mother and daughter should have the same hair color, wouldn't you agree?"

Right before their eyes, Sif's hair rippled, as if an unseen wind was blowing on it. Then, a split second later, the hair turned blonde.

"Much better," Gocri decided.

Sif nodded. "Good. Now, shall we? The longer we wait, the more humans we're going to have to deal with. There must be at least two dozen of them out there, waiting for us."

"The number is closer to four dozen," Zeira reported, as she gently lowered Jerica and Sif to the ground. "Sif is right. There's no time to wait. Jerica and Sif, you two are off to the village. Gocri, you and I are on perimeter."

"What are we supposed to be doing?" the Glacier dragon asked.

"We're patrolling the skies," Zeira explained, as they flew away. "We make sure nothing surprises us."

Skellig eyed the two bipeds. "I'll be nearby, should you require assistance."

Jerica gave him a wide smile. "Thank you. I appreciate all the concern, but this is my home. The only thing to fear here is being caught outdoors after sunset, or in a house that hasn't been powdered."

Not having a clue what that meant, Skellig lifted off, quickly rising past the tree tops and disappearing into the clouds. Then, he watched Zeira and Gocri bank to the west and disappear into the clouds. Adjusting his own altitude so that he wouldn't be seen, he slowly circled the human settlement. Regulating his breathing, and adjusting his course to use the high-altitude air current he had just discovered, Skellig opened his senses and sought out Jerica. Almost immediately, a picture formed in his mind. He was looking through her eyes, and listening to everything that was happening around her with her human ears.

Skellig snorted. If someone had told him several fortnights ago that he'd not only be traveling with a mismatched group of fellow dragons, but a female tribesman as well, then he would have laughed off the accusation. However, not only had he become close friends with the other dragons, he actually trusted his life with any of the four. And the tribesman ... er, the human? Nothing could have prepared him for how that one small girl had changed his life. His abilities, which had been a comforting constant his entire life, had changed the instant Jerica had come into physical contact with him. What was the result? Well, he was surprised to learn he was just as eager as everyone else to see what special hybrid power he had temporarily been given.

"I heard that," Jerica's voice softly exclaimed, in his mind. "Do you really mean that?"

"I will deny it under the most heinous of tortures," Skellig answered, "but yes."

"Don't worry," Jerica's voice said. "Your secret is safe with me."

A series of images flashed through Skellig's brain before he had a chance to get his thoughts under control.

"Are you all right?" Jerica asked hesitantly. "You're trying very hard to keep something hidden from me. Well, hidden from all of us, actually. Are you in some sort of danger?"

"My apologies," Skellig told the human. "Those thoughts were not meant for you. They're a problem I must deal with, on my own."

"But, you aren't on your own, are you?" Jerica countered.

Skellig grunted, but didn't answer.

"When you're ready to talk about it, we're here to listen," Jerica said.

"Seconded," Sif's voice added.

Skellig sighed. "Appreciated, but this isn't the time. Jerica, Sif, be on your guard. A group of humans is approaching you."

Sharing Jerica's senses, he felt her nervousness and fear, but thankfully, it only lasted for a few moments. Suddenly, Jerica's heartbeat exploded with activity and her pulse skyrocketed. Concerned she was under attack, Skellig prepared to drop from the sky, fangs bared.

"Hold," Sif softly murmured. "Jerica knows these humans. In fact, I think the one she is embracing may be her sire."

Indeed? Zeira chimed in. *Are we sure?*

"Well, I'm no expert in human biology," Sif began, "but it has been my experience that, when humans leak water on their face, that they are generally happy, isn't that so?"

What if she's legitimately sad? Gocri wanted to know.

Or emotionally distraught? Nuri's voice suggested.

"Oh, I didn't think about that," Sif admitted. "Perhaps I should … wait. They're pulling apart from one another. Jerica, are you well? Skellig, perhaps you could check on her?"

"I'm accessing her senses right now," Skellig announced. The young human's thoughts and emotions mixed with his own. Neither Gocri nor Nuri were right. Jerica wasn't crying tears of sadness, or distress. It was happiness! He could feel an overabundance of joy coursing through their human's veins. "She's all right. She's feeling happiness."

"I'm all right, guys," Jerica softly told her dragon companions. "Come, let me introduce you to someone. Father, this is Sifula, a, uh, new friend. Sif, I'd like to present my father, Hallis."

Watching through Jerica's eyes, as he was sure the rest of his gathering was doing, Skellig observed a larger, older biped with a thick torso and more facial hair than he had ever seen on a human, look down at Sif's small human form.

"And who 'ave we 'ere? Sifula, is it? What are ye doin' out by yerself, girl? Where are yer parents?"

I wasn't expecting to find my father so soon, Jerica thought. *Help me! What do I tell him?*

"The truth," four dragons answered, in unison.

To make matters worse, Sif looked expectantly at Jerica, as though she was her legal guardian.

"Some help you are," Jerica grumped, as she glared at the girl Sif had become. "Father, can we please go home? It'll be easier to explain about Sifula there, in private."

Skellig, watching the proceedings through Jerica's eyes, saw Hallis turn to his fellow bipeds and give them a curt wave. "There be nothin' to see here, lads. Thought it might o' been somethin' else. All's well. Go home. And you, girl, I be so damn glad to see ye! We thought ye dead, J! Are ye still travelin' wit' that big, scaly beastie?"

"Her name is Zeira, and I won't talk about her in the open like this. How's Mother?"

"Shoulda seen her, lass. When I told her that not only

were ye alive, but now in the company of a dragon … hoo boy. She accused me of makin' up stories. As for yer friend … Sif, was it? I still wanna know how come a wee lass such as yerself be allowed to wander the woods? Ain't ye afraid of monsters, girl?"

"Aren't," Jerica corrected, "and no, she's not."

Skellig grunted with amusement as Jerica let out an excited squeal.

What is it? Do you see something that offers you amusement?

No, it's not that, Jerica explained. *I can see my father's forge. We live above his workshop. I'm home, Skellig!*

We are very happy for you, Zeira told her. *Please remember, we are here for a reason. We must locate the wizard you told us about.*

Mage, Jerica corrected. *This won't be easy.*

Why? Gocri wanted to know.

Because he *was the one who initiated the lottery. He's the one who came up with the idea of human sacrifices in the first place.*

I would imagine that did not go over well with your gathering.

Village, Jerica corrected.

The door to her father's shop was less than two feet away. Before she could knock, or reach for the handle, the door suddenly flew open. Her mother, Nyssa, stood before her. Wide-eyed, mouth agape, she stared at Jerica for a few moments before physically yanking her inside and wrapping her arms about her.

"Jerica! Thank the Maker! We feared the worst! When Hallis claimed to have spoken with you, I thought he was making it up. I'm so sorry!"

Her mother collapsed into tears and sobbed into her shoulder.

"Told ye I wasn' lyin'," Hallis grumped, but not before wiping away a tear of his own.

"You must tell me everything!" Nyssa insisted. "I want to know how you escaped! How did you get off that cursed altar? I want to know … I want to know who this girl is. Hello, there. Who do we have here?"

Jerica turned to Sif and held out a hand. "Come on in. We need to close the door. Are you guys still with me?"

I am, Skellig confirmed.

We all are, Zeira announced.

"Of course we're with you," Nyssa exclaimed. "Such a strange thing to say."

Jerica glanced around the darkened interior of the forge and gave her father a questioning look.

"Why are the forges out? It's the middle of the day!"

"Been worried 'bout you, girl," her father confessed. "Baron 'lowed me a few days to grieve. If there be one person who felt worse than me after seeing what happened to ye, it'd be him. He and Theresa have been by every day, checkin' on us."

"If the baron was against the lottery, then why did he allow it?" Jerica angrily protested. "He's the baron! He could have stood up to Doolan."

Who is barren? Skellig heard Zeira ask. *And who is Theresa?*

"I was wondering about that, too," Sif quietly murmured.

"What was that?" Hallis asked, overhearing.

Jerica headed for the closest work station, pulled out the stool, and sank down on it. Her parents followed suit moments later. Sif moved close to Jerica's side and was content to watch the proceedings standing up.

Taking a deep breath, Jerica looked at her father first. "Dad, do you remember when you spoke with Zeira?"

Hallis nodded. Her mother looked at her husband and shook her head. "Who?"

"Zeira," Hallis repeated. "That's the name of the scaled beastie who rescued J from that blasted altar. I have half a mind to tear that thing down and burn it to …"

"Dad!" Jerica interrupted. "Let me finish, would you?"

"Sorry, J."

"As I was saying, Zeira turned out to be one of five different dragons who have banded together to try and stop the damage Thunder King is wreaking on our world."

"Don't say his name!" her mother hissed at her. "He's too powerful!"

No, he's not, Gocri argued. *He's just a maniacal human who thrives on instilling fear in others. Trust me, the first chance I get I'm tossing him down the hatch.*

Jerica giggled the same time that Sif snorted.

"What?" Hallis demanded. "What be so funny?"

Shrugging, Jerica smiled at her father. "All right, here we go. Gocri just said he was going to toss the Thunder King down the hatch at the earliest opportunity that he could."

"Who is Gocri?" her mother wanted to know.

"He's a Glacier dragon," Sif automatically answered.

"And how do you know that?" Nyssa wanted to know as she looked over at Sif.

"Because, she's one of the five dragons," Jerica explained. "This is Sifula. We call her Sif, for short. Sif is a vapor dragon, and just so happens to have the ability to change forms. None of them wanted me coming in here, unprotected."

"You be a dragon?" Hallis asked, as he turned to Sif. Unable to hide his skepticism, Jerica's father shook his head. "Prove it."

Sif's form turned grey, then expanded until she was the same mass as Hallis. A few moments later, Jerica's father was looking at his twin.

"What manner of devilry be this?"

"There's no devilry involved," Jerica said, placing a hand on her father's. "Sif has been a tremendous help to us with her transforming abilities."

"Help wit' what, exactly?" Hallis asked.

Suddenly, there was a knock on the door. Hallis gasped with alarm and immediately shoved Jerica behind him.

"They be not gettin' her again," he vowed. He snatched one of the heavy metal hammers off a nearby tool rack and gripped it tightly in his hand.

There are two humans on the other side of that door," Skellig reported. *One male, and one female. The female appears to be in distress.*

"Distress?" Jerica repeated, forgetting that her parents didn't know she was in telepathic contact with her dragon companions. "What makes you say that?"

Eyes are leaking water, breaths are shallow, and her attire is in disarray.

Hallis strode over to the door and yanked it open, as though he expected to see an armed detail preparing to storm into his shop.

"Theresa! What be you doin' here, girl? And ye brought the baron! What gives?"

While Theresa rushed forward, to throw her arms around her father, Jerica silently explained who the girl was, and the role her husband, the baron, played in their village of Cael.

He's the king of the village, Nuri decided.

That's not what she said, Zeira argued. *He leads the Gathering, yes, but he still answers to another.*

About to correct them, Jerica shook her head. It was close enough.

"There are dragon sightings!" Theresa exclaimed fearfully. "Is it not enough that they've taken Jerica? Is it not enough that three different girls have lost their lives? What more could those terrible reptiles want from us?"

"T, there be nothin' t' worry 'bout. Look …"

"Of course there's something to worry about!" Jerica's sister argued. "You lost a daughter! I lost my little sister! How is that not something to be angry and upset about?"

Baron Vyler Dartmoor, a short, stout man in his early thirties, leaned forward to tap his wife on the shoulder.

"Not now, Vyler. As I was saying, that infernal lottery needs to be abolished! No other family should go through what we did. No other family should … Vyler, what is it? Why do you keep tapping me on the shoulder?"

Hallis and Nyssa stepped aside, revealing that which Vyler had already spotted.

"Jerica!" Theresa cried, lunging forward to encompass her sister in an embrace. "What …? Where …? How did you get here?"

"With help," Jerica answered, as she held her sister in a death grip.

"From Zeira," Hallis grinned.

Theresa broke the hug and stared at her father. "Who?"

"Would everyone please sit down?" Jerica said, as she began to pace. "This will be easier to explain with everyone as relaxed as they can get. There. Vyler, it's good to see you again."

"Not anywhere near as good as seeing you alive," Vyler quipped, giving her a warm smile. "I would like to know how you came out of this ordeal with your life."

Jerica shrugged. "I had help."

"From Zeira?" her sister asked.

"That's one of them, yes," Jerica said, nodding.

Pleased he knew something his wife and other daughter didn't, Hallis leaned back on his stool and grinned at his wife.

"Zeira is a dragon," Jerica said, using as nonchalant of a voice as she could. "She's the one who started this quest we're on, so she's essentially the one in charge."

"What quest is this?" Vyler wanted to know.

"To defeat the Thunder King and save our world," Sif said.

Everyone turned to the young child.

"What? Did I say that wrong?"

"Who's the girl?" Vyler wanted to know.

"Oh, this is Sifula. Sif, you've met my parents. This is my sister and her husband."

Skellig watched as Sif nodded at the two newcomers.

"Sif is a vapor dragon," Jerica continued. "She's currently in human form as my ... Skellig, what did you call it?"

Backup.

"Right. Backup. Sif is my backup, in case I run into trouble."

"And who is Skellig?" her mother wanted to know.

"Our backup," Sif explained.

Nyssa shook her head. "No, I mean, *what* is he? Another dragon?"

"Oh, sorry. Yes, he's another dragon. In fact, he's a Spark dragon."

Hallis blinked a few times. "Spark? What be that?"

Lightning, Skellig said, sighing.

The corners of Jerica's mouth curved upward. "Lightning."

"He said somethin', didn't he?" Hallis said, scowling.

"That's exactly what he said," Jerica confirmed. "Lightning, although I get the impression he rolled his eyes."

I had hoped your sire was familiar with my species.

"He hoped you, Dad, knew what species he was."

"Don' know much 'bout dragons, sorry. Skellig, I thank

ye for protectin' my Jerica."

It's my pleasure. However, she really doesn't need any protecting from us. In fact, she's going to be in demand.

Hallis shook his head after Jerica relayed what was said. "I don' know what that means, neither."

"*Either,*" Jerica corrected. "It means I can bond with any dragon, regardless of region."

Her parents, sister, and brother-in-law stared at her with shock written all over their features.

"It's true," Sif added. "She's been able to splice our powers together and get quite a variety of results. My personal favorite is flaming poo boulders."

Why did you have to tell them that? Zeira groaned.

Jerica giggled. "As we keep telling you, you have nothing to be ashamed about, Zeira."

You haven't introduced all of us yet, came Nuri's voice.

High above their heads, Skellig was nodding as he passed over their location.

Precisely. If you would have us trust your human companions, they need to be informed about us. All of us.

Jerica's smile melted away. "You're right. I'm sorry. All right, here we …"

"You're sorry about what?" Theresa inquired.

"I haven't done a good job introducing everyone. So, we'll take it from the top. I told you about Zeira. She's a fire dragon, from Blaze."

"Where be that?" Hallis immediately asked.

"Please save all your questions until the end," Jerica said, giving her father a smile. "Next up is Skellig, a Spark dragon from Gale." Vyler opened his mouth, to presumably ask a question, when Theresa elbowed him in the stomach. "Then, we have Nuri, a valthan. She's a water dragon, and is, quite literally, the fastest creature you've ever seen. Also, probably the nicest."

Awww, thank you, Jerica, Nuri said, as she continued her underwater patrols.

Hey! Zeira protested. *I consider myself friendly!*

"You all are, all right?" Jerica quickly amended. She looked at her family and shrugged. "They're all quite nice, but can be touchy. Now, after Nuri, there's Gocri. He's a Glacier dragon. He lives under the ice, in Bliss."

I'm impressed you remembered, Miss Jerica.

"Of course I'm going to remember, Gocri," Jerica said, without looking at anyone in particular. "You're all my friends, and I am interested in all of you. Lastly, and I'm always wondering about that part, we have the one member of my friends you've met. This is Sifula, of Rokke, who has one of the neatest abilities I've ever seen. Did I get everyone?"

"I want to meet you lot," Hallis suddenly announced.

Jerica studied her father for a few moments before turning to her home village's leader. "Vyler, is there someplace you can think of where a meeting like that can happen? In private?"

"Hmm, we have the village gathering rooms," the baron responded, thinking hard. "That can easily hold several hundred people."

"We're not meeting people," Jerica reminded him, "but dragons. Big ones. There's no way for them to fit inside a building."

"I can," Sif announced, raising a hand.

"Besides you, that is," Jerica amended, giving the small girl a smile.

Theresa tapped her husband on the shoulder. "My dear, what about Kinzler's Point?"

Vyler looked back at Jerica and nodded. "You did say one of your number is a water dragon, right?"

"I did, yes. Kinzler's Point? How would that work? We'd be seen!"

"I don't know if you've noticed or not," Theresa began, "but it snowed last night. The water is frozen over. All the boats are currently moored, or have sought warmer waters."

"Oh. Mom and Dad, would you like to meet some dragons?"

Thirty minutes later, their small group was at the waterfront, at the most northern point in all of Cael. There was a small bay here, but it, too, was frozen over. Jerica stared at the snow on the ground and turned, incredulously, to her parents.

"When did it snow? There was nothing on the ground

when I left, and there wasn't any expected snow for at least another fortnight! What happened?"

Hallis and Nyssa both spread their hands. "Who knows?" her father answered. "It was such a surprise that we asked Doolan, only he don't know, neither."

"*Didn't*, and why am I not surprised?" Jerica muttered.

"This? This is the human we must ask for help?" Sifula asked.

A look of alarm passed over Hallis' face. "Ye will not get anywhere near 'im, is that understood?"

"We really don't have a choice," Jerica confessed.

"Explain that," Hallis ordered, growing angry.

At that exact time, the surface of the ice in front of them … exploded. Huge chunks of ice and snow flew out in all directions. Several of the larger pieces angled toward their small group, but before anyone could react, something huge and grey appeared, and swatted the chunks of ice aside, as though they were no more bothersome than a few flies.

"What the bloomin' hell?" Hallis cried.

The rest of the humans, with the exception of Jerica, whirled around and immediately took a few steps back. Standing behind them, in her much larger, *natural* form was Sifula. However, she wasn't looking at them, but at the tiny, frozen bay, except it wasn't necessarily frozen any more, since Nuri had rammed the sheet of ice. The valthan was slowly pulling herself out of the water, while Sifula wandered over to watch. As Nuri neared, a yellow speck appeared in the sky and grew steadily larger. Skellig touched down next to Sif and, together, they watched their aquatic friend approach.

"Did that hurt?" Skellig wanted to know. "Are you injured?"

"From frozen water?" Nuri asked, shaking her head. "No. I'm fine. Besides, I barely hit it, and the ice sheet wasn't that thick."

Two more dots appeared, one white and one red.

"Ah, here she comes," Jerica observed. "And, she's bringing Gocri with her."

Once the five dragons were standing together, Jerica turned to face her parents, only there was no one present.

Her parents, her sister, and her brother-in-law were nowhere to be seen.

"Oh, come on! Didn't I tell you that they are all harmless? Well, I mean, not all dragons are, but these ones are safe. They're my friends! Dad, Mom, Theresa—where are you?"

"How can ye feel safe 'round so many beasties?" her father's voice asked, as his grizzled head appeared from behind a tree. "Ye have to admit, girl, that seein' five o' them, in the flesh, is not for the faint o' heart."

Zeira approached first. She lowered herself to the ground and waited for Hallis to approach.

"Sire of Jerica, you have nothing to fear from us." Hallis slowly appeared, followed somewhat reluctantly by his wife. Theresa and Vyler appeared next, from behind the next tree over. Zeira's eyes shifted to Theresa's. "You. You are littermates with Jerica? I bid you greeting."

"I don't think I've ever seen, heard, or read about so many dragons being in such close proximity to one another," Vyler was saying, as he was the first to recover from the initial shock of their appearance. "How have you overcome disapparating? Aren't you worried you'll stray too far from your home regions?"

All five dragons immediately pointed at Jerica.

"Not as long as she's with us," Zeira said.

"What does my daughter have to do with any o' this?" Hallis wanted to know.

Zeira turned to look at their rider. "Jerica, did you not tell him about your abilities?"

"Well, I started to. I don't recall finishing."

"What abilities?" Hallis asked.

"Magic doesn't run in our family," Nyssa pointed out.

"It does with me," Jerica confirmed. She unbuckled the leather bracer she wore on her right arm and held it up. "See this?"

"What are we looking at?" Theresa wanted to know. "Your bracer? It was mother's, wasn't it? Oh, wait. You got tattooed? I was never allowed to have one. Why does she get to have one and I never did?"

"Because," Gocri rumbled, causing all conversations to

come to an abrupt stop, "that is no tattoo, young human. That happens to be the mark of a dragon rider."

Hallis whirled on her. "J, be that true? Ye be one o' them riders?"

"There's more," Skellig added. "What you say about the regions, and our fear of fading, is true. We are susceptible to dying if we venture outside our regions, just like you. However, since we have all bonded with Jerica, none of us are in any danger now. Jerica is what the kai call *kairie*."

"Y-you?" Vyler sputtered. "You're the one he wants? Do you have any idea how much danger you're in?"

"The fabled rider you were talking about?" Theresa asked, frowning. "You're talking about my sister? You will NOT be turning her in, thank you very much."

In the blink of an eye, the dragons had surrounded the small party of humans and had commenced growling.

"You will hereby swear, here and now," Skellig began, as he locked eyes on the village's leader, "that you will personally see to it no harm befalls Jerica, or her family."

Vyler swallowed nervously. "I love my wife, and I will never let anything happen to her or her family. Ever. You have my word, dragon. In fact, I pledge my support to your quest. If there's anything I can do, then I humbly beseech you to allow me to help."

"There is something you can do," Zeira began. After a few moments, she looked at Jerica and nodded. "Perhaps you should tell him?"

"Tell me what?" Vyler asked.

"We need Doolan's help," Jerica said, letting out a massive sigh.

"That won't be easy," Vyler groaned. "He's a Guild Mage. He may be old, and decrepit, but he doesn't answer to me and never listens to my advice."

"That's not what we needed to hear," Jerica said, shaking her head.

"Well, he's getting better," Theresa admitted. "Wasn't he receptive to your idea to bring Cerebus here?"

"Only because of how much Cael could use the gold," Vyler said. "Think about it. Do you know how many jobs it'll mean for our people?"

"What is a Cerebus?" Skellig wanted to know.

"I was curious about that, too," Sif admitted.

"It's the largest mechanical device to ever be constructed," Vyler boasted. "You see, we applied to be one of the next locations for Cerebus to visit, and I'm quite pleased to say we were selected."

"*What* is Cerebus?" Jerica asked. "Can anyone tell me?"

"It's this great, big digger," Nyssa explained. "To hear Theresa describe it, you'd think it was larger than our entire village."

"It is," Jerica moaned. She faced Vyler. "Baron, does Cerebus dig mines?"

"On a large scale," Vyler said, nodding. "Think of all the good it'll do for Cael! I've never been prouder to serve the people."

"He's so happy," Theresa exclaimed, giving her husband a warm smile. Unfortunately, it didn't last long. She caught sight of Jerica's horrified expression and her smile quickly melted into a frown. "What is it? Is there something you're not telling us?"

"This machine is going to dig a hole," Jerica began, using a hushed voice. "It'll strip away all vegetation and drive away all animals. But, more importantly, since we knew we had to come here, to enlist Doolan's help, and now we find out that Cael is to be the site of the next pit mine ... Vyler, we have to stop it."

"Cael needs the infusion of people, gold, and ... well, jobs," Vyler protested. "Not everyone can make their living on the sea, Jerica. Think of the people. This project ..."

"... will spell the end of our village," Jerica finished.

"You don't know that," Theresa scolded. "There's no need for the theatrics. If you ..."

"You don't understand," Jerica interrupted. "We saw, firsthand, what happened to Ponotoa. The Thunder King deployed Cerebus there, and now nothing is right. These jobs pay less than a bar maid earns. And the mineral they're looking for? If it's found, then they're going to turn it into lethal weapons. No, we cannot let this happen."

"And how do you propose to stop it?" Theresa asked.

"We need Doolan's help," Jerica repeated.

"Ye said that before," Hallis pointed out. "What do ye want him to do?"

"Yes," a new voice wheezed out. "I was rather curious about that myself."

A gaunt figure, no more than skin and bones, appeared. He was wearing the maroon robes and blue belt the Guild of Mages were known for. Long, stringy gray hair, several days' worth of growth on a bony face, and yellowing teeth completed the picture as Cael's one and only mage appeared next to the baron.

"Baron Dartmoor. A pleasure, as always."

"Doolan. What are you doing here?"

"I might ask you the same question, dear boy. Never have I been in such close proximity to a dragon before, let alone five. I sensed I could be of service, so I came to investigate." Two black, beady eyes lit with interest as they landed on Jerica. "Ah, Miss Barille. I am delighted to see you here. You need my help? Well, what can I do for you?"

"Oh, what the heck," Jerica muttered. Steeling herself, she took a deep breath. "If we bring you a goblet, could you make whoever drinks from it more … shall we say, *willing*, to do something we'd like him to do?"

"The power of suggestion," Doolan grinned, showing off his stained yellow teeth. "The ability to control another person is not an easy feat. The spell would have to be incredibly strong, and would undoubtedly need some type of enhancer present in your goblet."

"Something like … jhorium?" Jerica asked.

Doolan blinked twice, which — for him — was the equivalent of shock.

"And how have you come to know of this mineral, my dear child?"

Jerica felt those leering eyeballs staring at her, trying to penetrate her clothing. "I have my sources. So, tell me, is this something you can do?"

A lecherous smile appeared on the mage's face.

"I do believe I can, dear child. What's it worth to you?"

"What do you want in return?" Jerica cautiously asked.

"I know you seek a partner for marriage. You will be my wife."

For once, Jerica relaxed, since she had been able to see that request coming from miles away and had already prepared an answer.

"I can't, I'm afraid." She hooked a thumb at the circle of dragons, all of whom were growling at him. "I have other obligations. There must be something else."

"Very well. One full night with me, then."

"The bloody hell ye will, mage," Hallis growled.

The mage's eyes flashed once, turning completely white. "That is my price."

Chapter 2 - Mine

How many times do I have to go over this, Skellig? There's absolutely no way I'm going to agree to Doolan's demand. And yes, before you protest, I know it's only for one night. How can you not understand what he wants from me?"

"What *does* he want from you?" Skellig asked, confused. "A night of your time? How can that be a bad thing if it accomplishes our goal?"

"Skellig, he wants me to … to …"

"I'll handle this," Hallis interjected. "Listen, ye scaly beastie, my little girl is no' gonna be alone wit' that smarmy gromper for any amount o' time. Should he ever try, ye have my blessing to bite 'im in half. Do ye understand?"

"If the two of them are ever alone," Skellig said, as he slowly translated the scenario into something he could understand, "that would be considered bad, and … a personal attack on Jerica?"

Hallis grinned. "Aye, now ye got it. And if ye see 'im try?

What are ye gonna do?"

"Bite him in half," Gocri answered. "Skellig, this really isn't difficult to comprehend. This human, Doolan, is much too old to be considered a viable mate for Miss Jerica. But, that doesn't deter *him*. He has indicated his desire, and even though it would accomplish our goal, we must not allow it to happen. Can you understand that?"

Skellig nodded. "Perfectly. Why didn't someone just say so from the beginning?"

"They did say so, from the beginning," Zeira argued.

"You didn't understand what they meant at first, either," Skellig insisted.

"True, but I *am* a female, and the thought of an unsuitable mate does not appeal. Once I realized what was being suggested, I knew we had to find another option."

"There *are* no other options," Sif added. "We have a problem."

"Yes, we do," Zeira agreed. "Skellig, do you see it yet? How close are we?"

Skellig lifted his gaze from the ground, where he had been watching Jerica and her human family, and looked east. Jerica's home region was Terra, and her village, while on a peninsula stretching even farther north, was flanked by heavily treed hills and mountains. To the east, where the topography changed somewhat to allow a small bay to be nestled among the many trees, signs of human interference could already by seen. For starters, a huge swath of trees had been felled. Several large trails — hadn't Jerica called them roads? — could be seen running off in several directions. And there, in a large clearing south of the bay was a growing collection of ... of ...

"Of what?" Nuri wanted to know. "I'm almost there, so if there's something I need to know about, I'd just as soon hear it from you first."

"No, it's nothing dangerous. I think. There are boxes, open crates, and stacks of metal everywhere. And, I can see another shipment on the way."

"Are we too late?" Jerica sobbed. "It sounds like they're already assembling Cerebus."

"I was told Cerebus would take nearly a week to build and prepare," Baron Dartmoor's voice added.

Skellig's gaze shifted back to the group of humans and singled out the young male walking next to Jerica and her sister. This was a human king? Was the Thunder King someone similar? How could one human convey such fear? Why wouldn't the people rise up in rebellion?

"He's a baron," Jerica corrected. "He's not a king, Skellig."

"One of your dragon friends thinks I'm a king?" Vyler quietly asked.

"He doesn't understand the difference between baron and king," Jerica explained.

And I hear you just fine.

"And he hears you just fine," Jerica relayed.

"Using his ears or yours?" Vyler asked. "I haven't quite figured that part out yet. You say they can share your senses? And you share theirs?"

"Mm-hmm. All the time. Why?"

Vyler waved a dismissive hand. "It's strange, that's all. No, I see you frowning. I'm sorry, Jerica. This is all so new to me. It's taking me longer than I'd care to admit to cope with all of it."

"Not nearly as long as it took me," Jerica confided. "I had to ... oh no!"

Thinking Jerica was in peril, Skellig immediately dropped from the sky, where he had been flying in circles, to see for himself what type of foe had to be addressed. In this case, though, it was just Jerica, seeing for herself what was going to happen to her beloved home. Unsure of what to say, Skellig continued his descent and landed next to the kairie and her family.

"We won't let it happen here," the Spark dragon promised.

Jerica approached and wrapped her arms around his front foreleg. "Thank you, Skellig. That means a lot."

"By the Maker!" Nyssa exclaimed, as she saw for herself the extent of what was being assembled. She immediately rounded on her son-in-law. "Vyler, you were all right with them doing this to us?"

"Th-they promised g-gold!" Vyler stammered, as all

angry eyes were leveled at him. "And j-jobs! It's something Cael desperately needs! You have no idea if what happened to the other village ... what was the name of it?"

"Ponotoa," Jerica whispered.

"Right. Ponotoa. You have no idea that whatever happened there will happen here," Vyler insisted.

"He wants jhorium," Zeira announced, alighting next to Skellig. "He's already demonstrated he'll do whatever it takes to get it."

"How does he even know this mineral is here?" Nyssa wanted to know.

Jerica hesitantly lifted her hand. "I can answer that. We were sent here because not only is Doolan here, but so is the jhorium necessary to power the goblet. That's why the Thunder King is sending Cerebus here. He wants it, too."

The strange group of dragons and humans stared at the growing collection of supplies necessary to assemble the gargantuan digger and then eyed each other. After a few moments, all dragon eyes turned to Zeira.

"Well?" Skellig prompted. "How do we proceed?"

Zeira was silent as she considered. "Well, we know we must prevent the destruction that's going to happen should this Cerebus device be assembled. We all saw what will happen if it does, so we need to think of some ideas which could help."

The fire dragon looked expectantly at the others—both dragons and humans—and when no one volunteered any ideas, she sighed.

"All right, let me start. We're dragons. I say we simply destroy the mechanics as they're being built. That'll prevent the construction of this Cerebus device, wouldn't it?"

Vyler shook his head. "That wouldn't work. If you destroy something belonging to the Thunder King, then it'll just be replaced and the number of guards increased. Plus, based on everything I've heard about the man, he'll probably exact some type of punishment on the people here."

"Let him focus his anger on us dragons," Gocri challenged. "We're the ones inflicting the damage. Let him come after us and see how he likes it."

"True," Vyler admitted, "only he won't see it that way. This is our village. The punishments will be levied against *us*. Humans, that is."

"That's out," Zeira decided. "What else? Anyone have anything to add?"

"We drive away the humans responsible for assembling this mechanical beast," Gocri suggested. Before anyone could protest, the Glacier dragon sighed and shook his head. "No deaths. Not one human life would be risked in this venture."

"You want to drive us away without hurting anyone?" Jerica asked, hopeful. "Would that work?"

Zeira, Nuri, and Skellig were shaking their heads.

"If it looks like we dragons are attacking the humans," Skellig carefully began, "then what do you think will happen?"

"Relations with the dragons, while already strained," Vyler said, "would deteriorate. I think the Thunder King might use that as an excuse to target you dragons next."

"Or sic Dym on us," Nuri sighed. "I don't know much about him, but I do know he's not a dragon to cross. If his allegiance is to Thunder King, then we'd best avoid him."

"He's just one dragon," Jerica argued. "There are five of you. Wouldn't all of you be more than a match for him? Besides, Skellig, didn't you tell us Dym is a Spark dragon? One spark couldn't possibly be as dangerous as you've made out."

Skellig immediately growled and shook his head no. "I've seen Dym in action on more than one occasion. He isn't one to be crossed. While I have complete faith in my companions, I would not want to risk any of them."

Gocri grunted once and fell silent.

"It's still a good idea," Zeira pointed out. "All right, who's next? Any other takers?"

Sif perked up. "Couldn't we, well, you know, persuade the Thunder King to dig his mine elsewhere?"

"That would certainly do the trick," Zeira observed, "only none of us knows how to do that."

"I know how to do that," Jerica insisted.

Everyone fell silent.

"Go ahead," Zeira urged. "Let's hear it."

"We use the goblet, of course."

"The one that hasn't been created yet?" Skellig asked, frowning. "Let's not get ahead of ourselves. Until that goblet is created, forcing the mine to move will more than likely not be an option."

"Couldn't we create it now?" Jerica asked.

"You've heard what your wizard will charge," Zeira reminded her.

"Yes, that's true. I'm counting on all of you to find something else that will appease him. So, for argument's sake, let's say we *could* get this goblet crafted. Then, all we'd have to do is …"

"Wait a moment," Hallis interjected. "There be no way he's gettin' anywhere close to ye, girl. I won' allow it."

Jerica smiled at her father. "Thanks, Dad."

"Do you remember what Doolan said?" Vyler suddenly asked.

"About what?" Jerica asked.

"About what he'd need when you asked him whether or not he could create a spell to make it work," Vyler clarified.

Jerica nodded. "I do. He said he'd need some type of …?"

"… enhancer," Zeira finished. "That's when you mentioned jhorium."

"What *is* jhorium, anyway?" Vyler wanted to know.

"It's a special mineral," Zeira explained, "that happens to be imbued with magic. If you get enough of this material together, then magical weapons can be created, no doubt allowing the price to be set so high only a king would be able to afford them."

"This mineral?" Theresa said. "It sounds priceless."

Jerica nodded. "Based on what we've seen the Thunder King do in order to get it, yes, I think it would be."

Skellig pointed at the stacks and stacks of material being assembled that would, in the next few days, be assembled into Cerebus. "Thunder King obviously knows — or suspects — jhorium to be here, in this village. Can we all accept that as fact?"

The humans slowly nodded their heads.

"He knows there's jhorium here," Jerica said, "so our

next task becomes clear: we have to make sure we get it first."

"That's yer plan, girl?" Hallis asked, as he spun his daughter in place to face him. "Find this special mineral first? Then what?"

"Well, to be honest, we haven't gotten that far yet."

"We need to make sure the Thunder King knows it's gone," Zeira announced.

Hallis started nodding. "Ah, of course. If he knows what he wants be no longer here, then he be sendin' his machinery elsewhere, be that whatcher thinkin'?"

Skellig nodded. "It is, but to be clear, we're not sure how to do it."

"Do you know where to find this jhorium?" Theresa asked. "The sooner you get your hands on it, the sooner you can convince *him* it's no longer here. Then, all this will go away. It's perfect! How can we help?"

Zeira and Gocri landed nearby. Sif, at Theresa's request, was currently mimicking her and Jerica's mother. Walking side by side with Nyssa, even Hallis admitted he had difficulties picking out which one was which.

Vyler tapped his sister-in-law on her shoulder. "Jerica, what was the name of that other metal? The opposite?"

Hallis looked interested. "Ye be lookin' fer another metal now?"

Jerica nodded. "That's right! I had forgotten about what Zebulon said. We need to get our hands on some drininite."

"Never heard o' it," Hallis confessed.

"And that goes for everyone else," Jerica glumly reported.

"I certainly haven't," Vyler agreed. "But, oftentimes, there is more than one name associated to things."

"Are you saying this drininite might be called something else?" Theresa asked. "How clever! That's so smart of you to point that out, dear."

The baron beamed with pleasure. Hallis sighed, while Nyssa had to look away.

"Who knows the most about metal?" Jerica asked. "Dad, you're a blacksmith. You haven't heard the name before?"

"I have no idea what it is. Sorry, girl."

Sif turned to Jerica. "Is there anyone we can ask?"

"An elder, perhaps?" Skellig suggested.

Vyler, with his mouth open, paused. He looked at Theresa and shrugged. "How about asking Percival?"

"Who's he?" Zeira wanted to know.

"He's the school master," Jerica answered. "There's another not-so-pleasant fellow for you." She caught sight of the dragons all staring at her, and decided to elucidate. "The children are all afraid of him. He doesn't tolerate speaking out of order, tardiness …"

"… happiness, intelligence, compassion …" Theresa added, with a frown.

"Sounds positively delightful," Nuri decided. She swished her tail back and forth. "Where can we find him?"

Jerica and Theresa looked up at the exact same time. They each noticed and then giggled.

"Well," Jerica began, "he maintains his classes well past the noon hour. He's probably in his school, poring over ways to torture Cael's children during their next lesson."

"I never really cared for him," Theresa admitted.

"I don't think anyone did," Jerica said, nodding. "But, I don't think we'll find anyone who knows more about geology than he does."

"Who gets to be the lucky one to ask him?" Theresa asked.

Jerica pointed at her brother-in-law. "I say the baron should have that honor."

"Me?" Vyler sputtered. "Oh, come on. I liked him just as much as you two. I really think it should be one of you."

"I can do it," Sif volunteered. "I would just need guidance on where to find him."

"Being shown up by a dragon," Theresa scolded, as she gave her husband a sad shake of her head. "Thank you very much, Sif. Jerica knows the way. Sis, you'll show her?"

"All right, all right, I'll do it," Vyler grumped. "I'm not about to subject our guests to Percival's whims."

"Perhaps one of us should accompany you?" Zeira suggested. "Sif, would you?"

"Of course. I assume you don't want me using my natural form?"

Zeira nodded. "Correct. You should be in human form, so …"

"Just a moment," Skellig interrupted. "Perhaps we don't *want* Sif in human form."

"Why not?" Zeira asked.

"You heard the description about this unpleasant human. I think if another biped is present, especially a female one, then it'll just draw the attention of this person."

"Which will be bad," Vyler confirmed. "Very well, I'm curious. What do you have in mind?"

Skellig held out a claw and turned to Zeira. "Do you remember the form Sif took at the seer's suggestion? A species of dragon so small it could fit on Jerica's open palm?"

"The gyre dragon," Jerica recalled, nodding. "You want her to accompany Vyler? Disguised as a teeny, tiny dragon? I really don't think that'd be necessary."

"I can do this," Vyler said, still wearing his frown. He looked up at the sky and noted the sun's position. "I'd better get going before he's done for the day."

"Good luck!" Theresa exclaimed, as she threw her arms around him. "Isn't he the greatest?" she asked, as the baron trudged off, toward the village.

At that time, Zeira, Skellig, and Gocri returned to the air. Nuri dropped through the hole in the ice she had created and disappeared. That left only Sifula, who was already changing her form back to the tiny fist-sized dragon.

"He's just going to talk to his former teacher," Jerica pointed out. "You're making it sound like he's going to take on a dragon single-handedly. Why offer praise for something so trivial?"

"Maybe the human needs to hear it?" Sif suggested.

"I was just giving an example," Jerica said, as she turned to give the vapor dragon a smile.

"Why do you always belittle him?" Theresa asked, as she stomped over to her and then folded her arms across her chest. "He's the *baron*, which means he has a lot of responsibilities."

"You praise him like he's a child," Nyssa pointed out.

"You're taking her side?" Theresa demanded, growing angry.

"No one be accusin' no one else o' anythin'," Hallis proclaimed. "J, stop goin' at yer sister. She be meanin' no harm, do ye, girl?"

"She's just jealous," Theresa declared. "*I* found a good man, and she doesn't have one, so she's trying to find faults with …"

Jerica threw her hands up in despair. "I'm not having this conversation right now. Theresa, if you want to keep babying Vyler, you go right ahead. I won't say another word about it. Skellig, are you still up there?"

Of course.

"Are you keeping an eye on Vyler?"

Of course. He's already inside a structure with a pointed roof and a crenellated tower.

"Oh, good," Jerica said, sighing. "He's already at the schoolhouse. I wonder how …"

Now he's vacating the structure.

"What? That's way too soon. Does he look all right?"

He looks angry, Zeira reported.

"That can't be good," Jerica murmured.

"What is it?" Hallis demanded. Still clutching the hammer from before, he hefted it menacingly. "What is it wit' the folk lately? Has common courtesy flown out the window, like good manners? I have 'alf a mind to thump some common sense into that good fer nothin' …"

Nyssa placed a restraining hand on Hallis' arm and gently pushed the hammer down.

"You'll do nothing of the sort, my dear. We don't know enough about what's going on. My guess is that Percival simply wasn't there. Vyler must have stepped in, realized the school master wasn't there, looked around for a bit and then left."

"But, he was only inside for less than a minute!" Theresa protested.

Not true. He was inside the structure for, by my estimation, four minutes.

"Skellig says Vyler was inside nearly four minutes," Jerica relayed.

Nyssa started patting the air. "Now, let's not jump to conclusions. I'm sure everything is going to work out just fine."

A few minutes later, the baron appeared, walking briskly toward them. Skellig had been right. He didn't look pleased.

Of course I'm right, Skellig insisted. *I know what an angry tribesman looks like. Er, make that an angry human. I'm sorry, Jerica.*

"No offense is taken," the kai assured him.

Vyler joined their group, but before he could say anything, Theresa was there. Tapping his shoulder, she waited until he was looking at her before proceeding.

"Vyler, my love, what did you find out? Percival had stepped out, hadn't he? You went inside, saw that he wasn't there, and then left, didn't you? Isn't that what you did?"

Let the human speak, Skellig instructed.

Jerica held up a hand. "Theresa, just a moment. Vyler, what did you find out?"

Skellig, from his position in the sky, watched as their kai's packmate opened her mouth in what he guessed was going to be an angry retort, but thankfully, Jerica laid a restraining hand on each of her sister's shoulders and held her fast.

"Theresa, now's the time to hold off arguing. I …"

"Well?" Theresa interrupted, as she faced Vyler and ignored Jerica. "What did you find out?"

"He was there," Vyler reported. He leaned against a nearby boulder and shoved his hands in his pockets. "And, just as pleasant as ever."

"He refused to answer you?" Theresa cried, appalled. "What nerve! Why, I should …"

"You'll do nothing," Vyler said, frowning at his wife. "It's all under control, T. As for Percival, well, after I helped him locate a few geology tomes, we found the answer. There's a reason no one has heard of drininite. Turns out it's fairly rare."

Sounds like our luck, Gocri's thought grumbled.

Let him finish, Zeira said.

"How rare?" Jerica was asking.

"As rare as a jewel," Vyler answered. "In fact, that's exactly what drininite looks like in its natural form, a gemstone."

"A jewel, eh?" Hallis retorted. "How the blazes are we gonna get our hands on sumpin' like that?"

"*Something like that*," Jerica corrected, sighing. "And don't you worry. I have faith in my friends."

High overhead, Skellig joined Zeira as they continued to fly in circles above the village of Cael.

"Did you hear that? Jerica said …"

"I know what she said," Zeira interrupted, with a sigh of her own. "I don't suppose you know what gemstone they're talking about, do you?"

Skellig shook his head. He didn't. He focused his attention on their kai and waited for her to take a breath.

Jerica, ask Vyler to describe this jewel. We dragons are quite familiar with most gemstones. Perhaps we've seen one before. Maybe, one of us has one in their possession?

Jerica nodded. "Vyler, what else do we know about this gemstone? Er, what color is it?"

"Black," Vyler immediately answered, having anticipated the question. "Drininite is so black that it absorbs the light. That's what Percival was telling me. You'll know you have a genuine specimen when not even sunlight will be reflected from its many facets. I …"

"I don't think that helps us," Theresa interrupted, with a groan.

Jerica's mother suddenly straightened and a look of wonder appeared on her face.

"What is it, love?" Hallis asked. "Ye know where it is we can find some o' them jewels?"

"I'm not even going to try to correct that one," Jerica sighed, shaking her head.

Hallis stuck his tongue out at his youngest daughter before returning his attention to his wife.

"I believe I do. Vyler, how big does this jewel have to be?"

The baron held up his hands in a helpless shrug. "Who can say? Logic suggests the larger the jewel, the more sensitive it'll be. I really don't know."

"Mother, do you have one of these drininites?"

Vyler held up his hand. "I've actually …"

The baron was ignored.

Hallis crossed his beefy arms over his chest. "If ye have one o' them, then I wanna know how ye got it, 'cause I certainly did no' give it to ye."

Nyssa swatted Hallis on the arm, but not before she blushed. Jerica and Theresa both groaned and looked away.

"Of course not, you silly man. But, I have seen one before, in Cael!"

Everyone perked up, including all five dragons.

"Where?" Zeira asked.

"Who's got it?" Skellig inquired, at the same time.

Nyssa shook her head and turned to Vyler. "Percival does."

"I could've told you that," Vyler grumped.

"That's why he knows so much about them," Jerica sighed. "I *knew* I had seen one before. Mother, you're sure he still has it?"

Nyssa nodded. "I know he does. In fact, I'm the one who set the gem in the book."

She pressed the gemstone into the book? Skellig asked, clearly confused.

"She works with leather," Jerica explained. "If she says she set a black jewel onto a book's cover, then that's what she did."

Theresa suddenly nodded. "Now that you mention it, I think I've seen it, too. Was the book dark brown and had an engraving of a dragon on the cover?"

Vyler nodded. "I love how no one is paying attention to me. I *know* he has one of those jewels you're talking about. It was right there, in front of me. The book you're talking about is his personal journal. I don't think he's going to be giving it up anytime soon, I'm sorry to say."

Actually, I believe he will, Zeira argued. *Quite willingly, I might add.*

"Zeira thinks he can be bartered with," Jerica relayed.

"Balderdash," Vyler argued. "That's his most prized possession."

"Balderdash?" Jerica giggled. "You'd better watch your mouth, Vyler. Zeira, let's hear your idea."

It's easy. We have something I'm quite certain he'll want. Or, more appropriately, he'll want to use.

We do? Skellig asked, baffled.

Since when? Gocri added, equally amazed.

Why am I always the last to know? Nuri complained.

"Ye have somethin' ol' Percival wants?" Hallis asked, as he stared into Jerica's eyes.

"I have no idea what Zeira is talking about," Jerica protested.

"I be talkin' to the dragon. She can hear me, can she not?"

Of course I can.

"She can hear you. Go ahead. I'll relay what she says."

Hallis took a few steps and positioned himself in front of his daughter. "What do ye have in mind, dragon? Er, Zeira?"

Well, it just so happens I have an intact oron stone in my possession.

Skellig's eyes widened. He had forgotten about the seeing stone. Perhaps they could trade the stone for the jewel?

No, we are going to offer the human a chance to use the stone, Zeira corrected. *He doesn't get to keep the stone.*

Ah. Excellent choice.

"How the ruddy hell did the likes of ye end up with one of them stones?" Hallis demanded, once Jerica repeated their conversation.

It wasn't easy, Zeira, Skellig, and Gocri all echoed.

"Are you sure Percival will trade for a chance to use this stone-thing?" Vyler hesitantly asked.

Jerica nodded. "He should. Will you take me back to him? Sif, are you still there?"

An even smaller dragon emerged from Vyler's left breast pocket. It climbed up the baron's shirt and sat on Vyler's shoulder, like a parrot.

I do humbly apologize. I must have dozed off.

"What type of dragon is that?" Jerica wanted to know. "It's even smaller than the gyre one from before!"

I wish I knew, Sif admitted

Skellig descended from the clouds, landed near the humans, and leaned forward to better inspect the tiny reptilian form.

"I did not know we came that small," the Spark dragon decided.

"It be no bigger than a mouse!" Hallis exclaimed. "I really be envious o' you dragons. Think about it. Havin' a magical power. Oh, think o' the fun ye could have."

"Maybe later," Jerica scoffed. "Sif, can you stay like that for a little longer?"

The tiny black dragon nodded.

"Good. We're headed back to Percival's. Zeira, could you come down here? I need you to give me the oron stone for a little while."

Of course.

Twenty minutes later, Vyler, Sif, and now Jerica, were back at the large, circular building with a pointed roof. Just behind the round structure, attached to it, was the oddly mismatched square tower, which rose some thirty feet or so above the top of the school's highest point. And, as Skellig had pointed out, the top of the tower was crenellated. Did Percival feel a need to spy on the town from his perch atop the tower?

Before any of them could knock on the door, it opened, revealing a wrinkled, stern face. Percival was easily old enough to be Jerica's grandfather, and looked the part. His hair was solid gray, his clothes stank of mildew, and his teeth were stained brown, presumably from drinking too much tea.

"Back again, I see. Was I not clear enough the first time? And who do you have with you? Ah, Miss Jerica Barille. I remember you. Humor an old man and just tell me why you're here."

"I could be here, wanting to visit with you," Jerica began. "I …"

"Don't insult my intelligence, young lady. I know what I'm like. No one wants to spend any more time here than necessary. So, take it from me when I say you will have a far better chance of attaining that which you seek if you're simply honest with me."

Jerica took a deep breath. "Very well. I need drininite. I know you have a stone on the cover of your journal. My mother made the cover for it, and she remembers setting it in the carving of a dragon."

The school master's lips thinned as he studied her.

I stand ready to assist, Skellig declared. *I trust this not.*

He may be formidable, especially for someone my size, Jerica said, *but I think he's harmless. In fact, I think I'd even go so far as to say he's lonely.*

Sif's small black head emerged from within her front pocket. The tiny dragon appeared to study the older fellow before shaking its head.

I don't sense any malice from him, Sif reported. *Skellig, hold your position. We are in no danger.*

Skellig grunted once. *Understood.*

Percival turned to Vyler. "You told her?"

"I didn't tell her anything. They already knew you had a black jewel."

"I'm not giving you my jewel," Percival stated, as his mouth twisted into a frown. "I found it, therefore, it's mine! Why would I possibly …?"

The elderly teacher trailed off as Jerica unwrapped the oron stone and held it up. As expected, Percival's eyes widened with disbelief.

"Is that a …?"

"It is," Jerica confirmed, nodding.

"How did you …?"

"It wasn't easy."

"Are you really suggesting …?"

Jerica shook her head, sending her hair tumbling about.

"I'm not, actually. My oron stone is far more valuable than your simple piece of drininite. But, I'll tell you what. In exchange for your drininite, I'll let you use it. You *are* familiar with how an oron stone works, aren't you?"

Percival's expression said it all. Jerica shrugged off the scowl and held the crystal sphere aloft.

"This offer is only valid right now. And I mean, *right* now. If you don't want to trade your drininite for a chance to have one question answered, then so be it. I already told you that we needed a piece. If not yours, then we'll have to keep looking. So, what's it going to be?"

"You must allow me a full day with it," Percival insisted. "After all, my drininite is rare, and …"

Jerica returned the sphere to the cloth bag she had been using to carry the magical talisman, and then quickly tied the ends of the wrapping into a knot.

"Thank you for your time. We won't waste any more of it. Baron, Sif, it would seem we must …"

"All right!" Percival cried. He ducked inside his school and returned several moments later holding something clenched in his fist. After making sure everyone was watching, the school master opened his hand to reveal something nestled in his palm that was darker than the blackest of skies. "You win. Allow me to ask a question, and this is yours."

Well done, Jerica! Zeira's voice exclaimed.

From his position it the sky, Skellig nodded. *Well done, indeed. That's not bad for a human.*

"Give me the stone," Percival ordered.

"The oron stays with me," Jerica pointed out. "You may place a hand on it, but possession of the stone will not change. Now, if you will, please hand me the drininite."

Percival reluctantly dropped the stone into Jerica's hand. Or, he tried to. The small jewel acted as though it hit *something* in midair and ricocheted in the opposite direction. Unsure what had happened, Percival retrieved the stone and tried again to give it to Jerica. As before, the jewel started to fall toward Jerica's hand, but just before it was to make contact, it seemingly flung itself in another direction.

Having an idea what was happening, Jerica placed a hand on Percival's arm to prevent him from trying again.

"Don't worry about the stone. Leave it there, I'll get it after you're done."

"You're just going to leave it on the ground? Fine, whatever. It's your stone now, so you can do with it whatever you please."

Sif? Jerica called out. *Would you retrieve the drininite?*

Of course. I'm on it.

High above their heads, Skellig circled lazily about in the sky. He watched the tiny form Sif had become emerge from the kai's pocket. Proving the vapor dragon was quite adept at becoming familiar with foreign forms, Skellig watched Sif scamper down Jerica's dress and disappear into the thick grass surrounding the building. Ordinarily, he wouldn't have been able to watch such a tiny form from such a distance, but thanks to the extra-long grass field, he could track Sif's movements by watching the blades of grass rustle back and forth.

"May we begin?" Percival demanded.

Jerica blinked a few times and nodded. "My apologies. My mind was … elsewhere. Let's begin."

"I want to hold it."

"It stays with me," Jerica said.

"That wasn't our bargain," Percival insisted.

"I never said I'd let you hold it," Jerica said, shaking her head. "This isn't my stone, so I can't take the chance something will happen to it. But, just to show you that there are no hard feelings, I'll give you some advice which will hopefully allow you to use this stone better."

"You've used it," Percival accused.

"I haven't, no, but one of my friends did." Jerica tapped the side of her head. "Make sure you formulate your question correctly. What I mean is, try not to phrase it in such a way that an unwanted answer could be given."

"What do I have to do?"

Jerica unwrapped the oron once more.

"Lay your hand on it. Close your eyes, try to clear your mind, and when you're ready, ask your question."

Percival placed his arthritic hand on the stone. All present watched the teacher close his eyes and remain still for a few moments. Ten seconds passed in uncomfortable silence before the teacher's eyes opened. A blush formed on Percival's face as he stared at the ground.

"Why can't I find a good woman?"

What did he say? Skellig asked, uncertain he had heard the human correctly.

He wants to know why he, er, can't find a suitable mate, Jerica answered.

I feel your mirth, Skellig said. *What's so funny?*

It's a very personal question, Skellig. I would have thought he'd direct his question at the oron silently.

"What?" Percival snapped.

"You didn't have to ask out loud," Vyler explained. The baron was doing a fantastic job of keeping his face devoid of emotion. "Out of curiosity, did the stone answer you?"

Sullenly, the school teacher nodded.

"Will you tell us what it said?" a female voice asked.

Thinking Jerica was the one who had voiced the question, Percival rounded on her.

"That's a personal question, don't you think? What business is it of yours? Why would you want to know?"

"I don't want to know," Jerica stated. "I never said that I did."

"Well, someone did," Percival snapped. Without another word, he spun on his heel and left.

Sif, were you the one who asked? Skellig asked.

I'm sorry. I was curious.

Did you retrieve the drininite?

About that, Sif began. *I don't know what's going on, but it won't let me touch it. I reach for it, and it skirts along the ground.*

"I've been thinking about that," Jerica admitted. The young girl began walking in circles as she stared at the ground. After a few moments, she picked up several long sticks.

What are you doing? Skellig asked, curious.

"I'm looking for … ah! Here we go. All right, let's see if we can … yes! I have it! I have the drininite. Now, how am I supposed to carry this thing? Vyler, would you do me a favor and hold out your hand?"

Puzzled, the baron did as he was asked. Using the two twigs like a long pair of tweezers, Jerica dropped the black stone onto Vyler's open palm.

"I don't understand what the problem is," Vyler said, as he stared at the black gemstone. "Why couldn't you hold it?"

Jhorium! Zeira exclaimed. *Drininite repels jhorium! If jhorium is the source of magic, then that gem was repelled away from you due to the jhorium in your body.*

Jerica took a few moments to relay what Zeira had said.

"You're a kai!" Vyler exclaimed. "Of course! You couldn't physically touch the gemstone. How clever!"

A commotion to their left caught their attention. Something grey appeared and grew steadily larger. Several moments later, they were looking at Sif's natural form.

"That was why I couldn't touch it. I have magic in me, too."

"I would think all dragons should," Jerica said, shrugging. "Vyler, you're able to hold the drininite?"

"Much to my consternation, yes. I was rather hoping that,

deep down, I had some type of magical ability. It would seem I do not."

"You're still a fabulous baron," Jerica told her brother-in-law. "Don't ever forget that."

"Thanks, J."

Jerica, hurry back. We're all waiting for you.

"We're on our way, Zeira."

Ten minutes later, they were all back at Kinzler's Point.

"So, let's see this blasted jewel," Hallis said. "J, hand it over. I wanna see it."

Jerica turned to Vyler and nodded. Smiling, Cael's baron reached out and dropped the black jewel into Hallis' hand. As with Vyler, the black stone plopped onto Hallis' calloused hand without incident. Holding it between two fingers, Jerica's father held it up to the sun, fully expecting to be able to see light through the gemstone.

They couldn't. The smooth stone was too dark. Plus, there were no signs it was translucent. Hallis held the pebble this way and that, and tried to get the jewel to reflect sunlight. It didn't. Holding it close to his face while the others crowded around him, they could all see that the drininite was the size of a medium pebble, and from all outward appearances, must have been handled by a lapidarist, which meant the small stone had been professionally cut to resemble a jewel. It also explained the high number of facets.

"And you're sure this is what we're looking for?" Nuri asked, as she edged closer to the black gem.

Visible on Hallis' open palm, everyone who hadn't witnessed Jerica's interaction with the drininite gasped with surprise. The black jewel was starting to inch its way across Hallis' hand, heading away from the valthan. Surprised, Nuri hesitated, and, of course, the drininite hesitated as well.

"Don't you see what it's doing?" Jerica said. "It's sensitive to magic. Dragons are pretty much the embodiment of magic, so there's no way they're going to be able to touch the drininite. Well, maybe if it was in a bag, or something. Still, they'd have to have a firm hold on it, or at the first chance it gets, it'll fire itself out of there."

Hallis held the jewel aloft, which suggested that he was

ready to allow someone else to take a closer look. When no one said anything, Gocri shifted his weight to his other leg and leaned forward, intent on taking the jewel from the biped's hand. Unfortunately, the gemstone zipped away from Jerica's father and threatened to become lost on the grassy field, except it was nimbly plucked out of the air by a figure who seemingly materialized out of nowhere.

"Doolan!" Jerica cried, as she whirled to face the mage. "What are you …? Umm, you're holding my gem."

"This belongs to you, does it?" Doolan asked, as he brought the jewel up to his wrinkled face for a closer inspection. "I hope you didn't pay much for it, my dear. This is a jewel? It looks like a polished river stone. What stone is it, if you don't mind me asking?"

The smarmy mage leveled a lecherous smile at the girl and took a few steps toward her. Hallis instantly placed himself in front of Jerica and held out a hand.

"I'll be havin' that. It's a gift to my Jerica. Black onyx."

"Black onyx, eh? I'm sorry to say you've been swindled, my dear Hallis," Doolan crooned. "I have several specimens, and this is nothing like mine."

"Then, I'll be havin' words with that blasted salesman. Do ye mind?"

"Not at all." Doolan's long, bony fingers opened and allowed Hallis to retrieve the jewel.

"What are you doing here?" Nyssa asked.

"I'm just checking on dear Jerica," Doolan replied. "Perhaps she has an answer for me? Call off your dragons. I come in peace."

"Then leave in peace," Hallis ordered. "It'll be a cold day in …"

"I'm still considering all options," Jerica hastily informed the mage. "Thank you so much for checking up on me. Umm, my dragon companions have been known to be a bit testy, so I'd suggest you stay clear of them."

Doolan bowed low. "Of course. I can't wait to … that is, I look forward to conducting our business together."

"I haven't agreed to it," Jerica said, frowning.

If possible, Doolan's lecherous smile grew even wider.

"May I offer a compromise?"

Skellig squinted his eyes as he studied his companions. The humans were clearly taken aback, although he would happily make the unpleasant human lunch.

A growl formed, deep within his chest. It was loud enough to attract the elderly male human's attention.

"Now, just calm down, dragon," Doolan said, as he patted the air. "Hear me out. I may have a solution to your predicament."

Skellig took a single step and lowered his head until he and the human were at eye level.

"Speak quickly, biped."

Doolan nodded, and turned to Jerica. "I looked in on your problem. I believe I have another solution, one which both our parties will find acceptable."

"If it has nuthin' to do wit' my daughter, then let's hear it," Hallis ordered.

"Let's call it … *an exchange*. I give you information that will help you fulfill your quest for the jhorium to overcome the Thunder King, and you? Your company will procure something for me. Really, now, I can't believe I didn't think of this sooner." Doolan edged closer to Gocri and companionably rested a hip against one of the Glacier dragon's three-foot talons. "Trust me when I say you'll want to hear me out."

It was Gocri's turn to lower his head and stare at the human mage.

"Have I given any indication I was fond of you?" he rumbled. "Have I not made it clear that I intend to chomp you in half if you so much as threaten Jerica, or any other human she cares about?"

Jerica turned to look up at the ice dragon. "Aww, thank you! That's sweet!"

The tiniest of smiles appeared on Gocri's face. It vanished, though, as he turned to look at the mage once more.

"You have precisely three seconds to move away from me, or so help me, I'll squish you flat."

Doolan couldn't move fast enough. Once he had put a couple dozen feet between himself and the group of (growling) dragons, he patted the air once more.

"Again, it would behoove you to hear me out."

Jerica waved a dismissive hand. "Fine. You have something to say? Let's hear it. I make no promises that I'll take you up on anything you offer."

"Fair enough. Now, with regards to your mission, you won't be successful, I'm sorry to say, until you add your final member."

All five dragons perked up.

"What final member?" Zeira asked.

"He's lying," Skellig accused.

"We need another?" Zeira echoed, as she looked at her fellow dragons. "How could you possibly know that?"

Doolan bowed low. "Well, I am a senior member of the Guild of Mages, my dear dragon. I do know a thing or two."

Skellig let out an irritated snort, releasing electrical arcs from his wing talons. "You're making this up. It's not appreciated."

Doolan sighed. "Fine. I don't normally do this outside my shop, but I will for you. That's how much I want to be able to work with you."

The mage closed his eyes and fell silent.

"What's he doing?" Zeira wanted to know.

Theresa took Vyler's hand and gasped. "I've seen him do one of these before. They're …"

"… creepy?" Hallis suggested, after she trailed off.

"… unnecessary?" Nyssa asked.

"… staged?" Skellig said.

"… unsettling," Theresa decided. "He's placing himself into a trance. It's how he can make his predictions."

Doolan's eyes opened, but his pupils had disappeared, making his eyes appear solid white.

"He fears you." The mage's voice was flat, expressionless.

"What's going on?" Nuri asked. "I have no idea what's happening here."

"Hush," Zeira scolded.

Jerica hesitantly cleared her throat. "Er, Doolan, are you talking to me?"

"Yes. He fears you."

"What's goin' on, J?" Hallis whispered.

"*Why* does he fear me?" Jerica asked.

"He fears you," the mage continued, using an eerily monotone voice, "and he fears this party more than anything. He fears what you can become."

Gocri snorted once and tapped Skellig on his shoulder. "Is the maniacal biped referring to us?"

"Hush," Skellig scolded.

"Hmmph," Gocri grunted.

"Your party of seven must *never* be allowed to come together."

"Seven?" Jerica repeated. "Is this what you were talking about before? There's only six of us. Me and five dragons."

"The final dragon must never be allowed to join."

"Can it be any dragon?" Skellig asked. "Or is there one in particular?"

"You'll find him slumbering beneath the roots."

Skellig shared a look with the rest of his companions. "Huh? Our newest member is sleeping under a tree?"

Doolan suddenly let out a violent sneeze. His hat flew off his head. When he stooped to retrieve it, everyone could see the mage's eyes had reverted back to normal. The mage noticed everyone staring at him and bowed once. "Pardon me. It would appear I have allergies."

"I assume ye be done wit' yer trance?" Hallis asked, unimpressed.

"Oh, is that what I was doing? Well, if it was, then yes, that's all I've got, I'm afraid. I hope you were taking notes, my dear boy, because I have no recollection of what happened or what was said."

"You mentioned the sixth dragon," Jerica said, frowning. "Which tree are we supposed to find him under? Or her, I guess. What species of dragon is he, or she?"

"Didn't you hear me, my dear sweet girl?" Doolan asked, holding up his wrinkled, bony hands. "I have no idea what I said. If I told you something you need to do, then I would suggest you do it. Premonitions are not something I'm fond of, and I don't do it often, but I haven't been wrong yet. Now, do we have a deal? I gave you my services willingly. May I assume you'll procure that which I seek?'"

"And what is it ye be seekin'?" Hallis demanded.

"Four scales from your newest companion."

"We don't even know what type of dragon he will be!" Skellig protested. "What use could they be to you? Unless ... of course! I should have known."

"Should have known *what*?" Jerica asked.

Skellig pointed a sharp, pointed talon at Doolan. "Don't you see? He already knows what kind of dragon needs to join our group. You, out with it. Who are we looking for?"

Doolan shrugged. "Oh, didn't I tell you? If you want your quest to succeed, and I suspect you do, then you're going to have to find yourselves a sol."

Chapter 3 - Surprise

All right, the human mage is gone," Zeira reported. "Now, would someone care to explain to me why you four all let out a groan at the same time? What is a soul dragon? Does anyone know? I have to admit that I'm not familiar with that species. Then again, it really isn't too surprising. There would appear to be a lot of species I've never encountered."

"It is a *sol* dragon," Skellig glumly reported. "S-O-L."

"I guess it could be worse," Jerica was saying, after watching Doolan disappear around the bend. "A sol dragon? He — or she — sounds nice! I wonder what we ... Skellig, Gocri what is it? Why do the two of you have that look on your faces?"

"Not him," Skellig moaned.

"Maybe there's another?" Gocri asked.

"You know there isn't," Skellig argued. "He's the only one left."

"Who?" Zeira wanted to know. "Have I heard of this

dragon? And are they male or female?"

"Male," Gocri answered. "His name is Othos."

"I'm not familiar with him," Nuri admitted. "Would someone please elaborate?"

"Seconded," Zeira added.

"Othos," Skellig began, taking a deep breath, "is probably, without a doubt, the oldest dragon I am aware of."

Gocri held up a muscular foreleg. "For me as well."

Zeira shrugged. "So, he's old. That shouldn't make any difference, should it?"

Skellig shook his head. "No, it doesn't. Have you really never heard of Othos the Just?"

"Othos the Just?" Nuri repeated. "He has a title?"

"When you've lived that long," Gocri added, "you can give yourself whatever title you want. For us, he's Othos the Strong."

"I'm surprised I've never heard of him," Zeira said, looking helplessly at her companions.

"You're young," Gocri reminded her. "Othos the Strong. We are to seek a genesis. Incredible."

"A genesis?" Nuri repeated. "Is that what his species is called?"

"A genesis," Skellig whispered. "Ooo, I had forgotten about that." He glanced at Zeira and noted the blank expression. "The genesians are the oldest classification of dragons, having witnessed the birth of this universe. Only a few species can call themselves that. Othos is one of them."

"I'm surprised I'm not familiar with the term *genesis*," Nuri complained.

"What about *celestial*?" Gocri asked. "That's the classification we call him in Bliss."

A gasp of alarm sounded from the water. "A celestial? We're going to look for a *celestial*?"

Gocri turned to look at the water. "You know the term?"

"Yes, thank you."

"Excuse me?" Jerica asked, raising her voice.

Five dragons looked down at the small group of five humans.

"I'm sorry," Zeira apologized. "It was rude to ignore you.

Do you have a question?"

"I do," Jerica said, nodding. "What species is this Othos fellow?"

Skellig saw that Zeira looked expectantly at him. He glanced at Gocri, but the Glacier dragon was apparently locked in some type of silent debate with Nuri.

"Sol."

"Sol?" Jerica repeated, confused. "Yes, I heard you say that before. What is …? Wait. Isn't that another name for …?"

"The sun," Skellig confirmed. "Othos is a sun dragon. As far as I'm aware, he is the last of the celestials."

Their kai's face fell. "Oh, how sad."

"Sols are an ancient species," Gocri added. "They are also the largest known dragons."

"Bigger than you lot?" Hallis asked, amazed. "Er, dare I ask, how big are they?"

Skellig lowered himself to the ground and held out his claw. "You, human, could easily sit in my open palm."

"I can see that," Hallis said, nodding.

"And you've seen how big Sifula's natural form is?" Skellig asked.

"We have," Vyler confirmed. "She assumed her natural form just before Doolan caught the drininite jewel."

Skellig nodded. "That's right. Now, in that same vein, several of *us* could easily fit on the palm of a sol dragon, including Sif."

"They're that big?" Jerica asked, incredulous.

"Othos is the largest dragon who has ever flown," Gocri said. "I'm told it was truly a sight to see."

"I can't believe we have to find Othos," Skellig was saying, more to himself than anyone.

"How did he catch it?" Hallis asked.

Skellig's head jerked up. "What was that?"

Jerica laid a hand on her father's shoulder. "What did you say?"

"How did he catch it?" Hallis asked again.

Skellig turned to Jerica's sire and cocked his head. "I don't understand the question. Are you referring to your magician?

He's a human, so I would say … with his appendage?"

"He be our mage," Hallis stated.

Jerica shrugged. "So?"

Nyssa giggled. "I think what my husband is trying to ask is, if that black jewel is repelled by magic, why would someone who uses magic on a daily basis be able to hold it?"

Hallis nodded. "That's right. What she said."

Jerica frowned and looked at Zeira. "That's actually a good question. How was he able to do it?"

Zeira shrugged. "I cannot say. There must be more we don't know about that jewel."

"Jerica?" Nyssa called out. "What are your plans? Are you returning with your dragon friends?"

"Yes. They need me, Mother. We have to track down this … this … *sun* dragon, and if this one is anything like the others, it's going to be a challenge to free him."

"He isn't imprisoned," Skellig argued.

"That's good to know," Zeira said, sighing. "Wait. *How* do we know that?"

The Spark dragon held up a claw. "Well …"

"Well, *what*?" Nuri asked.

"He's sleeping," Skellig said.

"And he hasn't been seen in over two thousand years," Gocri added.

Skellig turned to Sif. "You mentioned you're older than the rest of us. Have you ever met Othos?"

Sif's grey head swung back and forth. "Met? No. Seen from a distance? Yes."

"And?" Zeira prompted. "Am I going to like this?"

Sif looked at Skellig and nodded. "It's as he said. Sol dragons are an ancient, powerful species of dragon. Nearly ninety percent of all dragons can say that the sol is a distant ancestor."

"Why hasn' he been seen in thousands o' years?" Hallis asked.

"I'm sorry, I don't have an answer," Skellig said.

"I do," Sif said.

Everyone turned to the vapor dragon.

"Some of us won't like the answer. The reason is humans,

I'm afraid. Humans have long craved power. You might be surprised to learn that some parts of a dragon have magical abilities. Therefore, for those humans who *don't* have power, or *can't* use magic, then possessing something, *anything* from a dragon can only elevate your chance of being able to either perform magic, or perhaps cast a spell."

Vyler snapped his fingers. "So, *that* is why Doolan wants those scales? He knows they have some sort of magical property. Do we have any idea what he has planned?"

"The only thing I know, now, is that he apparently wasn't born with a natural magical ability," Jerica said. "He must have to use spells and powder, like everyone else who can't perform magic."

Skellig turned to Sif. "What do you think? Can we trust what that human said?"

"He's said a lot of things I don't trust," Sif replied. "Perhaps you could narrow it down?"

"About where to find Othos," Skellig said. "Sleeping under some tree? Well, at least it goes with what I know about him."

"Which is …?" Nuri asked.

"I've heard he sleeps until he's needed."

Jerica held up a hand. "Umm, are trees bigger where you dragons live?"

Zeira shrugged. "Not really. Why?"

"You're telling me this sun dragon is so massive that any of you could fit on Othos's hand?"

Skellig nodded. "That is correct. Oh. I see where you're going with this."

"What is it?" Zeira asked. "What's going on?"

Skellig turned to their leader. "Zeira, if we are to believe what the human mage said, and that Othos slumbers underneath the roots of a tree, well, either there's one massive mountain with a single tree on top, or …?"

"… or Doolan isn't referring to a normal tree," Zeira finished. "I hadn't thought of that. Could it mean anything else?"

"It's something we're going to have to figure out," Skellig decided. "We should find a place to nest for the night."

"What about right here?" Vyler suggested. "I'll see to it that no one bothers you. It's the least I can do."

"Thank you," Jerica said. The teenager hugged her parents. "I'll let you know when we figure this out."

"If ye figure it out, ye mean," Hallis corrected.

Jerica shook her head. "I have faith in my friends. Together, we're quite formidable. This is just a riddle, I'm sure."

"It's so very good to see you alive and well," Vyler said again, as he gave the girl a quick hug. He turned to see all five dragons staring at him. "I was going to suggest you make sure she's safe, but I can see I don't need to. The five of you are already doing an admirable job of protecting her. Thank you."

Nyssa stepped forward, holding on to Hallis' hand. "Yes, thank you. If it wasn't for you, our Jerica would be dead by now. You have my eternal thanks."

"An' mine," Hallis confirmed. "Need anythin'? Ye have but to ask."

Once the six of them were alone, Skellig turned to Nuri and grinned.

"What?" the valthan inquired.

"Any way we could get fish for dinner tonight? Ever since all that talk about sturgeon, I find myself craving some seafood."

Nuri nodded. "It would be my pleasure."

Hours later, long after the sun had set, Skellig found himself with some free time and decided to indulge in his one and only foible: nocturnal flying. All dragons, by definition, could see in the dark just as easily as during the day. For him, a flight through the nighttime sky, when the only light came from the thousands of twinkling stars above his head, had become his absolute favorite pastime. With his wings at full extension, he did a quick check that they were functioning properly, and that he was well out of range of the nearest obstacle on the ground. In this case, he was at an altitude of several thousand feet. The world was dark beneath him, with an occasional pinprick of orange light visible far below, denoting a hearth somewhere in the small human settlement of Cael.

Casting his eyes toward their camp, he could see his glacial friend had scraped together enough snow to create a huge mound, and had burrowed his way into its heart. It made sense. After all, he *was* from the northern ice fields.

I still am, Gocri's thought came, chuckling.

Grunting, Skellig noticed that their kai, Jerica, was stretched out on the ground, near their fire, with Sif nearby, keeping watch.

As we agreed, let me know when you tire. I'll commence watch duties.

And as I told you, Sif returned, *vapor dragons don't sleep. I'll be more than happy to keep an eye on our human.*

I'm nobody's human, Jerica's thought came.

You know what we mean, Sif said.

I know. I'm just teasing you.

Get some rest, Jerica, Skellig told her. *We have a long day ahead tomorrow.*

Are you sure you want to simply fly around until we see something worth exploring? Jerica asked. *Do you know how long that could take? Remember, we don't have many days left until that huge digger is assembled.*

She has a point, Nuri's thought said.

Where are you? Skellig wanted to know.

About twenty miles from our nest. I smelled sturgeon, and decided to catch a few, for breakfast tomorrow.

An excellent idea. Where's Zeira?

I'm here, the youngest dragon's thought came. *I'm staying put, making certain Jerica is warm enough when she meditates.*

I'm not meditating. I'm trying to sleep.

Oh. Are you not able to sleep? Skellig asked, concerned.

Not at the moment, no.

Why's that? Skellig asked.

For starters, everyone keeps talking in my head. Do you really enjoy flying at night as much as you do?

I do.

I'd like to try it sometime.

I would be honored to give you a ride, Skellig formally announced. *Rest, Jerica.*

I never thought I'd say this before, but I think the stars are too bright for me to rest. Funny, I never had this problem before.

You've never slept outside? Zeira asked.

With my sisters, yes. We used to stare at the stars for hours. We always imagined we could see animals, people, and all manner of things hiding in the heavens.

Skellig turned his eyes skyward. The hundreds of thousands of bright lights winking back at him had him nodding. It wouldn't be difficult to imagine seeing shapes in the many clusters and arrangements. If he looked hard enough, he thought he could see a castle.

I see it, too, Zeira said. *Four towers and a lopsided moat?*

That's the one, Skellig said, smiling. *What else do you see?*

My mother, Zeira grumped. *I can just hear her telling me how I just need to let the teasing go and focus on other things worthy of my attention.*

Sif, what about you?

Well, I don't see anything that stands out. That could be a mermaid, but she's missing a tail. To the west, I see what looks like a tree, only the trunk is too small. Over there, farther north, it looks like a chimera.

Skellig suddenly roared with alarm as an intense wave of emotion washed over him. Within moments, Zeira joined him in the air, and there, gaining swiftly, was Gocri.

"What is it?" Zeira asked, as she nervously scanned the skies. "What do you see?"

"It's not what I saw, but what I *felt*," Skellig explained, "and what I felt came from Jerica. I … Gocri? I'm fine. Jerica isn't. We need to get back to the ground. Hurry!"

"What's wrong with Miss Jerica?" Gocri asked, as the three of them reversed course and plummeted toward the ground.

Wings snapped open and the three dragons impacted the earth with such force that Gocri's mound of snow collapsed and poor Jerica was thrown to her feet.

"I've got the north," Skellig growled, as he turned to the open water.

Nuri's head surfaced. "I'll cover any aquatic approach."

Gocri turned south. "I'll deal with any bipeds who …"

"Guys, guys!" Jerica cried, as she jumped up and down

and waved her arms in an attempt to be noticed. "I'm all right! Really!"

Thinking the threat was coming from the other direction, Skellig puffed out his chest and thundered past the diminutive kai and waited, fangs bared and wings extended. After all, as a dragon, one could never know when a hasty retreat to the sky would become necessary.

A few moments later, when absolutely nothing had happened or appeared, Skellig turned to Jerica with a *What's up?* expression on his face. Jerica, however, was pointing up at the sky.

"It's there! The answer is there!"

Zeira and Gocri appeared at Skellig's side and, together, the three dragons craned their necks to study the stars.

"Umm, I think I missed something," Zeira decided.

"There are no threats from the air, Miss Jerica," Gocri announced.

"I can't smell anything," Skellig added.

"There's nothing in the sea more dangerous than me," Nuri reported, from the water's edge.

"No. It's not us! Look at the stars! I don't know if you dragons have ever done it, but we humans navigate by them. Sif, weren't you the one who said it?"

Four heads, five if they included the human's, turned to Sif. Wide-eyed, the vapor dragon returned the stares and eventually dropped her gaze to the kai.

"I'm sure I don't know what you mean."

"The tree!" Jerica said, as she practically hopped in place with excitement. "When we all started to share what we thought we saw in the stars, what was the first thing you said?"

"The first thing? All right, that cluster of stars over there, near the horizon, looking like a half-eaten mermaid."

Jerica shuddered. "Oh. Eww. Very well, what's the *second* thing you said?

If possible, Sif's eyes opened even wider. She immediately turned to look up at the stars high over their heads.

"A tree! That's right! I did say that. Look, there. I still see it. If you look south, and then to the west, you can see that grouping of stars. That large cluster? To me, it looks like foliage. And just below it? What can you see?"

"A short trunk," Nuri said, nodding.

"I see it," Skellig said, nodding. "Hmm, it *does* look like a tree, but not any type I've ever seen."

"That's because we can't see all of it!" Jerica continued. "If we were to all head in that direction, what do you think would happen?"

Gocri grunted once. "I would say that, as the night progresses, more of that particular constellation would be revealed. Ah, I believe I comprehend. We keep flying in that direction until the roots of the tree are exposed. Is that where you're suggesting we'll find Othos's island?"

"Doolan called it," Jerica said, shaking her head. "And I, for one, am not about to tell him he was right. He said we'd more than likely find Othos *slumbering beneath the roots*. I think he was talking about *that* tree. What do you think?"

"It's an excellent place to begin looking," Skellig said. "We should all rest up. We have a lot of flying to do tomorrow. Nuri, it looks like there's nothing but open water in that direction. Do you know if there are any land masses that way? I would hate for one of us to become exhausted and have nowhere to land."

"Presumably, Othos's island is there," Nuri said. "But, I see where your concern is coming from. On the open sea, there are always islands and seamounts, so I wouldn't worry too much."

"Seamounts?" Zeira asked. "I am not familiar with that word."

One of Nuri's comically small front forelegs drew an imaginary line, angled steeply up.

"Think of it as an underwater mountain that doesn't breach the surface. They're usually formed by extinct volcanoes. There are parts of the sea where, inexplicably, the depth is no deeper than a few feet. I'm fairly adept at spotting them."

"You will be our saving grace," Zeira told the valthan. "If one of us becomes fatigued, we'll need to find a place to safely land."

Nuri nodded. "We'll be just fine."

* * *

"I'm just saying it's a bad idea."

"Why? Aren't you the one who said we should be traveling by night rather than by day? It makes perfect sense. We need to see the stars, so ..."

"That's not what I meant," Skellig insisted. "We can cover more ground with more sets of eyes looking for this island."

"Skellig, what happens if we get lost?" Zeira asked.

"Not everyone has your sense of direction." Skellig chuckled, but then sighed as he felt a sudden pang of embarrassment from the fire dragon he had come to call a friend. "I am so sorry. I can feel you mistook my intention."

"No, you're right to bring it to my attention," Zeira said, crestfallen. "I have proven time and time again that I have no business in ..."

"Stop it," Skellig ordered, growing angry. "I was teasing you, Zeira. There's no need to take offense when none was intended."

"It's just that ..."

"Let it go," Skellig ordered. "The only thing I'm going to argue with you about is splitting up. We need to make certain we stick together, at all times. Once we're out there, over the sea, we're essentially committing ourselves to finding this island as quickly as possible. If one of us heads off in another direction that dragon could become fatigued--what then? With nowhere to land, there's nowhere to go but *down*."

Zeira nodded. "Understood. Thank you."

Skellig looked at the fire dragon and cocked his head. "You're thanking me? For what?"

"For not being afraid to tell me I'm about to make a bad decision."

"You're welcome. Look. We're at the point of no return."

"What do you mean?" Zeira asked.

Skellig pointed south. "It's the last possible time to decide if you want to change your mind. See? The coast turns inward, headed southeast. Check the stars. We're going that way, toward the *tree*."

"I haven't changed my mind," Zeira said.

"Good for you," Sif said, overhearing. "I think our kai is correct. I think we'll find Othos somewhere *that* way."

"Who said I'm right?" a sleepy voice suddenly asked.

"You woke her up," Skellig accused.

Sif and Zeira flew close and peered at the individual stirring on Skellig's back. Noticing she was being watched, Jerica waved at the two dragons before drawing another blanket around her and snuggling deeper into the makeshift saddle Skellig had tied around his neck.

"Who said I'm right?" Jerica repeated.

"I did," Sif confirmed. "I was saying I believe you're right, in that we're on the right track. It seems … logical, I guess."

"Where's Gocri?" Jerica asked.

I've scouted ahead, the ice dragon explained. *It was decided one of us should fly ahead, in the direction we're traveling, to verify there are no threats.*

"That's a good idea, Gocri. Thank you."

"My pleasure," the Glacier dragon returned.

Skellig felt his rider fidgeting in place, trying to see what they were flying over.

"Nothing but sea, I'm afraid," he reported.

"Huh?" Jerica asked.

"You're trying to see over my side? There's nothing to see but the sea itself, I'm afraid. You'd better get used to that view. We'll only touch down when there's actually something to touch down *on*."

"Is Nuri down there? Nuri, can you hear me?"

Both physically and mentally, aye, the valthan returned.

"You're doing all right?" Zeira asked.

"I'm perfectly fine. Unlike the five of you, I'm in my element, and am safe should I stop moving. That reminds me, Zeira, would you like me to scout ahead, too? If Gocri went south, I can venture slightly off-course. We don't know which part of these *roots* Othos is under, so it couldn't hurt."

Zeira and Skellig were both nodding.

"It's a good idea," their group leader responded.

"What are we going to do after the sun rises?" Sif asked.

"We will find the first suitable place to set down and stay there, 'til sunset," Zeira told them.

"And if we don't find something?" Skellig asked.

"We will," Zeira promised. "I'm sure of it."

Three hours later, and one hour past sunrise, Skellig dryly noted, they found their first island. Thankfully, it was deserted, tiny, and offered enough open space to allow all of them to rest on dry land. Nuri promptly went in search of food, and once they were all fed, Sif shrunk down to a human form. Grouped together, their party's two largest members covered the entire lot of them with their wings, affording them some semblance of night, and they rested.

After nightfall had descended once more, the six companions set out. Flying in close formation, with Nuri effortlessly keeping up in the sea below, the four-winged dragons, and their kai, continued their trek south, but then — surprisingly — veered west after the celestial tree they were following appeared to have pulled up roots and moved on its own accord across the sky. Eyeing his companions, Skellig waited to see if anyone was going to challenge the sudden course correction. When no one did, he shrugged and dipped his right wing down, which resulted in a gentle right turn.

After another hour or so of flying, the strange phenomenon happened again. All of a sudden, they were all flying in the wrong direction, which necessitated another course correction. Once they all changed to a course heading southwest, Skellig decided to see if anyone else had noticed their course kept, well, changing course.

"Since when do constellations move?"

"It's moving now," Zeira answered. "The farther we fly, the farther we ..."

"Yes, I know enough about celestial positioning, and how it changes due to our movement," Skellig interrupted. He pointed a claw at the constellation they were following. "However, in this case, it's not what I meant. Yes, the trunk is getting bigger, which means we are getting closer. However, unless the four of us suddenly veered off course at the same time, how did all of us manage to find ourselves headed in the wrong direction? I have to wonder if some other force is at work. Nuri, it happened to you, too. Is there anything to report? Have you noticed anything?"

"Just the same as you," Nuri replied. "Granted, I don't use the skies to navigate, but I do know how to maintain a straight course. The constellation has changed direction twice now, when *we* have not. I'm with Skellig. There's something else at play here."

"Stay alert," Zeira ordered. "We all knew there would more than likely be some obstacle to overcome, and it would appear to be formidable."

"How do you know for certain?" Sif wanted to know.

"Othos has been asleep for hundreds of years," Zeira answered. "That suggests he's been undisturbed, which means whatever method he's using to hide himself must be very effective."

Skellig looked up at the skies. "I do believe we have our first sign of roots. Those stars, there and there. When applied to the rest of the tree, they could certainly be considered its roots."

"We must be getting close!" Nuri exclaimed. "How far now?"

Skellig shrugged. "Who can say? I think we should investigate the next island we find. Agreed?"

"Agreed," Gocri acknowledged.

"Agreed," Zeira added.

"That's going to be a problem," Nuri said.

Blinking with surprise, Skellig dropped his head and looked at Nuri, far below.

"What was that?"

"I said, *that* is going to be a problem."

"Why?" Sif asked.

"There's an island about twenty miles out," Nuri reported.

"Then, that one must be the one we're looking for!" Zeira exclaimed. "How wonderful!"

"Don't get too excited," Nuri warned. "That island can't possibly be the one we want."

Skellig felt Zeira's hopes fall and chuckled to himself.

"Why not?" the fire dragon asked.

"That island is so small that, if Othos was on it, he'd sink it."

Skellig stared at the tiny speck in the distance and waited for his eyes to unfocus. Taking several deep breaths, he concentrated on the image and waited for his vision to zoom in as far as it would allow. For a dragon, it was considerable.

Nuri was right. This particular island could easily hold the six of them, but there was no way a sol dragon would have fit. Conclusion? They had to keep looking.

Skellig felt Zeira's discomfort grow.

Don't lose faith, he sent to Zeira. *You've got us this far. We'll get you the rest of the way.*

What if it's the wrong way? What if we're following a wild phoenix chase?

Trust your instincts, young Zeira. I think you'll find that we are, in fact, headed in the right direction. Now, whether or not we can awaken Othos? That remains to be seen. Only time will tell, and if our luck holds.

Hours later, they caught a break. Skellig was tiring, his wing muscles ached, and he yearned to find a place to put down. Opening his senses to his companions, he could tell that all of them, save Nuri, had similar thoughts. A few moments later, all thoughts of exhaustion had been completely forgotten. And of all people to break the news, it was Gocri, who made the announcement.

"I have something," the ice dragon reported.

"I didn't even notice you had gone scouting," Zeira complained.

"You can't call it scouting," Gocri insisted. "Not when the island we seek is half an hour away."

"Which direction?" Skellig asked.

Gocri pointed in the direction they were all headed. "That way."

"How do you know it's Othos's island?" Zeira wanted to know.

"Once you see it, you'll know," Gocri assured her. "I cannot fathom how his island has remained hidden for as long as it has."

Skellig stared at the large white dragon. "How do you mean?"

"You'll know as soon as you see it," Gocri promised.

Skellig grunted. "You're being facetious."

The Glacier dragon said nothing, but Skellig *did* see a smile on his face.

Once the tiny island was behind them, and the new, larger one was in front of them, Skellig snorted with surprise. Gocri had been right. There was no mistaking this was the right island. How did he know? For starters, he could actually *see* Othos's massive body curled around the island's perimeter. Granted, to an outside observer, it simply looked like an island that was ringed with mountains. However, in this case, the overall shape of the mountains were what gave it away. It actually *looked* like a sleeping dragon. Othos was so large that the only access to the island's tiny bay was through a small opening between his front forelegs and the tip of his tail.

"Are you sure that's him?" Zeira asked. "Yes, before you scoff, I can see the shape of the mountains on the island. It *does* looks like a resting dragon, but no, it looks like solid stone to me. It could just be naturally shaped boulders."

"It's him," Nuri said, dropping her voice to a whisper. "I can feel his heartbeat. Each beat sends shock waves through the water."

"He really wasn't that difficult to find," Skellig decided. "Gocri is right. How is it he hasn't been found before?"

"Maybe he *had* been found before," Sif argued. "Found, but unable to be awoken?"

Surprised, Skellig turned to the huge mound of rocks encircling the island and hesitated. It made sense. Something that large, and distinguishable as a sleeping dragon, even *if* it looked like someone had molded the shape of a large winged reptile out of the very mountains, would be very hard to miss. He could only conclude that Sif was right: Othos had more than likely been found, but since no one could wake him up, his discovery hadn't been mentioned. So, what should they do? How would they wake him up?

"Look at the size of him!" Jerica exclaimed, suddenly sounding fearful. "He's so big! There's no way that could be him. By the gods, my father's forge could fit in his hand!"

"This was too easy," Gocri rumbled. "It took us less than a full day of searching. Was it supposed to be this easy?"

Skellig held up a claw. "We have yet to wake him up."

"How *are* we going to wake him up?" Zeira wanted to know.

Skellig pointed at his back. "I do believe we have the secret weapon that no one else had; our kai."

"Me?" Jerica squeaked. "How am I supposed to rouse something so much bigger than me?"

"I'm thinking your magic will play a significant part in this," Zeira said, eliciting nods from the others. "Which power do you currently possess?"

"Umm, I think it's still the lullaby, from when we fought the djinn."

Sif held up a claw. "Wait. Your magic changes with whomever you touch, correct?"

Their kai nodded. "That's right, Sif. Why? I haven't touched anyone else."

"Your sire?" Skellig said.

"Your dam?" Gocri offered.

"Your littermate?" Zeira suggested.

"The young male?" Nuri said.

"The old male?" Sif asked.

"Doolan? But … but … he didn't touch me! Umm, did he? Oh, it doesn't matter. We already saw that Doolan doesn't have a magical ability of his own. But the others? I know Vyler doesn't, and Theresa doesn't."

"Your parents?" Nuri pointed out. "You came into physical contact with them many times."

"They don't count," Jerica insisted. "They don't have any magic."

"That's what you said about yourself," Skellig reminded her. "What if one of them has a power, and they have just never used it before?"

Jerica crossed her arms over her chest. "I think I would know if my parents suddenly started doing magic."

Zeira pointed a long claw at their kai. "You insisted you didn't have magic when we first met. And now, you're a kai. What if your sire and your dam each retain some type of dormant power?"

Jerica spread her hands in a helpless manner. "How

would I know?"

"Well, you were able to summon the lullaby," Nuri recalled. "Try it now. Let's see if you still have the power to put someone to sleep. That'll let us know whether or not you'll be including your own magic with ours."

Skellig watched the human shrug, close her eyes, and concentrate. She implored her borrowed abilities to sound the lullaby, as it did when they were all battling the djinn on the other side of the world.

A single note sounded, as if someone had started humming.

"I don't hear the lullaby," Zeira reported.

"Then, that means I clearly don't have ... oh!"

Jerica's eyes snapped shut and she teetered on her feet. The swaying became more pronounced, and she would have fallen over if not for Zeira dipping forward and using her wing to stabilize the human.

"Oh!" Jerica exclaimed, as she kept her eyes shut. "This is amazing!"

"What is?" Zeira asked. "What's going on? Are you all right?"

"I'm fine, Zeira. Somehow, and I don't know how, I'm looking at ... this is really weird. I'm looking at a cross section of the sky and the water. But, it's just not the water. It goes down several hundred feet. I can see Nuri, the fish in the surrounding water, and even the contours of a nearby underwater ridge. How is this possible?"

"You must have touched me," Nuri said. "You just described my echolocation skills. It's how I navigate underwater."

"But ... you're a dragon! And I'm a human! I've touched all of you before, and I've never borrowed your abilities."

"She makes a fair point," Zeira decided. "Does anyone have any thoughts about it? Anyone at all?"

"No clue," Skellig admitted. "We'll have to worry about that later. For now? If Jerica has Nuri's power, then we need to learn how that can help us."

"What happens if she mixes her talent with one of ours?" Sif asked. "What if she touches Zeira? Any idea what fire and … Nuri, how would you describe your echolocational skills? Tonal?"

"I would, aye. And, for the record, I would love to see what happens when you mix my power with Zeira's. Jerica, will you try?"

"Of course. I just don't know if anything will happen. Would someone move me to Zeira's back?"

Five minutes later, they had their answer: Jerica was, indeed, mimicking the dragons' abilities. From the moment the kai's hand was placed on Zeira's back, a frown appeared on her face and she kept staring at her hands.

"What is it?" Skellig asked, flying close. "Is something the matter?"

"My hand is turning red. That *can't* be a good thing. Look! LOOK! There's a small flame dancing on my palm! My hand is on fire!"

"If you're worried, we can drop down to the sea," Zeira offered.

"No, thank you. It doesn't hurt. I think … I think I just borrowed *your* power, Zeira!"

"Not unless you suddenly have an explosive case of indigestion," Zeira said, shaking her head.

"She's right," Skellig said. Eyeing the sleeping form of the sol dragon far below them, he continued to circle above the island. "She must have touched Nuri last, and now with you, Zeira, she has the ability to summon fire."

"But, I've touched all of you before," Jerica protested. "I just don't understand why I borrowed, er, *mimicked* your powers this time. What's changed?"

"Lack of a human to mimic?" Sif suggested.

Jerica's mouth formed an O of surprise. "I did not think about that. All right, if that's the case, how do we best use this to our advantage to wake Othos up? I mean, look at him! Whatever we do must be as powerful as we can get it."

Skellig nodded. "Then, I think it's going to take all of us to do it. The combined talents of five dragons. Think about it. It should be more than enough to wake him up."

"Do we experiment, or do we all simply latch on and see what happens?" Nuri asked. "It's going to be a little harder for me, since I'm not able to join you up in the air. Not unless I'm carried again, and I really prefer not to do that, thank you very much."

"That means we'd all have to be on the island," Zeira said, as she looked down at the small piece of land surrounded by the sea. "The question becomes, how fast can we all clear out once he wakes up?"

"*If* he wakes up," Gocri said.

"True," Zeira acknowledged. "I think Skellig is right. Once we fire something at him that has all of our abilities combined, then I think it'll be enough to wake him up. Then, it'll be a matter of vacating the area. Just in case."

"Just in case?" Jerica repeated, frowning. "Umm, can I ask something? Is this Othos fellow friendly or mean?"

No one said a word.

"We don't know, do we?" Jerica moaned. "Fine. We've made it this far. We might as well see it through. Very well, if I'm going to splice everyone's power together, we'll need to find a way to all come into contact at the same time. After all, I may be riding Zeira, but if I wanted to add Skellig's spark, then …"

"I feel the alarm coursing through you," Zeira reported, growing concerned. "What is it? What's wrong?"

"How in Altaic's name are you doing that?" Skellig asked, genuinely curious.

"Who is Altaic?" Nuri wanted to know.

"It's not important. Jerica, how are you doing this?"

"What is it?" Gocri asked. He banked his huge white wings and flew over the three of them. "Do my eyes deceive me? Does Miss Jerica now have lightning sparking through her hands?"

"She does," Jerica whispered, as she watched the dancing yellow arcs of electricity intertwine through her fingers. "But, I haven't touched Skellig, either!"

"You're mimicking our abilities, but you're not physically touching us," Sif observed, amazed. "That is most impressive, Jerica. I didn't know you could do that."

"*I* didn't know I could do that. Are you telling me that I can switch between you five at will?"

"It would appear so," Skellig said, nodding his approval. "You are full of surprises, young human. Very well. Can you tap into more than one of our abilities at the *same* time?"

Jerica held up her hands. "I have no idea. I wouldn't know where to begin."

A blast of fire sprung from her left hand and streaked up, through the air, leaving a white trail of smoke. Shocked, Skellig watched their human stare at her appendages and then make a sudden shaking gesture with her right arm. A bolt of lightning arced through the air and came perilously close to striking one of Skellig's wings.

"That was definitely my power," Skellig said. "Thank you for confirming my theory. Do you know what this means?"

"What does it mean?" Jerica asked, in a quiet voice. "I'm not going to like this, am I?"

"Responsibility of awakening Othos falls to you, Miss Jerica," Gocri said, after receiving a nod of approval from Skellig. "You can manipulate our abilities into something else. It's up to you to find the right combination to awaken the sol."

"That's just great," Jerica grumped. "Fine. Let's see what it'll take. Now, let's think about this before you get me close. If I have Zeira's fire, Skellig's spark, Nuri's navigation, Gocri's frost breath, and Sif's ... what *is* your primary defense, Sif? What would I be borrowing? I certainly can't take your ability to shift your form. What else can you do?"

In response, Sif opened her jaws and spewed out a steady stream of a dark, almost black smoke.

"Smoke? How in the world would I wield smoke?"

Sif's large form shrank until she could pass for Jerica's twin. She neatly dropped onto Zeira's back and joined the kai.

"I believe you already are," Sif informed her.

"I am? How?"

Sif gently tapped her own nose. "You appear to be leaking smoke out of your nose, here and here. The smoke is dark, so I can only assume it's mine."

"Well, I'll be. You guys are really something."

"Does this help you?" Sif asked.

"I'm not sure," the kai admitted. "Look, let's think about

this logically. We have a dragon who's sleeping. Granted, he's much bigger than any of us, but it simply doesn't change the fact that he's sleeping. What do we have to do? Well, we need to wake him up. Of the five of you, one has the ability to send out a musical tone."

"Nuri's echolocation," Zeira said.

"That's right. So, I figure that one will definitely have to be part of this. Now, Skellig's power is spark. We might be able to shock him awake. But, combine the two together?"

"I thought we needed all five for this to work?" Gocri asked.

"Then, maybe it's the order they're all added," Jerica suggested, shrugging. "All right, let's give this a try. Starting with Nuri's, we're going to add Skellig's lightning. Then, I think we should add Zeira's fire. Who knows? He might be cold. Then, we can add Gocri's frost, which will act as yet another slap in the face. Finally, if none of that works, we add yours in last, Sif. Smoke."

"How are you going to effectively combine our abilities?" Sif asked, curious. "It's not as though they're tangible, physical objects you can manipulate."

Both of Jerica's hands suddenly flashed bright white. Then, they flashed again. Frightened, and thinking there was something wrong with her hands, she clapped both hands together a few times, and when that failed to extinguish the bright light, flicked them violently apart.

A pulsing orb of swirling colors was *pulled* into existence as Jerica separated her hands. Staring at the globe of energy with a look of awe on her face, she continued to slowly increase the distance between her hands and watched with shocked eyes as the orb was stretched larger. The glowing sphere grew until it was the size of her own head.

"What are you going to do with that?" Sif whispered.

Jerica looked at the orb and then down, at the sleeping dragon. Since all five dragons were tapped into Jerica's mind, they all knew what she was about to do. However, before she could release the glowing sphere, a brilliant flash of white arced dangerously close to her and Zeira, and before she knew what was happening, a crack of thunder rendered her senseless.

Skellig growled and immediately flew over Zeira and her rider, using his body to shield theirs from harm. A second jagged white arc of electricity crashed down, inches from his left wing. Knowing what was coming, Skellig immediately blocked his senses and waited for the ear-splitting clap of thunder to subside.

It would seem their luck had finally run out. Scanning the skies above, Skellig caught sight of a dark green figure slipping away into the clouds. He groaned aloud.

"What is it?" Zeira exclaimed. "Are we under attack?"

"Aye. He found us."

"Who?" Nuri asked.

"Dym."

Chapter 4 - Dym

Skellig, you and Gocri take the perimeter. Let us know if you see him come back. Nuri, you're our only hope if one of us is forced into the sea. Sif, change form and get on my back. You are Jerica's primary protector."

"You've come a long way, Zeira," Sif commented, as she changed forms to a dragon that was about the same mass as Jerica. Sif's new body coiled reflexively around their kai's form and nudged her a few times with her head. "You're sounding like a leader more and more each day. Jerica, are you all right? Please say something."

"Ooo, I have such a headache."

"You're alive! Thank the Maker! We were so worried."

"What happened, Sif? What was that ... what form are you now? You're a human-sized dragon? I like it!"

"I don't use this one often," Sif admitted. "I've never learned the name for it. It has the same mass as a gromper, so I simply refer to it as the scavenger dragon."

Jerica nodded. "Gromper, scavenger, it makes sense. Oh, why is everything spinning? I can't seem to get my bearings."

"The lightning bolt was much too close for a human to handle," Sif explained. "The resulting thunderclap rendered you unconscious."

"Skellig shot off a bolt of lightning?" Jerica asked, confused. "Why?"

"Not Skellig, but Dym," Sif solemnly stated. "Hush now. We must be careful. He's out there, somewhere."

"Where are the others?" Jerica whispered.

"Gocri and Skellig are searching for him now. I'm here with you, and Nuri is down below, in the event we have an, er, emergency water landing."

"Dym is a Spark dragon?" Jerica asked.

He is, Skellig answered, overhearing.

"He's just one dragon, right?" Jerica wanted to know. "There's five of you. Together, aren't you more than a match for him?"

Dym may be just one dragon, Skellig said, sounding out of breath, *but what he lacks in numbers, he more than makes up for in ferocity.*

A loud rumble sounded from overhead. Zeira and Sif immediately checked the sky to see if they were in danger of being struck by Dym's lightning bolts.

"That was close," Sif said. Her teeth were bared and she was doing her best to wrap her small wings around the kai's body.

A streak of green shot by them, going so fast that the nearby clouds practically exploded in the wake of the Spark dragon's passing. A split second later, another jagged white bolt of pure energy came dangerously close to striking them. Just in time, Zeira folded her wings and spun out of the way.

Dym rocketed by a second time, but this time Gocri was waiting for him. He huffed out a huge cloud of frost particles and then snapped his wings together, pushing the white cloud squarely into the path of their aggressor. Dym could do nothing but fly through it.

A roar of pain sounded.

Twin bolts of lightning snaked out from the nearest cloud

and streaked toward the jade dragon. Only by executing a twist in mid-air did Dym avoid getting struck. His wing talons crackled with energy and a pair of electrical bolts instantly fired back.

"Come now, Skellig," a sinister, hissing voice taunted. "I thought you were better than this. You know it's only a matter of time before I destroy your kai. Bring her out here and let's end this now, together."

Skellig dropped from beneath a large nimbus cloud and tucked his left wing tight against his side. Spinning wildly, he dropped like a stone, heading directly toward the sea. Nuri's head broke the surface of the water. She looked up at Skellig's hurtling form and growled.

Has he been hit? Skellig, are you injured?

Yellow wings sprang open a mere twenty feet from the water. Skellig glided across the surface of the sea without getting a drop of water on himself. With Dym watching, seemingly mesmerized, Skellig fired two more bolts at his opponent.

Most impressive, Nuri conceded. *How can I help?*

Stay out of this, Nuri, Skellig's thought came. *Dym is a vicious fighter. I don't want you hurt. Only attack if he somehow ends up splashing into the sea.*

If he does, it'll be the last thing he ever experiences, Nuri vowed.

Not seeing his adversary anywhere, Skellig cast his senses out and was immediately drawn to the left and nearly a thousand feet up, realizing Dym was speeding back toward him fully charged and ready to shoot. Cursing, Skellig closed his eyes and allowed his senses to ascertain Dym's location. He was close, no doubt about it.

Dym was suddenly flying behind Skellig, within biting range. In fact, he watched those green jaws open and prepare to sink into his tail, and sadly, there wasn't anything he could do about it. But suddenly, Dym rotated in midair and hurled two of his own lightning bolts—at Zeira!

"Watch out!" Skellig roared. "Zeira, bank left. Hurry!"

The inexperienced fire dragon didn't react in time, unfortunately. The first bolt sailed harmlessly over her head, but the second made contact with her abdomen and a huge explosion of sparks lit up the sky.

"Zeira!" Jerica cried, as she was thrown off the fire dragon's back.

Sif was already changing forms. Within moments, a second fire dragon appeared, plucked Jerica out of mid-air, and hurriedly sped off.

"I've got her!" Sif reported. "How's Zeira?"

"In a free-fall," Gocri grunted. "I don't think she's conscious. I've got this."

Skellig watched, dismayed, as Gocri tucked his huge white wings and *dove* straight down, catching up to Zeira as she tumbled snout over tail through the sky. The much larger ice dragon grabbed Zeira's tail and then snapped both wings open, attempting to slow the two of them down. However, the surface of the sea ended up being closer than anyone had thought. Without a doubt, Skellig thought angrily, the two of them would get dunked. On the verge of abandoning his fight with Dym, a peculiar sight emerged.

A swirling whirlpool formed in the water. Faster and faster it spun, until a fifty foot jet of water erupted straight up. Skellig grunted with approval. Nuri! However she did it, he was thankful. The water spray gave Zeira a thorough splashing, but their esteemed leader remained unconscious.

"I cannot maintain this," Gocri said, as his great wings flapped furiously. "I'm sorry, I have to set her down."

Nuri's head appeared. "Gocri, it's all good. On the count of three, let her go. I can manipulate the water to push her onto shore. Can someone make sure her head stays above the surface?"

Sif landed, set Jerica down, and began to swell in size. In record time, a second Glacier dragon had appeared and nodded her readiness.

Gocri nodded his thanks and, as Nuri counted it down, released Zeira's tail.

A second huge spray of water shot up, catching Zeira's falling form squarely on the chest, and true to Nuri's word, *heaved* the inert dragon onto the shore. Zeira landed ungracefully on her back, and her head would have cracked the ground — hard — if not for Sifula's quick actions. She snagged one of Zeira's horns and held the fire dragon's head tightly as she gently lowered it to the ground.

"Nice work, Sif," Nuri praised. "How is she?"

"Still out, I'm afraid."

"I'm off to help Skellig," Gocri said, and he disappeared into the clouds.

A second, much smaller jet of water suddenly splashed on Zeira's face. A roar of confusion and uncertainty sounded before the fire dragon shakily rose to her feet.

"What happened?"

"You were hit by a lightning bolt," Sif said. "Dym had targeted Jerica, but you were in the way. How do you feel?"

"Like I just flew into a mountain," Zeira assured him. "One of these days, I hope to repay Dym for his … kindness."

I'm working on it, Skellig reported, from somewhere above them.

"What about Jerica?" Zeira worriedly asked. "She was on my back!"

She's fine, Gocri said. *Sif switched to a larger form and took Jerica safely away.*

"Oh, good. Thank you, Sif."

"My pleasure."

"Where's Skellig?" Zeira wanted to know.

"He's engaging Dym," Nuri reported.

"Oh, I hope he's okay. Skellig, how are you doing?"

A little preoccupied at the moment.

Where are you? Gocri asked. *I am en route to render aid.*

I'm currently trying to keep my tail from being bitten off, thank you for asking. How are you?

Faring better than you, it would seem. Ah. You're close. Were you being pursued?

What do you mean were? Skellig demanded. *I've been trying to keep my tail out of his jaws, only he's a much better flyer than I am, and I can't seem to shake him.*

No one pursues you.

What? He was just there! This is not good. Everyone, be on high alert. I'm sorry to say I lost him.

Zeira turned to inspect the sky. Dym was gone. But she knew there was no way they were lucky enough to have the second Spark dragon give up.

I couldn't agree more, Zeira, Skellig told her. *I trust this not. He's been behind me the last five minutes.*

Casting his senses outward, Skellig's mind was drawn to an area above his head. The thick layer of clouds would be the perfect place to hide. Was Dym still up there, waiting to strike?

"Of course I am, Skellig," Dym hissed. A jagged bolt of lightning ripped out of the clouds and came dangerously close to one of Skellig's wings. "You know me much better than that. Now, I am in a good mood. I'll give you one chance to escape with your life. Consider your words carefully. Do you wish to pursue this foolish engagement or will you do the smart thing and surrender your kai? The longer you make me wait, the less jovial I become. Choose now."

Dym appeared out of nowhere and, to prove that he could, flew side-by-side next to Skellig underneath the thick, gray cloud. Flying casually, as though he believed he was in no danger whatsoever, Dym continued.

"There's no way for you to win this. Don't risk death over one of those ungainly tribesmen. Surrender her and you and your companions may yet escape with your lives."

A narrow red funnel, complete with swirling flames, suddenly shot up from the ground and slammed into Dym's left wing. The green dragon roared in pain and reflexively tucked his injured wing close to his side. He dropped straight down, like a stone.

Dym struck the sea with enough force to create a minor tsunami, which began rippling outward in all directions. By the time the waves neared the shore, the tsunami was nearly ten feet high and threatened to flood the beach, where Jerica and Zeira were resting.

However, as they watched, the wave collapsed in on itself and harmlessly washed over their ankles. Nuri's head surfaced moments later.

"Everyone all right?"

"We're good, Nuri," Jerica called out. "Thank you!"

"My pleasure. Now, if you'll excuse me, I see someone I'd like to say hello to."

Dym, desperately trying to extricate himself from the water, was beating his wings in a furious attempt to gain some altitude. Slowly, Dym's green body lifted from the sea. Roaring triumphantly, he rose above the surface. Believing himself to be clear to resume his attack, Skellig's adversary scanned the skies, evidently looking for him.

Now, Nuri chose to introduce herself.

The valthan's sleek, blue form arrowed out of the water and rammed Dym's abdomen with enough force to crack a scale or two. Dym's victorious roars switched to howls of pain and he dropped back into the sea.

Go get him, Nuri, Skellig said, as he grunted with satisfaction.

Nuri had said there was nothing in the sea faster, or deadlier, and she wasn't kidding.

Below, Skellig couldn't keep track of Nuri's location. One moment, the valthan was nearly a half mile out to sea, and the next, she swam circles around Dym. Skellig's eyes shifted to his fellow Spark dragon. Everyone could see Dym was exhausting himself with his repeated attempts to lift off from the water. With Nuri's speed and perfectly timed strikes, Dym's plight seemed hopeless.

The jade dragon roared in frustration and his two black wing talons crackled with power. It looked as though he was preparing unleash his power against Nuri! Worried, Skellig scanned the surface of the sea. Moments later, a ripple on his right caught his eye.

Worried about the green dragon's power, Skellig watched Nuri's long, sinewy form twist and turn in the water, rocketing through the small bay formed by the peculiar shape of the mountains. Every time it looked as though Dym had found leverage, Nuri would either slam into him with the force of a typhoon, or race past, pulling him underwater in her wake. Dym would surface, cursing and roaring his displeasure. But Nuri's currents were dragging Dym farther out to sea.

Dym roared a final time, sighted Nuri as she was passing by, and then blasted both bolts of electricity at her.

Nuri! Skellig called. *Tell me you're all right!*

A loud cry of pain, much more severe than anything that Dym had released before, echoed across the bay.

Now what? Skellig wanted to know. *What hit him?*

He fired off another blast of his power, Nuri explained. *And, it would appear he hasn't learned much about how various elements conduct electricity.*

He zapped himself, didn't he? Jerica's voice suddenly asked, joining the collective in Skellig's mind.

Aye. I think he's starting to learn Spark dragons and water really don't mix.

But, he has lightning powers, just like Skellig! Jerica protested. *I thought that, you know, if a bolt of lightning hits water, everything for miles around gets shocked. Isn't that how it works?*

No, Skellig argued. *If you want to stay safe during a lightning strike in the open ocean, dive as deep as you can go. Lightning travels along the surface of the water. It doesn't delve very deep at all. That's why so few fish are ever injured during lightning storms and why Dym keeps reacting every time he fires a shot. In essence, he's blasting himself.*

"Coward!" Dym roared. "You're afraid to fight me yourself, admit it!"

"What's the matter, Dym?" Skellig called out as he circled high overhead. "Have you figured out yet that you won't be able to beat the valthan?"

"Still sore I locked you in that prison on that deserted island?" Dym countered.

He's the one who ...? Jerica asked, shocked.

Hush, Zeira interrupted.

"Still sore?" Skellig mocked. "You left me there to die! And you think I'm going to give you preferential treatment now?"

"I need no preferential treatment from the likes of you," Dym sneered. "You are nothing but ... arrgggh! I swear to the Maker if your valthan pet touches me again, I will personally destroy her and her entire clan."

"The only one in danger of being destroyed is *you*, Spark," Nuri said coolly. "You're the one who imprisoned my companion? You're nothing more than a scourge on this world, and it will be my highest honor to rid the world of it once and for all."

"Skellig, are you going to let her do that?" Dym cried out, as he flapped his impotent wings in a futile attempt to remove himself from Nuri's path. "Are you really going to allow your gromper pet to kill your sire?"

"Why not?" Skellig roared back. "You left me to die on that island! I had only two days left before Fading would've taken me. My friends saved my life. Can you say the same for yours? Oh, what's that? You don't have any friends."

"I am DYM!" the green Spark dragon roared. "I answer only to the Thunder King!"

"The Thunder King is only a biped," Skellig scoffed. "You do his bidding! If you try to call it anything else, then you're more delusional than I had originally thought."

"You answer to a biped," Dym shot back. "You're no better than I."

"She is my kai," Skellig argued. "And does it look like I answer to her? Do any of us? You're the one in the water. You're the one who has an angry … what did you call her? A gromper pet? She is Nuri, and she's a valthan. She's also more than a match for you in the water."

"Whoever, or whatever she is, call her off," Dym snarled.

Seeing how Dym's struggling form managed to move closer to shore, Skellig landed at the water's edge and took his place next to Zeira and Sif. Moments later, Gocri touched down next to him and, together, they turned to regard the struggling Spark dragon who was still at least a hundred feet away.

"Why should I?" Skellig asked. "You've insulted her. You've made no attempt to apologize. I, for one, am not in a very forgiving mood when it comes to you, so … I will have to decline your generous request."

A smile appeared on Nuri's face and she immediately dipped below the surface. Moments later, Dym roared again as Nuri streaked by and lashed out, dragging him an additional twenty feet away from shore.

"You're a disgrace to Gale," Skellig began, as he began to pace along the shore. "You turned your back on your heritage!"

"What has Gale ever done for me?" Dym snapped. "Arrrgggh!"

Skellig spotted the trail of bubbles as Nuri sped away.

"You're pathetic," Skellig continued. "You have no honor. I'm ashamed to admit you are my sire."

"No one is more ashamed than I am," Dym clapped back, "for having sired such a disobedient offspring as yourself. Go on. Tell your gromper if she strikes me again, then I'll unleash hell on your scrawny tribesman."

"They call themselves humans," Skellig nonchalantly pointed out, "and I wouldn't recommend it. Nuri is quite protective over our 'scrawny tribesman'."

For being in the sea, Dym moved blazingly fast. His left-wing talon suddenly thrust out of the water, and a jagged bolt of lightning streaked toward Jerica. Dym roared in pain as, enraged, Nuri targeted the Spark dragon again and lashed out with her considerable strength.

"Look out!" Sif shouted.

Huge white wings appeared and swept everyone out of harm's way. The lightning bolt blasted harmlessly at the very spot where Jerica had just been standing.

Rising to her feet, and making a play of brushing herself off, Jerica tapped Gocri's foreleg.

"Thank you for your quick thinking. Now, would you step aside? It's my turn."

A huge grin split the Glacier dragon's face. "Of course."

Dym sneered as he saw Jerica calmly walk to the water's edge.

"What are you going to do, biped? Do you think I'm afraid of you?"

Jerica flung her arm out. The same strange red funnel, complete with swirling flames, shot out from her right hand and hit the tip of Dym's exposed right wing. The wing talon, which had been crackling with energy, poofed out and, roaring with pain, Dym attempted to shift his injured wing out of harm's way. But the strange magical ability tracked his movements, and his wing continued to burn. Roaring with frustration, Dym dove underwater in an attempt to hide from the strangely shaped red flames.

There was a swirl of water, and an explosion of bubbles. Dym's body was *thrown* to the surface, revealing the freshly scarred right wing and the small hole it now contained.

"Ooo, that looks painful," Skellig mocked.

"You have no idea who you're dealing with," Dym glowered, as his head rotated in the water until he was looking straight at Jerica. "He will see you *burned*. Everyone you know, everyone you care about will be taken from you. You think you know pain? Every time you ..."

"Oh, give it a rest," Skellig sighed. "The more you ramble, the more we tune you out. Do you think we're scared of your master? He fears us. He's right, because all of us, together, are formidable. When you see him, be sure to tell him you're alive only due to our generosity."

"You're sparing me?" Dym spat. "Save your pity. I don't need it."

"You were beaten," Skellig informed him. "You know it and I know it. Now, tuck your tail between your legs and go."

"How? I'm stuck in this blasted water."

Skellig turned to Nuri. "Would you?"

Do you trust he'll go? Nuri asked, switching to their shared mental connection.

I do. But, be ready, just in case.

Nuri's head vanished, and the surface of the water became choppy. The sea exploded outward, flinging Dym end-over-end, into the sky. Two charred, green wings started beating the air. Once Dym had regained his balance, he turned to face the six of them, snarling in anger.

Skellig braced for the worst. Had he made a mistake in releasing his sire?

A glint of color caught his attention. When Skellig looked, he could see that Jerica was there, hand outstretched, and the swirling red mass was dancing around her arm. She looked up at Dym and shook her head.

"I've hit you twice now. The next shot will make a hole five times the size. You'll be unable to use that wing for months. So, think long and hard about what you do next."

"*He* will not stand for this," Dym said, baring his fangs. "You and your pets *must not awaken Othos*."

"How does he even know who we're looking for?" Zeira wanted to know. "Am I the only one who's worried about that?"

"You have no idea who you're messing with," Dym growled.

"At the moment," Sif began, "we're dealing with a bully. Get going, before I change my mind."

"You cannot do this," Dym vowed.

"We can and we *are*," Skellig assured him.

"You will regret this," Dym said, as he rose into the air.

"Consider this a learning experience," Zeira told the petulant dragon.

Nuri's head surfaced and she stared at Dym. "Should we meet again, it will not go as favorably for you."

"Why would you regret sending him away?" Jerica wanted to know. "Will he be back?"

Skellig nodded. "Without a doubt."

"Do you?" Zeira asked, edging close. "Do you regret it?"

"I already do," Skellig spoke softly, as he watched the retreating form disappear into the clouds.

Gocri got to Skellig first. "You neglected to mention you are an offspring of Dym."

"Why didn't you tell us?" Nuri asked, as she pulled her long body out of the water and slowly made her way up to the five of them.

"And tell you what?" Skellig asked, sounding glum. "That my sire was the one responsible for placing me in the ice prison? That he views me as a waste of scales, since I won't join him in serving that ridiculous biped? Er, no offense, Jerica."

"None taken, I assure you," their kai responded. "Umm, was he really your father?"

Skellig reluctantly nodded, and then shrugged. "I've long moved past trying to apologize about my sire. He is who he is, and I'm thankful to say, it hasn't affected who I am. Dym tried to overthrow Lord Myrdaynth, and when that failed, he was branded an outcast and expelled from Gale. I had to fight for my name, as they wanted to throw me out based only on my connection to *him*. I actively renounced my ties with Dym, and when he learned about my betrayal, he vowed to make me suffer as I've never suffered before."

"I'm sorry you had to go through that," Zeira said. "But,

let's look on the bright side."

Skellig tilted his head at their leader. "And that would be …?"

"We drove off Dym! Plus, look around! I think we all believe those mountains to be the one and only Othos, asleep for literally thousands of years. Then, we have our kai, who has proved to be quite resourceful. In fact, I do believe she still has the sphere that should awaken Othos, even though I do not see it. It's exciting! Isn't it exciting? Aren't you feeling the excitement here?"

Skellig finally smiled and, after a few moments, nodded his head. "Your enthusiasm is contagious, young Zeira. Jerica, are you ready to see if that ring of mountains is, in fact, a sleeping dragon?"

"How do you want to do this?" Sif asked.

Zeira fell silent as she gazed at the mountains towering far above her head. Now that she was faced with confronting, and awakening, a being so old and so large that her mind struggled with trying to put its sheer size in context, she hesitated. Wordlessly, she turned to Skellig, who nodded his support. Going around their ring of friends, each nodded their readiness. Swallowing loudly, Zeira turned to their human rider.

"Jerica, do you still have that orb you created earlier?"

Skellig watched their kai reach into a pocket and retrieve the glass sphere, still swirling with various colors.

"I do. I didn't know what else to do with it."

"We should leave this place," Zeira decided. "If this is actually Othos, and he really is disguised as the mountains, the last place we want to be when he wakes up is right here. So, Jerica, you're with me. Skellig, Gocri, and Sif—let's all stay close together. And Nuri?"

"I'm here," the valthan confirmed.

"I have no idea how far away from this island you should be. I know you're fast, but I also don't want to take any chances."

"Understood. I'll be well out of range."

"Good. Everyone ready? Let's go."

Once the flyers were airborne, and Nuri had exited the

small bay and was now watching from nearly a mile away, Zeira dipped her wing and started her approach.

"How does it work?" Zeira asked, as they neared what she thought of as Othos's head. "Do you invoke the spell? Throw it? Break it open, like an egg?"

"I was just going to drop it," Jerica confessed. "It's strange, but I get the feeling the only thing that needs to happen is for this globe to break, and for Othos to be close by. I say we fly over him and just drop it on his head."

"If that's his tail," Skellig began, pointing at the other side of the bay, "and his body is there, with those swells looking like wings, then this formation we're headed toward would have to be his head."

"If this is instantaneous," Zeira nervously began, "then I'm thinking the rest of you should fall back. If something happens to me, then I certainly wouldn't want it to extend to you, too."

"I'm staying," Gocri flatly declared.

"As am I," Sif added.

"We're with you, Z," Skellig informed their leader. "What happens to you will happen to us. If this goes badly, then ... well, let's just say I'm honored to have fought alongside each of you."

Gocri grunted in agreement.

Zeira twisted her neck so that she could look back the way they had come. "Nuri, I can't see you. Are you clear?"

Yes.

"Good. We're over him now," Zeira reported. "Jerica, if you're going to do this, now's the time. I'm banking, so you'll be able to drop the orb straight down."

Once Jerica was certain they were flying directly over what had to be Othos's head, she dropped the sphere. Almost immediately, four flyers and one valthan reversed course and headed in the opposite direction. Jerica twisted around to watch the orb fall. It was only a matter of time before contact.

What happened? Nuri wanted to know. *Is it Othos? Is he waking up?*

"Nothing is happening," Skellig reported. "Either the spell didn't work ..."

"… or it didn't break," Sif finished. "I'll swing by and take a look."

"I'm closest," Skellig argued. "I'll do it. Hmm, I can't see anything. I'll drop lower and see if I can tell what happened to Jerica's orb."

"Be careful," Zeira advised.

"It's only flying," Skellig said, as he banked his wings and dropped lower. "There isn't a single thing happening. The mountain still looks like a mountain. I don't see the spell anywhere. Perhaps we are mistaken. Could this be the wrong island?"

"I can tell you what's wrong," a gravelly voice announced, on Skellig's left. Gocri pointed down. "I see the spell lying there, in the open. It's intact. No wonder the spell didn't work. It didn't break. I'll go down and just smash it myself."

"Gocri, wait," Skellig urged. "I have a better idea. Be ready to fly like the wind, my friend."

"What are you going to do?" the ice dragon inquired. "Oh, I see. Plan to throw a lightning bolt at it, huh? I don't know, Skellig. It's a small target, and it's quite a distance from here. Do you really think you can hit it?"

Skellig's nose lifted. "Hmmph. Just you wait and see. Watch this."

He sighted the tiny orb, felt his power surge, and then heard it crackle ominously. He was ready to fire. Holding his breath, Skellig sighted the glowing orb and fired both bolts.

There was a flash of light so bright that it was impossible to comprehend. Nuri let out a roar of warning, but it was too late. Everyone's senses short-circuited and just like that, they were rendered unconscious and began a freefall to the sea, hundreds of feet below.

That is, all but *one*.

"What happened?" Skellig asked. "I can't see anything! Why won't my eyes work? Is everyone all right? Hey guys? Someone please answer me!"

They are unconscious, Spark.

"Who's there? I don't know your voice."

No, but I know yours, Skellig. You may call me Othos.

Chapter 5 - Othos

Skellig blinked furiously, but nothing but blurred images appeared. However, his other senses told him several things. First off, he was no longer in the air. Second, he hadn't splashed down into the sea. Third, he appeared to be by himself, as he couldn't sense any of his companions. But … he did sense *one*, an unfamiliar presence. The stranger's mind was so strong and so powerful, that he briefly wondered if he might be simply imagining it.

"No, you didn't. I am no figment of your imagination."

"Are you really Othos?"

"That is one of the many names I have gone by."

"Oh, uh, I am …"

"… Skellig, yes, I know."

"How do you know me? We haven't met before, have we?"

"We have not."

"You sound exasperated," Skellig accused.

"Because, just for once, I wish we could skip this part and go straight to the pleasantries."

Skellig blinked with surprise. This was a celestial? He sounded so … normal.

"So, why do *you* sound so surprised?" the voice wanted to know.

"Well, I, er, never met a, er, genesian before," Skellig admitted. "Or is it celestial? And, it'd be better once my vision is restored."

"It's only been a few minutes. Give it a few more. You'll be pleased to hear the effects aren't permanent. As for my species, I'm technically a genesian, but I'm also a celestial, so either will work. And before you ask, yes, all genesians are celestials, and no, not all celestials are genesians. Confused?"

"Admittedly, yes, but I can let that go for now."

"Good. For the record, there's so much more to discover when you're not relying on your visual acuities."

"What the blazes is that supposed to mean?" Skellig demanded.

"It's just a suggestion. Now, let's see. There we go. How's your vision now?"

Skellig blinked his eyes a few more times and then grunted with surprise when they both cleared and he was able to look around.

He was back on Othos's island, only this time the ring of mountains was noticeably absent. That wasn't too surprising, as he was supposedly addressing Othos himself. In fact, now was as good of a time as ever for a proper introduction. However, when he turned to face the acclaimed sol dragon, both eyes shot open with surprise.

There was Othos, staring at him with equal fascination. The sun dragon was — surprisingly — a dark, charcoal gray color. His chest and undersides appeared to be white, he also had small white blotches here and there, across his body. On his back, he had two sets of wings: a larger, primary pair and a much smaller, secondary pair. Both were folded flat against his back. And finally, both of Othos's horns were spiraled, and twisted out from either side of his skull, looking very much like a biped who was ready to embrace another of their species, as they were wont to do.

Othos remained motionless; alert. The sun dragon was facing him, but that wasn't what had surprised him. At the moment, it was because the two of them were the same size!

"Confused?" Othos good naturedly asked. "I get it all the time."

"But … you're tiny! Look at the mountains! They were here, and now they're gone! Wasn't that you, in disguise?"

"It was, aye."

"Why are you so small now?"

"Would you prefer I go back to being my natural size?"

"You can shift your size, too?" Skellig sputtered, impressed.

"Well, obviously. Aren't you going to ask about your companions?"

"Yes! Where are they? What happened to them?"

"Yeah, about that. They passed out once I decided to stop pretending to be asleep. Too much light can overwhelm the senses, which is exactly what happened to them. Oh, you're looking for them? They're over there, where I put them."

"Over …?"

Othos indicated everyone was behind him. Hurrying around the celestial's body, being careful not to tread on his tail, Skellig saw for himself what had happened. There were his friends, splayed out before him. To Skellig, they appeared to be sleeping on the soft grass. Even Nuri was there, spread out in a circle. He was surprised to see that his valthan friend was almost long enough — provided she was stretched out in such a way that her snout was resting against her the tip of her tail — to wrap around their entire group.

"No wonder you don't come out of the water often," Skellig said, keeping his voice low and soft. "I certainly don't remember you being that long."

"Fear not for your friends," Othos said, coming to stand beside him. "They're fine."

"Are you keeping them unconscious?" Skellig asked. "Please allow them to awaken. I don't like seeing them like this."

"As you wish."

In unison, five sets of eyes snapped open. Gocri made it to his feet first. He sniffed the air, bared his fangs, and immediately turned to face Skellig. The Glacier dragon's eyes widened as he noticed Othos resting complacently nearby, as though the two of them were the best of friends.

"What happened?"

"You were rendered unconscious at the same time, by *him*." Skellig motioned Gocri over. "I'd like to present Othos. Othos, this is Gocri, from Bliss. Next to him is Zeira, from Blaze. We also have Sifula, from Rokke, and Nuri, the valthan. And finally, sitting between Zeira's front forelegs, is our kai, Jerica."

Othos rose to his feet, took several steps forward, and then lowered himself back to the ground, directly in front of the human girl.

"So, you're the one who's causing all this fuss."

"Excuse me?" Jerica stammered. "I haven't created any fusses, thank you very much."

"She really hasn't," Zeira confirmed. "Not yet, anyway."

Othos fixed Jerica with a stare. "Answer me this, human. Did you, or did you not, come to your companions' aid when you borrowed the abilities of three different dragons? Did you not come up with a powerful weapon no one has ever seen? And, before you respond, did you — or did you not — use that power against Skellig's sire?"

"You know he's my sire?" Skellig groaned.

"You know I can splice together their powers?" Jerica said, at the same time.

"I'm waiting for an answer," Othos said, as he stretched a leg up to his head and picked his fangs with one of his talons.

"Yes, I may have done that," Jerica finally admitted.

"Uh huh. And, do you know of any other humans who have the ability to do what you did?" Othos continued.

Jerica sighed. "I do not, no."

Othos turned to Skellig. "Of course, I knew he was your sire. Your markings match his. No one else noticed?"

"What markings?" Nuri wanted to know.

Othos pointed at Skellig's chest. "Skellig and Dym bear the exact same markings on their chest and abdomen. Come,

come. Can you see the black marks against his yellow scales? Those markings. Dym has the exact same marks, in the exact same places. That's what gave it away for me. No, don't look at me as though I'm using some special power. I've always been an astute observer."

"I didn't notice," Zeira confessed. "I was too busy being worried about everyone's wellbeing to look at the marks on Dym's back."

"And that's what makes you a good leader," Othos observed. Then, he sighed and turned to Skellig. "Your sire is not particularly fond of you, is he?"

"You noticed?" Skellig scoffed. "He's been that way for as long as I can remember."

"I was watching the entire time," Othos replied. "It was refreshing to watch the lot of you working together so efficiently. Good for you."

"It's only good for us if the blathering idiot actually returns home," Gocri grumbled. "I'm not convinced he has."

"Nor am I," Nuri added.

Othos closed his eyes. When he opened them, everyone was shocked to see his pupils had vanished and his eyes had turned completely white. The sun dragon turned his head to look east.

"Skellig, you'll be pleased to know your adversary has … how did you phrase it? 'Tucked his tail between his legs'? It would appear he has done precisely that."

"Wait, you can see him?" Zeira asked.

Othos nodded. "I will say he is by no means hurrying, but at least he's headed away from here."

"You're able to see what others are doing?" Sif asked, shaking her head. "Does that, er, include *everyone*?"

Othos shrugged. "It may."

Jerica shuddered. "Well, that's a little …"

"… creepy?" Skellig finished.

"… unorthodox?" Gocri added.

"… unsettling?" Nuri said, adding her voice to the others.

"Is this something you've always been able to do?" Zeira asked.

Othos nodded. "Yes."

"Do you do it often?" Sif asked.

Othos grinned. "What, spy on others? Only when necessary. A dragon has to stay entertained somehow. Anyone else?"

After a few moments of uncomfortable silence had passed, Nuri gave a slight cough and raised a thin foreleg in the air.

"I'm still confused. If you're actually Othos, how is it you're so small?"

"I already asked him that," Skellig said.

"And?" Nuri asked, turning to him. "What'd he say?"

"I *am* right here," Othos said, as a huge grin split his face. "I must admit, I truly missed this."

Skellig held up his own foreleg, with one claw extended.

"Just a moment. We'll come back to that. Earlier, I asked the question and I do believe you didn't answer. How is it you're so small?"

"I really don't have any idea," Othos confessed, chuckling. "It's something I've always been able to do."

"Then why increase your mass to something the size of a mountain range?" Sif asked.

"Because I started out resting," Othos said. "I fell asleep. When I do, if enough time passes, I revert to my natural size. Or, if I've adopted a smaller form and I get angry, then it's harder to hold the size. The mountains are my natural size. But, since that would probably intimidate everyone present, I thought it best to present myself on the same scale as you. Satisfied?"

"And when you said you missed this?" Skellig reminded him. "What did you mean?"

Othos drew a circle in the air with a claw. "This. This right here. You have to understand, I haven't conversed with anyone for a very long time. And the last time I did? The only thing I was asked was whether or not I'd restore the sun."

"The sun?" Skellig repeated. He turned to look up at the fiery ball of light in the heavens. "What about it? What needed restoring?"

Othos chuckled. "Well, in his defense, it became dark in the middle of the day, and I might have suggested he had done something to anger me."

"Did he?" Jerica asked, wide-eyed.

"Of course not. I was merely teasing him. And …"

"And what?" Zeira prompted.

"Well, I was hungry, and I had just returned from Tonlaos, and was in no condition to hunt, so I insinuated the sunlight would return if he made an offering to, well, to me. Foolish, I know, but there you go."

"It was nothing more than an eclipse, wasn't it?" Sif snorted, between bouts of laughter.

Othos grinned. "Maybe. All he had to have done was wait an hour or two and the daylight would have returned on its own. But, that's in the past. What's done is done."

Skellig held up a claw. "Wait, where did you say you had been?"

"Tonlaos."

"I don't know where Tonlaos is. I've never heard of it."

Othos waved a dismissive claw. "Oh, I see. Your confusion is justified. It's about as far away from here as you can get, which means you'd have to fly to the other side of the world if you wanted to see it."

"Is it on the third continent?" Jerica asked.

Othos turned to her and knelt down so that he was practically nose to nose with the girl.

"The third continent? I don't … wait. Oh, I see. If the one we're on now is the first, then by your reasoning, the third would be several continents away?"

"Right," Jerica said, nodding.

"Yes and no," Othos said, smiling.

"How can it be yes *and* no?" Zeira asked.

Othos sighed. "Think about it. If this world only has three continents, then that means if you fly that way," and pointed west, "the first continent you find after crossing one of the seas will be the second. Then, do it again, and since you won't be on this continent, you'll be on the third. With me so far?"

Everyone nodded.

Othos turned and pointed in the opposite direction. "Now, if you fly *that* way, you will encounter another expanse of water, another ocean. Cross it, and which continent will you encounter?"

Skellig's mouth opened as he prepared to answer, but then a dawning notion occurred. Realization struck and he was rendered speechless.

"Ah, I see our Spark friend has come up with the answer. Tell them, Skellig. I think it would sound better if the explanation came from you."

The group turned to Skellig.

"He's saying," Skellig began, "if you fly west, you'll hit what we think of as the second continent. After it, then the third. But, if we head in the opposite direction, we'll encounter the third continent, then the second, and finally, we're back where we started from."

"Well, color me blue and call me a gromper," Gocri exclaimed, as he snorted out a small cloud of frost. "I did not see that coming."

Skellig looked around their group. Slowly, one by one, his companions came to the same conclusion as he had. The world was round! Of course, if they had headed in the opposite direction, they would have encountered the third continent first. Still, it was a huge undertaking, and not one they could have accomplished any time soon.

"Forget about land masses for now," Othos said, as he rose to his feet. His wings stretched out and remained that way as he walked around. "Sorry, when you are as old as I am, getting up from the ground becomes an ordeal. Don't let anyone tell you otherwise. There's nothing dignified about growing older. Now, we should be off. Skellig, I still see you moping. Thinking about your sire? Well, don't. There's no guilt to be had for his actions. Dym chose his own path, as have you."

"I really don't want to meet up with him again," Zeira said.

"But, you will," Othos insisted. "One of the drawbacks of being a celestial is that we were all gifted with the powers of premonition. I have already seen what happens when Dym returns."

"Who wins?" Skellig wanted to know.

"I will not say," Othos announced. "The future is not set. There are many paths our destinies can take. Only you can decide what will happen."

"Are you going to help us with our mission?" Zeira asked.

Othos nodded. "Yes."

"Why?" Skellig asked. "You're a celestial, a sun dragon. Surely, you have way more important things to do."

Othos made a circular gesture with a claw. "Like what, turning into a mound of rocks? Counting the fish jumping in the sea? No, I think I'm going to like this."

"What about your scales?" Nuri asked. "Can you tell us why a human would want some?"

"My scales?" Othos repeated, as he looked down at his chest. He gave his lower abdomen a few errant scratches. "What about them?"

Zeira stepped forward. "We were wondering if, er, your scales are due for a sloughing anytime soon?"

"Perhaps. When I'm awake, I'll usually slough my scales once every other year or so. But, as you know, I have been asleep for a good spell. Why do you ask?"

Skellig glanced over at their kai. How much was she going to tell him? A frown appeared on the biped's face and suddenly, Skellig knew Othos was about to get an earful.

"Back home," Jerica began, "there's this mage. We need his help, so in order to secure that assistance, and to keep me from jumping into the jaws of the nearest dragon, we have to bring him back several scales. He specifically named you, and scales that come from a genesian. So, my question to you is, why would one of us humans want one of your scales? Is there something we don't know?"

Othos nodded. "I think I know where you're going with this. Might it be something about … this?"

Othos vanished.

"What just happened?" Skellig demanded. "Where'd he go?"

"Trust your senses, and you'll have your answer," Othos's voice announced.

"Invisibility?" Jerica incredulously asked. "Are you suggesting the holder of your scales would be given the power of invisibility?"

The air shimmered and, just like that, the sun dragon was back.

Othos shrugged. "It's the only thing I can think of. Just a moment. Let's test it." He used his right leg to scratch at his left and kept at it until several scales fell off. Stooping to pick them up, he offered them to the human. "Take these. I will admit, you've made me curious. I would personally like to see if anything happens when they come into contact with a biped."

Jerica held up a shield-sized scale in front of her and shrugged.

"That makes two of us. I get the impression Doolan wanted to make something out of them. I mean, it's light enough, so would that be a possibility? Zeira, what's the matter?"

Everyone turned to Zeira.

"Perhaps if you could share my senses right now, Jerica, you'll be able to see what I'm seeing."

As their kai closed her eyes and attempted to establish a mental connection, Skellig repositioned himself next to their leader, and right away, saw what Zeira wanted to share with Jerica. When the scale was held just so, it became invisible, as did everything that it was covering. Right about then, Skellig felt Jerica's presence inside their minds. She looked through Zeira's eyes and, as Skellig had expected, gasped with alarm. Unfortunately, it didn't take a scholar to determine what Doolan's intentions were.

"Why, that disgusting, smarmy, perverted ..."

"So, this mage wants the power of invisibility," Zeira said, ignoring Jerica's rant. "Would it be so bad to give it to him?"

"... creepy, egotistical, repulsive ..."

Skellig turned to Zeira and shook his head, a fact which didn't go unnoticed.

"What? What am I missing?"

"Zeira," Skellig patiently explained, "if that human obtains the ability to become invisible at will, what do you think he'll do with that power?"

Zeira shrugged. "Go hunting? I don't know where you're

going with this."

Gocri stepped forward. "Allow me."

Skellig nodded and took several steps back.

"We've already established this human's desire for Jerica as a mate," Gocri began.

"... maniacal, sickening, leering ..."

Zeira reluctantly nodded.

"So, what will happen if he's now given the ability to have his way with the females, with or without their knowledge?"

Zeira's eyes widened. She quickly looked at Skellig. "He wouldn't."

"That is *precisely* what he wants," Skellig assured her.

"... excuse of a human being!" Jerica finished. Their kai was flushed, her eyes sparked with anger, and she looked as though she was ready to release another round of insults. "If that ..."

Skellig held up a claw. "We get it. Giving him Othos' scales is out of the question. We won't let anything happen to you, or any other human female because of those scales."

"Th-thank you."

Othos picked up the scales Jerica had dropped. "What should I do with these? Am I to understand you no longer desire them?"

Jerica nodded. "Yes. Please, dispose of them. We can't let those fall into the wrong hands, can we?"

Othos nodded, took several steps back, and leaned forward, so that all four legs were on the ground. Lifting his front right foot, he smashed his claws down, sinking his talons deep into the earth. A few moments later, the splotch of white scales directly over his heart began to glow. Within moments, the glow had spread to every single scale on his body. The light rippled a few times, suggesting whatever power Othos was accessing was building. Growing in intensity, the light traveled down Othos's front foreleg and approached the ground.

"Better cover your eyes," the genesian warned.

Not needing any encouragement, especially after falling victim to Othos's power earlier, everyone squeezed their eyes shut.

"It's done. You can open your eyes now."

"What did you do?" Jerica wanted to know.

Othos pointed at the ground. "I used my essence to dig a hole. Once I was sure it was deep enough, I dropped those scales down."

"How far down is it?" Skellig wanted to know.

"Well, it was, perhaps, one tenth of my full power, so I'd say probably only three or four …"

"… feet deep?" Nuri asked. "You run the risk of someone digging them up."

"Hundred," Othos clarified.

"Three or four hundred feet deep?" Sif repeated, incredulous. "And I thought Nuri was a fast digger."

"I'm not," Nuri admitted. "At least, not on dry land. Othos, how did you do it? You never mentioned you excelled at digging."

"I have long since learned," Othos began, as though he was lecturing a group of dragonlets, "that sunlight, in highly concentrated doses, can be a very effective tool."

"Amazing," Nuri breathed.

"No more so than being able to outswim anything that lives," Othos said, turning to give Nuri a nod of acknowledgment. "So, this is your quest, and I wish to join. Therefore, where are we off to now?"

Zeira held up a claw. "Would you give us a moment?"

Othos nodded. "Of course."

Zeira motioned everyone over for an impromptu huddle.

"He wants to join us!" Zeira furiously whispered.

"We were told our mission wouldn't succeed until a sixth had joined the group," Skellig reminded her. "This just makes it easier for us."

"Am I the only one who's intimidated by him?" Nuri asked.

Sif, currently resembling Zeira, raised a claw. "I am, too. Can we trust him?"

"He's a celestial," Gocri began, "If he wanted to inflict harm, he would have done so by now. We need him to join, and he wants to join, then who are we to argue?"

"I hate to be the one to say this," Jerica began, "but we

cannot let any of his scales fall into Doolan's hands. That's our stipulation. Othos can't give Doolan any scales until we figure out how to keep him from using them."

Skellig's head jerked up as a notion occurred. He gave his companions a reassuring smile before motioning Othos over.

"Yes?" Othos politely asked, as if he was anticipating the question.

"Can you do something to your scales that would prevent them from being used in a ... let's say *untoward* manner?"

The sun dragon grunted once. "I've never been asked that before. I honestly have no idea. You're proposing I alter my sloughed scales so that this biped I keep hearing about cannot use them against anyone?"

Jerica's face lit up. "That's exactly what we need to know! You don't understand. This human is a bad person. We can't let him get an advantage over anyone."

"If he's so bad, why don't you just dispatch him?" Othos challenged.

"Umm, I don't know how you treat other dragons," Jerica began, "but we simply do not do that to other bipeds, er, humans, no matter how much they may deserve it."

"It would make our lives easier," Gocri admitted, nodding. "Say the word, Miss Jerica, and I'll ..."

"... toss him down the hatch?" Jerica wryly finished. "Don't tempt me."

Zeira spread her wings, which prompted the others to do the same.

"Where are we off to?"

Skellig pointed at Jerica. "Back to Cael."

* * *

"All I'm saying is we need to find a way to neutralize Othos' scales," Jerica was saying.

"I'm sure we will," Zeira said.

"I'm with Gocri," Nuri announced, far below them. "Let's just dispatch him after he creates this goblet and be done with him."

"We can't just go around killing humans," Jerica reiterated.

"It's not something we do. We'd be thrown in the dungeon. Well, I would be. There are no dungeons large enough for you guys."

"I'd like to see a biped try to stop a dragon," Gocri scoffed. "It takes a dragon to stop a dragon."

"We come in all shapes and sizes," Zeira announced, flying close. "Othos is proof of that. And Sif."

Gocri nodded. "The point is conceded."

Skellig looked down, at the open water below them. "Nuri, how are you faring?"

"It gets boring swimming this slowly. I've already explored the area. Not much to report, so we should …"

"Did Nuri just trail off?" Zeira asked, when their valthan companion fell silent. "Nuri, are you well?"

There was no answer from the surface of the sea.

Sif switched forms, returning to her natural state.

"Nuri? If you don't answer, then I'm going to head down and try my hand at becoming a valthan."

I'm fine, Nuri's voice said, switching to their shared mental connection. *But, there's something down here you need to see.*

Skellig eyed the others and, when everyone nodded their readiness, he tucked his wings and dropped like a stone. Once he was gliding less than a hundred feet from the surface, he saw that Nuri was now pacing him, swimming below the surface.

"What is it?" Skellig wanted to know.

Vessels.

"What?"

Human vessels.

"You mean you found some boats?" Jerica asked, from her place on Zeira's back. "That's not so unusual. We're over the sea, so … no? I can actually sense you disagreeing with me. You think it *is* unusual? Why?"

Not for who it contains, but what. *You flyers had better gain some altitude. Until you at least see what I'm talking about.*

Once they were high enough, the flyers followed Nuri's instructions until they could see for themselves what had been found. The valthan was right. There were three large, flat-bottomed ships, cruising the coast in close formation.

The ships, Skellig could see, were long and wide, almost as if they were designed to carry cargo, and not passengers. That must be what alerted Nuri. And what cargo were these boats carrying?

It's Cerebus! Jerica whispered, in shock. *At least, there are parts of it. Look, do you see that section there, on the closest ship to us? There's a curved section with scooped buckets for teeth. It's part of the digging wheel! These ships are going to Cael! Are we too late?*

Nuri? Skellig asked. *Based on their speed, how soon before they get there?*

Less than two days, Nuri guessed.

It's not enough time, Skellig lamented. *They will have their contraption assembled before we are ready!*

You all act like you're concerned, Othos's voice broke in. *If you're that worried about those floating pieces of wood, then ...*

Let me guess, Skellig interrupted. *You'd just as soon take them out?*

Of course.

As dragons, we cannot get involved, Zeira miserably pointed out. *We cannot jeopardize any of the truces that exist between our species and that of the bipeds. We're trying to save lives, not risk them.*

And if they didn't know dragons were responsible? Othos casually asked.

How would they not know? Sif asked. *Oh! You're suggesting ...?*

Now, wait a moment, Zeira began. *There's no way we could ...*

We're listening, Gocri interrupted. *What do you, a genesian, know about covert attacks?*

It might not be covert, Othos admitted, *but it certainly wouldn't look like a dragon attack.*

This isn't wise, Zeira said, worried.

Let's hear him out, Skellig suggested. *We need more time. If we create that, then we still have a fighting chance. What do you think, Z?*

Very well. Othos, what do you have in mind?

Their new friend appeared on Zeira's right and pointed at the distant ships far below.

I may not be familiar with modern-day truces or allies, Othos began, *but it occurs to me that these alliances and truces wouldn't be compromised if no one knew dragons were behind the attack. Am I right?*

The only way we could do anything to those vessels is if we're within striking range, Sif pointed out, *and that, I'm sorry to say, would mean we'd be seen.*

Not if the area is blanketed by fog, Othos suggested.

There's no fog out today, Zeira protested.

Or smoke, or steam, or clouds, or …?

What do you know that we don't? Nuri asked. *If you have an idea, please share it with the rest of us.*

Othos grunted once and shook his head. *They're young, they're inexperienced. Don't get frustrated. Just smile and be pleasant.*

Are you talking to yourself? Zeira asked.

Mm-hmm. Listen, you are Fire. Sifula is Smoke. Gocri is Ice. Do you know what happens when you mix fire and water? No one? Do you, or do you not, have a kairie present? Combine your powers. Target the vessels. I think you'll be surprised at the results.

How do you know …? Forget that. Zeira twisted her neck to look at her rider. *Jerica, is this something you can do? Are … are you asleep?*

Jerica's eyes opened. "I just finished. Oops. I mean …"

I just finished. Fly over them and let's see what happens.

They might see us, Skellig warned.

I think not, Othos countered.

Flying as high as she could, while still keeping the floating vessels in sight, Zeira banked her wings and put herself on the same course as the ships.

Ready. We're flying much faster than they are moving. What are you going to … it's working! Look! You're emitting smoke from your hand!

It's steam! Skellig corrected. *What happens when fire and water meet? You get steam! Now I see what Othos was trying to explain.*

I'm right here.

He said if we can prevent anyone from knowing dragons are involved, then we can delay these ships and buy some more time.

He knows us better than we know ourselves, Sif commented.

And I can still hear you, Othos said. *I believe a few more passes will provide enough cover to blanket the vessels in mist. They'll never know we were here.*

You're enjoying this, aren't you? Skellig accused.

Guilty as charged, Othos admitted. *I haven't had this much fun in centuries. Now, shall we?*

Shall we what? Zeira asked.

Let's go see what we can do to ruin their day, Skellig translated. *Othos, this is your idea. After you.*

My pleasure.

Will no one address the flaw in our plan here? Zeira complained. *The bipeds won't be able to see us, but that doesn't mean we'll be able to see them! How are we supposed to mount an attack on an opponent no one can see?*

Relax your eyes, young Fire, Othos instructed. *A dragon's gaze can penetrate a great many things. Tiny droplets of water is one of the easiest. Once you know what you want to see, ignore the rest.*

I wish it was that simple, Zeira grumbled. *And I'm not that young.*

Do you wish to hear how old I am? Othos challenged.

No.

Good, because even I don't know the answer to that. If I was told to guess, then it'd be ... what the ...?

They all felt a brief flash of alarm as Othos's presence vanished from their minds.

Othos, where are you? Are you all right? Zeira, I think we need to abandon our attack!

Skellig's right! Until we know what happened to Othos, we need to retreat! There's something here we weren't counting on, so ... arrrgh!

Zeira! Skellig called out. *Talk to me! Where are you? Where's Jerica?*

They're in the water! Nuri cried out. *Hang on, I'm on my way!*

What's going on? Gocri demanded. *Are we being attacked by the boats? If so, then I'm dropping all pretenses and am outright attacking them.*

I'll be right there with you, Sif vowed.

I've got them, Nuri announced. *Jerica is unresponsive, but alive. I can feel her heartbeat. I have her on my back and I'm pulling Zeira through the water, but I can't go that fast. I have to keep her head above the waves, which makes it difficult to swim. Like Jerica, she appears to be unconscious. What's this? Her wings have been tied together? How is that possible? I think ... I think there's some type of weapon on that boat. They must have suspected an attack by dragons and were ready for us. How is that possible? I swear before all of you that I'm going to personally sink each and every one of those miserable …*

Nuri! Skellig mentally shouted. *Worry about that later! Get Zeira to safety. And what about Othos? Did he end up in the water, too?*

Not yet, he hasn't, their valthan friend confirmed. *I would have been able to tell the instant they … oh, no! Now he has! He is unconscious, too! I can't help both of them at the same time! What do I do?*

We risk exposing ourselves, Skellig answered. *Safety is our main concern, but I fear we don't have any choice.*

Where are you now?

South of the vessels, Nuri reported. *I'm approaching the shore as quickly as I can.*

Look behind you. Those ships are in trouble! You're telling me that's not you?

Skellig, I trust this not. I fear for Zeira and Jerica's safety. I have to get them to shore! I don't know what's causing that disturbance.

Agreed. Sif, Gocri, help Nuri!

What are you going to do? Gocri wanted to know, as he tucked his wings and dropped lower to the surface.

I have to see if I can help Othos. We … what in the name of Cerephles?

What is it? Gocri asked, concerned.

Turn around and see for yourself.

The waters surrounding the three barges had become so turbulent that pieces of the Thunder King's precious digger were breaking their restraints and sliding off the ship to splash into the sea. A huge, jagged spike thrust upwards, as if someone below was trying to skewer one of the boats. Impossibly, the huge spike moved through the water with ease. A second spike appeared, three boat lengths away. The spikes started growing larger.

It's Othos! Sif exclaimed. *It has to be!*

As the two spikes were exposed, it became apparent they were spiraled, just like Othos' horns. It was, indeed, the sol dragon. The base of Othos' skull appeared as the celestial emerged from the water in his natural size.

The impossibly huge figure continued to rise out of the sea as he stood on the seabed. Towering above them, Othos leaned down and glared at the three boats. One of them was shooting something at him, but the weapon was never intended for a target so large. Projectiles bounced harmlessly off his chest.

Othos scooped the boat up in his right hand and lifted it up, off the surface, hundreds of feet in the air. Only when the boat was at eye level did the gargantuan dragon speak.

"I do believe you've made a foolish mistake."

Cries and shouts could be heard coming from the boat. Tiny specks, undoubtedly humans, flung themselves off the ship, figuring they had a better chance of survival in the water. Othos watched the frantic activity for a few moments before he grew angry and held the boat upside down. Making sure all the humans—and cargo—were off the boat, he crushed it in his hand.

Long oars appeared on either side of the two remaining vessels. In a coordinated effort, the boats began to pull away. Two steps was all it took for the massive dragon to bring himself into range. Before anyone knew what was happening, both ships met the same fate as the first.

"Your vessels are forfeited," Othos told the humans. "Begone, you damnable, irritating bipeds."

Othos caught sight of Nuri, struggling to pull Zeira up onto a distant shore. The mammoth figure disappeared, and in his place rose the much smaller version of their new friend.

"How is she?" Othos asked, as he touched down on the shore. "You, human, you are well?"

"Yes, thank you."

Skellig, Gocri, and Sif touched down moments later.

"What happened to being discreet?" Skellig asked, as he looked over at Othos.

"What can I say?" Othos shrugged. "Those bipeds caught me off guard. I never knew they had a weapon to pin our wings back. Thankfully, for me, I have two sets and was quickly able to revert to my full size. What irritates me is, well, those humans knew we were coming. In fact, I'd say they were counting on it."

Chapter 6 - Fallout

You know, I really thought he'd be bigger," Vyler was saying, after witnessing the arrival of the newest dragon. "I mean, from what you guys all told me, I thought you were going to be so big that you'd take up the entire area."

"He would if he was his typical size," Zeira countered, as she landed beside the sol dragon and folded her wings against her back. "As it turns out, Othos has the ability to change his size, among other things. Oh, where are my manners? Othos, there are some humans here I'd like you to meet."

Cael's baron looked appreciatively at the newcomer. "Othos, huh? Baron Vyler Dartmoor, at your service."

Othos took several steps forward and lowered his head until he was no more than a few feet from the baron.

"You are the one responsible for the humans dwelling in this area?"

"Aye, that's one way to look at it."

"Then, you'll be pleased to know we--that is, the seven of

us--have done your village a great service today."

"Er, all right. What would that be?"

Jerica raised a hand. "Perhaps this isn't the right time for this?"

"Please," Othos scoffed. "I'm told that you, Barren, were dreading the arrival of a large mechanical device. Well, you can rest safely, knowing the pieces of that contraption are now on the bottom of the sea."

"Baron, not barren," Vyler sighed. "B-A-R-O-N. They may sound the same, but I just *know* you used the wrong one. Wait. Pieces of *what* contraption? Are you talking about Cerebus? Why would … you didn't…?"

"Those vessels were no match for my talons," Othos boasted, as he held up a foreleg. "I held the boats aloft, rotated them until they were upside down, and once they were empty, reduced them to splinters. You're welcome."

All the color drained from Vyler's face. "You didn't."

"I most certainly did," Othos insisted.

"What's going on?" a new voice demanded. The owner of the voice pushed his way through a thicket of trees and shrubs separating land from water. "Did I hear that right? Did something happen to our equipment? There'll be hell to pay if it's so."

"You guys had better hide," Vyler warned, lowering his voice. "The last thing we need is for them to find a bunch of dragons sitting here in broad …"

Cael's baron trailed off as he turned to behold an empty clearing. There was absolutely no sign of the six towering dragons. Where could they have gone? There was nowhere to hide, and from the look on his wife's face, and Jerica's, none of them knew where they had all gone, either.

"I'm Vyler Dartmoor, Baron of Cael. Who might you be, soldier? Where do you hail from?"

"Lieutenant Marek Thrombeaux. I have been placed in charge of security. Did I hear that right? Cerebus is going to suffer a construction delay?"

"I, er, that's right, I guess," Vyler admitted. "I was just informed that the supply barges met, ah, a watery end and all cargo was lost."

"Informed by *whom*?" Lieutenant Thrombeaux asked suspiciously.

Vyler shrugged. "I'm a baron. I have many informants. Does it matter?"

"Where are they now?" Thrombeaux asked.

"Who?" Vyler asked, trying to sound—and act—innocent.

"Your informant," Lt. Thrombeaux snapped.

"You forget who you're talking to, soldier," Vyler responded, growing angry. "I am the appointed baron of this area. You may be in charge of security for this monstrosity, but here in Cael, *I* am in charge."

"This project has been placed under my jurisdiction," Lt. Thrombeaux stated, crossing his arms over his chest.

"By whom?" Vyler scoffed.

"By decree of His Majesty, Emerus Dinty."

Vyler blinked his eyes. "Who's that?"

Emerus Dinty ... Zeira wordlessly repeated, and then in perfect harmony with Vyler: *Who's that?*

"That's not the name of the Terran King," Vyler pointed out. He saw the soldier take an angry breath. "But, before you say anything else, I do know he fell, in battle, to the Thunder King. Is that his real name? Emerus Dinty? I can see why he prefers his chosen title."

A grin appeared on the lieutenant's face, but was gone a split second later.

"Better get used to it," Lt. Thrombeaux grumbled, sobering. "His Majesty isn't going to tolerate the loss of his supplies. More will have to be shipped. Delays are unacceptable, and any reports which include a delay are usually met with high levels of anger and pain."

"Believe me," Vyler began, "I don't want to put you through ..."

"Oh, it won't be me updating him this time," Marek interrupted, "but *you*."

What's wrong with him? Skellig inquired. *He has gone quite pale.*

It's not too difficult to believe humans, too, fear this Thunder King person, Gocri suggested.

"It's impossible," Vyler insisted. "They call him Thunder King for a reason. This is Terra. His region is Spark. Do you know what that means?"

Whoa, wait a moment, Sifula protested. *This human Thunder King? He's from the same region as Skellig?*

Sad, but true, Skellig admitted. *Hmm, have I not mentioned this before?*

No, you haven't, Gocri returned. *It does explain why your sire is beholden to that blasted biped. Er, no offense, Miss Jerica.*

None taken, Jerica's voice said. *Where is everyone? How were you able to hide so effectively as quickly as you did?*

Fear not, Zeira said, as she projected what she hoped was a feeling of emotional assurance. *You are in no danger. We are still close.*

"Our Thunder King isn't planning on coming *here*," the soldier continued, with a smug look on his face. "However, that doesn't mean he won't, especially when I report this loss of materials to him. Be prepared, baron."

"That's just swell," Vyler groaned.

Lt. Thrombeaux started to turn away when, as an afterthought, he faced Vyler once more. "I do hope you have a suitable excuse ready. After all, *you* are the one who is responsible for all equipment being shipped here. If only we had arrived sooner, we might have been able to prevent this disaster. Well, that's on your head, not mine. I hope you get to hold on to it."

Theresa, who had been clutching Jerica's hand tightly in her own, rushed to her husband and threw her arms around him, sobbing. "What are we going to do?"

"Everything is going to be just fine," Jerica began.

Theresa whirled around, a look of anger on her face. "This happened because of *you*! If you and your pet dragons hadn't interfered, then my poor Vyler wouldn't be losing his head!"

"I haven't lost it," Vyler stammered. "And, if I have anything to say about it, I plan on keeping it that way."

A large grassy knoll, situated close to the water's edge, suddenly shimmered and morphed into Zeira. Similar landmarks in the area, including large boulders and fallen trees, disappeared as the dragons emerged from hiding. Skellig dropped the image of the large mass of stone he had been employing and stood up. Stretching his neck, then his back, and finally, extending his wings out to their fullest potential, he took several steps forward and lowered his neck until he was eye-to-eye with his kai's littermate.

"No one will be harmed. Yes, this appears to be our fault, there's no getting around that."

"What are we going to do?" Jerica asked.

Zeira turned to Jerica and her reptilian features hardened. "I think it's obvious. We find the jhorium first. That enormous mechanical device must not be allowed to destroy this land. Therefore, we must act quickly."

"Perhaps," Othos' deep voice rumbled, "it wasn't a good idea to destroy the humans' boats?"

Skellig turned to see the sol dragon rising up, out of the water, this time in his much smaller form. Moments later, Nuri's head popped up, and studied their group standing quietly by the shore.

"Er, no offense, Othos, but I think that's the general consensus of our group. The vessels should have been left, unmolested."

Othos' mouth opened for an angry retort.

"I know they had weapons which were designed to fell a dragon," Nuri hastily added, "but that doesn't mean they should have been destroyed."

"Perhaps you're right," Othos sighed. "Very well. I will concede that I *might have* caused this ... dilemma, so I will pledge myself to supporting whatever solution is necessary."

"*I knew it!*" a voice cried.

Within moments, streams of soldiers flooded the area. They took one look at what was waiting for them and came to an abrupt halt. Five dragons, with the head of a sixth in the water, turned to regard them as if they were pesky insects. Lt. Thrombeaux came to an immediate stop and started sputtering like a schoolboy.

"I, er, umm ... oh, boy."

Othos reared to his full height and stepped forward. He pointed a claw at the lieutenant; four nearby soldiers fainted dead away.

"You. Human, come here."

Gone was the soldier's swagger, his confidence, and quite frankly, his wits. Marek reluctantly approached the huge celestial and refused to look him in the eyes.

"I was the one who destroyed your precious boats," Othos began. "You will not ... kindly extend me the courtesy of looking at me, would you? There, that's better. Seeing how I was ... you're doing it again. Look up at me, would you? What's the matter, have you never seen six dragons before?"

"Not at the same time," Marek whispered. "Please don't eat us."

"Eat you?" Othos scoffed, raising his head. "Eat you? Why in the world would I ... oh, I get it. You're a human, and I'm a dragon, and therefore, it's in my nature to feast upon your entrails, is that it?"

Three more soldiers fainted.

"Well, haven't you before?" Marek challenged, as he turned to look at each dragon. "Don't lie to me. Everyone knows we can't trust dragons."

"I chewed, but I never swallowed," Othos insisted. "There's a difference."

"Not helping," Jerica muttered.

The majority of the soldiers began inching for the water's edge, as though they thought they'd be able to swim to freedom in the event of an attack by the dragons on land. Most, however, did not notice Nuri's head watching quietly from the water. Those soldiers who were more observant let out cries of alarm and, once they realized they were surrounded, dropped to their knees and held their swords over their heads in surrender.

"Get up," Vyler scolded. "No one is demanding you surrender your arms. *They* aren't going to hurt you, provided you don't do anything stupid. Lieutenant, would you mind?"

Still eyeing the dragons, but trusting the baron to know what he was talking about, Thrombeaux motioned for his men to get on their feet.

"How...?" one soldier began.

"I'll handle this," Thrombeaux informed the soldier,

stepping in front of him to address the baron. "Why do they…? How do they…? Why don't they…? I don't know what to ask."

Vyler turned to Jerica and held out a hand. "They answer to her, it would seem. She's their kai."

"You!" Thrombeaux cried. "You're the one, aren't you? You're the rider Thunder King fears! I should've known!"

"I am," Jerica confirmed. She walked over to one of Skellig's forelegs and leaned companionably against it. "You needn't worry about them. They're harmless, unless you threaten any of us. Then, they'll eat you all for supper."

Zeira turned to Jerica with a look of horror on her face. *What? We most certainly will not.*

Jerica let out an audible sigh. *I know this. You know this. But* they *don't* know this, *get it?*

Ah. I've got it. I think.

"We will do nothing to alarm your pets," Thrombeaux began. Then, raising his voice, he faced his men. "None of us will."

All six dragons growled menacingly. Skellig took a few steps forward with his fangs bared.

"They're companions," Jerica corrected. "They're quite nice, once you get to know them. Now, about that shipment … the dragons only attacked because your guys attacked first. A weapon on one of those boats launched a projectile at my friends. As a result, one was immobilized. What you have to understand is, if you attack one dragon, you've pretty much declared war on *all* the dragons."

"They lost our shipment," Thrombeaux argued. "You know as well as I that the Thunder King will not sit still for this."

"Perhaps," Othos falteringly began, "that is, maybe there is something we can do to rectify this situation?"

Thrombeaux's gaze swung over to the celestial and let it linger there.

"What do you have in mind?"

"Some type of reimbursement?"

"I'm listening."

Othos turned to Jerica. "What do humans value more

than anything else?"

"Power."

"That doesn't help us. Anything else?"

"Umm, gold? Jewels? Treasure?"

Nodding, Othos turned back to the soldiers. "Interested?"

Thrombeaux stared at the dragon towering over him. "Are you serious?"

"As a set of fangs."

"Just a moment."

What are they doing? Othos asked, switching to their shared telepathy.

I don't know, Jerica admitted. *I think they're tempted, but why they can't say that is beyond me.*

I'm close enough to hear them, Nuri reported. *They're saying something about horns.*

Zeira looked puzzled. *Horns? What about them?*

I don't know, Nuri admitted. *Look, they're done talking among themselves.*

"You, dragon," Thrombeaux began, addressing Othos, "you say you destroyed the three barges?"

"Barges?" Othos repeated, confused.

Boats, Jerica translated.

"Ah, yes. Boats. That was me. I will admit it was foolish." *Yet, those imbeciles had it coming*, Othos mentally added, eliciting snorts of amusement from Gocri and Skellig.

"Here's what we'll do, dragon," Thrombeaux said. "We will attribute the loss of the vessels to natural causes."

"That would be wonderful!" Jerica exclaimed, but sobered instantly. "Oh, I'm so sorry about the crew."

"Most have already joined my men here," Marek explained. "A few are unaccounted for, but those have most certainly fled. As I was saying, we will report the boats were lost at sea."

"But, won't the Thunder King want a better explanation than that?" Vyler asked.

"Against the forces of nature?" Thrombeaux asked, shaking his head. "No, he'll be angry, but he won't pin the blame on anyone. But, before we do that, we *must* collect the horns."

"Horns?" Zeira repeated, as she reached up to touch her own horns. "We're not giving you our horns."

"Huh? No, that's not what I meant. Each boat sailing under the Thunder King's crest carries with it a qiin horn. These horns will …"

"What's so keen about it?" Jerica wanted to know. "That seems a funny way to describe a horn."

"A qiin horn?" Thrombeaux repeated. "What is so odd about that? Our mages have learned the horns of a qiin have the ability to …"

Vyler held up a hand. "I'm sorry, would you spell the word?"

"What, qiin? Q-I-I-N. You don't have them here? Whatever. Their horns have the ability to record audio, so ships will have one on board to document any emergencies. In the case of a boat sinking, a recording of the circumstances will be left on the horn, detailing weather conditions, choppiness of the water, and so on. A recovery effort will always be launched to recover the horn so that it can be determined who, or what, was at fault. So, in this case, we have to find those three horns and make sure they're destroyed."

"You haven't indicated what you want yet," Jerica pointed out.

"I'm getting to it. So, is it possible? One of your number is a water dragon. Can you retrieve those three horns?"

In response, the dragons turned to look at the sea, where Nuri was visible.

"I'm on it," the valthan reported. "If they weren't crushed, I'll be able to locate them."

Jerica waved at Nuri as her head vanished beneath the surface.

"Do you think it'll be able to locate those horns? It typically takes us months, if not years, to locate a horn from a submerged ship."

"Her name is Nuri," Jerica added, as she frowned at the soldier, "and as she said, if they're there, she'll find them. What do you want in return for this arrangement?"

The soldier's response was immediate. "Dark tears. We've all heard stories that they can be found in these waters."

Jerica turned to her brother-in-law. "Do you know what he's talking about?"

Vyler nodded. "I do, actually. Black pearls. They are found in only four places in the entire kingdom. And Kinzler's Point is one of them. That isn't something we advertise. How did you hear about it?"

Thrombeaux shrugged. "You wanted to know what we want in exchange for our cooperation, well, that's it. Each member of our team will require one dark tear."

"How many men are there?" Vyler asked, sighing. "How many do we need to find? A dozen? Fifteen?"

"Twenty-four."

At that moment, Nuri's head broke the surface of the water. She slowly made her way to the water's edge, where the entire group gathered to meet her.

"You didn't find them," Thrombeaux guessed.

Nuri unfolded her front legs and carefully made her way out of the water. Well, at least, the first quarter of her. Looking at the soldier, she lowered her neck and spat something at their feet—three short, gray horns. One of them had a huge crack running from base to tip.

"How the ruddy hell did you find them so fast?" the lieutenant wanted to know.

Nuri approximated a shrug. "Once I learned what to look for, it was easy."

"Ever hear of something called *dark tears*?" Sifula asked.

Nuri turned to look at their vaporous friend, who was now the spitting image of Zeira. "Dark tears? I do not think so. What are they? Is this something else we're looking for?"

Skellig nudged Marek with the tip of his smallest talon. "You. Tell her what these things are. If they're in the sea, Nuri will know what they are."

"They're from the sea?" Nuri said, shaking her head. "I'm sorry, if that's true, then I haven't heard of …"

"Black pearls," Marek reported. He held up a clenched fist. "They're a little bigger than my fist, perfectly round. They …"

"… have flakes of green, gold, and red embedded within the sphere," the valthan interrupted. "Some have more colors than that, but those three are the most common."

"You know what they are!" Jerica exclaimed, delighted.

"You could say that," Nuri returned.

Skellig, noting Nuri's hesitation, inched forward. "Nuri, is there a problem? What aren't you telling us?"

Nuri held up a tiny claw. "First, who wants these, how many are needed, and how much time do I have to find them?"

Jerica pointed at the group of soldiers, which was growing steadily larger.

"They do. It's in exchange for them not reporting us. Why? What's the matter, Nuri, are you all right?"

"I'm told they aren't difficult to find," Thrombeaux said, in a tone of voice bereft of his usual harshness. "Is this not the case?"

"It is so," Nuri confirmed, sighing. "I don't know how many are left."

As one, the entire group turned to their valthan companion and waited for an explanation.

"They, er, are quite tasty," Nuri began.

"What?" Marek demanded. "You've been eating them? It's a pearl! They're not even edible!"

"Sure they are," Nuri countered. "Crunchy on the outside, chewy in the middle. Once you break through the crunchy exterior, you'll find it's quite … that's not the point, so there's no need to bring that up. I'm sorry, I've been snacking on them. I didn't know I should have been leaving them alone."

"Just see how many you can find, would you?" Zeira asked.

Nuri nodded. "Of course."

"Poor Nuri," Jerica moaned. "It feels like we're punishing her. She's had to find the horns, and now we've sent her after these black tears."

"Dark tears," Thrombeaux softly corrected. "Each is worth the equivalent of four times a soldier's annual pay."

"Why do you call black pearls dark tears?" Jerica wanted to know. "Is there some myth associated with them?"

Thrombeaux shook his head. "No myth or legend, I'm afraid." Gone were the harsh looks and stern body language.

"It's just what they're known as, to us. Oh, no. Where did *that* come from?"

Thinking a threat had manifested, Gocri and Skellig stepped around the humans and faced north, to the sea. Sif immediately reverted to her natural size and spread her wings in an attempt to shield Zeira and the humans.

"I'm more than capable of fighting," Zeira grumped, from somewhere behind Sif's right wing. "You don't need to keep doing that."

"What are we looking for?" Gocri wanted to know.

"No idea," Skellig admitted. "You, human. What do you see?"

Thrombeaux and the rest of the soldiers had retreated farther inland, and were pulling Jerica, Theresa, and Vyler along with them.

"Look out!" Marek called. "A rogue wave approaches!"

Skellig turned his gaze to the north. Yes, a large wave was approaching, and it was coming in *fast*. It *had* to be Nuri.

Well, of course it's me. I was trying to hurry, wasn't I?

"It's Nuri," Skellig reported. "No need to fear."

"No need to fear?" Thrombeaux shouted. "It's nearly twenty feet high! It's going to wash away your village! We need to alert the guards! We need to …"

"Just a moment," Jerica interrupted. "Watch. I think you'll like this."

Faster and faster the wave traveled, zeroed in on their location. Huge plumes of seawater shot skyward as the wave broke upon the reef, only a few seconds from shore.

Ten feet from making landfall, the wave collapsed in on itself, sending tiny rivulets of water in all directions, splashing only a few drops of water on everyone's shoes. Lifting her sandal, Jerica looked at the soldiers and smiled.

"It's a long story."

"What the bloody hell happened?" Thrombeaux demanded. "You wield a power strong enough to neutralize a destructive rogue wave?"

Nuri's head surfaced as she carefully walked up the beach. With half of her body exposed, she lowered herself to the ground and rested her head on the sandy shore. Far behind, her tail lazily swayed left and right in the water. After a few moments, her jaws opened and she dropped a mouthful of black, circular objects at their feet.

"I hope this is enough. I had to check the western coast to get the rest. But, there you are. Two dozen nuggets of goodness."

Skellig reached down to pick up one of the pearls. "You seriously eat these things?"

"Mm-hmm. Thankfully, I'm full, or I probably wouldn't have been able to control myself."

Skellig stared at the smooth black sphere. It was tiny in his hand, and he could barely tell it was there. Shrugging, he turned to the closest soldier and held it out. The biped looked nervously up at him, and then checked with Thrombeaux to see whether he should accept it.

"Of course, idiot," the commanding officer scolded. "I'd hurry before he eats it himself. I'd say he's sorely tempted."

"Perhaps," Skellig confessed, as he dropped the pearl into the soldier's outstretched hand. "But, I'll save that for another time, when no one is watching."

"Is there enough for everyone?" Jerica asked.

"There should be," Thrombeaux said, as he inspected the pile of black orbs. "Oy, you lot. Line up."

One by one, the smiling soldiers were given one of the dark tears. Once everyone had their treasure tucked safely away inside pockets, or bags, or whatever, Thrombeaux faced his troops and snapped his fingers a few times.

"Everyone? Eyes on me. These gifts are from the dragons. Are we ever going to divulge what happened here?"

"No, sir!" the men chorused.

"What *did* happen to the supply barges?" Marek asked.

"Went down in a storm," one soldier said, shrugging.

"It was a terrible loss," another added.

Satisfied, Marek turned to look at Othos, who had been sitting on his haunches, watching the humans.

"You're covered, dragon. Othos, was it? You … well, all of you, have made believers out of us."

Othos settled himself to the ground and stared at Thrombeaux. "Believers? You didn't think dragons existed?"

"That's not what I meant," the soldier said, shaking his head. "You've shown us that dragons can be trusted. I hope you can say the same for us."

"You answer to the Thunder King," Jerica said, which—surprisingly—caused the soldiers to drop their heads with shame. "Why would we ... what are you doing? Why do you all look like that?"

Thrombeaux cast a furtive look over his shoulder, and then quickly to the right and left, as though he suspected someone could be eavesdropping.

"It's not as if we want to. We have no choice! We know what he's doing is wrong, but there's not a lot we can do about it. No one wants to put their life in danger, and that's exactly what will happen if you oppose Dinty."

Skellig snorted. "Doesn't really inspire fear, does it?"

Jerica's eyes widened. "Maybe you could help us?"

"I believe we already did," Thrombeaux pointed out. "But, we will if we can. What do you require?"

Vyler approached and sighed heavily. "We need Cerebus to dig elsewhere."

"That's not going to happen," Lt. Thrombeaux replied. "The dig site has already been determined. That's why Cerebus is on its way here, I'm afraid."

"Will it really create havoc and devastation?" Vyler asked.

Thrombeaux sighed. "On a scale which you would never believe."

"How can we make it go away?" Vyler asked. "Is there hope?"

"The King won't order Cerebus to be dismantled until it finds every last bit of some type of metal."

"Jhorium," Jerica breathed. "That's what we were planning to do. We are going to find this metal first."

"That won't stop him from ordering Cerebus to dig," Marek said. "Tell me that is not your plan."

"Is it not a good plan?" Sifula asked. "I thought it was. Find this metal, make it known we found it, and then leave the area, which will then make this Thunder King lose interest in Cael."

"*That* is our plan," Jerica confirmed.

"How do you plan on locating this jhorium before Cerebus does?" Thrombeaux asked.

"We have a small piece of drininite," Jerica said. "We'll use it to locate the jhorium before Cerebus can be assembled."

Thrombeaux surprised them again when he held out his hand. "Good luck to you. We will try and stall them from our end. The loss of equipment will probably buy you four days, maybe five. I'd get moving if I were you."

The soldiers were all smiles as they moved off, many continuing to bow at them as they backed away from them.

Jerica eyed the sol dragon. "You got lucky."

Othos shrugged. "Perhaps. I really didn't mean to make a mess of things. I thought I was helping."

"I know you did, Othos. Well, if you really want to help, we need to figure out where the jhorium is hiding, extricate it, and do it as quickly as possible."

Othos straightened and picked idly at his fangs with one of his talons. "When you *do* locate this mineral, you need to be certain your Thunder Boy knows about it?"

Jerica giggled. "Thunder King, but yes, we do."

"So, you might say you want to make a spectacle of it."

Intrigued, Skellig inched closer. "You have an idea, don't you?"

"I do, Spark. I do."

"Let's hear it," Zeira urged. "What do you have in mind?"

Othos turned to Jerica and nodded. "Well, this is entirely based on what you've told me about *her*."

"They haven't told you anything about me," Jerica insisted. She turned to Skellig for confirmation, but saw that the Spark dragon was tapping the side of his head. "Oh, you mean using mind speech? I'm surprised I didn't hear it."

"He didn't," Othos confirmed. "I accessed his memories. Then, not believing what I saw, I accessed Zeira's, and then the rest. All confirm my suspicions. Therefore, what we need is for you to work your magic, so to speak."

"I will, of course," Jerica said, "but that doesn't mean I know what to do."

Othos' grin exposed every fang in his mouth. "I believe two of us ought to do it. With you, that is. Nuri, are you ready?"

Nuri's head lifted. "Me? Uh, sure, I can be ready. I *am* ready. What do you need me to do?"

"Who else do you need?" Gocri asked. "I'm not sure how I can help, but I will gladly volunteer my services."

"Same here," Skellig added.

"That goes for me, too," Sif said.

"I'm here as well," Zeira reminded everyone. "I'm more than happy to help."

Othos shook his head. "Appreciated, but unneeded. The second will be … me."

"You?" Zeira repeated, surprised. "Jerica can only manipulate powers of those she has bonded with. Wait. You're suggesting you want to bond with her?"

"We already have," Othos announced. *I can hear your thoughts, kairie.*

But … that isn't the same as bonding, is it? Jerica protested. She looked at her dragon companions. *Can all of you hear me?*

Six dragons nodded.

Nuri rose to her feet and began backing into the water. "My powers of echolocation, with your powers of … wait. What ability will Jerica be adding to my own?"

"Illumination," the sol dragon answered. "If I'm right, then Jerica, holding the piece of drininite, while tapping into your echolocational skills, Nuri, and my powers of illumination, should reveal the location of the jhorium."

Skellig cocked his head. "Are you sure? I don't see how that will work."

"Admittedly, much of the tweaking will come from Jerica," Othos said. "She has to properly voice her expectations before she can expect the magic to function properly."

"And how am I supposed to do that when I have no idea what I'm doing?" Jerica objected.

"Perhaps *I* could be of assistance?"

The seven of them whirled around to see a lone human walking their way. Jerica couldn't help it. She groaned aloud.

"Doolan. What are you doing back here?"

"It's not often so many dragons can be found in one place," the elderly mage began. "As such, I find myself keeping an eye on this place, in the hopes that your group will return and need some help. Now, if I heard you correctly, my dear Jerica, you seem to be in a predicament."

"I'm not offering you anything," Jerica snapped. "My friends will figure this out *without* your help."

"Then, could I give you a few pointers on spells and their creation?"

"Why would you help us?" Vyler wanted to know.

"Because, it's in my best interests to do so," Doolan smoothly replied. "Oh, I know all about your quest to find a way to appease me without fulfilling your agreement."

Jerica's mouth opened. "I ... I...?"

"Let us not worry about that right now," Cael's mage said, clasping his hands behind his back. "I see a sixth dragon has joined your ranks. Excellent! And you'd be the sol dragon? There's no need for introductions, my scaly beastie. Now, young Jerica, if I may. Stand there. Close your eyes."

"Nuh-uh. Not a chance."

"Come, come, dear girl. I'm trying to instruct you in the fine dynamics of spell-casting. Now, do you want to learn or not?"

Jerica's eyes widened in disbelief. "You want to help me? Since when? Why are you being nice all of a sudden?"

"What angle are you playing at?" Vyler demanded.

"My dear baron," Doolan soothed, "I only have the noblest of intentions."

Skellig immediately slammed an arm down between his kai and the creepy male human.

"You want to help? Fine. You, stay there. Jerica, come over here, next to us."

"This will work better if I am able to physically touch her," Doolan insisted. "Yes, that sounds bad, but I assure you, I ..."

"I will personally bite off anything that comes into contact with her," Gocri vowed.

"Not if I get to him first," Skellig said, giving the Glacier dragon an appreciative nod.

"I'll do one better," Othos stated "You, human. If you harm anyone here, I'll personally make you lunch. What? Skellig, why do you make that face?"

"Gocri has already used that same threat."

"Oh. Well, it still stands. We could share, I suppose. I get the top half and you the bottom? Observe. The human doesn't appear so cocky now, does he? You may proceed, biped."

"I, er, very well. Jerica, close your eyes."

"No one will harm you," Skellig told her, using a soft voice.

"Thanks. All right, they're closed. Now what?"

"You're looking for something? Do you know what it is?"

"I do, but I don't know how to find it. Who has the, er, black stone?" Jerica asked, raising her voice.

"Your father had it last," Vyler said, stepping forward. "He gave it to me for safekeeping. Here. I've got hold of the crazy thing. I can feel it pulling away. If you take it, will you be able to, I don't know, *keep* it?"

"Yes, I think so. I just have to keep my hand closed."

Jerica carefully took the piece of rare mineral and admired the many polished surfaces. She also felt the pull of the stone as it tried to put some distance between itself and her. She looked back at Doolan.

"Now what?"

"That is the stone I observed before? I will admit to being insanely curious about it now. It's not important. With your eyes closed, open your senses. You'll have to craft the spell in your mind, giving it an exact set of instructions on what to do. Bear in mind, if you aren't specific, and aren't clearly thinking about what you want it to do, the spell will backfire, or give unexpected results. Does that make sense, my dear?"

"Yes, I think so." *Guys, I have no idea why he's being so nice. He's really starting to freak me out.*

You're perfectly safe, Zeira assured her.

I won't let any harm befall you, Miss Jerica, Gocri added.

Thank you. All of you. All right, Othos, are you there?

Always, came the celestial's powerful thought.

What do I do? What's your plan for making this work?

It's easy. With Nuri's echolocation skills, we send her power out to explore the area. In this case, with you holding that stone of yours, and with what I've divined of its purpose from everyone's minds, you can specify Nuri's power to look for areas it'll want to shy away from.

Clever, Sif murmured.

With that in mind, using my powers of illumination, you would then add in the ability to show us what areas are specifically being avoided, or are being attracted. Does that make sense?

How would that work? Jerica wanted to know.

I'd say … well, let's see. If you're using my powers, you could use sunlight for the location of this mineral you're looking for. All the others can stay in darkness.

But it's light outside!

Then, you'll have to think about using bright sunshine. My power is capable of burning holes through the densest of materials. No, I feel your alarm. There's nothing to worry about. Right, ready to try it?

No.

Will you try it anyway?

If I must. Is everyone ready?

We're ready, Zeira said.

Jerica sighed, took a deep breath, and reached out to Nuri. She felt the valthan's rapid heartbeat, and felt the cool, refreshing water on Nuri's back. Then, keeping those feelings prevalent, she cast her senses out to Othos. Even though he had told her she was already bonded with him, she didn't remember sharing any of his senses, so was unsure what to expect. But, as soon as his presence filled her mind, she gasped with shock. Here was a dragon who was old, so very old. His power and experience made the others pale in comparison. This was a dragon who had seen the birth of the known universe, and had probably been around even longer.

I have, Othos chuckled.

Concentrating on the simple fact that Othos was a sun dragon, and confident she had added the celestial's powers to her own, Jerica clutched the drininite tightly in her hand and sent out a blast of Nuri's unique sound waves. This time, she imagined the strange black gem as the source of the sonar blast. She waited to see what was going to happen.

Nothing did. Jerica turned to Othos.

"Well, that was a dismal failure. Do you have any other tricks you'd like to try?"

Chapter 7 - Doolan

This isn't working, Skellig," Jerica complained—quietly— two hours later. "I've tried everything Doolan suggested. I tried everything Othos wanted to try. I've even tried following a few of my own hunches. Why won't it work? How are we supposed to find the jh—er, *mineral*, if none of these spells work?"

"Don't despair," Skellig said, as he lowered himself to the ground next to his kai. His kai. He really should refer to her as everyone's kai. He twisted his long, yellow neck and spotted the human mage near the water's edge, sitting on the ground. His eyes were closed, he appeared to be rocking, and if Skellig wasn't mistaken, he could hear the mage humming to himself.

"He's meditating," Jerica said, looking up at the Spark dragon. "Maybe … maybe he doesn't know, either?"

"It's a possibility," Skellig conceded. "Have you tried …?"

"The problem is," Jerica continued, "that I have absolutely

no idea if I'm doing these spells right. After all, I've never done them before, and I seem to recall going on record that, prior to meeting you dragons, I have never done any magic before in my entire life. That has to mean something, doesn't it?"

Skellig took a breath. "Well …"

"And then there's Othos," Jerica interrupted. "He says I've bonded with him, but I certainly don't recall doing anything of the sort. After all, with you, Zeira, and the others, I actually had to try and see if I could sense your thoughts, almost like … well, almost like two blindfolded people stumbling around to see whether they'll eventually connect."

Skellig tried again. "Maybe …"

"Oh!" Jerica interrupted, for a third time. "We mustn't forget that we have no idea what this mineral looks like, so what's to prevent us from walking right by it? Or flying, as it were? Skellig, do you have any input? Why aren't you talking?"

Skellig grunted. "I've tried. Several times. Look, we all know you are no spell caster. But, in this case, the human wizard appears to be giving his assistance. Freely, as it were."

"Yeah, about that," Jerica said, frowning. "How do we know he's not trying to further sabotage us? He is not known for his … well, let's just say *compassion* for his fellow humans. I simply don't trust him."

"If you don't trust him, then I certainly won't, either," Skellig vowed. "Come. Let us find out what your wizard thinks of this situation."

"Eww, I'd rather not talk to him. I can't stand the way he continually leers at me."

"If he does, I'll squish him flat," Skellig promised. "There he is. Looks like Nuri has been keeping an eye on him. You, human. Er, Doolan. We'd like a word."

The mage's eyes opened, he yawned once, and then slowly made his way to his feet.

"Yes? Oh, it's you, Jerica. What may I do for you, my darling dear?"

"I'm the one you're dealing with," Skellig snapped, causing the elderly human to jump with surprise. "We've tried numerous variations of your spells. I've heard you rephrase, reword, and even try singing the spell."

"Of course, my dear dragon, of course. Is there a question in there?"

"Since we seem to be stuck on determining whether or not the spell is working, tell us what's supposed to be happening. What should we be looking for?"

As the frail human began to explain the nuances and complexities of spell-casting, Skellig noticed the rest of his fellow dragons, save Nuri and Othos, who were in the sea, had crowded close.

"I tried to tell my dearest Jerica that spell-casting is not for the uninitiated. It's a very complex skill to learn. Mistakes are bound to happen during the first attempt. And the second. Probably the third, too."

"Just tell us what we should be looking for," Sif urged. "Since it's logical to assume what we seek is buried, will the ground have a big X on it? Maybe an arrow that points to the exact location?"

Doolan finally sighed. "I am not privy to what is going inside that young girl's head. Spell-casting isn't for the faint of heart. A very precise set of instructions must be created, with no chance for loopholes, before it'll work. I've known mages who have spent their entire lives on their craft, and never managed to master it. Dear girl, don't be upset if you are unsuccessful. Most are, I'm afraid."

"Our kai is powerful," Skellig said, growling loud enough to be heard by all. "If anyone can do it, she can. Now, assume she knows what she's doing. What should we be looking for?"

"Well, that depends on how she phrased it," Doolan insisted. "What can you tell me about it?"

"I'd say it's more about which powers I used," Jerica countered.

"That makes no sense, my dear child," Doolan crooned. "Spell-casting builds a foundation from the words you speak or think, and then …"

"Look," Jerica snapped, unable to hide the exasperation in her voice. "I used her power and his. That, coupled with the properties of this thing I've got clenched in my fist, I'm fully expecting … I don't know, sunshine, maybe, to light the way? I don't see anything like that, so somehow, I've done something wrong with the spell. But I've also changed the wording around at least four times."

"And did it work?" Doolan eagerly asked.

"Do you see anything lit up around here?" Jerica asked, unable to keep the sarcasm from her voice.

"Er, no."

"See? It isn't working."

"Perhaps we should try something else?"

"Why are you doing this?" Jerica asked, rounding on the gaunt old man wearing the bright red robes of his guild. "You've never been this nice, not once in all the time you've been in Cael, which is as long as I've lived there."

"Can't a person want to help out their fellow villager?" Doolan asked, as he gave her a wide-eyed, innocent look.

"Not when it's you," Jerica said. "You're up to something."

"Let's hear your other suggestion," Vyler said, trying to defuse the situation. "You said we should try something else? Like what?"

"Well, if this was me, I'd use a familiar," Doolan said, offering a smile which showed off his brown, stained teeth.

"What does that mean?" Theresa asked. "He wants to use a familiar *what?*"

Doolan carefully lowered himself to a squat and gently placed a hand on the ground.

"A familiar," the mage explained, "is a living creature who will temporarily be … *pressed* into service."

This caught the dragons' attention. Skellig growled. The Spark dragon also noticed that every other dragon, save Othos and Nuri—who hadn't heard Doolan's definition— were now glaring at the human. In fact, his ice dragon friend was advancing on the biped and, if he wasn't mistaken, was about to take a bite out of the human.

"You subvert other beings to do your bidding?" Gocri snarled.

"Never dragons," Doolan hastily added. "I assure you, the familiars mages like myself use are harmless creatures, such as insects, or … or … birds."

Gocri calmed down, but not by much, Skellig noticed.

Then again, had Gocri really wanted to take a bite out of the person their kai despised, who was he to argue? In fact, he'd probably join in, just to show support.

Gocri cast him an appreciative look.

Thanks.

Skellig nodded back.

"What I do," Doolan explained, as he nervously eyed the dragons crowding around him, "is I search for a suitable familiar. Once I find one, in this case, I sense there's an earthworm less than a meter from the surface, I'll exert my influence over the worm, and ask it to take a look around, so to speak."

Vyler cleared his throat. "Uh, er, earthworms don't have any eyes. How would they do that?"

Doolan paled. "All right, bad example. Let me search for a ... there! I do believe I just found an ideal specimen to be my familiar."

A speck of color became visible above their heads as it circled around and around, clearly reluctant to venture closer, but apparently the mage's control was strong. A blue bird appeared and descended into their midst, landing on Doolan's outstretched arm. It chirped nervously as it stared at each individual dragon.

A thought occurred as Skellig eyed the skittish creature. His forked tongue appeared and he deliberately ran it along his teeth. Sure enough, the bird tweeted with alarm and then defecated all over Doolan's robed arm.

Sif appeared next to him.

An interesting reaction. Jerica is now fighting to control her giggles. What prompted you to do that?

I have no idea, Skellig admitted. *The notion occurred, I acted on it, and, well, I was amused.*

I'm so sorry, Jerica's voice said, causing both dragons to look her way.

Was that you? Skellig inquired. *How did you ... you're not even looking at us.*

If I look in your direction, I'm going to burst out laughing. I was just thinking, wouldn't it be funny if that bird got scared enough to poop all over Doolan's arm? Then, you licked your fangs. I guess I forgot our minds are linked, and without realizing it, gave you a suggestion.

Are we agreed? Sif said. *No harm done?*

No harm done, Jerica said, nodding.

"Now that he's completely under my control," Doolan was saying, "I can have him fly wherever I want him to go. Since he's my familiar, I'm able to see what he sees, so in essence, this bird has become an extension of me. Yes, Baron? You have a question?"

Vyler pointed at the bird. "How is *that* supposed to help us find that which we know is buried in the ground? Does this bird have some type of power we're not aware of?"

Doolan nodded and turned to Jerica. "Ah, a very valid point. You mentioned before you possess something to help you locate that which you seek? What *do* you seek? I do not seem to remember."

"That's because we haven't told you," Jerica said.

"But you *do* have a method of detecting this object, don't you? May I see it, please?"

Skellig watched Jerica hold up a finger, indicating he was to wait, and then turned to face them.

How much do we trust him? How much should I tell him?

He clearly wants something he knows he normally wouldn't be given, Zeira said. *And, he must think his best chance of success lies with us. I think his offer to help is sincere. You can offer him the drininite, but you don't necessarily have to tell him what it's for.*

A good point. Thank you, Zeira.

My pleasure.

Taking a deep breath, and making sure her grip was tight, she held up the polished black drininite.

"You've seen this before, remember? You caught it when, well, it was *tossed* through the air."

"Ah, yes. That stone is what you plan on using to detect your mystery mineral?"

"How do you know it's a mineral?" Skellig asked, suspicious.

"If you don't want me to know it's a mineral, my dear dragon," Doolan began, "perhaps, you should keep that bit of information to yourselves. Now, if you'd be kind enough to pass over this stone. There, thank you. What I'll have to do is tie the properties of this stone into a simple location spell, and then persuade my familiar to approach any area it is clearly uncomfortable with."

Without realizing it, Skellig nodded.

"Your plan is ... *sound*. How long will it take?"

"Oh, aren't you silly, my dear dragon. I've already finished. At the moment, I'm trying to persuade my familiar to fly away, only it is extremely reluctant to comply. Maybe it's because of the presence of six dragons? Oh, look at that. The poor thing has relieved himself. On me. Again. Go on, now. Start your search."

Skellig watched the bird defecate a third time and scramble like mad to put as much distance as possible between it and the dragons. Once it was gone, Skellig turned back to the mage.

"Do you have a prediction just how long this will take?"

"Too many variables, my scaled beastie. There are too many variables to consider. The bird may find the location in the next five minutes, or it might take it days."

"We don't have days," Jerica pointed out. "Besides, we wouldn't want to keep that poor bird enslaved for that long. I assume you'd look for a new familiar?"

"Whatever for?" Doolan asked, genuinely curious. "When a suitable familiar is found, why would it be prematurely released when the objective hasn't been obtained? That doesn't make much sense, does it, my dearest young Jerica?"

"Oh, that poor bird," Jerica lamented.

"I don't see what the problem is," Doolan said, growing angry. "After all, aren't your dragons doing the exact same thing to you?"

"What was that?" Skellig snapped.

"Excuse me?" Gocri asked, jerking his head up.

"We are not," Sifula added, at the same time.

"Of course you are," Doolan insisted, oblivious to the dragons' rising ire. "You found yourself a human, have determined she's suitable for your purposes, and have then corralled her into doing your bidding. How is this different than this example? I found a familiar and am using it in similar ways."

"We are not alike," Skellig insisted. "Our kai is not imprisoned. Our kai has a choice. She can return home to her family at any time."

"Do you really expect me to believe that?" Doolan dryly asked. "I know full well how difficult it is for you dragons to find a suitable rider. Now, for some reason, my sweet Jerica has proven herself suitable to the likes of you five. Er, *six*. Additionally, I can see that some of you are not from this region, but I'll let that go for the time being. Answer me truthfully, dragon. If your rider decided she was done *adventuring*, what would that do to this delightful soiree you've been having? Face it, you'd all disband and return to your respective regions. Am I right?"

Just let me eat him, Gocri implored.

You have to admit, Othos began, *that it's very tempting. If you don't want to eat him, let's just see how deep into the ground he can be hammered. Anyone interested? Just me? Spoilsports.*

"No one is holding me against my will," Jerica declared, as she stepped in front of the mage. "These dragons have shown more honor than most humans I know."

"Oh, sure," Doolan said, waving a dismissive hand, "you're told you can leave at any time. No, there's no need for threats and intimidation by your scaled companions. I'm suggesting that, should you decide you'd like to, say, return home, then your companions would find some way to talk you out of it. All without using any type of coercion, of course."

"Not true," Sif said.

Skellig turned to look at Gocri. Detecting movement, Gocri's head swiveled until he was returning the look.

I trust this not. This human is up to something.

I agree.

If I didn't know any better, then I'd say he's stalling.

I agree, but for what?

I think the two of us need to figure this out.

The ice dragon's head was nodding, even before Skellig had finished his thought.

What do you have in mind?

Skellig turned to look at the open bay.

What would you say to checking the area? If someone was trying to sneak up on us, I'd certainly like to know about it.

Gocri nodded. *I'm on it.*

Giant, white wings were unfolded and snapped down, a split second after the Glacier dragon leapt up. Disappearing into the clouds, Skellig felt the eyes of his companions on him.

He's going to do a little investigation, that's all.

Can I help?

Skellig turned to Nuri.

Gocri is checking to see if there's anything out there we need to know about.

Another set of eyes would be helpful in a situation like this, the valthan pointed out. *Gocri can check the air. I'll check the water.*

It was Skellig's turn to nod. *Good. Please do.*

Nuri's head slipped under the surface and disappeared. Ripples appeared in the water as evidence of her discreet departure.

Is everything all right? Zeira asked. Skellig felt the worry emanating from their leader. *Is there anything you need to tell us?*

Only that Gocri and Nuri are checking the area.

For what?

For anything that shouldn't be there, Skellig said.

Ah. Understandable.

Guys? It was Jerica. *Look at Doolan. I think we have a problem.*

Skellig glanced at the human mage. Yes, Jerica was right. Worry lines had appeared on Doolan's face, and he was gritting his teeth in anger.

"What is it?" Skellig asked, causing the human to flinch. "What's wrong?"

"I've lost my familiar."

Jerica slapped a hand over her mouth in horror.

"It's not what you think," Doolan was quick to add. "It's still alive and well, only …"

"It broke free of your control," Vyler guessed.

"Yes. I cannot fathom what happened."

Zeira made a circular gesture with her arm. "Well? Try again."

"The bird was perfect," Doolan lamented, as he squatted

down to place a hand on the ground. "It could fly, it could … hmm. I may have found a replacement."

In spite of himself, Skellig had to admit he was impressed. "What did you find, wizard?"

Something small, about the same size as the piece of drininite, darted past Jerica's head. Skellig watched as his kai flung her arms up and started waving them around, as though she had discovered she was on fire.

"What is it?" Sif asked. "May I be of assistance?"

"Only if you can make it go away," Jerica said, as she ducked behind Zeira's leg. "What … is *that* the new familiar?"

"It is," Doolan said, as he demonstrated a supreme amount of disinterest by holding out his hand and waiting for the creature to land on it.

It was a large hornet. It sat there, in the middle of Doolan's wrinkled hand, cleaning itself. After a few moments, it buzzed its wings a few times and turned to face the mage. Then, much to Doolan's surprise, and Jerica's dismay, three others appeared and landed on the open hand. The new arrivals swarmed over their enchanted companion, no doubt wondering what had happened to it.

"They came to its aid," Skellig deduced. "Interesting. I didn't know such creatures had that capability."

The three additional hornets suddenly froze in place. As one, their wings were lowered and they turned to face Doolan.

"Why settle for one when you can have four?" Doolan gloated. "Now, give me a moment and I'll send my new helpers out to explore the area."

"What is the largest familiar you have ever used?" Zeira suddenly asked.

Disinterested, Doolan didn't bother looking up from the creatures in his hand.

"A centaur, but don't ever tell anyone that I did that." The mage cackled to himself as he whispered instructions into the insects' minds. Just then, Doolan's eyes widened. "Out of curiosity, why do you ask?"

"No worries. You should be all right."

"About …?"

Jerica pointed up. "*Them.*"

There, maybe twenty feet above Doolan's head, was the rest of the hive. They swirled and looped around in the air, looking as though the hornets were flying erratically, but when studied from afar, Skellig could see that the tiny insects were protecting themselves by keeping in a tight formation. Perhaps, if the mage could do it, making an entire swarm of hornets as familiars was probably a brilliant idea, not that he'd ever admit that to the mage.

"Well, well, what have we here? Yes, you'll all do just nicely. There. Tiny minds are so easy to manipulate. Oh, dear. Did I say that out loud? My apologies. Go now, my little minions. Let us see if we can find whatever it is my dear, sweet Jerica is yearning."

The swarm obediently flew away.

"I've asked you to stop calling me that," Jerica said, as she scowled at Doolan. "I'm not your dear, sweet girl. I am no one's girl, is that understood?"

"Perfectly, my … apologies. Of course, Jerica."

"Why are you being so nice?"

"Can't an old man try to be decent every once in a while?"

"Not unless it benefits him in some fashion. What do you get out of this?"

"Nothing but the satisfaction of being able to help you, of course."

He's lying.

Skellig looked up. *Nuri, you have found something?*

As have I, Gocri's voice broke in. *Nuri, you first.*

A large vessel approaches from the south.

Intent on getting Jerica's input, Skellig turned to their kai, only to see her hold up her finger to the mage, who had begun spouting nonsensical explanations for his actions once more. Jerica turned to him and nodded.

Describe what you see, Nuri, Jerica urged.

Water vessel, not as large as the flat ones Othos destroyed.

Hey, I said I was sorry, didn't I? Othos's voice interjected.

What else? Jerica asked.

Two masts, one at the front and one at the ship's back. Sails are blue, with a yellow mark through the center.

Are there cannons? Jerica wanted to know.

What is a cannon? Describe it.

Metal. They're typically as long as I am tall. They are cylindrical, and are usually sitting on some type of base, whether it's wooden or metallic in nature.

I don't see any ...

Or ... I'm sorry, I just remembered that these types of ships have their cannons concealed. Do you see any square panels on the ship, on either side?

Yes, I've seen them. Nearly twenty to a side. That's not good, is it?

It's one of the Thunder King's warships, Jerica groaned. *Somehow, Doolan must have sent out a message. I just don't ... the bird! That's where he sent the bird! He gave it a message and sent it south. Wanloo is to our south. That's why Doolan was stalling. I'm sorry, everyone. He was calling for help.*

How soon before it arrives? Zeira's voice asked.

Based on its speed, Nuri voice said, *maybe an hour. Possibly less.*

That's so soon! Jerica cried. *How is it moving so fast?*

Sails are all slack; wind is non-existent here, yet the craft moves, Nuri reported. *I do not know how the craft moves.*

Magic or mechanics, it doesn't matter, Skellig said.

I can still sink it, Nuri decided. *The bigger they are, the easier they are to hit. Say the word, and I'll ...*

It's my turn, Gocri's gruff voice interrupted. *Mine is just as dire, I'm afraid.*

Let's hear it, Zeira said, sounding glum.

Dym has been spotted. He's on his way.

We were able to take him on before, Sif recalled. *We can do so again.*

He's not alone, Gocri added. *I see four others with him. All, I might add, appear to be Spark.*

What? Skellig demanded. *He travels with four other Sparks? Are you sure?*

Yes. They all have markings, like yours.

Blast, Skellig grumbled. *When will they arrive?*

About the same time. They appear to be keeping pace with the ship Nuri has located. For protection?

It must be, Skellig said, sighing. *Very well. We need to ...*

"My, you've all grown quiet," Doolan observed. "Is everything all right? I do hope there's nothing that ..."

Othos strode over to the mage and raised a clenched claw. "Allow me. It's the least I can do."

Doolan's eyes widened with fright. But, before he could do — or say — anything, he suddenly let out an exclamation of surprise and slowly turned in place to inspect the surroundings.

"What is it?" Jerica asked.

"I do believe we might have something!" His eyes were closed and when he stopped rotating, Skellig saw he was facing southeast. "Yes, I'm sure that must be it. I'm sensing ..."

"... you're about to be eaten?" Othos growled.

Doolan's eyes widened once more.

"Get pounded into the ground?" Skellig said, raising a clenched claw.

"Wait a moment," Zeira interjected. "Wizard, you appeared surprised just then. Those insects found something, didn't they?"

Doolan dropped his gaze to the ground but refrained from saying anything.

"He's about to turn you into goo," Sif helpfully reminded the biped. "If you don't want that to happen, you'd best tell us what they found."

"There's something to the southeast," Doolan wailed. "About two miles. That's all I know, I swear!"

"You're looking awfully panicked for a human," Skellig observed. "Might you be guilty of doing something and you're worried we'll find out about it?"

"I ... I ... have no i-idea what y-you're talking about."

"And you're stuttering," Zeira observed. "Nervous?"

"You didn't send the bird out to help us," Jerica accused. "You sent it to Wanloo, didn't you? You told them about us and where we are. Why?"

"I'm terribly sorry, my dear girl. I had to. I'm under orders. You and your team of misfits must *never* be allowed to find that jhorium. He needs it for ..."

"He needs it for what?" Vyler repeated. Then, a look of surprise spread over his face. "You know all about what's been happening, don't you? The rising tension between species, the fighting, and the ... what did you call it, Jerica?"

"The imbalance. Forget about that for right now. He knows about the jhorium!" Jerica looked up at Othos. "All right, you can smash him."

Othos grunted once and hammered his claw onto the ground. Such was the force that Jerica was knocked off her feet. However, when the sol dragon lifted his claw, everyone could see that the canny mage had vanished. There, in the soft grass, was the small pebble of drininite. Pocketing the rare mineral, Jerica looked helplessly up at her companions.

"Damn him! What are we supposed to do now?"

Skellig pointed southeast. "That's easy. The reinforcements haven't arrived yet, which means we still have a little time. But, it also means we need to move. Zeira, we need to find the jhorium — and retrieve it — before *they* get here.'

Zeira nodded. "Agreed. Jerica, hold still. You're on my back. Vyler, I assume you'll return to the village?"

"Yes. I'll try to hold them off as long as I can. Jerica, you and your friends stay safe."

"Where are we heading?" Skellig asked, once they were all airborne.

"Southwest," Zeira reported.

"You're assuming the wizard is not leading us astray?" Skellig asked.

"He seemed surprised," Sif added, flying close. "Maybe even disheartened. I feel as though his role was to stall us for time, and it didn't play out that way."

"This jhorium is supposed to be buried in the ground," Skellig reminded everyone. "I'm not sure how we'll find it."

"Just get us to, what was it? Two miles? Take us two miles southeast of where we were," Jerica said.

"We're approaching that right now," Skellig announced.

Jerica's eyes widened. "That was quick."

Skellig flew up and over Zeira, moving from her right side to her left. "It's the most efficient way to travel."

"Are we landing?" Gocri asked.

Zeira nodded. "Yes."

"Where?" Sif wanted to know. "There's no area large enough for all of us."

Gocri snorted. "Allow me. I'll go first."

The Glacier dragon flapped his great white wings as his momentum slowed. Touching down lightly, Gocri immediately began making a clearing large enough for all of them to stand. Trees were snapped off at their trunks. Fallen logs and various shrubs were swept aside as Gocri used his wings to wipe the area clean. Once there was nothing left but tree trunks and tufts of grass dotting the landscape, he signaled his readiness.

"Nicely done," Skellig said, as he landed next to his large friend. "Do you think we'll have to dig?"

Gocri eyed his talons. "I hope not. But, if we do, so be it. I ... do you see that?"

Detecting the alarm in Gocri's voice, Skellig whipped his neck around.

"What do you see? Which direction?"

"West. Behold. I do believe we're in the right location."

Skellig was confused. "What makes you say that?"

Gocri pointed. There was Zeira, who had just placed Jerica on the ground. But, as for Jerica, she was facing north, and both of her eyes were glowing. In fact, they were so bright that they cast twin beams of light on anything she looked at.

"What is it?" Jerica asked, as she started to turn to look at them.

Every dragon present jerked their head away and held up claws to shield their eyes.

"I believe you should look away, human," Othos said, grinning. "Looks like we had it right the first time, just not the location."

"What are you talking about?" Jerica wanted to know.

Othos brought up a claw and touched the side of his skull, near his eyes.

"I do believe it's safe to say your eyes are emitting pure sunlight."

"They are? I can't even tell."

"Don't look at your friends," Othos cautioned. "You could irreparably damage their eyesight."

The twin beams of light suddenly vanished.

"Well, don't close your eyes now," Othos scolded. "It's up to you to locate the mineral you seek."

"But … I don't want to hurt my friends!"

"Then, be sure they're behind you when you're looking," Othos advised.

"Oh. Very well. Can someone tell me which direction to face?"

Skellig, with his eyes tightly shut, made a spinning gesture with his claw.

"Perhaps you should take a quick look around and see if you can determine which direction you need to be looking?"

"How will I know?" Jerica questioned.

"Othos, she's borrowing your powers, isn't she?" Zeira asked.

"She is, yes."

"So, does that make you immune to the sunlight? If she happens to look straight at you, would you be injured?"

"Hmmph. I hadn't thought of that. I am immune to sunlight, so she should be able to."

"Test this," Zeira directed. "I don't want to needlessly put anyone at risk."

Othos gazed at the human. "Jerica, make a quarter turn to your right and open your eyes. Everyone is behind you."

"They're open. What are you going to do?"

"I'm going to walk around you to see if your eyes will … no, I'm fine. You just looked directly at me."

"Perfect," Zeira was saying. "So, as Jerica is inspecting the area, we'll need you, Othos, to determine if there's any change in Jerica's eyes. That way, we'll know we're close."

"We already know we're close," Gocri argued.

"True," Zeira conceded. "I can only assume something will happen once Jerica is looking directly at the area we need to dig."

Something certainly did happen. After ten minutes of looking this way and that, Jerica turned to inspect a nondescript section of the ground when she announced a startling discovery.

"What's going on?" Jerica called. "Everything has turned red! No, wait, it's gone. No, I'm sorry, it's back. I … oh, I get it. I think I found the jhorium! Or, at the very least, I think I know where we need to dig!"

"What do you see?" Othos asked, inspecting the grassy floor for himself.

"Tell us," Zeira called out, from her position behind Jerica.

"Her eyes have become fire," Othos reported. "If she looks at a specific place on the ground, then the sunlight becomes red and ... arrrgh! It's hot! I see what your new power is doing. If you move away from the location, the sunlight fades. But, once you look at the right position—fire. It's hot and cold."

"We should mark the area, so we know where to dig," Sif suggested.

"That won't be a problem," Othos chuckled.

"What's so funny?" Jerica asked.

"The spot we need to dig," Othos said, pointing at the ground. "is nothing but a big scorch mark. Two, actually."

"Jerica, can you close your eyes?"

"They're closed, Zeira," Jerica announced.

"I see what you mean," Zeira was saying, as she stared at the marked ground. "X marks the spot!"

Chapter 8 - Jhorium

Am I the only one who sees the problem here?" Skellig asked, as he turned to his companions. "Yes, we know where this mysterious metal is supposed to be. Yes, I have every faith that it's there. Rather, I know it's *down* there."

The seven of them were staring at the twin scorch marks Jerica had left when she tapped into Othos' power. Ironically enough, the two marks had made a crude X, as if to further illustrate the area where the jhorium was hiding. Jerica approached the mark and scuffed it with the toe of her sandal.

"All right, Skellig, let's hear what you have to say."

The Spark dragon grunted once and then pointed at the scorched earth. "We know the jhorium is there, somewhere beneath that mark."

"We all know this," Gocri reminded him.

"And you don't want to?" Skellig guessed. "That's fine. Some of us are better diggers than others."

"Oh, no you don't," Gocri said, as he gripped Skellig's tail and forcefully pulled him backwards. "I wasn't refraining from adding my name to the list of potential diggers."

"Good to hear," Skellig said, nodding his appreciation. "This jhorium. Whomever digs it out needs to know what to look for."

"What's the problem?" Sif asked. "We dig, we retrieve, and we skedaddle before anyone else gets here."

"And we're looking for?" Skellig prompted.

Jhorium, Nuri answered, from within their minds.

"How close are you, Nuri?" Zeira asked.

I'm at the mouth of a small river, the valthan reported. *It's freshwater, so I cannot proceed. Therefore, I'm waiting here until you return. Or, if you head in another direction, I'll follow along as close as I can.*

"Good," Zeira replied. "Thanks, Nuri. Skellig, you were saying?"

"That mark." Skellig said, as he pointed at the scorched earth. "We have no idea how far down we'll have to dig, and on top of that, we don't know what jhorium even looks like. How would we know we've uncovered it as we dig?"

Sif's eyes widened. "A very good point. I can only hope we'll know when we see it. After all, if this jhorium is the source of magic, and all of us are magical by nature, then wouldn't we know if we come into contact with it?"

"I think that's our saving grace," Skellig decided. "Now, who's the best digger?"

Othos looked at Jerica. "I say, *she* is."

"Oh, please," Jerica scoffed. "Look at the difference in size between us. There's no way I'm better at digging than you are, Othos. Why would you think I am?"

"Because, young human, you have the ability to take our powers, mix them together, and see what happens."

Skellig watched their kai look at the ground and frown.

"We're talking about digging! I don't think there's any combination of magical abilities I could borrow that would let me out-dig a dragon."

Zeira looked at Othos. "What about you? You're a sol dragon. Can you use your abilities to dig through the earth?"

Othos was shaking his head. "I tried once, and it was an unmitigated disaster--too destructive. I tried a second time and attempted to keep the sunlight to a minimum."

"What happened?" Sif wanted to know.

"Nothing. That's all that happened--sunlight, shining upon the ground. Look, perhaps there *is* a way, but more than likely, there isn't. You take the risk of destroying the jhorium when you use my powers. It's your call, of course."

"What about Jerica?" Nuri asked. "She's used a mix of our powers before. Is there something that might work in this situation?"

"What human power do you have now?" Zeira asked.

Jerica shook her head. "I'm fairly certain that the only power I still have, and I'm deathly afraid to turn it back on, is the sunlight-through-my-eyes bit. And, as you can imagine, it's not something I'd care to repeat anytime soon."

"There are no other humans around," Zeira sighed. "I'm out. Fire is too destructive. Like Othos said, we'd run the risk of damaging the jhorium."

"I'm out," Skellig added. "I have no idea how an electrified spark would help us dig."

Perhaps, Nuri began, *that's the point.*

The group fell silent.

"What do you mean, Nuri?" Zeira asked.

Doesn't this sound like one of the obstacles we faced earlier?

"I'll give her that," Skellig agreed. "You're saying that this particular challenge *must* be dealt with by the normal physical means. Ugh. That means we'll have to actually dig."

I would advise you to hurry. Remember, we have some unwanted friends headed our way.

Skellig nodded. "Acknowledged. Who's best at digging?"

Gocri groaned. "That'd be me. I may as well get started. If you'll …"

"Excuse me," Sif interrupted. "I do believe *I* am best suited for digging."

"You're too large, Sif," Gocri began, as he pivoted in place until he was facing the smoke dragon. "That's why it's easier for me to do it."

"Gocri, look at me."

The ice dragon turned and, once he saw Sif, his mouth gaped open with surprise.

"What are you? What form is that?"

Detecting awe in Gocri's voice, Skellig turned to see for himself what was happening. There, standing beside Gocri, was Sif, only this time, his vaporous companion was using a form Skellig had never personally seen before. There was a collective gasp of astonishment as the rest of their group noticed Sif's transformation.

Sif had become a dragon the same size as Gocri, but that was where the similarities ended. Sif's new form was heavily muscled, was jet black, wingless, and was also without horns. Her front forelegs were much longer that her back two, which made it look as though she was perpetually looking skyward when she walked. Attached to Sif's front forelegs were enormous three-foot-long, curved talons. Sif's tail was also remarkable, in that it resembled a long pillar of rock that tapered to a point.

The rest of the dragons might not have recognized the form, but Jerica did.

"It's Terran! Sif has become a Terran dragon! Oh, that makes perfect sense. Earth dragons are known for digging through the ground. That was a wise choice, Sif."

Sif's huge head dipped low. "Why, thank you, Jerica. Gocri, may I?"

"Be my guest, Sif. I'll be right here if you need me."

Sif shuffled over to the scorched earth, raised a curved claw, and began to dig. Right away, Skellig could see Sif had come up with the winning idea. The form of the Terran dragon tore through the earth as easily as a sharp blade piercing unprotected flesh.

That's a grisly thought.

My apologies, Jerica. I'll come up with a better analogy.

That's quite all right. You've made your point.

Skellig watched as Sif, in Terran form, leaned forward and started digging as fast as she could. Rocks, sand, bits of gravel, and larger stones landed in a rapidly growing pile. Soon, practically all of Sif's large form had disappeared from sight as the hole deepened considerably.

"Where was she when I had to dig you out?" Zeira wondered aloud, as she grinned at Skellig. "I know I'm not the best digger, either, but compared to that? I may as well stick to flying."

"I know what you mean," Othos said, as he watched several stones bounce harmlessly off his chest. "Terrans are known for their strength and their tunneling abilities. They may not be the brightest star in the sky, but they are very efficient workers. Observe. Your clever companion has dug so deep that we can no longer see her."

"I don't know what we'd do without her," Zeira admitted. "Or any of you, for that matter."

"Still feeling overwhelmed by the discovery that you are the leader of this group?"

"Admit it, Zeira," Skellig said, "you're finding this easier than you would have thought possible."

"Telling others what to do? That's not in my ..."

"Caste?" Othos offered. He watched a larger boulder head toward Zeira, but she wasn't looking. He deftly caught it in mid-air before casually discarding it over his shoulder. "Are you not a member of the Phoenix caste, living in Blaze?"

"I never told you that," Zeira said, amazed. "You must have picked that up from my thoughts. Or Skellig's. He knows where I'm from."

Othos shook his head. "When you are as old as I am, you have to invent ways to entertain yourself."

"What is that supposed to mean?" Zeira demanded. "Have you ... can you ... were you watching me?"

"In a manner of speaking, aye. When a Fire, who cannot produce fire, yearns to be something more, then who am I to turn down such a rare opportunity to watch the development of a fine leader?"

"You're talking about me?"

"No, he's talking about Dym," Skellig scoffed.

"Oh. Well, he's ..."

"... of course he's talking about you!" Skellig said, shaking his head. "Zeira, look how far you've come! When I first met you, you were embarrassed about your unique condition."

"I still am," Zeira muttered.

"You were hopelessly lost …"

"… thank you for bringing that up," Zeira interrupted.

"… yet, you didn't turn back. You kept going, even though it was away from your home. With the danger of Fading closing in, you continued on your mission, rescuing us along the way. We owe you our lives, Z."

Zeira smiled. "Z. You haven't called me that in a while."

"Sorry. If you prefer Zeira, then I'll call you …"

"Z is fine," Zeira said, cutting him off.

A decent sized rock flew through the air and collided with Zeira's chest. By itself, it wasn't remarkable. However, a muffled *WHUMP* sounded, and everyone, including Zeira, turned to look down.

"That sounded … different," Skellig decided. "What hit you?"

"It was a stone," Zeira said. "I'm sure of it."

"They typically don't sound like that," Gocri added.

"Perhaps you should find it," Othos suggested.

The three of them, along with Jerica, turned to regard the celestial.

"You know something we don't?" Skellig asked.

"Perhaps. Like I said, I would suggest you locate that rock."

"We need to find that stone," Jerica said, with growing excitement. "Was it a piece of jhorium?"

"Might've had a piece embedded within it," Skellig said.

"We won't know until we …" Gocri held up a piece of broken stone—tiny in his claw—to the rest of the group. "I think this might be it."

Skellig leaned over to look. "What makes you say so? Oh, hello! Yes, I think you're right. Do we all see this?"

Gocri held the tiny rock between two talons. Then, remembering one of their number was the much smaller biped, held it down so Jerica could take a look.

"I don't see what … oh! Is that what we're looking for? There's some kind of green vein running through this rock."

"I do believe it's glowing," Skellig said.

Jerica squinted her eyes. "How can you tell?"

"We dragons are more susceptible to light than humans,"

Skellig explained. "This rock, with the green embedded within, is glowing brighter than the daylight. Not much, mind you, but enough to be noticed."

Jerica turned to the huge, imposing hole where Sif had begun digging and pointed.

"Someone needs to let her know. Look around. I don't see any more of that green anywhere. Somehow, Sif hit the area where the jhorium was resting and unearthed a piece. We need to get her to backtrack."

"An excellent idea," Skellig said, as he looked over at Zeira, who nodded.

Sif, it's Skellig. Can you hear me? We need you to stop digging.

There was no answer. No sound except the relentless digging and the inevitable barrage of debris that would pour up and out of the tunnel every couple of minutes when Sif removed the loosened earth. Sure enough, nearly ten seconds later, another stream of broken boulders, stones, and clumped earth flew out of the hole.

Sif, are you there?

There was no answer.

"I'm not able to reach her. Perhaps someone else might have better luck?"

Sif, it's Jerica! We need to talk to you!

Sif, it's Nuri! Please stop! You've found a piece!

"What about you, Othos?" Zeira challenged. "Can you get her attention?"

"Well, she's not answering you, but she *is* there. I can hear her. Can't you?"

"We can *all* hear her," Gocri scowled. "It's kind of hard to miss."

"Not with your ears, but up here," Othos said, touching the side of his head. "Once you hear her, you'll be able to talk to her."

"Why are you acting so cryptic?" Skellig demanded. "The more she digs, the farther away she moves from the jhorium deposit. We need her to stop, now!"

"Then, you, Skellig, should be the one to tell her. No, don't argue. *Listen.*"

Skellig sighed, closed his eyes, and tried to tune out the

scraping sounds coming from the hole. As he waited for his senses to clear, a strange sound appeared in his mind.

Up and down, and through the night,
Too much power doesn't make a right,
Winds blow hard, moving you 'round,
Out she rushes, but can't be found.

Neither here nor there, nor anywhere,
All have searched, 'cause they care,
Who would've thought what they saw,
Was nothing more than an empty claw.

Riding the winds through the night,
Gathering all who …

"She's singing!" Skellig exclaimed. "How didn't I notice that before?"

Zeira's eyes promptly closed, as did Gocri's. After a few moments, the ice dragon was smiling. Zeira, on the other hand, couldn't hear her.

"I am so over being the last person to be able to do anything," the fire dragon crossly said. "Why? Why can't I hear her? Othos, do you know?"

"I do, young Fire, but …"

"… I'm not going to like the answer, am I?" Zeira sighed heavily before growling. "Fine. Tell me."

"You expect that you can," Othos answered.

"Of course I do," Zeira said, confused. "I'm a dragon."

"And that's why you cannot," Othos argued. "Until you're able to open your senses and train your body to do what you want it to do, without *expecting* it, then you will continue to struggle."

Zeira groaned. "That's just great. We'll circle back around to that. Skellig, did you let her know?"

"Oh, of course. Sorry. Just a moment."

They all heard it. Almost immediately, the scraping stopped and they heard a loud shuffling sound, presumably Sif's Terran form. After a few moments, it got progressively louder as it reversed out of the tunnel. Ten seconds later, the spike that was Sif's tail appeared, followed by the bulk of Sif's body. Once she emerged, she gave herself a good shaking, and then turned to Skellig.

"What is it? You said I found a piece? Where is it?"

Jerica held the stone up. "It's this, Sif. Do you see the green vein?"

"Oh! It's glowing!"

"So I'm told. This is what we're looking for. Somehow, you must've stumbled across it."

"Hmm. How long ago was it dislodged?"

Skellig looked at Zeira, and then Gocri. "Ten minutes?"

"I'd make it fifteen," Gocri said.

"Between ten and fifteen minutes ago," Sif murmured. Her huge Terran form actually started to pace. "That was when I made a course correction. Something didn't feel right, so I changed course, but only marginally. I think … I think this stone came from the point in which I veered off. Just a moment. I'll check."

Her curved talons hooked onto the rim of the hole and she hoisted herself up. Giving the group a quick smile, Sif hopped into the hole. The scraping began anew, not nearly as loud, suggesting Sif was carefully digging in a select few locations. Ten minutes later, they heard her shuffling toward them. When she emerged, she was clutching a handful of stones. Depositing them at their feet, Skellig could see that there were no fewer than forty or fifty small stones, each with a piece of the green ribbon running through it.

"That's all there is," Sif reported. She looked at the hole and started to move toward it. "I really shouldn't leave it like this. Give me just a moment, and I'll fill this back in."

"No," Skellig said.

"Wait!" Zeira shouted, at the same time.

Skellig motioned for Zeira to continue.

"Leave the hole as it is. Remember, we need to make certain the humans know *we* have extricated all the jhorium from the surrounding area. They need to know that it's too late and that there's nothing for them here. It's the only way to keep that giant mechanical contraption away from Jerica's home."

Sif shrugged. "Leave it like it is? You got it."

The Terran dragon turned gray and then morphed into a mirror image of Jerica. Together, the two humans sat at the edge of the rock pile and began inspecting them.

"You're sure this is all?" Jerica asked.

"I am. That's what took so long. I dug away from the main deposit area, in all directions. There's no more to be found.

"Well done, Sif!" Zeira praised. "We have the jhorium!"

Jerica selected a small stone with a thick green ribbon running through it.

"Well, you have to admit, it *is* a rather pretty shade of green. It reminds me of the forest canopies we were flying over earlier."

Skellig approached and gazed at the rock pile. A growl formed, earning him a look from his companions.

"What's the matter?" Zeira wanted to know. "Why are you upset? Look, we accomplished our objective: we have the jhorium!"

"What we have is a considerable number of rocks that we are now going to have to move. I had no idea there'd be so much of it. What are we supposed to do with all of that?"

Jerica held up a piece of stone that had a very visible streak of green running through it.

"This? This isn't jhorium. I mean, at least it isn't *pure* jhorium."

All six dragons let out a collective groan.

"Wh-what?" Zeira sputtered.

Skellig's growl grew louder. Gocri sighed, and Othos simply sat down on the ground and shook his head.

Jerica, perhaps you could explain what you mean? Nuri requested.

"This is ore. The jhorium is clearly the green stuff riddled throughout the stone, but obviously, we don't need the non-green material."

"How are we supposed to remove the excess stone?" Zeira wanted to know. "Do we have to break it up and pick the pieces of jhorium out of it? I can't even begin to think of how long that would take."

"There's a much easier way to do it," Jerica assured her.

"It's something my father calls *processing*. The ore needs to be melted down. The raw stone will either burn off, or can be skimmed off. What you're left with is a much purer form of jhorium. The more times it's processed, or refined, the purer it gets. All of this ore is probably no more than a pound or two of jhorium."

"That's why the devastation from that pit mine was so extensive," Skellig said. "That machine ate the entire landscape looking for more of that blasted mineral."

Jerica nodded. "Exactly. You're right, Skellig. We need to make it known that we have the jhorium, but we also need to clear out. Didn't you say Dym was on his way?"

Gocri looked up, noting the position of the sun.

"I'd say we have no more than thirty minutes at most, Miss Jerica."

"How can we move all of this stone?" Sif wanted to know.

"I'd like to know what we're going to do with it. It needs to be … what did you call it, Jerica? Processed? Where can we take it to be processed?"

Jerica beamed a smile. "That's easy. My father."

"I thought your sire was a blacksmith," Zeira said.

"He is, but part of blacksmithing is working with metal. Oftentimes, the only way to get that metal is to skim off impurities, as my father would say. He doesn't do it often, but he has the equipment. That's what's important."

Zeira nodded, pleased. "Excellent. Very well. We need to get this material to him. Ideas?"

"Build a container," Gocri suggested. "Then, we could give it to Miss Jerica's sire and let him do what needs to be done."

"Something big enough to hold all of that?" Jerica asked, dismayed. "I don't think we have that kind of time."

"What do you suggest?" Zeira wanted to know.

Jerica was silent as she considered. "Nuri, how close are you?"

Less than two miles. I'm in a tributary less than two miles from the bay.

Jerica nodded and looked up at her companions. "New

plan. We need to get these stones to Nuri."

And what am I supposed to do with them?

"We're going to build a raft and float them back to Cael. Would you be able to meet my father with it? I can tell him where to meet you so he can get the stones back to his shop as quickly as possible."

Won't it be obvious what I'm doing? The jhorium is quite noticeable.

"We'll have to cover it with something. Am I right to assume you can get it to Cael the quickest?"

Pulling a simple raft? Of course.

Sif pointed at the pile of rocks. "Why can't we just carry it back ourselves?"

"Dym is out there," Skellig reminded her. "Quite frankly, I'm astonished he hasn't arrived yet. Whatever is on that ship must be worth protecting. Regardless of that fact, I don't want to push our luck. I'd just as soon be far away from here. Jerica is right. We need to get rid of this pile, but do so in a way that doesn't arouse suspicion."

Othos and Gocri each scooped up a large handful. Seeing how a few small leftovers were still on the ground, Sif hurried over and, while still in human form, retrieved the four stones that were visible. Then, looking over at Jerica, she nodded once and took the smallest piece of ore and deliberately returned it to the ground.

"Why did you do that?" Zeira asked.

"In case they don't figure it out," Sif explained, as she pointed at the large nearby hole. "Once they see this, there will be no doubt what we did here, and what we took."

"Good idea. Are we ready? Let's go find Nuri."

Once they were reunited with their valthan companion, and the dragons deposited the ore onto the beach, Gocri announced he was going on patrol, and launched himself into the air.

"Words cannot express how hopeful I am in getting away from here unseen," Jerica murmured, as she watched Nuri hold several fallen logs in place while Skellig tied them all together using vines.

"I'm sure we will," Sif murmured. The vapor dragon had switched forms, morphing from an exact image of Jerica into that of her mother, Nyssa. "Can your sire really remove the jhorium from these stones?"

"He should be able to," Jerica confirmed, nodding. "I know it's not his favorite thing in the world to do, seeing how it requires extensive time monitoring a smelting pot, but ... oh, wait. I need to tell him. Umm, I don't suppose you know how I can reach my father, do you? Zeira did it for me once before."

"Your sire? Let me see. Just a moment." Sif's eyes closed, but almost immediately opened. "That was easier than I thought. Your essence is strong, Jerica, just like your sire's."

What's this? I be hearin' voices in me head? Not again. I must really lay off the ... wait! Are ye one o' them dragons? Do ye have Jerica wit' ye?

You are *hearing voices in your head. I'm here, Dad. So is Sif. Listen, I need you to do something for me. It's urgent!*

Consider it done, my girl. What do ye need?

We're sending Nuri back to Cael. She'll be towing a raft that will be loaded with jhorium ore. I don't need to tell you how important it is that this doesn't fall into the wrong hands.

Jhorium? That be what yer searchin' for, right?

It is. We found it. It's a vein of green material running through the local rock.

Ah, ye need it processed, don' ye?

Yes! Can you do it?

I'll dust off me smeltin' pot, girl.

Thank you so much, Dad! I ... do you have access to a wagon?

A wagon? Oh, for transportin' it to the shop. Aye, I can find one. How long b'fore ye arrive?

Nuri, are you here? Can you answer that?

I'm here, Jerica. The raft was just finished. It's crude, in terms of vessels I've seen on the surface, but it'll do. They attached a lead rope, so I can pull without surfacing. I'll be back in your village in about ten minutes.

I figured ye'd be quicker than that, dragon.

I have to follow the shoreline, sire of Jerica.

Ah. My mistake. Call me Hallis. Where do ye want to meet?

Pick an empty spot on the shore. I'll find you. Jerica, they've finished loading the raft. I'm heading off.

Thank you, Nuri. And Dad? Thank you. I'll be in touch. Stay safe! I don't know if Vyler told you, but there's a warship headed toward Cael, with a number of Spark dragons.

Aye, Theresa told me. The warship has already passed, but I did no' see no dragons with it.

Oh, no! I have to go. Love you, Dad!

Jerica? What ...?

Sif terminated the connection.

"Jerica, if your sire is correct, it means Dym and his companions are on their way here. We need to go!"

"Did the rest of you hear that? We're going to have company! Gocri? Can you see anything?"

I'm watching them now, Gocri's thought came. *They do not yet know they're being watched.*

"Where are they?" Zeira wanted to know.

At the dig site. They've found the leftover piece of jhorium, and I can tell you they aren't happy about it.

"And Dym?" Skellig asked.

He's beside himself with rage. Has Nuri left with the jhorium ore?

"She has," Zeira confirmed. "We even took Skellig's advice and covered the raft with branches and tree limbs, to make it look as though we were hauling a load of lumber."

I'm in trouble! Nuri's panicked voice announced.

"What is it?" Skellig asked, baring his fangs. "I'm heading your way. I'll ..."

No, Skellig, wait! Bring Jerica! Sif, switch to a human form. Get both of them out to me. Hurry!

Skellig's head snapped up. "What? Why would you ...?"

Othos shrugged. "Maybe she needs your kai to work her magic?"

Zeira groaned. "Of course! She needs humans visible on the raft, or questions will arise. I didn't think about that! Take us out there. Hurry!"

Skellig snatched up both Sif and their kai and took to the air. Flapping as hard as he could, the three of them quickly rose into the air. However, the Spark dragon suddenly growled with dismay and tucked his wings, dropping them straight back down. Barely skimming over the treetops, Skellig oriented himself and headed north.

"What'd you do that for?" Jerica wanted to know.

"If we rise too high, we'll be visible to everyone, including those to the south. Look. The enemy ship nears. Do you see Nuri? She's directly ahead of us, keeping herself close to the coast. Prepare yourself. I'm going to place you directly on the raft."

"We're ready. Thank you, Skellig. I wouldn't be able to do this without your help."

"It's a team effort," Skellig added.

Swooping over the raft and timing it so that Jerica and Sif were dropped onto the leafy branches covering the rocks, he waited for at least one of them to wave at him before he angled himself to return to the others. Growling to himself and beating his wings to increase his speed, he could only hope he could return before their time ran out.

He didn't make it.

We're under attack! Zeira's panicked thought announced. *Gocri, watch your back! You've picked up a visitor! Othos, can you…!!*

What is it? Skellig asked. *I'm on my way, Z.*

Gocri has been hit! He's been knocked out and has fallen through the tree canopy. I have no idea if he's all right.

I'm here. Where are you, Z?

Skellig, I'm heading east, but I don't know how far I can make it. There's two of them following me. I don't know what to do!

First off, don't panic. That's what they're hoping you'll do. I see you. I'm following the two of them. Look out! The closest one is preparing to fire! When I say turn, bank hard left. I'm going to even out the odds. Now! Turn left!

Zeira pulled her left wing against her body and made a sharp left turn. The bolt of lightning flashed so close that she could feel her scales tingle with alarm. A second lightning bolt arced dangerously close to her, but thankfully missed. Then, she heard a roar of pain. Turning to look behind her, she saw one of the Spark dragons spiraling out of control before slamming into the trees far below.

I don't know if I can shake him.

Zeira, I've taken one of them out. The other is for you.

They're behind me! How am I supposed to …?

Think about that statement, Skellig interrupted. *Of all of us, you are the one uniquely situated to fire off a blast in the opposite direction. You are more than capable of removing your pursuer.*

My flames! How could I have forgotten about my flames!

So, you forgot. Worry about that later. For now, you need to ...

Skellig, you don't understand! I've never gone this long without thinking about my disability!

Congratulations. Don't celebrate just yet. You need to take care of your aggressor. Hurry! I think he's building up a charge to throw your way.

Ooo, this still isn't very dignified.

And being pursued and fired upon from behind, is better? Let him have it!

A huge bout of flames erupted from Zeira's backside, bursting into an enormous wall of flames. The rogue Spark dragon furiously tried to avoid the surprising fire, but ended up clipping his wing on one of the treetops. Spinning and crashing, he dropped from sight. Zeira and Skellig flew away.

"I grow tired of this, Skellig." The voice hissed like a sinister snake, and seemingly came from everywhere.

"Dym. What do you want?"

"What else? You will return the green metal to me. Now."

"Or what?" Skellig challenged. "None of us are afraid of you."

"Is that so?" Dym sneered. "Where is your backup? Where's the water-worm? What about the icicle? Your friends have deserted you."

"My friends have deserted me?" Skellig stated. "What about you? Didn't you arrive with a few followers of your own, the ones who are now gone?" Skellig heard Dym let out a low growl. "What's the matter? Not used to a fair fight?"

"You're no match for me, dragonlet. Besides, two of my companions are still out there. They're on their way here, now."

"I thought I was no match for you?" Skellig taunted, tucking and banking right. A lightning bolt lanced the now-empty space. "Come, come. This will never do. Surely, you're able to fight your own battles, aren't you?"

Out of the corner of his eye, Skellig spotted one of the two remaining Spark dragons, but, a split second later, a dark grey form slammed into the hapless Spark, smashing him through the green canopy below them. Broken branches, snapping trunks, and bellows of pain followed.

"One down and one to go," Skellig announced, in a sing-song voice. "Do you dare call for assistance? Behold, your companions are being picked off, one by one."

"Again, I don't need anyone's help in taking you down, you pathetic excuse of a Spark. I ..."

The fourth Spark dragon appeared, but this time, as the dragon dropped near the treetops, it was keeping an eye on the clouds. It didn't know where Othos was hiding, but was taking no chances.

As the fourth Spark dropped even lower, a white, heavily muscled foreleg reached out of the canopy, snagged it by its tail, and yanked it down. It happened so fast that the poor Spark didn't utter a sound.

Gocri, that was excellent timing, my friend. Are you all right?

I took a blast to my chest, but I'll survive. It was a smart move, flying back over this area. They thought I had been incapacitated.

Well, there's still one more.

Can you handle Dym or do you need assistance?

I think I can take him, Gocri.

I'll be watching. If you falter, I'll be there.

Thank you.

"And now there are none," Skellig announced. A quick barrel roll to the left, smiling as a second bolt of lightning flashed by. "You're becoming predictable, Dym. Leave now, while you still can."

"Or what?" Dym snapped. "You have something that doesn't belong to you. Here's my offer. Hand over the jhorium, and I will make your death quick and painless."

"Here's my counter offer," Skellig began, watching one of his companions fly north, out over the sea. He automatically turned in the same direction. Over water now, he looked back to verify his sire was still following—and he was. Skellig tried a final time. "Leave now, while I still permit it. Linger, and you'll be filled with nothing but regrets."

"Don't make me laugh. You are in no position to dictate threats to me, dremmling."

"As you wish."

The waters erupted from below. An impossibly huge claw rose from the sea and plucked Dym out of the air. With his wings blotting out the sky, Othos brought his claw up to his face to stare at his prisoner. The celestial turned to Skellig.

"What would you like me to do to him? Bite his head off? Pinch off his wings? I've done less to others who have been more of a pain than this one."

Feeble bolts of lightning bounced harmlessly off of Othos' chest. Dym, finally realizing his predicament, fell silent. As he was brought up to the titan's face once more, he hissed with alarm. "If you're going to do it, then just do it."

"You don't deserve to live," Othos accused.

"Then, finish me off," Dym said, lifting his nose high into the air. "I will *not* beg."

"Very well."

The great jaws opened, and Othos made as if he was about to toss the unrepentant dragon down the hatch.

"All right! Don't do it! I don't deserve to be eaten! H-have mercy!"

Skellig's eyes widened with disbelief. The fearsome Dym was begging for his life? Since when?

"Why should I?" Othos thundered. "Why should I spare a pathetic miscreant such as yourself? Skellig, what say you? What should I do?"

Dym's frightened eyes sought out his. "Look, I know we have our differences, but are you going to let this behemoth treat your only sire as ... well, nothing more than a tidbit??"

"You haven't given me a reason to keep you alive," Skellig said. *Othos, may I land on your palm?*

Which one? The one holding your sire?

Yes.

Of course.

Skellig perched on one of Othos' curled fingers. He peered down at his sire and shook his head. "Well, he's not wrong. You are a pathetic miscreant."

He heard Dym growl angrily. "You know what? Go ahead. If it means I don't have to look at your gloating face anymore, then I'm all for it. Do your worst, cretin."

When the killing bite never materialized, Dym cracked an eye.

"Still here," Skellig announced.

"If you won't kill me, then you can release me. Just know this. If you don't kill me now, you'll never be able to rest. I *will* put an end to this abomination to my bloodline. You will always wonder if this is the day Dym will enact his revenge."

He shared a look with Othos and gave a perceptible shake of his head.

"You're being released," Skellig told his sire. "And do you want to know why? It's because of this: I'm not like you. At all. If you want to be a murderous, traitorous example of our species, then so be it. I, for one, am proud to say that I will *never* follow in your footsteps. You are a pitiful example of a Spark, and I will continue to strive each day to be the best I can be."

At the signal from Skellig, Othos opened his hand. Dym immediately launched himself up. Belying his size, Othos smoothly snatched the green Spark dragon out of the air, as nimbly as one would do to a pesky insect. Once more, Othos brought the unlucky dragon up to his face.

"*He* might not have any interest in killing you, but that doesn't mean I don't. Be gone, cretin. Do not let our paths cross again."

Dym gasped with alarm. The moment the giant claws opened, Skellig's sire pumped his wings for all he was worth as he tried to put as much space as possible between them.

Is everyone all right? Jerica's voice suddenly asked.

I am. Othos is, too. Gocri is the one I'm worried about.

Those sparks do pack a sting, Gocri's strained voice announced. *I'm all right. I just lifted off from the ground.*

We're heading back to Cael, Zeira announced. *We have to protect the jhorium!*

Chapter 9 - Blacksmith

"Did you really have to get everyone to pitch in and help?" Jerica asked, amazed. She was standing in the middle of her father's shop and was just trying to find a spot where she wouldn't be in the way. Two lines of laborers were streaming in and out of her father's shop. One was carrying pieces of the jhorium-infused stone in, and the others, empty-handed, returned to get another armful. "How much more could there be?"

Hallis appeared. "There be plenty, an' that's no lie." Her father plucked a stone from a passing worker. "See this, J? This vein runs shallow. There be not much of yer green min'ral."

"You're thinking there's a lot less here than it looks, is that it?"

"Aye."

The front doors slammed shut. Hallis leaned around her to study the back of his shop. "Good job, lads. No one can see what be back there."

His men grunted by way of acknowledgement as they prepared to return to their work that had been preempted by the delivery of the jhorium.

"Jus' a moment, boys," Hallis called. "I think it be … noticeable if one part of the shop be workin' on refinin' these chops and the rest of ye be working with metal."

"You want us to help?" one man asked. He was a beefy fellow who was hefting a hammer Jerica knew to be almost as heavy as she was.

"Nay. There be various scraps ou' back. Grab a smeltin' pot and get to refinin'. It'll draw suspicion off o' me."

"What do you want us to make?" another asked.

"I don' know, Julius. Make some shovels, or horseshoes, or …"

"Nails?"

Hallis snapped his fingers. "Perfect. Listen up, ev'ryone! I trust each an' ev'ry one of ye with my life. What I'm 'bout to do be fraught wit' peril. We must keep what we be doin' a secret. Understand?"

There were a chorus of ayes and yessirs. A tear sprang to Jerica's eye as she watched her father's workers start up mini-smelting pots at their stations, disguising her father's actions. After all, if the entire shop was doing the same thing, an outside observer wouldn't look twice.

There was a knock at the door. Everyone froze and, in unison, turned to look at Hallis.

"Don' just stand there. Open 'er up. We don' wanna appear uncivil, do we?"

There were gasps and several cries of alarm as, once the door was opened and it revealed a perfect replica of Jerica. One by one, the workers turned to stare at the real Jerica, before turning back to the clone. Jerica groaned with dismay.

"What is it?" Sif asked. "I can feel your … why is everyone staring at me?"

Jerica hurried to her side. "Look who it is! My cousin is here! Wouldn't you know, everyone always says we look alike. Well, in this case, when we, uh, are wearing the same outfit, it sure looks like we're twins, doesn't it?"

The laborers started nodding and then returned to work.

"Quick thinkin', girl," Hallis said, as he appeared by her side. "I did no' think o' that. Sorry. Come wit' me."

"Did I do something wrong?" Sif asked, with genuine innocence, as she turned to follow Jerica and her father deeper into the shop. Near the back, Sif turned to Jerica with a questioning look on her face.

Jerica shook her head. "Sif, this is what happens when you choose the same form as me, and then proceed to show up at my father's shop still looking like me."

"What happens now?" Sif wanted to know.

Hallis beckoned them over to a work station situated in the far corner. The vent flaps had been opened beneath the metal grate, and a smelting pot — his largest — was sitting on the open flames. The bottom of the pot was already glowing red.

Jerica selected a stone and tossed it in with a resounding clang.

"Wha'? No, girl. Not yet!" Hallis retrieved a pair of tongs and fished the stone out.

"But … the pot is ready! Don't we have to melt the stones down?"

"Do ye know how long it'd take doin' it like that?" Hallis asked. He shook his head and then pointed at a machine set up on a temporary table. "We have to use that first, girl."

"I don't remember that device," Jerica said. "What is it?"

"It be a rock breaker," Hallis answered. "Put the rock there, spin that wheel there, and this arm be lowered until it smashes the rock. Then, we take the smaller bits and put 'em in the pot. Julius, come 'ere, lad. Will ye man this for me?"

Julius, the big, beefy youth from before, nodded, eager to please. Hallis went through the motions of what was expected and then watched as Julius broke the first stone apart and swept the remains into a waiting container. When there was enough material, Hallis would then empty the container into the pot.

"Ev'rything gets dumped in," Hallis explained, as he upended the container into the smelting pot. "It'll all get so hot that it'll melt into goo."

"Magma," Jerica translated.

"Right. More than likely, the green will melt at a different temperature. Either we will have to remove the goo …"

"… magma," Jerica corrected.

"… magma," Hallis amended, sticking his tongue out at his daughter, "from the pot, which will leave us wit' what I'm guessin' is a layer o' slag on top."

"Slag?" Sif repeated, confused.

"It's the leftover bit from the stones that need to be skimmed off. Dependin' on what melts first, it could be the stone, or it could be that bit o' green there. Either way, it will go there, in that smaller pot on the table."

"How long will all of this take?" Sif asked.

"It depends on the composition of the stone," Jerica said.

Hallis pointed at her. "Right. What she said."

Jerica dropped her voice to a whisper. "If the jhorium melts first, great. But, based on everything we've gone through thus far, I really don't see that happening."

We'll have to do this the long, hard way, Zeira said. *It needs to be done right.*

Jerica nodded. "Exactly."

Hallis looked up. "Eh?"

She pointed at Sif. "They're listening, either through Sif's ears or mine."

"Ah. Yer friends are wit' us, so to speak. Er, hallo! Can ye 'ear me?"

"Keep your voice down," Jerica scolded. "Remember, we don't want it known the dragons are involved."

"O' course, o' course. Sorry."

Sif and Jerica pitched in to help fill the space next to Julius with stones. Once enough had been moved to keep Julius occupied for the next several hours, Jerica returned to her father's side. Her eyes had started watering and a sharp, acrid smell filled her nostrils. Waving a hand in front of her, she noticed that her father was dumping a white powder into the pot and giving it a few stirs with a thick, metal hook.

"Are yer eyes botherin' ye? This can give off some noxious fumes, an' that be no lie. Tell the boys to open the windows."

While Jerica relayed the instructions, Sif wandered

close to the pot and leaned over to see for herself what was happening. She had casually rested a hand against the pot as she was watching the contents slowly melt.

"Watch yer hand, girl!" Hallis scolded.

Surprised, Sif turned to the blacksmith. "Are you talking to me? What's wrong?"

"Yer hand! How bad are ye burned? Lemme see. It can … what be this? There be no burn!"

Sif turned to look back at Julius, who was busy working the rock breaker, and leaned confidentially toward Hallis. Noting her behavior, he did the same.

"I may look like a human, but I assure you, I am *not*. I am a dragon, and these sights and smells do not affect me. Neither does heat, for that matter."

"Be that as it may, girl," Hallis said, "don' let the others see that. A pretty girl like ye would get a nasty burn. Remember, these lads don' like magic too much."

Jerica reappeared, followed closely by a waft of fresh air.

"All the windows are open. Everyone is going to know what we're doing."

Hallis nodded. "Good. This be a blacksmith shop wit' a workin' smeltin' contract with the village. Should be no surprise we got a fume or two comin' outta our windows."

An hour later, Hallis beckoned them over to the large crucible. He pointed inside and had an expression of delight on his face.

"There be yer answer, J!"

Jerica pulled a stool over so she could see inside. "I'll have to take your word for it. I can't get too close or else I'll get burned. What's happening?"

Hallis' voice dropped to a whisper. "That green metal of yers be finally melted. It took damn near forev'r. I can see it, floatin' on the top. Look, lemme do this."

He pulled a lever situated next to the pot, which partially closed the vent, and then selected a long-handled ladle with visible holes riddled throughout. He walked over to a large wheel with a handle on it and rotated it a few times, which had the effect of lowering the vent and pot to a more manageable position. Reaching in with the ladle, Hallis carefully stirred the contents a few times. Grunting irritably, he returned the ladle to a wall full of hanging tools and selected a ladle without the drainage holes. After a few more moments of stirring, Hallis nodded.

"I've got some o' it collected. Movin' to the crucible on the counter. Steer clear, girls."

Jerica hooked an arm through Sif's and pulled her out of the way, just as her father swung the ladle over a much smaller metal container, no larger than a bucket, sitting on the metal work counter. He poured something glowing red-hot into the crucible. Julius deposited the next load of crushed stone into the smelting pot and the process started all over.

"How much do you think we'll end up with?" Jerica wanted to know.

"O' that green metal? Ye be lucky if ye get a single bar's worth, J."

"What? Didn't you just scoop an entire ladleful into that smaller bucket?"

"It's no more than a spoonful at best. This be a process that takes its sweet time. I'm guessin' we be done by sunset."

And there's no way to speed things up? Zeira asked.

"No," Jerica automatically answered. When her father gave her a questioning look, she tapped the side of her head. "I've seen what has to happen, Z. It's not a quick process if we want it done right."

"Right," Hallis declared, giving her a wink.

They heard a bang from the other room, the one with the laborers. Hallis muffled a curse and turned to Jerica.

"Stay here. Both of ye. I'll see what be goin' on."

Before he could take a step, Vyler burst into the room. Catching sight of Jerica, he made his way over to her, completely ignoring Hallis.

"We have a problem."

"What is it?"

What's the matter? Zeira wanted to know.

"The *Pymbro* just berthed at our pier!"

I don't understand. Someone named Pymbro just birthed a deer?

Despite the serious announcement, Jerica burst out laughing. Vyler rounded on her.

"You think having a warship docked at one of our piers funny?"

"I'm sorry, Vyler. Umm, Zeira was trying to decipher what you said, and what came out was super funny."

Vyler leaned close to her and dropped his voice to a whisper.

"Zeira, that warship is here. I thought it would simply turn around, but no! Soldiers have been pouring out of that ship for the last hour. It … that Cerebus. Apparently, there are enough parts here to commence assembly and they're doing it now! What do we do? I'm told Cerebus will begin digging two days from now!"

"It didn't work," Jerica breathed, as she felt the color drain from her face. "Z, what do we do?"

We watch and observe.

If I may?

Othos, go ahead.

There's no need for concern until their intentions are clear. Perhaps they don't know the jhorium has already been claimed?

Jerica relayed the celestial's thought. "That's why the warship is here, and that's why Cerebus is still on track for assembly tomorrow."

I thought this mechanical beast took days and days to assemble? Skellig protested.

Jerica's mouth opened with surprise. "I do remember someone saying that. Vyler, doesn't it take weeks to assemble Cerebus? Now you're saying it'll only take two days? Did they get extra man-power?"

"From the *Pymbro*," Vyler confirmed. "The quartermaster informed me that fifty people were offloaded at the docks. All had been assigned to the assembling and day-to-day activities necessary to keep Cerebus running at top efficiency."

"That's a very precise description," Jerica observed.

"That's a direct quote," Vyler said, shrugging. "I don't understand what went wrong. They know you have whatever it is they're looking for, don't they?"

Jerica turned to Sif. "What if they don't? What if Dym told a different story?"

Dym is no fool, Skellig said. *If he thinks he can cause us grief by reporting false information, then yes, this is something he'd do.*

I don't think so, Zeira argued. *It would mean looking bad when the Thunder King learns about the theft.*

High above Jerica and Sif, Skellig nodded. It made sense. As much as he didn't like his sire, he had to admit Dym could never be considered foolish. Everything he had heard about this human Thunder King suggested he had a temper on him, and would frequently lash out at those he commanded. A dragon would be no different.

"That's not the end of the bad news, I'm afraid."

Everyone turned back to Vyler, who was now staring at the floor.

"Out wit' it, lad," Hallis ordered. "What be goin' on?"

Vyler's voice was barely a whisper. "Those three barges, the ones destroyed by that huge dragon? Well, replacements are already on the way. They're due to arrive in three days, which means Cerebus will be at full strength!"

"The ships arrive in three days, plus we have at least two more until it's fully assembled," Sif said. "That will give us …"

"It doesn't give us anything," Jerica insisted. "Didn't you hear what Vyler said? Cerebus will begin to dig in two days. We have two days to figure out how to drive them away."

The stakes have changed, Zeira declared. *There's no logic in assembling this contraption when the mineral they seek has already been found and removed.*

It's a ploy, Gocri said.

Exactly. We need to find out why they're really here.

Does it matter, Zeira? Skellig asked. *They're here, and they're intent on digging, regardless of the outcome. No, there's something wrong. They wouldn't do that unless … of course! It's a set-up. They must suspect we're still in the area, so they're hoping we attack the digger in an attempt to stop it.*

If we did, Othos began, *how would they stop us?*

"Only a mage would know," Jerica murmured.

"A mage? Wha'? Ye won' be callin' Doolan anytime soon, J. Ye 'ear me?"

"I don't plan on it. We have to be ready. The dragons think the ship is here, waiting for us to do something foolish to keep Cerebus from being assembled."

"Would ye?" Hallis asked.

"Would I *what*?" Jerica wanted to know.

"Try sumthin' foolish with yer dragon friends?"

"I don't know. Right now, we can't do anything that would draw attention to ourselves. We have to wait for the jhorium to be finished."

Hallis made a shooing sound and ushered Sif and Jerica to the door.

"It be not safe 'ere, girls. I recommend ye find yer dragons and hide wit' them. Come back at sunset. The task should be done then."

The two of them nodded politely and hurried outside, followed by Vyler. The baron bowed once and hurried off. Sif looked around the quiet village and took Jerica's hand.

"We won't let anything happen here."

"Thank you. I hope you're right. Where should we go? Back to Kinzler's Point?"

That's where we are, Zeira confirmed. *Well, most of us. Gocri is flying patrols. He's convinced Dym is somewhere out there.*

He isn't, Othos reported.

What? Zeira sputtered. *Why didn't you say so before?*

You didn't ask. I do not sense any other Spark dragons beside Skellig. In fact, the only dragons I sense are the six of us.

"That's good news," Jerica said, looking at Sif.

Later that evening, Jerica returned to her father's shop, with Sif in tow. Gently pushing the door open, she poked her head inside and saw that all of the laborers had gone for the day. Since none of the stations were occupied, the vents had been closed, and the overall temperature in the shop was easily thirty degrees cooler than before.

A clatter sounded from up ahead. Someone was moving about, and from the sounds of it, had just dropped a pair of tongs.

"Dad? Is that you?"

"J? Come in, come in. Be Sif wit' ye?"

"I am here," Sif called.

Working her way through the many stations until she reached her father's private area in the back, Jerica came to a stop. Hallis stood before her, with a look of triumph on his face. As the two of them approached, Hallis turned to grab something behind him and then eagerly held it in his open hand.

Jerica smiled. Her father was holding a lustrous green bar no larger than her fist. Surprised, she looked up at her father, who nodded.

"That's all there was, J. We went through ev'ry rock, swept up all the bits and pieces, and dumped 'em in. Will this be enough for ye?"

Jerica took the bar and hefted it in her hand. Her mind told her the bar was metal, and should therefore be heavy, but it was only a fraction of the weight. She handed the bar to Sif, who had the same reaction as she did.

"It's so light. I've never encountered a metal with so little weight."

"That makes two of us," Jerica said.

Hallis raised a hand. "Three. Where are ye off to now?"

"We need to get this to my, uh, friends," Jerica answered. She wrapped the bar in a piece of cloth and tucked it into a pocket. She could barely tell it was there. "It's late, Dad. Go on home. And thank you. This means the world to me."

"Yer welcome, J."

"Thank you, sire of Jerica," Sif added.

"I told ye to call me 'allis."

Thank him for us, too.

"Zeira says thanks," Jerica said. "They all owe you."

"Never had dragons indebted to me before," Hallis mused. A grin split his face. "I kinda like the notion."

"Skellig says if you ever need anything, you only have to ask."

Hallis nodded. "Now that I think about it, there be somethin' I'd like."

"What?" Jerica asked, curious.

"An emerald. A big one."

Puzzled, Jerica stared at her father. "You've never indicated you liked jewels before, Dad. Why the change of heart?"

"Not fer me, J, but yer mum. She loves emeralds. I'd love to get her a big one."

Jerica's eyes widened. Even now, when faced with the possibility of untold riches, the only thing her father asked for was a jewel he could give to her mother?

Her eyes filled as she embraced her father in a tight hug.

"Love you, Dad. I'll be in touch."

Hallis' face reddened as he caught sight of Sif smiling at him.

"Aw, heck. Love ye, too, girl. Sif, keep an eye on her."

Sif nodded, and then followed Jerica to the door. Outside, the two girls veered north, following the main street until it dead-ended at the piers. Turning right, they moved east, past the many empty vendor stalls, until they could see Kinzler's Point in the distance.

"You should see this street during the daytime," Jerica was saying. "There are so many vendors lined up here, and here, that you can barely walk."

"What do they sell?" Sif inquired.

"What *don't* they sell?" Jerica laughed. "Fishing poles, nets, ropes, dried fish, dried fruit, powder, jewelry, animals, meat, cheese, and the list goes on and on."

"I'm sorry we missed them," Sif said, sighing. "I do believe I'd like to see that."

"Well, sunset was probably a half hour ago. Once the sun goes down, that's their cue to close up shop until tomorrow. Do you smell something?"

"I can smell quite a bit," Sif said.

The two of them came to a stop. They were still on the cobblestone road, but they were far enough out of town where they were essentially by themselves. Jerica looked behind her, in the direction they had come from, and then — lifting a foot — checked the bottom of her sandal.

"What is it?" Sif asked.

"I smell something rotten, something foul," Jerica decided.

Sif took a few cautious sniffs. "I smell it, too. It smells like ... meat?"

Jerica held a hand over her nose. "If that's meat, it's from an animal long dead."

"Smells great, doesn't it?" Sif said, nodding.

The winds from the north picked up, and with it, the foul stench was carried away. For the next ten minutes, both Sif and Jerica continued down the worn street until Jerica came to a sudden halt. Again.

"It's back, and it's stronger than ever. What could be making it?"

A look of alarm spread over Sif's face. "I know that smell. It's …"

A bolt of lightning lanced down from the sky and struck the ground less than five feet from them.

"It's Dym!" Sif cried.

A streak of color flew by overhead, disappearing into a bank of clouds in the southern sky.

"That dragon was dark, almost black," Jerica said. "Whoever that is, it wasn't Dym."

A roar sounded from above. The dark dragon sped by again, and right on cue, a second bolt of lightning struck dangerously close.

What is it? Zeira asked. *I can sense your alarm!*

We're under attack! Jerica sent back.

Is it Dym? Skellig snarled. *I'm on my way!*

As am I! Gocri added.

The foul stench returned. Jerica's eyes widened as she realized the scent was their attacker. She turned to Sif, to shout a warning, but Sif was no longer there. Sensing motion from above, Jerica looked up in time to see the strange dragon streak toward her. Its wing talons crackled with energy as it prepared to fire.

Motion erupted behind her. Turning, Jerica watched as Sif's new form sprouted four legs, wings, and a tail. When the attacking dragon was less than thirty feet away, Sif leapt into the air, gave herself a violent twist, and snapped open a wing. The unexpected slap knocked the dark dragon senseless, where it crashed into the ground and fell still.

Two flashes of color, one yellow and black, and the other white, streaked overhead. The two separated and approached from opposite directions. Skellig landed first, followed closely by Gocri. Both adopted defensive positions and carefully watched the sky.

Gocri, seeing the dark grey Spark dragon sprawled on the ground, moaning, gave a snort of surprise. He turned to Sif, who had just landed.

"What did you hit him with?" Gocri wanted to know.

Sif shrugged. "Just my wing."

"Your wing did *that*?" Skellig said, admiring the number of smashed tree limbs and broken trunks. "Remind me not to get into an argument with you."

"I would never hit you with my wing," Sif promised.

Skellig nodded. "Good to know."

"Maybe my tail?" Sif suggested, as she waggled it on the ground.

"Ha ha. Can we …? Jerica, what is it?"

"I don't smell it anymore."

Skellig blinked a few times. "What was that?"

Their kai pointed at the inert form of the unconscious dragon. "I can't smell him."

The three dragon companions stretched their necks over to the unconscious newcomer and sniffed.

"I smell a dragon," Skellig decided. "Definitely Spark. I'd say … current?"

"Like you?" Jerica asked.

"I'm plasma," Skellig clarified.

"What's the difference?" Sif asked.

"Strength of power," Skellig answered. "Plasmas are much stronger than … all right, now I can smell it."

Jerica's eyes widened. "Does that mean …?"

A lightning bolt slammed into the ground at Skellig's feet. Skellig let out a growl of warning, but it was too late. Two more bolts struck, throwing Jerica to the ground. Sif flipped head over tail and landed, unconscious.

Gocri roared a challenge and took to the air. Skellig did the same. Spark and Glacier flew in close, protective formation.

"And here I thought Spark dragons were rare," Gocri grumped, as they extended their wings and executed a near perfect one-hundred-and-eighty-degree turn.

"How many are there?" Skellig asked. He was using every ounce of strength, and every trick in the book, to stay close behind their attackers. "I only see the one."

"There are three," Gocri reported. "Four if you count

the one Sif took out."

"The one Sif took out," Jerica repeated, from the ground.

Sif appeared at her side, shaken, but alert. She had shrunk herself down into a much smaller dragon, still easily three times her former mass.

"Jerica, are you all right?"

"Where's that other dragon? The one you knocked out?"

Sif turned and pointed. "Over there. Still out."

"Follow me. Hurry!"

Jerica hurried over to the unconscious dragon and slapped a hand on its leg, then hurried back to Sif's side and nudged her back the way they had come.

"Just confirming a theory. Come on, we need to help Skellig and Gocri."

"How? I cannot leave you alone."

"And I'm not asking you to. Now, do you see the guys?"

Sif looked up. "Yes. It would seem *they* are now the ones being pursued."

"There's magic involved here," Skellig insisted. "I may not be the best flyer, but I can hold my own. With these three it's all I can do to keep my tail out of biting range."

Sif spotted Gocri trailing just behind Skellig. It looked as though neither dragon was willing to desert the other.

"Perfect!" Jerica cried, picking up their thoughts. "Skellig, do you see me down here? I need you to do a flyby."

"That would put you in danger," Skellig argued. "That's a bad idea."

"I have a plan. Gocri, are those three still following you?"

"Yes."

"Follow Skellig."

"Will do, Miss Jerica."

"Sif?"

"Yes, Jerica?"

"Let me know when they're close. I'll need about a five second head start."

"A head start for what?" Sif asked.

"You'll see."

Sif tapped Jerica's shoulder. "Get ready! I see them coming!"

"Is Skellig still leading?"

"Yes. Gocri is just behind him."

"Good. Skellig and Gocri, when I say *now*, take deep breaths and hold it."

She felt their confusion, but neither dragon was willing to disobey.

"They're close!" Sif shouted. "Now's the time!"

Jerica tapped into Sif's powers, remembering the one defensive ability she could employ, and then applied it to what she had borrowed from the unconscious Spark dragon.

"Now!"

A blanket of dark smoke gushed forth from Jerica's open hands. It rose and quickly spread, creating a dense blanket of dark fog. Sif's eyes widened as she caught a whiff of the foul stench.

Skellig reached the cloud first. He punched through it, unscathed, as did Gocri. Their pursuers, unfortunately, were caught with their mouths open. All three dragons gasped for breath, began hacking, and spiraled out of control. One crashed through a line of trees and fell still. The second and third actually collided with one another, crashed to the ground and came to a stop after sliding the last thirty or forty feet, sending up plumes of grass, plants, and a few shrubs.

"What was that cloud?" Skellig asked. "Jerica, did you do that?"

"Yeah, sort of. I borrowed Sif's breath and that noxious smell coming from the other dragon. You and Gocri didn't breathe it in, but the others, well, you saw what happened. They were knocked out!"

"That's some quick thinking, Jerica," Sif praised.

Nicely done, Jerica! Both Othos and I were on our way, but since you have everything handled, we're headed back.

"Yes. Wait. Skellig? I have a question for you."

"I'm listening."

"Exactly how many Spark dragons did you say there were? There's you, there's your father, and now these three. I get the feeling that all of Gale is against us. That can't be true, can it?"

"I haven't visited Gale in several years," Skellig admitted.

"Who knows what has happened there in recent times?"

"Does it make you want to go back?" Zeira asked.

"Yes and no."

"Guys? Can anyone hear that but me?"

"I hear something," Zeira reported. "Bangs, twigs snapping, and ... yes, I can feel the ground trembling. Is it a terra tremor?"

You guys might want to see this.

Othos? Where are you?

You and your companions should return to the site where the jhorium was taken. Crouch behind the ridge visible to the northwest.

What ...?

Trust me, young Zeira.

They didn't have far to go. Crawling along the ground, keeping themselves as flat as possible, the group of five dragons — and one human — edged ever closer to the ridge's edge.

"They're assembling Cerebus!" Jerica softly wailed.

A large boulder suddenly lifted itself from the ground and dropped into a discard pile of broken tree trunks, huge rocks, and other uprooted material.

"What's making the stones move like that?" Sif whispered. The vapor dragon had returned to the much smaller human form, and was now crouched on the ground, next to Jerica.

"I wish I knew," Jerica murmured.

They watched the frantic activity below them in utter silence. Humans, like a busy ant colony, ran every which way. Everyone seemed to have some place to be, and a task. One person was holding vines, another an armful of documents. Another kept pointing at various objects to be marked and disposed of.

Another stone went sailing by, as though it had wings. Jerica traced its trajectory and saw something that made her blood run cold. She tapped Zeira's leg and pointed at the rim of the hole they had dug earlier.

"Do you see those two humans next to the hole?"

"What about them?" Zeira wanted to know.

"They're wearing robes of red," Jerica pointed out. "Do you know what that means?"

The dragons stared back at her.

"They're mages, like Doolan. Why would they bring more mages?"

"Probably because of what they fear we can do," Zeira said. She stared at the activity for a few more moments, a look of resolution on her face. "Since the humans have chosen to assemble this mechanical device regardless of whether or not the jhorium is in the ground, our choice becomes clear: it must be destroyed."

"Dragons shouldn't indulge in the affairs of humans," Othos said, adopting a regal tone.

Zeira, Skellig, Gocri, Sif, and Jerica all turned to stare at the sol dragon.

Trust me, Nuri's voice said, *if I was there, I'd be staring, too. We cannot sit by and do nothing.*

"I said that only because I felt obligated to say it," Othos continued. Lowering his neck, and his voice, the sol dragon eyed all of them. "But, that doesn't mean we have to listen. Young Zeira is right, as is Miss Nuri. We will not stand by, not when we have the power to stop this."

"What do you suggest?" Skellig asked.

Othos suddenly turned to look at Jerica. "That answer lies with you, Jerica. What are you willing to do to protect your home?"

Skellig watched a look of determination appear on their kai's face.

"Just tell me what you want me to do."

Chapter 10 - Cerebus

Dawn's first light began to show over the ridge, and Jerica felt no closer to an answer, even as the busy workers below continued to assemble the fearful Cerebus.

"Last night, Othos suggested you were the key to this," Skellig said gently. "I say he could be right. You, Jerica, know our powers and have the ability to manipulate them. Have you reached any conclusions?"

Jerica sat on a nearby fallen log and fell silent. "Smoke, lightning, fire, frost, echolocation, and ... and *sun*. There must be something you can create. This would be easier if I had a base power to work with," she softly mused.

Skellig's head jerked up. "Oh? Are you saying you need to find a human with a suitable magical ability again?"

Jerica smiled sheepishly. "I'm sorry, everyone. I can try to come up with something just by borrowing from all of you."

"But ours are just basic powers," Skellig pointed out. "I think you are right, in that you'll need to borrow a human's magic. After all, they're the ones who get the strangest powers. I'm sure you will be able to fashion something useful once you have that."

"Oh, sure, no pressure there," Jerica sighed. "Very well. You guys, stay out of sight. I'll head back to Cael and talk to Vyler. He's the baron, so he just might have a registry somewhere which shows who has what."

"You're not going alone," Zeira announced. "Sif, would you?"

The smoke dragon, currently in the form of another fire dragon, nodded. Her body turned grey, shrunk to three times its former mass, and morphed into a human. This time, a young girl—about nine or ten years of age—was looking back at them with wide, unblinking eyes. Her hair was black, she was wearing a light blue dress, and had a red ribbon tied in her hair.

"Where'd you get *that* form?" Jerica wanted to know. "I've never seen it before."

"We passed a herd of small humans yesterday. This form was one of them."

"A herd? Hmm, do you mean you passed a group of school children?"

"Isn't that what I said?"

"Well, we don't want any unwanted attention, and with that warship still docked at Cael, we need to take all precautions."

"Do you wish for me to change to another human?"

"No, we should … do this. Make your hair yellow."

The girl's long locks became the color of straw.

"Now, make your nose slightly bigger. Good grief, Sif, I didn't say to make it look like a banana. There, that's better. Finally, can you change the eye color from brown to blue? There, that's perfect. There are no girls living in Cael who look like that. We can say you're my little sister. Are you ready? We're off. Z, we'll be back as soon as we can."

"We'll be right here," Zeira promised.

Thirty minutes later, Jerica and Sif walked into the large three-story building that constituted Cael's municipal building. She knew her brother-in-law's office was on the top floor, so she immediately moved to the stairs and, making certain Sif was still following, climbed to the third floor. Pushing open the closed door at the top of the staircase, she and Sif emerged into a circular open area with a middle-aged woman seated before a huge desk. She looked up at the two of them as they emerged and immediately frowned.

"Visiting hours are from one to three every other day, and never on Fridays. You can come back then. Would you like to set up an appointment?"

"I'm Jerica Barille. I'm here to see Vyler, er, the baron."

"Baron Dartmoor is currently preoccupied," the woman informed her. "If you'd like to come back at …"

Vyler's door opened and her sister's husband appeared. "Jerica! I thought I heard your voice. As I've told you before, Mrs. Flechin, whenever a member of my family comes to see me, you're to usher them in regardless of what I'm doing. Their presence here means there's something that needs my attention. Do try and remember that in the future."

Jerica saw that the frown remained plastered on Mrs. Flechin's face as she was escorted into Vyler's office.

"Jerica? Who's your friend? No, wait. Sif? Is that you?"

"It's me," Sif confirmed.

"Are you two all right? What can I do?"

"Cerebus will be functional in just a few hours," Jerica quietly explained. Vyler might have trusted his secretary, but she sure didn't. "More mages were brought in, and I can only assume they're helping."

"Blast," Vyler swore. "What do you need from me?"

"I need to borrow someone's magical ability," Jerica explained. "Do you have a list here of folk with powers?"

Vyler hurried over to the closest bookcase and slid out a narrow notebook. He opened it as he sat down at his desk. Flipping through pages, and skimming paragraphs, Vyler finally let out a victorious grunt and slid the book across his desk to Jerica.

"All right, do you see this page? That's where the last census was notated."

"There aren't many of them," Jerica sighed, as she skimmed through the various names and a brief description of what they could do. "I was hoping there'd be more."

"Magic-wielders are getting hard to find lately," Vyler said, nodding. "That's why I decided to keep track. Do you see anything that might work?"

"Let's see. Here's one who can play a flute without touching it. Here's someone who can make water boil. And here's a lady who can see through walls, provided they're thin enough. I don't ... oh, wait! I think this one will work. It says here he's a horse breeder. Can you bring him here?"

"Mr. Varry? He must be near eighty years old. Are you sure you want him?"

"I'm positive. Thanks, Vyler."

Twenty minutes later, the elderly horseman was standing in front of Vyler with a look of confusion on his wrinkled face.

"I don't recall the last time I was in here," Edmund Varry stated, as he looked around. His frail, arthritic fingers latched onto one of the chairs in front of Vyler's desk and slowly pulled it out. "My strength isn't what it used to be, baron, so please excuse me."

Sif leapt to her feet and pulled the chair out for him.

"Why, thank you, little princess. What's your name?"

Sif looked at Jerica for confirmation she should answer, to which she was given a nod.

"Sif."

"Have you met Jerica before?" Vyler asked. "If not, allow me to make the introductions. This is ..."

"Oh, I remember Hallis' pretty daughter," Mr. Varry said, letting out a soft guffaw as he waved off Vyler's request. "It's a pleasure to see you again, Jerica. It's been a while, hasn't it? Last I saw you, you were no higher than my knee. Glad to see you all grown."

The look on Jerica's face suggested she had no recollection of ever meeting this particular person before, but she also didn't want to make an issue of it. Rising to her feet, she held out a hand. After a few moments, Mr. Varry took it.

"You have been mentioned several times by my parents over the years."

"Is that so? Well, you young filly, can I ask in what context was I mentioned?"

"Umm, well, we ... have ... been, uh, envious? Yes, that's it! We were always envious of the lucky buyers of your wonderful horses. I've always dreamed of owning a horse."

"I have a beautiful gelding for sale right now. He's yours, young miss."

Jerica's eyes widened. *That* was going to take some explaining to her parents.

"Such, er, wonderful news! Mr. Varry, before I forget, could you explain to me how long you've been a practicing magic-user?"

The elderly villager's wrinkled brow lifted with surprise. "My magic? No one has asked me 'bout that for ... gosh, at least forty years."

Vyler peered at his notebook. "It says here you're able to keep your grounds free from moles? Can you explain that?"

"Damn, pesky rodents," Varry grumbled. "They burrow every which way, riddling your land, causing swells and depressions. It doesn't take much to trip up a horse, and if a horse becomes injured or breaks a leg, well, that seals the poor creature's doom. Not once has any of my mares, or my stallions, thrown a shoe, or got so much as a sprain on my land."

"How does it work?" Jerica asked, adopting as innocent a tone as possible.

Mr. Varry shrugged. "It's nothing remarkable. I could lay my hand on the ground, find one of their tunnels, and force the little monsters to the surface."

"Is it an electrical charge?" Jerica asked. "Is that how you get them to move?"

"I don't really know," Mr. Varry admitted. "I can tell you it only works underground, never above."

Jerica held out a hand. "Thank you so very much. You've been extraordinarily helpful."

Surprised, the horse breeder took the hand, gave it firm shake, and made his way to his feet.

"Baron. Girls. Have yourself a good day."

Once the elderly gentleman had left, Vyler pulled Jerica aside.

"Do you believe his magic will work?"

"For what I have in mind, yes. Thank you so much. Sif and I are headed back. Hey, before I forget, will you keep this for me? I don't like carrying it around on my person."

Jerica produced the small jhorium bar, still wrapped in cloth, and gave it to her brother-in-law. "Tell me you have a safe place to keep it."

Vyler nodded as he took the bar. "What is it? Never mind, I don't want to know. I will keep this safe. As baron, I have access to … it's not important. It'll be waiting for you when you get back."

Once they were outside, Jerica hooked her arm through Sif's and hurried as fast as they could away from Cael. Once they were beyond the outskirts, with nothing but open water to the north, Sif switched back to a dragon form, choosing a white dragon this time, which suggested she was trying her hand at becoming an ice dragon. Whatever the color, this form had wings, and was able to cover a lot of distance in a very short amount of time.

Approaching from the northeast, and landing well shy of where Cerebus was being assembled, Jerica and Sif returned to the small ridge to watch the proceedings below. Nearby, a large pile of twigs and branches shimmered and faded away, to be replaced by Skellig. A huge mound of earth, looking very much like the discard pile from where they dug out the jhorium in the first place, became Gocri. And finally, having not yet mastered the art of illusion, Zeira emerged from behind a copse of trees.

"We were only gone for less than an hour," Jerica groaned. "I cannot believe how much they accomplished in a short amount of time."

Centered in the valley below, the Thunder King's massive digging machine, Cerebus, was nearing its final assembly stages. Resting on giant wooden wheels that were probably higher than Gocri was tall, the complicated contraption resembled the cranes employed to empty cargo ships.

Cerebus' main body had a radius in excess of a hundred fifty feet. The control cabin was four stories high, to hold a crew of twenty-five. An elongated arm was attached to one side of Cerebus' square body and stretched out nearly three hundred feet. Embedded into the end of the arm was a huge spinning disk, which had scoops large enough to hold five humans each, all along the edge. On the direct opposite side of the digging arm was a much smaller arm with large metal weights hooked to it.

Running the length of the elongated arm was a conveyor belt, which conveniently caught the recently dug soil and ferried it back to the main control deck. From there, it was sorted into bins, and those bins would then be transported off site, presumably to a waiting ship.

Cerebus' lower section, directly beneath the control deck, had the oddest piece of equipment yet: the largest wooden wheel anyone had ever seen. What was something like that doing on a digger? It looked like a water wheel, but there was no river nearby! What could it be possibly used for?

Casting the thought aside, she focused her attention on the large metal blocks on the flip side of the digging arm. If those happened to be what she was hoping they were, then there might be a chance to use them against the Thunder King. She could only pray that the magic she borrowed would work as well as she hoped.

What are you looking at and what do you hope they are? Skellig thought to himself.

"Counter weights," Jerica said, as she picked up the dragons' questioning thoughts. "If those weren't there, then the weight of the digging arm would tip Cerebus over."

"Can we use that to our advantage?" Zeira asked.

Jerica shrugged. "Possibly. I really don't know what'll happen when I unleash our surprise for them. Wow. I can't even imagine what will happen when the other three arms are attached."

Two nearby trees shimmered and then merged into one. Othos appeared a few moments later. "What was that? There are more arms?"

"Look at the base of that thing. You see how the one arm is attached and there are the counterweights on the opposite side?"

"Yes."

"I remember Vyler saying there were multiple arms. Think how efficient that thing would be if there were digging arms on all four sides."

Skellig pointed north. "Did you see the pipe?"

Jerica blinked at him. "Huh?"

Gocri helpfully pointed a talon northeast. "In the time you and Sif were gone, these huge pipes were set up. They are so long that I think they are anchored in the bay."

"Are you looking at it now?" Jerica asked.

Gocri nodded. "I'm opening my senses."

"Look at the size of it!" Jerica cried. "That pipe is big enough for a human to walk through it without having to stoop. How in the world did they get something that big installed so fast? It's humanly impossible."

Gocri turned back to Jerica. "You mentioned humans in red robes ... wizards? They are responsible. They lifted each pipe into place, all the way to the water."

Jerica nodded. "You're right, it's in the bay. I think ... of course! It makes perfect sense now! I set something similar up for my father in his shop. I think they're planning on piping in the water to Cerebus!"

"The beast needs to drink?" Sif asked, confused. "I was under the impression it was a mechanical device."

"It *is* a water wheel," she breathed, snapping her fingers. "I thought that looked like a paddle wheel from one of our mills. Don't you see? That's why the pipe is there. They're going to feed the water to the wheel! It'll turn, which will spin those gears. That, in turn, spins the large digging wheel at the end of the arm."

"What happens to the water once it has been used?" Vyler wanted to know. "Is it piped back to the bay, or is it recycled?"

"There's only one pipe," Skellig reported. "That can only mean the water is not being collected and it is being allowed to soak into the surrounding area."

Jerica groaned. "The soil can only absorb so much, not to mention that they're using sea water. It'll poison the land, trees, and the native wildlife! We cannot allow them to do this."

Jerica and the dragons fell silent as they gazed at the

abomination in the center of the small valley. A horrible grating sound had begun. Skellig noticed the huge disk at the end of the long arm was slowly starting to spin. As the noise grew progressively louder, the digging wheel accelerated until it was almost a blur. A klaxon sounded, and with that, the entire arm descended until the scoops made contact with the ground.

The terra tremors began almost immediately. Trees were shaking so badly that most lost their needles and leaves, with many losing their branches. Flocks of birds rose noisily into the air, voicing their displeasure. Herds of various animals scrambled to put as much distance as possible from the metal behemoth and themselves. However, the dragons all noticed that none of the fleeing beasts and animals were able to make it over the inlet pipe. Frantic, they fled in the only direction they could, which was north, toward the bay.

"This is a disaster," Zeira decided. "Nuri, are you there?"

Yes, I'm here.

"Are you safe?"

Of course.

"You've no doubt noticed the large metal tube sucking water out of the bay?"

I have. There are no safety precautions to prevent it from snatching up fish, plankton, or seaweed. I've been trying to see what it would take to destroy it. It's made of metal, which can withstand much more than any other medium I've dealt with. I'm afraid I won't be much use against it.

"Just steer clear of that thing," Zeira ordered. "I don't want you anywhere near it. At least, not until we know what we're going to do with it. Jerica, it's begun. If we're going to do something, now's the time. What's your plan?"

"Well …"

"What power did you end up choosing?" Skellig asked, unable to hide his eagerness.

"What will you be able to make us do?" Gocri asked.

"I've always wondered about a mixture of fire and ice," Sif said, sighing.

"I'd love to be included in your plan," Othos added.

"I'd love to be able to destroy that pipe," Nuri wistfully said.

Jerica had to laugh. "Don't get your hopes up. Remember, we need to make sure you guys stay hidden at all times. We can't raise the ongoing tensions between everyone."

Othos nodded. "She's right. You must all remain hidden."

"That includes you," Skellig pointed out. "More than anyone."

"What's that supposed to mean?" Othos asked.

"You have a tendency to bite first and then ask a question or two later," Zeira told him, in as friendly a tone as she could.

"Hmmph. We'll see."

Skellig thumped his tail and pointed at their kai.

"I do believe Jerica was going to tell us what power she was able to borrow. J, go ahead."

"Mimic," Jerica corrected, with a smile. "And, well, it's, uh … scoff if you may, but I think this will work. The magic I found is very effective at removing moles."

Skellig held up two claws barely an inch apart. "Small rodent, digs underground, and isn't even a mouthful? You're kidding."

Jerica dropped into a cross-legged sitting position on the ground and closed her eyes.

"No, I'm not. This man's magic happens underground. That means that whatever I end up splicing this power with, it's going to stay underground."

Skellig's eyes widened. "They won't be able to see what's coming!"

"Exactly. So, let's add Zeira's fire, Skellig's lightning, and a dash of Othos' intensity and see what we get."

A small orb appeared in her hand. It was predominantly red, but it did have yellow swirls if held up to a light. Giving her friends a nervous look, Jerica rolled to her knees, and placed a trembling hand on the ground.

"Well, here it is, and before anyone asks, no, I have no idea what's going to happen."

"We should test it," Zeira decided.

"How?" Skellig asked. "On Cerebus? Will they be able to place any of the blame on us?"

Everyone looked at Jerica.

"Don't look at me. I really don't know. Zeira's right. We

should test it. Very well, you guys be prepared to clear the area at a moment's notice, all right?"

"We'll be ready," Skellig assured her.

Remembering how Mr. Varry had described his powers being used, Jerica placed an open palm, face down, on the dirt. Holding the red orb tightly in her other hand, she pictured the monstrosity that was Cerebus in the valley below and imagined inflicting damage. Carefully, she set the orb on the ground.

The red sphere melted into the earth. Moments later, a disturbance in the valley below caught their attention. Something was there, moving fast, as it headed directly for Cerebus. In fact, the object was moving so fast under the ground that it was sending up a plume of dirt and debris as the earth swelled upward as it passed by.

"Where'd it go?" Gocri asked. "Did it misfire? Did anything happen?"

Skellig was already pointing at the valley below. He nudged his white companion and looked pointedly at the disturbance, which even from this distance, didn't need a dragon's eyesight to be visible.

Jerica turned to Skellig. "Was that …?"

"I believe so, yes."

"If someone follows that line, then it'll lead them right back here, right?"

Skellig nodded again.

The rest of the dragons were ready.

"We need to change locations," Zeira said, having already come to that conclusion. "We cannot be discovered here."

A distant explosion sounded. Hurrying to the edge of the ridge, Jerica and the dragons saw a pillar of dark smoke rising from Cerebus' base. One of the giant wooden wheels was lying on the ground, knocked off its axle and split in two.

The dragons looked at their kai as she was placed on Zeira's back.

"Start making more," Skellig urged. "And tell us how to use them."

"You can't be seen!" Jerica insisted, as Zeira turned tail and hurried — on land — away from Cerebus.

"And we won't," Skellig assured her, as he and the others fell into step behind her. "No human eye can match the speed with which a dragon can fly."

"Or swim," Nuri added. The valthan had surfaced and was watching them approach.

By the time they reached the shore, Jerica had made nearly a dozen of the altered spells. Handing several to each dragon, Jerica explained what she did to make the last one work.

"Think about what you want it to do," their kai explained. "Then, drop it on the ground. Now, whether or not this works from the air, I don't know."

"They're incredibly small," Gocri observed, as he stared at the tiny orbs rolling around in his palm. "I think the only way I can do this is to do one at a time. One in each hand. My talons are much too big to try and drop just one if I was holding more in each hand."

Zeira nodded. "That's a good plan. If each of us has two, and we're able to make successful hits, that should buy us a few days."

"Is it safe to carry them in my mouth?" Nuri wanted to know.

Jerica looked at her valthan friend and shrugged helplessly. "I don't know, Nuri. I think the spell triggers when it touches the ground. I just don't know if you want to take that risk."

"I want to be helpful, so yes, I'll risk it."

Nuri swam close to shore and walked a few feet out of the water. Jerica reached up and, as carefully as she could manage, placed two of the orbs in the valthan's mouth.

"You be careful," Jerica sternly told the dragon. "Do not hurt yourself trying to attack that thing. In fact, that goes for all of you. Be careful, all right?"

"They won't know what hit them," Skellig promised.

Once everyone had two spells, one in each hand (unless you were a valthan), the dragons took to the air — and the sea. Skellig rose steadily; his wings beating slow, powerful strokes. Once he was concealed in the clouds, he opened his senses and peered down, at the valley, which lay to the left. The giant mechanical beast was making an unbelievable amount of noise as the humans scurried around it to try and repair the broken wheel.

This was going to be fun. All he had to do was make sure he was thinking about the destruction of the mechanical contraption and voila, he would drop a sphere. There was six of them, each armed with two spells. If each of them scored hits, there was a better than average chance they could destroy the monstrosity once and for all. In addition, thanks to their kai's quick thinking, no one would suspect any dragon was involved in the beast's destruction.

As he readied his approach, Skellig increased his velocity until he was nothing more than a blur in the sky. He eyed his closed hands and smirked as he imagined the destruction he was about to deliver to the threat of Jerica's home village. Perhaps if they targeted those large wheels enough times, they could knock it off its perch? Maybe get it to tip over? That would definitely cause a delay or two.

Picturing explosion after explosion happening to Cerebus, Skellig released his first orb as he passed over the ridge where they had been hiding before. However, this time, as he banked north, he noticed something new.

A flash of blue caught his eye. Turning his head to pinpoint where he had seen the color, he detected not just one speck of blue but a dozen. They had been arranged in a grid-like pattern, and were about a hundred feet above ground.

Spells.

Two more blue spheres rose from the ground and took their places in the sky, and one let out a pulse of light, then a brilliant bolt of blue-colored lightning. It arced through the air and slammed into the red subterranean spell he had dropped moments before.

There was a loud BOOM. Skellig saw that his spell had been destroyed.

"Uh, oh," the Spark dragon groaned.

Two more orbs pulsed, followed immediately by more blue lightning bolts. These two sped off, in opposite directions, resulting in identical explosions. Two pillars of dark smoke rose angrily from the ground, twisting and turning against the bright blue sky.

We have a problem, Zeira reported.

Mine didn't make it to the device, Gocri reported.

Let's do this, Skellig suggested. *We all release our second spell at the same time. Let's see if these blue orbs can handle that many simultaneous attacks.*

It could. Quite easily, in fact.

As trails of disturbed earth streaked toward Cerebus from six different directions, six blue spheres pulsed. Six bolts of lightning fired off, and sure enough, six different explosions shook the area. Echoes from the blast bounced around the canyon for a good ten seconds afterward.

We definitely have a problem, Skellig irritably grumped.

What are those blue things? Jerica asked. *They're offering protection for Cerebus, aren't they?*

One of the orbs pulsed a final time and as they were watching, a blue bolt snaked out and slammed into the ground, as yet another of the modified red spells streaked toward Cerebus.

Sorry, Nuri apologized. *I had one left. You never know until you try.*

I want a closer look, Skellig decided.

Steer well clear of those things, Zeira told him. *I don't want to see anyone hurt.*

Someone has to do it. We need to see if there's a way to nullify these spells.

I'll go with you, Gocri decided. *We are both skilled flyers.*

Thank you, my friend.

Always. Now, let's approach from the east.

Why the east? Skellig inquired.

Heavily treed, more mountains. We may be able to approach in stealth.

Ah. Very well. You take lead.

Skellig grunted once, pleased. He and Gocri flew out over the water, and then turned east. Once they were far enough away, they both turned south for a few moments and, once they were lined up, turned west.

Skellig started increasing his speed; Gocri did the same. Seeing Cerebus in the distance, Skellig turned to his companion and pointed left.

"I'll go this way, you go *that* way."

"Acknowledged."

The moment both dragons entered the valley, all fifteen of the blue orbs pulsed and became illuminated. Skellig barely had time to execute a quick barrel roll before nearly half of the orbs fired at him. Twisting and turning in the air, Skellig maintained his course, knowing that in just a couple of seconds, he'd be out of range. Even so, lightning bolts sizzled dangerously close by long after he should have been out of danger.

"Tell me you're all right," Skellig implored.

"I am," Gocri muttered, "barely. If we're going to do something like that again, then I clearly need to fast for a while. That was too close for comfort."

"Agreed. We need to neutralize those blue orbs before we can try attacking again."

Gocri flew close. "Any ideas how?"

Skellig shook his head. "None, I'm afraid. But, I firmly believe that there is always a way. We might need to consult with the others, but I'm sure there's a way to take those spells down."

"I say we try."

"We try *what?*" Skellig asked,

"I say we try to take one of those things down ourselves."

"We wouldn't be taking on just one, but all of them," Skellig pointed out.

"We wouldn't be attacking all, just one," Gocri argued.

"We didn't attack them at all," Skellig countered. "All we did was try and get a closer look. Every one of those large orbs targeted us and tried to kill us."

"If you're too scared to try, then it's all right. I can try this alone."

"Really? You appeal to my sense of pride? Blast. Fine, let's go. You realize Zeira isn't going to care for this?"

"We need to bring down this defense system. I'd like to know what it's going to take."

Skellig and Gocri turned left and flew south for a minute or two. Eyeing each other, each daring the other to back down, both dragons nodded once, circled about, and adjusted course to fly near the humans' digging machine. The array of blue spheres began to glow dangerously.

Skellig sighted the closest orb, felt his power increase, noticed tiny arcs of electricity running up and down his wing talons. Taking a deep breath, he locked his eyes on the nearest orb and fired off two bolts, which slammed into the sphere.

His yellow bolts exploded the moment they touched the blue ... spell? Orb? Sphere? Whatever it was, it caused his own power to discharge the moment it made contact. The only thing that happened was a brilliant flash of light, and then ... nothing.

The light faded, allowing his eyes to return to normal. Blinking a few times, he turned his neck to see what the status was. What he saw made him groan with dismay: the orb was there, undamaged.

"So much for that," Skellig grumbled.

"My turn."

Skellig turned in time to see Gocri spin in the air and launch an object. What was it? Another spell? Some type of defense weapon?

"It's just a stone I selected," Gocri explained. "I've had it ever since we departed. I thought it might come in handy."

There was a brief flash of blue as one of the orbs targeted the incoming stone and shot it neatly out of the sky.

"Blast," Gocri grumbled. "They can neutralize all manner of threats."

"We should head back," Skellig suggested.

Gocri opened his other hand and displayed a much larger stone, almost the size of Jerica. Hefting the boulder in his hand, he lowered his neck and applied his icy breath to the stone, not stopping until it resembled a snowball.

"What are you doing that for?"

"Maybe they're heat sensitive?" Gocri said, shrugging. "As Nuri has said, you never know until you try. Come, we make a final pass."

This time from the north, Skellig held back once Gocri started spinning. His glacial friend released the stone on the fourth revolution.

Much of the frost flew off the stone as it sailed through

the air, but it remained a bluish, frozen color. Gocri veered off, well away from the terrible blue orbs. Skellig turned to watch the stone fly unerringly toward one of the protective spells. They began to light up, which clearly meant the orbs recognized the threat. But there was a slight delay. Could that mean ...?

The frozen stone slammed into the intended orb and smashed it into a thousand pieces. A barrage of lightning bolts suddenly flashed toward them. Ducking, dipping, twisting, and turning, both dragons fled. Gocri roared in pain, his wing hit.

Skellig dropped into a free fall and caught Gocri's tail, but Gocri was simply too big for him to save. Roaring with frustration, Skellig snapped his wings open and pulled for all he was worth.

Chapter 11 — Evolution

Come on, don't fail me now! Gocri, wake up! I need your help to get us out of this! Gocri, can you hear me? Wake up! We're too high!"

His glacial friend was unresponsive. What to do? Skellig worked his wings frantically, trying to break their fall. Voices shouted in his mind.

No time at the moment, guys!

Get over the water, if you can.

He eyed the sea, jerking his body in that direction, holding onto the much larger dragon's tail for all he was worth. "Wake up, Gocri!" he implored, watching the approaching shoreline. Suddenly, it was now or never.

"Hold on!" Skellig cried, as he tucked his wings against his body. "We're about to touch ..."

Both dragons hit the surface of the water, striking the seabed and becoming mired in the thick layer of silt. Seawater rushed in and huge waves pounded their bodies. Struggling helplessly against the pulling water, Skellig expended the last of his energy and passed out.

When he came to, he was startled to see that he was now on shore, and based on the gouges in the sand behind him, had been dragged out. His first thought was Gocri. Was he safe?

"You both are," a calm, soothing voice told him.

Skellig shook his head, but waves of pain slammed through his skull. He groaned and dropped back to the ground.

"Where's Gocri?"

"He's here," the voice said. "His injury is being tended."

Skellig's eyes still refused to focus well. Too much seawater. "Who pulled us out?"

"You can thank *me* for that," the voice said, clearly shaken.

"Nuri?"

"Yes, it's me."

"Are you all right? You sound shaken."

"I sound shaken, Skellig? I watched two of my friends slam into the sea. I thought both of you had drowned."

"Tell me you helped Gocri first," Skellig implored.

"Only because I found him first."

Zeira, Sif, and Jerica arrived. The kai ran up to his snout and threw her arms around it.

"Oh, I was so worried! I'm so very, very, very glad to see you're all right. Don't ever do that again!"

Zeira approached next. "Skellig? Are you uninjured?"

"Waiting for my eyesight to clear."

Nuri reported, "Your eyes were probably open on impact, and got a thorough spraying. We brought freshwater and have been rinsing your eyes as you slept."

Skellig blinked and rose unsteadily to his feet. "You have? Thank you. I'm not sure what to say to that."

"You should try *thanks*," Sif suggested. "I've never seen Nuri move so fast. She was worried, Skellig. We all were."

"How's Gocri?" Skellig asked.

Zeira and Sif both turned to look up the shoreline. Gocri

was there, spread out, with one wing bent at an unnatural angle. Skellig winced as he studied the broken wing and then hung his head.

"It's all my fault. I never should have gone for a closer look. But, I feel I should tell you that …"

Zeira held up a claw. "As much as I'd like to know what happened, we really need to vacate the area. Do you hear that? There's a warning klaxon going off. It's no secret that the humans know we were involved with the attack on their contraption."

Skellig groaned again. "They know? How?"

"I'd say it has something to do with the destruction of one of the blue spheres," Sif said.

"You know about that?"

Sif nodded. "We all do. The only thing we don't know is who threw the rock that destroyed the orb? More importantly, *how* was it thrown?"

Skellig stared at Sif for a few moments. "I don't follow."

"Let's save that for later," Zeira said. "We need to get out of here, and fast. Plus, we have an unconscious ice dragon. I need ideas, everyone."

"How are we supposed to move him?" Skellig wanted to know.

"That's why I'm requesting ideas," Zeira said. A note of alarm had crept into her voice. "Flying is out. He needs to rest his wing."

"Swimming?" Nuri asked.

"Only as a last resort," Zeira decided.

"What about being carried?" Sif asked.

"Carried?" Zeira sputtered. "By who? Perhaps if all of us held on to a limb, we might be able to …"

"No," Sif interjected. "I'm talking about *him*."

All eyes turned to the large, grey head that had appeared next to Nuri's.

"Othos! Where have you been?"

"My apologies, Zeira. I'm really not allowed to be actively participating in skirmishes. It would appear I was taking sides, which is forbidden."

"Wow, I had no idea that …"

"Let me finish," Othos interrupted. "It doesn't mean I won't, though. You six are my friends. When someone wrongs us, is it not understandable to seek revenge?"

"What are you going to do?" Zeira asked. "Scratch that, we have bigger problems to worry about."

"If you were your normal size," Sif began, "you'd be able to carry him, wouldn't you?"

Othos nodded. "I could, yes. Where?"

"We need to find someplace quiet," Zeira said, "and out of the way, but not too far."

"There are islands all over the place," Nuri reported. "Couldn't we go to one of them?"

A loud clamor had started in the south and was starting to get louder.

"They're getting closer," Zeira said. She looked at Othos. "Will you? Carry Gocri to one of the islands?"

"Of course. In my natural size, we *will* be seen, of course."

"That's true. So, the sooner the better. Nuri, would you find us somewhere to go?"

"Y-yes, of course. I just … can you g-give me a minute?"

"Nuri, I know you were spooked," Zeira began, "but right now, please focus. I need you to find a safe place for us to regroup. Is there anywhere nearby?"

Nuri nodded. "Yes. I'm sorry, I just … never mind. Let me think. We need to stay away from prying eyes, so we should look northwest. I seem to remember a large, uninhabited isle there that should have room for us. I'll go verify its location."

"Thank you. Othos, you're up."

"Just a moment." The sol dragon turned in time to see Nuri go zipping off to the north. Satisfied she wasn't returning anytime soon, he spread his wings and flew off. "Be right back."

Watching the celestial disappear into the afternoon sun, Zeira turned to Skellig, who shrugged. Then, they heard a faint splash as the sol dragon had seemingly decided to go for a swim.

"I don't know what he's doing, either," the Spark dragon confirmed.

The water erupted upward. Twin spikes reappeared as

Othos lifted himself from the sea. Blotting out the sun, and casting a huge shadow over the land, Othos reached down with one of his forelegs and scooped up Gocri's inert form, careful to position the ice dragon's wings so they wouldn't be further injured. Turning promptly on his heel, Othos started walking away, traveling almost faster than any of them could fly, and to think he wasn't even hurrying!

"How are your wings?" Sif asked Skellig, lowering her voice to a whisper. "Can you fly?"

He nodded. "They're sore, but they're functional. Come on. Othos is pulling away from us. If we don't hurry, we'll be left behind."

As they flew in silence next to Othos' giant, striding form, Skellig got the impression that Zeira wanted to know more about their impromptu attack on Cerebus. Sighing, he turned to their group's leader and saw she was watching him. Well, both she and Jerica were.

"Out with it. I know you have questions. Fire away, Z."

"Can you walk us through what happened?"

Skellig nodded, and using a softer than normal tone, described in as much detail as he could what happened during the attack. Should they have done it? No. Gocri wanted to test his luck, but he advised against it. He also admitted that he probably could have stopped Gocri at any time, so the fault of the attack should fall with him and not with their injured friend.

"But you were able to destroy one of those orbs," Zeira said, impressed. "I thought they were able to sense motion?"

"They can, and they do," Skellig confirmed. "Gocri threw that first stone at it and it was vaporized long before it could make contact. And don't forget the spells Jerica made."

"What about the spells I made?" Jerica asked.

"The defense system protecting Cerebus could see those attacks coming, and they were doing so underground! We even flew by it with no thoughts of attacking, and those blue orbs lit up, as though they detected a threat. Whatever they are, and whoever put them in place, they are more powerful than we had thought possible."

"Tell me about the rock that destroyed the orb," Zeira

urged. "What was different about it?"

"It was frozen," Skellig recalled. "Gocri breathed on it, which made it look like a large snowball. I should also mention it was larger than the first stone that was thrown, if that makes any difference."

"I would think that, the larger the stone, the easier it would be spotted," Sif countered.

Zeira nodded. "My thoughts exactly."

"I was skeptical that this one would have any better luck than the previous ones," Skellig continued, "but much to our surprise, the orbs weren't lighting up. I don't think those orbs spotted the incoming rock until much later than normal."

"And this is from Gocri breathing on it?" Zeira asked.

"Yes."

"For how long?"

"Maybe four or five seconds, no more."

"I've seen him breathe on something that long before," Zeira recalled. "Yes, it turns white, but even he has said that whatever he uses his breath on doesn't freeze solid. That is, unless he spends an inordinate amount of time on it."

Skellig shrugged. He didn't know what else to say than what he had personally witnessed.

"We're here," Nuri announced.

Skellig turned to look back at the mainland, to get an idea on how far they'd come, but he couldn't see anything. Following a gargantuan dragon striding through the open sea as easily as he would wade through a shallow stream must have been more distracting than he realized, seeing how they were now a number of miles away.

An island appeared in front of them. Predominantly consisting of forested land, the western shore opened into a large bay, with a wide-open beach. For humans, it would have been perfect. For dragons it wasn't quite big enough.

"Allow me," Othos said.

Making sure Gocri remained motionless in his left hand, he used his right to swipe along the coast. Trees, stumps, rocks, and vegetation were swept out of the way. Othos plucked a dozen broken stumps free and tossed them into the forest. Then, being uncharacteristically gentle for a dragon his size, he set Gocri down on the recently cleared shore and shrank down to his much smaller form.

"He needs some help," Sif decided, as she stood over Gocri's inert form and inspected his wing. "His right wing appears to be broken in several places."

"How do we help him?" Jerica asked, as she looked up at Zeira. "He's a dragon. You're a dragon. Uh, is there, I don't know ... a dragon healer?"

"Not that I'm aware of," Zeira reported. She looked at Skellig. "What about you? Do you know of anyone?"

"I don't," Skellig confirmed.

"What happens if one of you gets sick?" Jerica asked. "What happens if one of you gets hurt? Who do you turn to for help?"

Zeira shrugged. "That's a good question. I guess it'd be ... my mother?"

"That doesn't help us, Z," Skellig said.

"There must be something we can do!" Jerica implored. "We can't leave poor Gocri here in pain! Look at his wing! It's broken! There must be something we can do to help him!"

They all felt the low growl before they heard it. As one, the companions turned to Gocri, who was starting to show signs of consciousness. Jerica hurried over and waited patiently for the ice dragon to open his eyes. When he did, Skellig could see the eyes burning with pain.

"Where's Skellig?" Gocri managed. "Is he ... all right?"

"I'm here," Skellig reported, as he approached Jerica. "How are you, my friend?"

Gocri turned his neck so that he could see his right wing. "Well, that explains a few things. Ouch. Remind me not to try that again. What happened?"

"What do you remember?" Zeira asked.

"Throwing a frozen stone. It ... you already know what happened, don't you?"

"She saw it," Skellig confirmed.

"I take full responsibility for what happened," Gocri began. "I pressured him into joining me during my attack. I shouldn't have done it."

"No, you don't," Skellig said, shaking his head. "You

wouldn't have been there if I had left things alone. I said I wanted a closer look. The fault lies with me."

Spark and ice eyed each other, each of them wondering how to disprove the other.

"You both feel guilt, and I'd say you're both partly at fault," Zeira began. "But, that's not important. What *is* important is that Gocri figured out how to defeat those blue orbs."

Gocri's head jerked up. "I did?"

"Yes. You froze the stone you threw, which meant it wasn't detected right away. By the time those orbs figured out they were under attack, it was already too late. Well done!"

"Oh, well, it was nothing."

"We need to tend to your wing," Zeira said. "A grounded flyer is not going to do us any good."

"I agree," Gocri glumly added.

"Do you have someone you'd turn to if you're injured?" Jerica asked.

"It is exceedingly rare for one of us to get injured," Gocri reported. "As such, I'm afraid I'm at a loss as to what to do."

A splash from the sea had Gocri and the rest of the gang turning to look at the water. Nuri had slapped her tail on the water, and based on her expression, hadn't realized she had done it.

"Sorry. I was just thinking. I might know of something that could help."

Skellig perked up, as did Gocri.

"Let's hear it," Skellig urged. "What do you suggest?"

"Let me see what I can find. I'll be back."

Nuri's head disappeared and a series of ripples signaled she was no longer in the area. Jerica wandered over to Gocri's side and sat companionably next to him. Skellig, unsure of what else could be done, lowered himself to the ground and rested.

"I wonder what she has in mind," their kai mused, as she leaned back against Gocri's white scaled abdomen. "I'm sorry you had to go through all of that."

"I'm sorry for putting our mission in jeopardy," Gocri grumbled.

Zeira approached. "Can I ask a question, Gocri?"

"Sure. What's on your mind?"

"The stone you threw, the one which destroyed one of those orbs? How big was it?"

Gocri shrugged and then looked at Jerica. "It had about the same mass as her, I'd guess."

"Skellig says you froze it solid."

"No, I simply coated it with my breath. I thought perhaps the orbs respond to body heat."

"And they did," Zeira said. "My question, though, is about your powers. Your icy breath. Have you ever frozen something before? I mean, froze it completely solid?"

"I have, yes."

"And ... how long did it take to do that?

The ice dragon fell silent as he considered. "It depends on the object. The larger it is, the longer it'd take to freeze it. Why do you ask?"

Zeira shook her head. "Just ... humor me, if you would. How long does it typically take to freeze an object of that size?"

Gocri's eyes shifted to Jerica's. "I'd say maybe fifteen seconds. Why?"

"You froze that stone in less than four," Skellig recalled.

Gocri moved his gaze to him. "Are you sure?"

"Yes. I thought for certain there was no way this would work, but you proved me wrong."

"Four seconds?" Gocri repeated. "That would be a record for me."

Nuri's head broke the surface of the water. She was holding some type of plant in her jaws. She then spat the plant at her feet and nodded at Gocri.

"Eat that. It'll help with the pain."

Gocri eyed the plant, which included leaves, stems, and roots, and remained silent.

"It's a variant of the eucalyptus plant," Nuri explained. "It will help you to deal with the pain."

"I think I'd rather deal with the pain," Gocri said, without breaking eye contact with the plant.

"Nonsense," Nuri insisted. "Jerica, would you take the plant to Gocri? It'll help him feel better."

Jerica nodded. "Of course."

If it was possible for an ice dragon to turn green, that would be Gocri as he eyed the plant nearing his face.

"It's a plant. I don't eat plants."

"There, there, this will help you," Jerica soothed. "If Nuri says it'll help with the pain, then that's exactly what it'll do. Here, open up. Gocri, you're not opening your mouth."

"I. Don't. Want. It," Gocri hissed, doing a remarkable job at both speaking *and* keeping his jaws tightly sealed at the same time.

"Oh, come now," Jerica tsked, as she held the wet, drooping big-leafed plant in front of Gocri's snout. "I know such a big and powerful dragon like you is not afraid of a little plant like this, is he?"

Skellig snickered. Gocri shot him a dark look.

"Especially when you know it'll help you feel better," Jerica continued. "Do this for me? Please?"

The white jaws reluctantly opened. Jerica stuffed the plant in between his fangs and then stepped back while the jaws closed. Kai and dragon eyed each other.

"It won't help unless you eat it," Jerica said.

"No swallowing it whole," Nuri warned. "It must be chewed. The juices from the plant are what is essential in relieving your pain."

Another titter sounded from Skellig.

"One word, Sparkles, and you'll be eating your own plant."

"Haven't said a thing," Skellig said, as he looked away. "I'm just minding my business."

Gocri sighed and finally chewed. A look of utter disgust appeared on his face as he glared at Nuri, then Skellig, and finally, Jerica. But, moments later, his eyes opened wide with surprise.

"Is it helping?" Jerica asked.

"I … the pain is gone."

"Your wing is still broken," Skellig said. "How could there be no pain?"

"Nuri, this plant was incredibly helpful," Gocri said, turning to the valthan. "I apologize for resisting."

This time, Nuri wore the frown. The rest of the dragons noticed, too.

"What is it?" Sif asked. "Nuri, is something the matter?"

"That plant has the ability to lessen pain," Nuri said, "but not remove it entirely. Something is wrong."

"Well, I'm not complaining," Gocri said. "I may not be able to move my wing, but at least there's no pain."

All eyes turned to Jerica. "Wh-what?" the kai stammered. "I didn't do anything. All I did was feed it to Gocri. Why are you all looking at me like that?"

"If that plant only helps with the pain," Skellig began, "but won't remove it entirely, doesn't that suggest something happened to it? Somehow, it's healing powers have been, I don't know ... *amplified*?"

Jerica held up her hands. "Again, don't look at me. I still have the underground rodent exterminator magic I took from that man in Cael. Does one of you have some type of healing magic we don't know about?"

There was a chorus of no's.

Everyone turned to Nuri.

"How certain are you of that plant?" Zeira asked.

"Utterly," Nuri stated.

The group turned back to Jerica.

"You must be doing something," Skellig insisted. "No, I see you want to argue. Hear me out. We've proved you wrong before, about wielding magic. Could this be another facet of your power?"

Jerica allowed her hands to drop helplessly to her sides.

"If it is, this is a new one on me. Look, Gocri might not be in pain, but his wing is still broken. Our problem has not resolved itself. What are we going to do?"

"I may have another idea," Nuri said.

Five reptilian heads — and one human — turned to the valthan.

"If we go under the assumption that Jerica did something to the plant ..."

"... which I didn't," Jerica insisted.

"... then it stands to reason if we can locate something designed to help with injuries such as this, then with its power amplified thanks to Jerica, or whatever it is she's doing …"

"… and I still don't know what I'm doing to it," Jerica quietly insisted.

"… then we might be able to locate something *stronger*, perhaps, which could completely heal him?"

"Like what?" Sif asked.

"Who has heard of the healing powers of certain crystals?"

"Please," Skellig scoffed. "That's nonsense."

Jerica was shaking her head. "No, not really. I've seen Doolan use crystals before. Since we now know he doesn't have the ability to work with magic, that means he must use talismans and spells in order to get his work done. Nuri, what did you have in mind?"

"Bright yellow crystals," Nuri began. "They …"

"Let me stop you right there," Jerica said, growing excited. "I actually know about this. You're talking about the shards of Vander?"

"Who's Vander," Skellig asked, "and what do shards have to do with anything?"

"It's just a classification," Jerica explained. "A mage by the name of Vander Sorrell. Now that I think about it, I think he must've been like Doolan: couldn't use magic. So, he started looking for items that were imbued with powder naturally. He discovered magic-infused artifacts could be found practically anywhere, but there's a stronger likelihood that you'd find it in a gemstone, or crystal. He discovered a bright yellow crystal which had healing properties. Place it on your skin, and it could heal a scratch."

"A scratch?" Skellig repeated. "We're talking about something more serious than a mere scratch."

"The larger the specimen, the more power it had," Jerica said. "That must be what Nuri is looking for. Oh, if I only had some powder. We'd be able to heal Gocri in hardly any time at all."

"What is this 'powder' you keep referring to?" Zeira wanted to know.

"It's a rudimentary form of magic-infused dust that allows non-magic folk to wield magic. The only thing the people of

Cael use it for is to ward off predators and monsters at night. We prefer to live a simple life otherwise."

"You can ward off monsters with powder?" Skellig clarified. "How?"

"By sprinkling it around your house in an unbroken circle," Jerica explained. "The problem with Doolan was, he kept making powder more and more expensive. The Guild of Mages don't care what they charge the people. If you wanted to sleep easy at night, then you had to pay for it."

"That's …"

"A rip-off?" Jerica replied. "I couldn't agree more."

"I was going to say that humans are strange creatures."

"Seconded," Gocri added. "No offense, Miss Jerica."

"None taken. Nuri? Do you think you can find a Vander shard?"

Nuri nodded. "I'll certainly try."

"How many are there?" Gocri asked.

Jerica looked up. "What was that?"

"Vander shards. How many are there?"

"There isn't a set number," Jerica explained. "When we say Vander shards, what we're really talking about are the yellow crystals. There aren't a set number of them."

"Crystals like that are typically found in deposits of igneous rock," Nuri proclaimed. "I've seen them before. Not around here, unfortunately, but that doesn't mean I can't look."

"In *what* kind of rock?" Gocri asked.

"Volcanic," Zeira translated. "We have an abundant supply of such deposits in Blaze." She sniffed the air. "I don't smell any trace of ash in the air. I don't think there are any volcanoes in these parts."

Othos stirred. He lifted his head and sniffed. "I can detect traces of ash."

Four dragons immediately tried. Skellig shook his head. Having been near an active volcano as recently as last year, he could smell no traces of one nearby.

"I don't smell anything," Sif said.

"It's there," Othos confirmed. "I'd say it was at least eight hours away."

"As the dragon flies or the human walks?" Zeira cautiously asked.

"As the dragon flies," Othos said.

"In which direction?" Gocri asked.

Othos pointed west, out over open water. "That way."

"Too dangerous," Zeira decided.

"Which is precisely why I'm going to be the one looking," Nuri informed them. "I *can* detect traces of ash. It's faint, but it's there."

"You can?" Zeira asked, amazed. Then, her eyes widened. "In the water. What would we do without you?"

Nuri nodded her head and dipped below the waves.

"She's proving to be more useful than any of us," Sif said, sighing. Her form shrank until she could have been mistaken for Jerica's sister. "While she searches, maybe this would be an ideal chance to test Gocri's newfound abilities?"

"What newfound abilities?" Gocri wanted to know.

"The ability to freeze something solid in less than half the time it would normally take you," Zeira answered. "I've seen you use your breath before."

"And?" Gocri prompted.

"Have you ever frozen something solid in a few seconds?"

"The stone wasn't that big," Gocri insisted. "There is no merit to this."

Skellig selected a large boulder easily three times the size of Jerica and held it up, then offered the stone to his friend.

"What do you think? Can you do it?"

"In a normal world, I'm obliged to say no," Gocri stated. "However, no one will say these are normal times. Very well. Place the stone down and move away."

With the gang gathered on the other side of their glacial companion, Gocri sighted the stone, took a deep breath, and expelled a steady stream of his icy breath at it. Right before their very eyes, the stone turned light grey, frosted over, and then became a large snowball. Surprised by the sudden appearance of the rock, Gocri held his breath and cocked his head at the sight.

"That was, what, five seconds?" Skellig reported. He took a few steps over to the boulder, gingerly touched it, and growled in pain. "Well, that was stupid. Serves me right, I suppose."

"What happened?" Jerica asked.

Skellig held up his claw. "The stone is cold. Painfully so, I'm afraid. Well done, Gocri."

"Excuse me?" Jerica said, raising a hand. "Can I ask a question?" Without waiting for an answer, their kai pointed at Skellig. "Why did that hurt you? Don't you have scales? Aren't you protected by fire? Why would a little cold bother you?"

Curious, Skellig cocked his head. It was a good question. *How* had he been burned by a super-cold stone?

Grunting, Gocri reached out to touch the stone. The moment his claw made contact, his eyes widened. He snatched the stone off the ground and held it up to his eyes.

"No one else touched this but me?"

Skellig nodded. "Only you. What's the matter? Why so surprised?"

"My abilities lack the strength to freeze something this thoroughly."

Once again, everyone turned to Jerica. "Hey, I didn't do anything this time. I didn't touch Gocri, nor did I even *think* about splicing powers together."

Skellig sat back on his haunches and considered. "A plant wipes out all of Gocri's pain and a frost dragon who, up until now, couldn't quickly freeze something solid."

Gocri turned to Skellig. "What are you thinking?"

"I'm thinking it appears our abilities are growing in strength. I think we should all test our powers. I'll go next if there are no objections."

There weren't. Nodding, Skellig leaned back in order to lift his wing talons from the ground, where he had them resting. Looking around the deserted island, he spotted one of the stumps Othos had yanked out and discarded. Ramping up his power internally, and hearing the signature crackling noise his power made when it was ready to be released, he targeted the stump and let his power fly.

Twin bolts of lightning shot out from his talons, only to fuse together less than two seconds later. The resulting white bolt of power was thick, jagged, and crackled with energy. It lanced out with deadly accuracy and hit the stump head on.

The stump exploded. Bits of broken wood and splinters rained down on them from all directions. As one, the dragons — and their kai — turned to Skellig.

"All right, that was new," Skellig was forced to admit. "The strength of that blast was at least two levels above my own."

"I'll pass on testing my flames," Zeira said, with a sheepish look on her face. "I'm going to assume you're right, Skellig, and excuse myself from this particular test."

Skellig chuckled. "Spoilsport. All right, Sif? Care to try?"

"I'm not sure what I *can* try," the vapor dragon retorted. "I can exhale a noxious smoke if necessary. I guess I could try that?"

Sif returned to her natural form. Looking down at them all, she faced the other direction, the same in which Skellig had destroyed the stump, and spat out a steady stream of jet-black smoke. It immediately expanded to cover the ground and steadily spread out in all directions. Unfortunately, that meant theirs, too.

"It's coming this way," Skellig warned. "Sif? Can you call it off?"

Sif shook her head. "My smoke? Since when have you heard of a smoke that will stop on command?"

The smoke obediently froze in place. Sif gave it a curious look before turning to her companions.

"It's never done that before. What is it doing?"

"You told it to stop," Jerica recalled.

"How does this help us?" Sif asked, perplexed.

"You gave it a command," Jerica pointed out. "Try giving it another."

"To my smoke? Nothing will happen. Fine, you want me to try? Observe. Smoke, retreat in on yourself."

Much to her surprise, Sif's smoke seemingly reversed course and began withdrawing into itself. Seconds later, it vanished.

"How is this possible?" Sif breathed, amazed. "No smoke dragon has ever had control like this before. Jerica? What have you done?"

"I swear to you, I haven't done anything!" their kai insisted.

"What about shifting forms?" Gocri asked. "You switch forms all the time. Is there anything different there?"

Sif switched to the tiny gyre dragon, then to a mirror of Jerica, then Nyssa, and finally to the large, unique plant dragon she had become on the back of that giant bug, back when they started their quest together.

"That was much faster," Skellig observed.

"Actually, it was," Sif agreed. "If you had seen me six months ago, you would barely recognize me."

"I think it's safe to say we've all improved ourselves," Skellig said, eliciting nods from those listening. "Where's Othos? Where has he gotten to this time?"

Zeira glanced around the open bay. "When was the last time someone saw Othos?"

"I'm right here," came Othos' reply.

"Where were you?" Zeira asked. "I was just looking in that direction. You were not there."

"I haven't left the island," Othos confirmed. "Although, I will say I was snoozing just a little bit ago."

"Here?" Zeira asked. "On the beach?"

Othos pointed farther inland. Sure enough, they could actually see the depression Othos had made in the ground when he was sleeping.

"You were invisible," Skellig said.

"I won't go invisible unless I allow it. You all probably just overlooked me."

"No," Zeira insisted. "I can see where you were, on the ground. We were looking right at you. I therefore think it's safe to say your own powers have been growing."

"From exposure to your kai? I think not."

"Exposure to our kai?" Skellig repeated. He looked down at Jerica at the same time she looked up at him. "You're saying all of this is happening because of our kai?"

"Because she is a *kairie*," Othos said. "They are known to have the absolute strongest magic in all the land. No one really knows what they're capable of doing, since no one has ever bothered to chronicle their abilities."

Nuri surfaced. She unfolded her thin front legs and slowly walked out of the water. Once she was a little more than halfway, and facing the group, she lowered her head and placed some stones at their feet.

"I didn't find a yellow crystal, but I did find a number of other colors. I decided to bring them all."

"Good thinking," Skellig praised, as he selected a stone. It was a deep purple color on one side, and the other looked as though it had been dipped in white liquid. Skellig held the half purple half of the stone aloft and nodded. "Amethyst. I'd recognize it anywhere."

"Any healing properties?" Zeira wanted to know.

Shrugging, Skellig held it against Gocri's injured wing. After a few moments, the glacial dragon shook his head.

"Apparently not," Skellig decided. "What's next?"

In this manner, they worked their way through the rest of the stones. One was a ruby, the other a diamond. Nuri had brought a beautiful specimen of obsidian, and had even found a fire opal. None, however, had any effect on Gocri's wing.

"What is this one?" Skellig asked, as he selected the last stone. Unlike the others, it wasn't shiny, nor was it polished smooth. It was a large lump of granite. "Why is this one here?"

"I was trying to break that one open," Nuri confessed. "I found many of these stones hidden within others, such as that. I tried and tried, but lacked the leverage to break it open. I'm hoping that one of you can."

Smirking, Gocri held out a hand. "Allow me."

Wanting desperately to be the one to try first, Skellig reluctantly passed the stone to his friend. That's when he noticed that Nuri motioned Zeira over. Intrigued, he leaned close.

"Something odd happened," Nuri reported, lowering her voice.

"What is it?" Zeira asked, growing alarmed.

Nuri looked at the gems scattered along the beach. "I found the gemstones near an active volcano."

Zeira nodded. "You did mention there were some in the

area because you could taste the ash in the water, right?"

Nuri shook her head. "No, I'm talking about *above the water*. When I couldn't find the source of the ash underwater, I expanded my search and followed my senses. These gems were collected from lava flows *he* described."

Skellig, Zeira, and Jerica all looked at Othos, who returned the stare. A smug look fell across his features.

"Wait," Skellig protested. "Didn't he say that the nearest volcano was nearly eight hours away?"

Nuri nodded. "That's what I'm trying to tell you. I was already a fast swimmer, but now? It feels like there's nothing I can't do."

"You, too," Zeira breathed. At Nuri's questioning look, the fire dragon launched into a little more detail. "All of us have experienced strange things. We appear to be growing stronger. I was going to ask you about it when you returned, but you beat me to it."

Mollified, Nuri could only nod.

There was a loud *CRACK*.

"Got it," Gocri exclaimed. He held out his claw and allowed the others to pick away the broken bits of granite to see what was there.

"We've got something," Skellig declared, as he held up a pale green stone. "Does anyone know what this is?"

Sif pointed at Gocri. "Let's see if it does anything."

Skellig gently held it against the injured wing. When nothing apparent happened, Skellig pulled away, only to be stopped by Gocri himself.

"Just a moment. Do that again, would you?"

"What, hold it against your wing?"

"Yes. I … *felt* something."

Skellig returned the stone to his friend's wing. He waited a few moments to see if anything happened. The entire group waited on bated breath for Gocri to make the announcement.

"Something is happening," Gocri finally decided. "I just can't tell what."

Zeira leaned over Skellig's claw to study the stone. "I don't think I've seen that type of stone before. Can anyone identify it?"

No one could.

"Well, here's hoping it has some sort of magical abilities," Skellig said.

"Could I have that a moment?" Jerica asked.

Skellig eyed Gocri, who nodded.

"What do you want with it?" the Spark dragon inquired.

The kai held up her left arm and pointed at a small laceration just above her elbow.

"If this has healing properties, then let someone who was hurt give it a try."

"How did you get hurt?" Zeira asked.

"I scratched it on a bush a few days ago," Jerica said. "It's nothing. But, it's an actual scratch. Let's see what this stone can do, shall we?"

Skellig gave her the stone, which was a little smaller than her two clenched fists, and watched as the green deposit was held against Jerica's left elbow. No one moved, and no one said anything.

"What are we waiting for?" Skellig quietly asked.

"To see if this does anything," Jerica answered. "It doesn't feel like it did, so we're going to have to … huh. Would you look at that?"

Three dragons rushed forward, all intent on seeing for themselves what had happened to Jerica's arm.

WHAM.

"Ouch," Zeira cried, shaking her head. Then, she ran a claw along each of her horns, verifying they were undamaged. "That hurt."

"I cannot believe we just ran into each other," Skellig moaned.

"Don't look at me," Sif said, shaking her head. "I'm in my natural form. You couldn't physically hit me even if you wanted to."

"I am so glad I witnessed that," Gocri chortled.

"Look!" Zeira exclaimed. "Look at Jerica's arm! Her wound is practically gone!"

"It's still there," Jerica contradicted, "but I will admit it's better. This stone has healing properties, but it isn't very strong."

"That's not going to do us any good, is it?" Skellig sighed.

Jerica held the stone firmly against her chest and closed her eyes. "Maybe, and maybe not."

"What are you doing?" Zeira asked.

"I'm trying something. Give me a second, will you? I want to see if what you all are saying is true." After a few minutes of silence had passed, Jerica wordlessly held the green stone up. "Would someone give this back to Gocri?"

Skellig nodded, took the stone, and then — with Gocri's nod of approval — held the green rock against Gocri's wing. Everyone held their breath as they trained their eyes on Gocri's injured wing. Five minutes passed, and as far as anyone could tell, nothing had happened.

"It was a good attempt," Gocri conceded, as he fidgeted on the ground. "It almost feels like my wing is ... what's this? How in the ...? Miss Jerica, it worked!"

"I stared at that wing the entire time," Skellig insisted. "It doesn't look any different to me."

"That's because you're looking at the wrong wing," Sif chuckled. "Gocri? Can you confirm your wing is healed?"

The frost dragon rose to his feet and extended his wings. He gave them several powerful flaps before folding them against his back. He turned to Jerica and bowed low.

"It would seem, Miss Jerica, that you've become a wizard."

Chapter 12 — Retaliation

Y ou do realize that there's no backing out now, don't you? Thunder King will clearly know the dragons are going to be responsible for this."

"I'm sure he already knows, Zeira," Skellig said. "Gocri? How's the wing?"

"Perfectly healed."

"Excellent."

It was the following day, early morning. The sun had risen less than an hour ago and the six dragons — and one human — were on their way back to Cael. Because, according to Gocri, it was time for some good old-fashioned revenge.

"We were trying so hard not to be linked to the attacks," Zeira moaned.

"True," Skellig admitted. "Now that everyone knows, there's no point in hiding it anymore. The only way we're going to be able to save our two species, the dragons and the humans, is if we can successfully defeat Thunder King and all of his minions."

"What about Dym?" Zeira asked. "Would you really sacrifice your sire?"

"I'd sacrifice my sire and not think twice about it," Skellig said. "I stopped thinking of him as my sire many years ago. Dym deserves everything that's coming to him."

"How do you want to do this?" Gocri asked, as they approached Cael's coast. "Direct, frontal attack?"

"There are still those lightning strikes to contend with," Skellig reminded him. "I may be Spark, but those blasts do hurt. No, we'll do exactly what we planned: approach in stealth, take out as many of those orbs as we possibly can, and when we finally have the advantage, we destroy that huge beast."

A wave of alarm washed over Gocri. Skellig, flying side-by-side with his friend, glanced over, worried. "Are you all right?"

Gocri pointed southeast, in the direction they were flying. "It would seem we are expected. Look, the number of orbs has doubled."

"Doubled?" Zeira groaned. "We need to call off the attack. There's no way we can …"

"We can still win," Gocri declared, cutting her off.

"How?" Zeira demanded. "Those orbs nearly killed the two of you last time."

"True," Gocri admitted, "but we know how to destroy them. Plus, they will never expect a direct attack. We have the advantage. We should use it."

Zeira increased her speed until she was flying next to the two of them.

"If that which we need to destroy has doubled in number, then it would make sense to have as many on your team as possible, correct?"

Both Gocri and Skellig shook their heads no.

"You are protecting our kai," Skellig reminded her. "We cannot simply set her down somewhere and expect her to be safe. Not only that, I cannot split my attention between this attack and wondering whether or not Jerica is safe. That is where *you* come in."

"Agreed," Gocri rumbled. "And, what's more, you will have your own protection. Sif, you volunteered to be their backup?"

A second ice dragon dropped down next to Zeira and nodded.

"Absolutely. No one will touch either of them."

Skellig nodded. "Good. You three, find someplace safe to wait this out. Gocri and I will handle this."

Once Zeira and Sif, along with Jerica, had flown off, Spark and ice dipped their wings and banked east. Flying alongside, but well away from Cerebus, they made their first pass, just to see what had changed in the single day they had been gone. What they noticed, unfortunately, wasn't good.

Assembly had been completed. Thankfully, Cerebus was still undergoing testing before being ramped up to full production, but the tests were still horrific to see. Gone was the hole that Sif had dug. In its place was a pit fifty feet wide and over thirty deep. Animals, vegetation, and insects had all been stripped away, leaving nothing but bare rock to signify where Cerebus' digging scoop had been. If this was the damage one day could make, Skellig couldn't imagine what an extended period of time would do.

"Sure you can," Gocri argued. "Ponotoa, remember?"

"That was a terrible disaster," Skellig recalled. "You're right. We cannot let that happen here. Jerica would be devastated."

Gocri dropped low and snatched stones from the ground as he passed over. Skellig did the same, a fact which didn't go unnoticed by his glacial friend.

"You're not throwing rocks, are you?"

"Only if I have to," Skellig scoffed. "I'm thinking I should be able to take the orbs out with my own abilities now. I can hand these to you when you are ready."

"That's going to be a lot of lightning bolts headed our way," Gocri said.

"Don't worry about me. I was able to avoid them last time. You're the one who was hit, remember?"

Gocri turned to Skellig and stared — hard — at him. "That's how it's going to be, is it? Very well. I do believe a wager is in order."

"To see who can destroy the most orbs?" Skellig asked. When Gocri nodded, Skellig let out a chuckle. "Very well. Challenge accepted. We go on the honor system. We each will report the number we destroyed."

"And the winner?" Gocri asked.

They had flown far enough east and circled around, gaining speed.

"Bragging rights, of course. But, I also propose we place our finest piece of treasure up for collateral."

"How did you know I have a treasure horde?" Gocri asked.

"Pssht, we're dragons," Skellig chided. "Who among us doesn't?"

"I accept. I will place my prized sapphire against your …?"

"A spiraled ruby."

"A spiraled ruby?" Gocri repeated. "You're kidding. I've never heard of such a thing."

"I would be just as skeptical as you. It is literally twisted, like this." Skellig made a circling motion with his claw. "It has to be one of the strangest jewels I have ever found."

"Very well, it's a wager. I look forward to adding it to my collection."

"It's never going to happen. In fact, *I* will be admiring my new sapphire before you know it. Do you want to split up or should we stick together?"

"I say we stick together. We know what those orbs *were* capable of, but that doesn't mean additional measures haven't been taken. I'd rather not be surprised, thank you very much."

"Agreed."

The two flyers dipped their wings to bring Cerebus and its blue orbs in range. Skellig watched his friend take a deep breath and blow into his right hand. Satisfied the stone was frozen, Gocri briefly locked eyes, Skellig nodded his readiness, and then started spinning in the air, building up momentum. At the same time the stone was released, Skellig sighted one of the orbs and released twin lightning strikes.

The first orb shattered into a million pieces after the stone slammed into it with enough force to punch through a castle wall. It even had enough momentum to carry through to the next orb, which it also destroyed. Gocri was ecstatic.

"Hah! Did you see that? Two of them with one shot. This is going to be easier than I thought!"

Skellig's bolts lanced through the first orb, splintering off to hit the neighboring orb, and then sprayed out a thin web of tiny arcs, making the orbs go inert. The second bolt behaved much like the first, destroying three before dissipating into the network of nearby orbs. Four of the protective globes went dark.

"Are you seeing this?" Skellig asked.

"You destroyed more than I did," Gocri reluctantly admitted. "Go ahead and gloat. It was a fine shot."

"That's not what I mean. I … uh-oh. Look out! They're firing!"

Both dragons dove out of the way as a cascade of streaking blue electrical bolts flew by them. Much more alert this time, both ice and Spark were able to keep themselves out of the line of fire.

"After my second bolt destroyed a few of the orbs," Skellig continued, as they raced away from the dangerous orbs, "there must have been some residual power left over, because it reacted with surrounding orbs. They went dark! I think that means they won't — or can't — fire at us."

Gocri nodded. "An intriguing notion. Come, we make another pass."

"Wait," Skellig said, as an idea occurred. "How well can you control your breath?"

"Elaborate."

"What I mean is, we know you can freeze something solid in a matter of seconds. What if you didn't want to do that? Could you just, you know, revert back to the power you had and just give it a little frost?"

"Why would I want to do that?" Gocri demanded.

Skellig tapped his chest. "If those things can't see cold objects, and if the two of us just happened to be colder than normal, then …?"

"We might be invisible to them," Gocri finished, his eyes widening. "Too bad we didn't think of this before we attacked."

"Do you want to try it?"

"You're asking me to coat you with frost?"

"Yes. Can you?"

"Indubitably."

"Mm-hmm. Will you?"

"Only if you let me know if it gets too cold."

"Oh, don't you worry about that. If it gets too uncomfortable, I'll be the first to sound the alarm."

Skellig remained as still as possible while Gocri circled him, blowing his breath. After the second pass, Skellig, satisfied, was now covered from head to tail in a soft blanket of ice particles. Gocri looked down at himself and scowled. Thinking fast, the ice dragon expelled a huge cloud of white mist and flew through it, circling about to fly though a second time, and then a third. Gocri's already-white scales were coated with a layer of frost, too. Together, they altered their course to take them back to Cerebus.

"Round two," Gocri said. He held out a hand. "Give me one of the stones you're carrying. I'm going to try to hit them with two this time around."

Skellig held out a stone. "Good thinking."

The second time around, once Gocri announced he was ready to throw, Skellig held back to watch the much larger dragon position himself. Gaining altitude before the dive, Gocri snapped his wings closed, spun around to build momentum, and in a span of less than three seconds, flung both stones.

Deciding he should strike at the same time as his companion, Skellig was ready. He targeted a section of orbs in the northeastern corner and blasted for all he was worth.

"How many did I get?" Gocri asked.

"Six. Four with the first, and two with the second. It's more than me. I was only able to get three. You should have told me I had a bad angle lined up."

"Don't pin the blame on me," Gocri chuckled, as he automatically began flying in errant zigzags across the sky. The lightning bolts flashed by, but without a direct course to target the attackers, Cerebus' defense system was pretty limited in what it could do. "Did you notice? We were able to approach even closer. Heat is definitely a factor with those orbs."

"I *did* notice," Skellig said.

It's not helping us at the moment.

Skellig perked up. *Zeira? Are you safe?*

Two orbs are pursuing us, Sif reported. *Or, more specifically, Zeira.*

They're ignoring you? Skellig asked.

For the time being. They seem intent on only taking her down.

Because of Jerica? They're coming after you because of her?

Not while I still breathe, Gocri vowed. *I'm on my way.*

No, stay where you are, Zeira instructed. *They're behind me. I think I have this under control.*

What are you going to do? Sif asked. *I don't think those orbs would be affected by my smoke.*

Two enemies? Flying behind me? Oh, I've got this. Nuri, I owe you big.

I am so very pleased to be of help, Nuri said.

Moments later, Skellig felt a powerful wave of exhilaration flow through their leader. Zeira must have been successful in eliminating their pursuers!

Yes, I was, Zeira confirmed. *Let's just say they weren't planning on a blast of fire shooting at them from that direction. We're safe for now.*

You ventured too close, Skellig accused. *That's the only way you would have picked up your pursuers.*

The two dragons flew in silence for a few minutes before turning about and beginning their third run.

"May I make a suggestion?" Gocri said, as he hefted his last rock. Eyeing an approaching lake, he dipped low enough to snatch a large rock sitting near the water's edge. Once he had returned to Skellig's side, he continued. "Don't try to destroy them."

"What? Why not?"

"You've proven you're able to disable them better than hitting them. If they're disabled, then that means they can't …"

"… fire back at us," Skellig finished. "I can do that. I would need to be closer, to hit anything with such a broad shot."

The three of us are clear, Zeira reported. *We are about as far away as we could get while still keeping the two of you in visual range.*

Good. It'd be hard to concentrate on what we're doing if Gocri and I have to worry about you three.

That goes for me, too, Gocri agreed. *We're preparing for our third attack now.*

Excellent. Able to destroy many of those orbs?

Yes, but …

They both felt Zeira's alarm.

Skellig? What's the matter?

The number of orbs doubled from yesterday. I would imagine the Thunder King didn't like knowing one of his precious blue orbs was destroyed.

Please be careful.

Always, Gocri added. He looked at Skellig and nodded once. "Are you ready?"

Skellig took a deep breath and signaled his readiness. Gocri repeated the process of cooling themselves down. Once Skellig saw the frost coating his wings, he knew they were ready. Focusing on his wing talons as they neared, ordering his abilities to *not* focus on a target, he prepared to launch his power. He imagined a loud burst of electrical energy spraying in all directions, which is precisely what he wanted.

"Stay clear," Skellig ordered.

He dipped a wing, dropped nearly fifty feet, and then rolled onto his back, so that he was looking *up* at the floating orbs and the blue sky beyond. Gritting his teeth, he let his power build until he couldn't contain it any longer. Twin pulses sprang forth from his talons, but without a specified target, the powerful bolts of energy looked for the first tangible object they could find. In this case, small tendrils of lightning shot out in all directions. Once he knew both talons had fired, he quickly righted himself and sped out of the area.

Gocri was waiting for him.

"Nice. That was much more effective. Do you have any idea how many of those orbs you just eliminated?"

"I don't, no."

"Nearly a dozen!"

"I think this might—"

A blue bolt of electricity flashed dangerously close! Both dragons veered sharply away.

"Where did that come from?" Skellig growled. Turning, he saw something that struck fear in his heart. "Gocri, they're following us!"

"What? How is that possible?"

"You've got three on your tail! Evade! Evade!!"

The ice dragon tucked his wings and dropped like a rock. Three orbs, trailing after him, also dropped. Hoping his friend could take care of himself, Skellig risked a second glance behind him. Not one, but four orbs!

You're in danger! Zeira cried. *I can feel it!*

We both are, Skellig snapped. *There's no time to talk.*

I can see you. Those orbs? They're following you!

I noticed, Skellig sourly stated.

What are you going to do?

I'm working on it. An idea formed. *Nuri?*

I'm here, at Kinzler's Point. What can I do?

I see you. I am headed your way.

So is Gocri, the valthan announced. *I do believe he's planning to—*.

Figure out whether these confounded orbs are waterproof? Yes, I am.

Skellig sensed, rather than felt, the next attack. He executed a quick barrel roll, just as two bolts of lightning blasted the open space he had just vacated. Roaring with frustration, he dropped low getting both wing talons wet as they skimmed along the top of the water.

Nuri's head broke the surface, easily keeping up with him. She made eye contact with him and smiled. "Would you like some help?"

"If you wouldn't mind."

"Sure thing."

Nuri vanished, as did all four of the orbs. Moments later, she was back.

"You were wondering if they like water? Well, they don't. There were a few flashes of light when they hit the water, then they went dark. I don't think they were designed to come into contact with seawater."

"Where's Gocri? How is he faring?"

"He told me he was on his way here, but I haven't seen him yet."

Skellig paled. "Blast. He's in trouble. I need to go."

"May I make a recommendation? Physical violence."

"Huh? What about it?"

"I don't think those blue orbs like physical violence."

Skellig nodded. "Thank you. I'll see what I can do. Gocri? Where are you?"

North. I'm ashamed to say I am unable to rid myself of these blasted spheres.

I see you. Stay where you are. I'm on my way.

What happened to yours? How did you get away?

I had help, which is precisely what I'm going to do for you.

Why are you holding a …?

Don't move!

Skellig had pumped his wings, gaining altitude and speed. Meanwhile, the orbs following Gocri started inching closer. The closest leveled a blast that almost reinjured his right wing.

Hefting a broken tree trunk like a club, Skellig thrust his nose down and dropped like a stone. On the way past his companion, Skellig swung the trunk as hard as he could.

A loud crack echoed sharply over the valley. Two of the orbs crashed against the ground and exploded. The third tried firing a bolt of lightning at him, but he blasted it out of the sky with his own lightning bolts.

"Do you know what we could really use about now?" Skellig asked, as he returned to Gocri's side.

"What's that?" the ice dragon inquired.

The two of them had resumed flying east as they considered how to attack the orbs next.

"One immensely large celestial."

"Where *is* Othos?" Gocri asked. "Why isn't he here, with us?"

"He always seems to be disappearing, doesn't he?" Skellig commented. "We can't worry about that now. Look! There aren't many functioning orbs left. I say we focus our attention on the southwestern corner."

"Agreed. A final run should do it."

All in all, it took another four passes before they could confirm all of the remaining dozen or so orbs had been rendered inert. Not willing to take any chances, Skellig continued to use his makeshift club to smash the non-functional orbs to bits. He was so effective that Gocri abandoned his rocks and selected a fallen tree for himself. Twenty minutes later, it was over.

I do believe we destroyed them all, Skellig announced.

Outstanding! Zeira praised. *What happens now?*

Now? Gocri questioned, as an overwhelming sense of smugness washed over the glacial dragon, *It's time for some revenge. Skellig, the first of us to inflict damage on that machine is the winner of our wager. Fair?*

Sure, sure.

What? What's wrong?

You already lost. See the smoke? I just set the spinning disc on fire.

That doesn't count! I didn't see you!

We'll decide it later. Jerica, this is for you.

Thank you so much! their kai returned.

Skellig returned his attention to the unprotected behemoth. Verifying Gocri was nearby, he turned to line up a course which would take him straight to Cerebus. Skellig stared at the monstrosity and chuckled to himself. Without those nasty orbs to protect it, the bulky contraption was wide open for the taking.

Skellig's wing talons crackled with energy as he readied a blast of power. Sighting the same area as he had before, the spinning disk, he focused his attention on the joint physically attaching the disk and arm. Destroy that, and Cerebus would be digging no more.

"I'm on it," Gocri announced, picking up his thoughts.

The two of them separated as they dropped lower for their approach. Skellig released his power just as Gocri flew by the multi-seated area where Cerebus' many operators worked, expelling a tremendous cloud of ice particles.

The top floor of Cerebus' operation level frosted over. Machinery ground to a halt, the large boom arm stopped swinging, and the great wooden wheels that were slowly moving the enormous device across the valley floor came to an abrupt stop. Skellig zoomed by next, firing another set of coordinated blasts at the digging disk.

The disk was now actively burning, but it wasn't showing much damage.

Just then, a klaxon started up, followed by another, and then another. Looking at each other and wondering what was behind it, Skellig suddenly felt something touch one of his wings. Whipping his head around, he was startled to see a rope wound tightly around the base of his wing, along with several round weights.

Skellig's eyes widened. This was an example of one of the throwing weapons that had been used against Othos a few days ago! Skellig had lucked out, in that the weapon had failed to pin his wing down.

He detected motion from the valley floor below. Two more of the spinning weapons were on their way up. Skellig folded his wings and spun, as he had seen Gocri do several times. Both weapons sailed harmlessly by him.

"Gocri? Watch out for …!"

"I know, I know," Gocri angrily spat. "I've already dodged four. Where are they coming from?"

"Somewhere down below," Skellig answered, growling with frustration. "I don't want to think what will happen if one of them lands on me. What should we do?"

"Our mission has not changed," Gocri reminded him. "Destroy that contraption!"

Skellig roared and fired another blast of power at Cerebus' digging arm. The disk was now fully aflame, and they heard a loud *CRACK* as it began to slip out of position.

"We should hit this thing with everything we've got before these damnable bipeds fire anything else at us."

"Agreed." Gocri swooped low and selected a few more stones. "You destroy the arm. I'll start working on the large cube with the wooden wheels."

Skellig nodded. "Deal."

Dipping right, and firing bolt after bolt at the digging machine, he watched the disk drop to the ground. Refocusing his attention, Skellig shifted his gaze to the opposite side of the giant cube—what Jerica called the counterweights. Whatever the name, their kai had explained that, without them, the weight of the arm would topple the device. Good plan!

Just then, the klaxons ceased. Was something else about to happen?

Unfortunately, the answer to that was *yes*.

A new siren began wailing, higher-pitched and incessant.

"That can't be good," Skellig mumbled.

It wasn't. He and Gocri watched as tarps were thrown off several small metal devices. Smaller than Cerebus, the devices were situated on wheels. Groups of four humans each spun the devices until they were aimed at …

"What are they doing?"

"I don't know," Gocri answered. "Miss Jerica? Are you able to determine the function of these new, smaller devices?"

Yes! They're cannons! Get out of there! They're going to fire!

"They're going to shoot something at us?" Skellig asked, only slightly concerned. "What could they possibly …?"

The first cannon detonated. A round, hurtling projectile, traveling impossibly fast, narrowly missed punching a hole in one of his wings.

"Important safety tip," Skellig shouted, as he tucked his right wing out of the way after another cannon shot. "Steer clear of those things. They are lobbing huge metal balls at us with enough force to tear your wings."

"Noted. Should we retaliate?"

"I'd say we'd be fools if we didn't, and I happen to know the two of us are *not* fools."

Skellig managed to take out a cannon, but since his blasts were more target-specific, he was only able to cripple one of the strange weapons at a time. Gocri, on the other hand, was able to freeze several of the cannons solid with a single breath, which amusingly enough, had the bipeds hopping around in pain, clutching their cold appendages, and squawking like harpies.

Skellig resumed his attacks, focusing his efforts on the counterweights. Bolt after bolt had no effect. "This is getting me nowhere. My target is metal, not wood. My power is ineffective."

Gocri flew close. "I see what you're trying to do. Follow me. I have a better idea. The device is unprotected, is it not?"

"I see no more shooting devices," Skellig reported.

"Good. Follow my lead."

Gocri landed on the surface of Cerebus and crawled around until he located the rack of counterweights, then struggled to pull them free. Skellig's eyes widened, and a grin formed. He landed on an adjacent side. Together, they worked on freeing the many weights currently preventing the digging machine from tipping over.

The first weight dropped to the ground with a resounding *thud*. Cerebus trembled, and creaked ominously. A second fell to the ground, followed immediately by a third.

The entire mechanical contraption teetered in the direction of the long metal digging arm. Working quickly, the dragons freed an additional four weights before they knew they had done enough. The digging arm shook and the back wheels were slowly lifting from the ground.

"It's starting to tip!" Skellig shouted. "We've done it! We need to get clear!"

A series of small explosions startled them both. Six minor bangs sounded, all on the opposite side of Cerebus, the one with the digging arm. Once the sixth charge blew, the digging arm collapsed noisily to the ground. The huge machine returned to solid ground.

Clinging to the side of the massive machine, both dragons looked at each other and then, realizing that humans *inside* the control tower had been responsible for blasting away the digging arm, leaned close to the windows so they could peer inside.

What Skellig saw was a group of frightened bipeds cowering close together as they made loud wails and cries of alarm.

"There's your problem right there," Skellig sighed. "This thing is still crawling with bipeds. They chopped off the beast's arm so it didn't tip over."

"I say we get them out of there," Gocri said.

"How?"

Gocri leaned close and held his eye to the nearest window.

When none of the humans were willing to look him in the eye, Gocri broke through one of the windows with a talon.

"This is addressed to all you humans," the ice dragon formally began. "This structure is about to be demolished. Obviously, that can happen with or without you in there. My companion and I will give you one chance to flee with your lives. Stay, and there's a strong likelihood you will perish. Do you understand? Favor me with a thumbs up if you do."

"Much better," Skellig observed. He punched a hole in the window he was leaning against and looked through. "He means you, humans. You have five minutes to vacate this beast."

It only took them twenty seconds.

Minutes later, the dragons were airborne. Circling Cerebus as though they were facing down the djinn once more, both dragons began unleashing their fury on the mechanical device. Windows were blown out. Gocri threw huge chunks of whatever he could lift through any window that was still intact. Battered and beaten, Cerebus began to list to the side.

Ten minutes later, it was over. The wooden wheels were broken and burning. There wasn't an unbroken window anywhere on the massive control center. The base of the machine split apart and half of it slammed onto the ground. Off balance, the entire contraption tilted over and fell to the ground, sending up huge plumes of dust and smoke. Moments later, it exploded.

Yes! Zeira cried. *Gocri and Skellig, well done! You did it!*

We all did it, Skellig returned.

Do we even know who won our wager? Gocri wanted to know.

Skellig shrugged. *Phooey. I don't. I was looking forward to claiming my prize. Your sapphire intrigues me.*

As does your twisted ruby, Gocri added.

I have two, you know.

Indeed? Would you be interested in a trade?

I think that would be perfectly acceptable. Your sapphire for one of my twisted rubies.

Excellent!

"You have no idea what you have gotten yourselves into." The voice, shaking with rage, came from somewhere nearby, and did not come from anyone Skellig knew. Scanning the area near and around Cerebus' burning hulk, Skellig spotted a small group of humans. One of them was watching him and Gocri and was shaking an angry fist at them.

"You have incurred the wrath of the Thunder King! There is nowhere you can go where you'll be safe from the likes of him!"

Skellig executed a tight turn and touched down less than a hundred feet from the humans. They gasped with alarm and fled—all but the one who had been shaking his fist at them.

"Have something to say, human?"

"Do you know what you have done?"

Skellig nodded. "I should say so. We've done this area a service. I've seen what these infernal devices can do. They should not be allowed."

"You have destroyed property belonging to the Thunder King," the older human male cackled. "You have signed your own death warrants. He'll come after you with every weapon in his arsenal."

Skellig nodded. "Good."

"Good?" the human scoffed. "The Thunder King will declare war on you dragons!"

"Good," Skellig said again. "That means he'll be coming after *us* and not humans."

Chapter 13 — Revelation

This isn't going to end well for us," Zeira was saying, nearly two hours later. "Yes, we managed to destroy the great mechanical beast, but no, we were unable to keep our presence from being discovered. The Thunder King undoubtedly knows we're here by now."

The dragons had converged at Kinzler's Point once again, and rendezvoused with their human counterparts: the town's baron, his wife—Jerica's sister—and her parents, Hallis and Nyssa. Once all of them were together, minus Othos, of course, Zeira spoke.

"We were supposed to avoid making things difficult for us. We were supposed to *not* jeopardize our alliances with one another. And now it would appear we've done the exact opposite."

"Don' be so hard on yerself," Hallis said, placing a hand on Zeira's foreleg. "Ye took care o' that huge digger, didn' ye? An' I still don' know why ye invited that contraption to Cael,"

Hallis finished by staring—hard—at Vyler.

"I had no idea the level of destruction it was going to cause," Vyler insisted. "I did not regret my actions then, nor do I now, when it's burning."

"There'll be hell to pay," Hallis said, drawing nods of agreement from the dragons.

Skellig held up a claw. "But … it'll be directed toward *us*, and not you humans."

"That Thunder King be one wicked sum bi—"

Nyssa elbowed her husband in the stomach. "Watch your language, Hallis. There's no need to talk like that."

"Sorry. I just be worried 'bout ye lot, that's all."

Skellig nodded. "It's appreciated. We'll be fine."

"I wonder how long it'll be until the Thunder King finds out what we did here?" Jerica mused.

"He prolly already knows," Hallis grumbled.

"His retribution will be swift," Vyler groaned.

"All the more reason we should be on our way," Zeira said.

"What if Cael is targeted?" Vyler asked. "What if, when Cael needs protection the most, none of you are here to help us?"

"Since when have dragons been around to protect us?" Theresa asked, confused. "We've lived our lives for years here, all without the interference of dragons. We've made it this long, I'm sure we can …"

"We won't let anything happen to this village," Zeira interrupted.

"Oh, thank heavens," Theresa exclaimed, letting out a pent-up breath.

Jerica gave a nervous laugh and then looked at Zeira. "What do you think will happen?"

Zeira tapped her chest. "To us? Oh, I'm sure we're going to hear about it. After all, even though he didn't expressly say not to aggravate the situation, I happen to know Darazok Aeogan isn't going to care for how this has been handled."

Skellig grunted. "Darazok Aeogan is your king?"

"He is the Fire Lord, aye."

"Have you spoken with him before?" Jerica asked.

"Oh, absolutely not," Zeira sputtered. "Why would he bother associating with the likes of me?"

"Because you're a member of the Phoenix caste," Skellig reminded her. "Every dragon's opinion counts, and if he's too stupid to realize that, then he doesn't deserve your input."

Flushing with pride, Zeira nodded. "Thank you. What about you, Skellig? What would your king do if he found out?"

"My king wouldn't care less," Skellig sighed. "He's opinionated, anachronistic, and still thinks the whole world revolves around Gale. I know Lord Myrdaynth likes to appear as though he cares about his subjects, but I assure you, he does not."

"And yet you're still loyal," Gocri guessed.

"He may be belligerent, ignorant, and arrogant, but he's still my king."

"That's very noble of you," Zeira observed. She turned to Sif. "What about you? What's your king like, in Rokke?"

"Queen, actually," Sif corrected. "Lady Chrys. I've met her twice and spoken with her once. She's very wise, and very intelligent. It saddens me to think of how she'll react."

"I assume you have an explanation for your actions, dren."

Gocri's head jerked up, as did everyone else. There, not far from where Nuri was resting by the shore, was a disturbance in the water. A small section of the sea had started bubbling, as though it was boiling, although from the way Nuri was staring at it, it was something she hadn't ever seen before. Larger and larger bubbles appeared, and as each one rose into the air and popped, it released a small amount of mist. Soon, it resembled a small fog bank, but oddly enough, it retained its shape instead of spreading out. The mist withdrew into itself until it resembled a sphere, and then a shape became visible: a regal, reptilian head, and it was *white*. The head ignored everyone except for one person, and that person had started to fidget.

"I am waiting."

Gocri took a single step toward the sphere and then bowed his head. "My Lady. How may I serve?"

"I do not recall meeting you before."

"You haven't, My Lady."

"What are you doing here, dren?"

"His name is Gocri," Jerica stated, growing angry.

The head shifted until it was staring at the human.

"Biped. Who are you?"

"I am Jerica. "

"What are you doing with one of my dren?"

"I'm his kai."

At this, the eyes widened with surprise and turned back to Gocri. "You did it? You were able to find a suitable kai?"

Gocri nodded. "Quite by accident, but yes, I did."

"Gocri? Are you going to introduce us?" Jerica asked.

The ice dragon swallowed nervously.

"Ah, well, My Lady, this is Jerica, my kai. Jerica? This is my queen, Freriss."

Freriss' head slowly turned, as if she noticed others were present for the first time.

"You travel with mixed company … Gocri. I see Fire, Smoke, Spark, and Water. Do you all have kai?"

Skellig nodded. "Yes. Kind of."

Freriss rotated her head until she was facing Skellig.

"Explain, Spark."

"My name is Skellig, Lady."

"Aren't you supposed to address her as *My Lady*?" Jerica whispered.

A faint smile appeared on Freriss' face.

"She's not my lady," Skellig pointed out. "It's actually the correct way to address her."

Jerica looked at the leader of the ice dragons. Freriss nodded.

"It's true." Lady Freriss' face grew firm. "Are the stories true? Were you part of a coordinated attack on a mechanical device belonging to the human Thunder King?"

"Told ye," Hallis softly muttered.

Gocri nodded. "I am."

"I will speak with you in private."

"That's our cue to leave," Skellig quietly told their kai.

"But, it's not fair he gets into trouble," Jerica protested.

"He was doing what had to be done!"

As she was about to protest further, Skellig scooped the human up in his claw and deposited her on Zeira's back, just as she was passing by.

"Hey! Wait a minute! You can't …!"

"Gocri is a glacial dragon," Zeira quietly reminded Jerica. "What did he call his home? Bliss? Well, in Bliss, obviously Freriss is in charge. If she says Gocri has done something wrong, there's nothing we can do."

"I don't like it," Jerica stated, crossing her thin arms across her chest. "He needs someone to stand up for him."

"We all stand with him," Skellig said, overhearing. "But, Zeira is right. This does not concern us."

Raised voices caused them to look over at their white companion. Gocri's head was hanging with shame, and the poor fellow refused to lift his eyes from the ground. Skellig growled once, looked at Jerica, and pointed at the ground.

"Stay. I'll be right back."

"… abolishing decades of peace and all for what? To destroy some mechanical construction created by the humans?"

"It was actually my idea," Skellig interjected. "Gocri participated, aye, but only at my insistence."

"You, Spark. You stand behind him?"

"I do, aye. He's my friend. I will not stand by as you unfairly judge him." Skellig detected movement in his peripheral vision and noticed Sif was now standing by his side.

"That goes for me, too."

"And me," Nuri added, from the water's edge.

Zeira appeared next and nodded her eagerness to assist.

"Your concern is duly noted, but without kai, I don't see how you can …"

"We only need one kai," Zeira stated, eliciting nods from the others. "Jerica has bonded with all of us."

"One human and all of you? Impossible."

"It's how we're able to travel together," Jerica explained. "Let me recap. Zeira rescued Skellig. The two of them found Nuri …"

"… I actually found them," Nuri helpfully pointed out.

"… they rescued Gocri, and then, together, they all

defeated the strangest set of obstacles anyone had ever seen. That, as it turns out, was Sif's doing."

"A kairie," Freriss whispered, impressed. "Is it true?"

"That's what everyone tells me," Jerica said, shrugging. "I can share any of their senses, I can splice together their abilities and my own, and I can prevent any of them from feeling the effects of the Fade."

"Gocri, you're here of your own free will? You're not being coerced in any fashion?"

"I am not," Gocri stated.

Freriss' eyes softened. After a moment, she bowed to Gocri. "Why didn't you tell me this earlier?"

"You didn't ask, My Lady."

Freriss turned to Skellig and smiled. "I would like another private word with Gocri."

Skellig nodded. "Of course."

Ten minutes later, it was over. While they could have been able to hear what was being said, should any one of them open their senses, Skellig had decided against it, declaring any attempt to eavesdrop in poor taste. So, they waited.

It happened so fast that one minute, Gocri was there, giving monosyllable answers to a peculiar small cloud floating just above the water. Then, the cloud vanished. After a few moments, Gocri returned to their side, saying nothing.

"Are you all right?" Skellig cautiously asked.

"Yes."

"Did she get over her anger?" Zeira asked.

"I'm surprised to report that she did."

Zeira's head nodded approvingly. "I'm glad to hear it."

"You haven't heard all of it."

Zeira's head lifted, as did Skellig's and Sif's.

"She … *thanked* me. Part of me still feels like she made a mistake."

"What did she say?" Nuri prompted.

"That she was proud of me for standing up for my fellow drens."

"Drens?" Jerica repeated. "What's that?"

"Er, consider it a term of endearment."

"Do you?" Skellig challenged.

"Drens are …" Gocri trailed off as he looked at Jerica. "Think of them as villagers. Peasants, even."

"Citizens," Skellig translated.

Gocri nodded. "Precisely. My queen praised me for sticking up for all those who couldn't and for being the first dren to ever have a kai."

"That must make you feel good," Vyler said. "It's how I feel whenever I do something for the people of Cael. It's actually what I *thought* I was doing when I agreed Cerebus should be situated here for the next several months. I am so very sorry I ever persuaded them to come here."

"You didn't know," Nyssa said, placing a comforting arm around her son-in-law's shoulders. "You were doing what you thought was best. No one can fault you for that."

"Except mebbe do a lil' more research b'fore ye agree to let outsiders dig up our village," Hallis nonchalantly suggested.

Jerica noticed her parents had taken a seat on a log that had been placed on the beach to act as a bench. She joined them, which prompted Vyler and Theresa to take the next bench over.

"What would yours say, Nuri?"

"My queen? She would probably ask just what I was thinking, aligning myself with foreign dragons and a group of humans."

"And what would you tell her?" Nyssa curiously asked.

"That I've never been associated with such a noble and honorable group of friends before, and I'd lay my life on the line, if necessary."

"The circle of friends here is unusually strong," a powerful, male voice declared. "What you have together is to be commended."

Skellig nodded. "Othos. I was beginning to wonder where you were."

They all turned to see the sol dragon rising slowly out of the water. Nuri was staring at him as though he had sprouted a second head.

"What is it?" Othos prompted.

"There was no one in the water other than me," Nuri insisted. "I would have known. Where did you come from?"

"I was needed elsewhere."

"Who needed you?" Jerica asked.

"No one you would know," Othos told her.

"Would we know of this person?" Zeira asked.

Othos turned to silently regard her. Zeira immediately lowered her gaze.

"Apologies. It is none of my business."

"Don't apologize, fire," Othos instructed. "You have no idea what I've been doing, and I'm a part of your group. I … what is it? You, ice. You look as though you've seen a ghost. Was Freriss not pleased with your involvement?"

Gocri gave a little jump. "How do you know my queen?"

"I've known her since she hatched, but that's another story." Othos lifted his nose and sniffed. "So, you all were successful? Has the mechanized digging machine been destroyed? I can smell ash in the air."

"Probably 'cause it's still burnin'," Hallis chuckled.

Nyssa thumped him in the stomach. "Be quiet!"

"Sorry."

Nuri swam to the water's edge and addressed the celestial. "For my own peace of mind, will you admit you weren't in the water just a few moments ago?"

Surprisingly, Othos nodded. "Of course. Several moments ago, I was nowhere close to the water."

"Is this relevant?" Skellig asked.

Othos shrugged. "I guess it could be construed as relevant. To answer your question, valthan, I was conversing with an old friend I lost contact with a number of years ago. Sadly, he isn't the dragon I remember. He's become bitter, and twisted with jealousy. He wants to send kill squads after this group, and I told him I'd dispatch any who tried. I'm sorry to say, that was the end of that particular friendship."

"Who are you talking about?" Zeira nervously inquired. "And dispatch kill squads? I may not know what those are, but they certainly don't sound pleasant."

"They're not," Skellig said, becoming glum. "Othos, you were talking about Lord Myrdaynth, weren't you?"

"I was. He's become bitter with envy and jealousy. He sees anyone more popular than he is as a threat to his rule.

Even one who has sat by his side for hundreds of years has become the bitterest of enemies: Dym. You, Spark, are Dym's offspring, are you not? I can smell the blood in your veins. It's the same as his."

"Did you see him?" Skellig asked, shocked.

"Briefly. He was trying to rally others into becoming followers of the Thunder King. He saw me coming and fled."

A notion occurred, causing Skellig to hold up a claw. "Hang on a second. You were just at Gale?"

"Yes."

"Gale, home of the Sparks?" Skellig clarified.

"Yes, home of the Sparks, your home. What of it?"

"It's on the other side of the world," Skellig said, confused. "How did you cover such a distance in such a short amount of time? How did Dym? We saw him here not that long ago, and it certainly wasn't enough time to get all the way to Gale."

"I can't speak for him," Othos began, "only for myself. I, for one, have an agreement in place with Ana, which allows me to use her medium the same way she does."

"Who is Ana?" Skellig wanted to know.

"She's had many names," Othos explained. "I know her as Anahita, only I will call her Ana for short."

"And who is Anahita?" Zeira asked.

"Think of her as, well, someone responsible for the well-being of the sea."

Skellig sat back on his haunches and scratched the side of his face. "I'm getting a headache. Go back to your comment about using her medium the way she does. What does that mean?"

"I use water to instantly transport from one location to another."

Nuri looked down at the water lapping in the shore in front of her.

"You use this to move around? Without swimming? What a unique concept!"

Othos scratched at an errant itch on the side of his leg. The sun dragon ended up scratching the area for close to half a minute, which resulted in several scales sloughing off. Jerica hurried over to one of the fallen scales, which was the size of a small shield, and turned to Zeira.

"This reminds me, we need to start thinking about what we're going to do about Doolan. We cannot let him have a single scale, let alone four. He'll want to ... Skellig, what is it?"

The Spark dragon was pointing at her. "That scale? When it's held up to your body like that, it allows us to see through it."

"We know this, Skellig," Jerica told him, "and no one liked that notion very well, did they?"

"But, you were using more than one scale," Skellig pointed out. "I believe you said your mage wanted four of them. If one will allow him to be rendered invisible, then why would he need four?"

Heads began turning. Within moments, everyone was looking at Jerica.

"I wish I could tell you why, but I can't. One scale will obviously render the holder invisible, so why the need for more?"

Dragon and humans alike turned to regard Othos, who shrugged again. After an awkward silence, the sun dragon started scratching his other foreleg, and didn't stop until half a dozen more scales plopped to the ground. Jerica, Vyler, and Hallis stepped forward to collect the scales. Holding them this way and that, the humans tried to figure out why a mage would covet them as much as he did.

"The best person to answer that," Zeira said, as she turned to look at Othos, "is *you*. You knew about invisibility. What else can you do that a human might desire?"

Othos looked thoughtful as he considered.

"Who can say? It's akin to describing everything you're physically capable of doing, and determining which — if any — stand out. Your mage wants four of my scales? And we know invisibility is one of my traits. I don't know ... let me think."

"Something only a sol dragon can do, and no one else can," Zeira added.

"Increase mass?" Gocri suggested.

"Shine with a light more brilliant than anything known?"

Skellig said.

"I really don't know," Othos admitted. "I'm so very … wait. What about vision?"

"What about it?" Sif asked. "Are your visual abilities more pronounced than ours?

Othos shrugged. "I don't know what others can and cannot do. As for me, I can watch other dragons regardless of location."

It became so quiet that the lapping of waves on the shore sounded like herds of galloping centaurs.

"That must be it!" Zeira cried. "Jerica? What would Doolan do if he could watch whomever he wanted, whenever he wanted to do it?"

"The possibilities would be endless," Jerica breathed, horrified. "This is worse than becoming invisible! Or, at the very least, it goes hand-in-hand with it. Oh, the tenacity of that man! He cannot be allowed to collect those scales."

"Wait a moment," Vyler protested. "Simply possessing those scales grants the holder the power of invisibility or this supreme visual power? How is that even possible?"

"He's a mage," Jerica said, sighing. "He's clearly found a way to make them work, which is why he can never be allowed to touch them."

"I can always snap his fingers off," Hallis suggested innocently. "Right 'ere, at the base o' the knuckle."

Nyssa chuckled, but didn't reprimand him.

Othos held one of his forelegs out; a few scales were in the midst of sloughing off. He selected one and brought it up to his face for a closer study.

"I fail to see how my discarded scales will allow a human to possess my strength of vision."

"None of us do," Skellig said, drawing grunts from his dragon companions. "Regardless, we need to be certain all of your scales are properly disposed of, including the one you're holding."

Othos nodded. "I seem to remember depositing the others into a hole. I can always …"

The others looked up as the sol dragon trailed off.

"What is it?" Skellig asked, growing anxious. "Is someone

coming? Is it Dym?"

Othos' gaze focused on Sif. "Prepare yourself."

Currently holding the form of a human, Sif quickly reverted to her natural state. "What is it? Is there …?"

Sif trailed off as a vent opened in the ground at her feet and steam hissed out. Instead of dissipating, the steam coalesced into a pulsing mass that slowly began to take shape. Ordinarily, the group would have started backing away from such a strange sight, but since they just saw something similar less than an hour ago, no one so much as blinked an eye. The steam pulled itself together to form another head. Spiraled horns sprouted, up and then sideways, away from the skull. The head rippled, momentarily losing its cohesion. Soon, the ripples vanished and two silvery eyes opened. The head then turned to Sif.

"So … it's true."

Sif bowed her head. "My Lady."

"I didn't want to believe it. You have declared war on the biped known as Thunder King. You may not know this, but he has amassed enough power to challenge any of the regions, and you hand him ours. Tell me why you shouldn't be banished. Tell me why I shouldn't cast you from our region as I have been pressured to do."

Sif refused to raise her head.

"Oh, enough of this," Skellig snapped. He purposefully stepped next to Sif, on her left. Gocri approached on the right. "Look at us. No one is from around here. I am from Gale." The Spark dragon went through the remaining introductions being careful not to pause so Sif's queen could object. "Sif has been an invaluable ally. You should be proud. You're, what, in Rokke? May I ask who I'm addressing?"

"You *must* be Skellig," the wispy apparition of a head decided, after a few moments of silence had passed.

Skellig's jaw opened with surprise. "You've heard of me?"

"I just spoke with Lord Myrdaynth," the image stated. "Let's just say he does *not* speak fondly of you."

"I can't imagine he would. If you've talked to him, then I am sorry you had to deal with such a …"

"… vindictive little carrion feeder?" the image finished.

"I am Chrys, ruler of Rokke."

Skellig nodded once. "It's an honor. And a carrion eater? You're too forgiving. He doesn't even deserve that title."

A smile flitted across Chrys' ghostly face. She returned her gaze to Sif and she sobered. "Why would you challenge a human who wields more power than he can handle? We all know what happens when a biped gets too much power. And now there's another biped, who wants some scales? Scales from whom?"

Sif immediately bowed. "My Lady. How long have you been listening?"

"Ever since I learned a whisp was involved. How were you coerced into participating?"

"I wasn't, Lady Chrys. I volunteered."

"This quest of yours was never sanctioned by me," the leader of the smoke dragons snapped. "You have implicated Rokke and made all whisps look bad. You are to return to Rokke immediately."

"She's a very important part of our mission," Skellig said. "Honestly, I shudder to think how we'd proceed if Sifula wasn't part of our team."

"What can a mere whisp do that the rest of you can't?" Chrys challenged.

"Her shapeshifting skills are second to none," Zeira said, coming to their defense. When Chrys' silvery eyes looked her way, Zeira nodded. "She can fool us, and she can even fool her kai's parents into thinking there are two of them."

Chrys' head lifted. "Kai? What about a kai? Are you saying one of my whisps has earned herself a kai?"

Jerica stepped forward and raised a hand. "That'd be me. And I think we need to show you something. Sif, become me, would you?"

Sif nodded and instantly shrunk in size. Less than ten seconds later, there were two matching human girls, complete with identical clothes. As expected, Sif's queen perked up.

"Wait. What is this? Since when can a whisp imitate flesh-colored skin tone?"

"Oh, that be nothin'," Hallis announced, stepping forward. "When Sif be lookin' like my Jerica, or my wife, I cannot tell 'em apart. Even when they speak, ye can' tell."

Chrys' pale eyes focused on Sif.

"You've mimicked her perfectly! And even when you talk, you're still able to pass yourself off as one of them! How is this possible?"

"I had some help," Sif admitted. "We encountered a human seer who seemed to know all about me. He was able to give me some pointers."

"Is this something that can be taught to others?" Chrys wanted to know.

"I should think so," Sif said, nodding. "If I can do it, then so can anyone."

The Queen looked around at everyone present. "I don't often find myself admitting I was wrong, but I will do so now. I was wrong to jump to conclusions. You, Sifula? I am going to tell you something. Before I reached out, I had no idea who you were. I thought for certain you were just some ... *outcast* doing everything they could to make their home look bad. However, I am pleased to say you are doing an admirable job. I'm still not happy about the possibility of going to war, especially with a biped, but should that become a necessity, Rokke will respond. If you need anything, you have but to ask."

The leader of Rokke nodded at all of them, then the cloud of mist vanished.

"That must make you feel good," Jerica said, looking at Sif and giving her a friendly nudge. "Your queen just said she was proud of you and offered her support. It doesn't get any better than that."

"Indeed," Sif admitted. "My mind is spinning. I ... I really have no idea how to process that."

"There's one more I've been stalling," Othos said, as a section of air shimmered and the sol dragon reappeared. "I've put it off long enough. He wants his turn."

"What?" Skellig snorted, as he turned to look at their newest friend. "Would you care to run that by us again?"

"I may—or may not—have the ability to subtly suggest a course of action," Othos said, shrugging. "What everyone doesn't know is that all of these leaders essentially reached out at the same time. Had their attempts been successful, you wouldn't have been able to stand up for one another. So, I saw to it that they took turns. The last one who wants to talk is about to make contact."

"Is it mine?" Skellig asked glumly.

"It could be my queen," Nuri said. "Although, for the record, she's the one who said there wasn't anything we, the valthans, could do. Since I have effectively proved her wrong, I doubt very much she'd show up here."

Othos turned to Zeira, whose face immediately fell. "It's my king, isn't it?"

"The Fire Lord wants a word," Othos said, nodding. He stepped back a few paces and immediately vanished, with: "Good luck, Zeira. Fear not, you'll do well."

A tiny red spark appeared in the air before them. It began spinning, growing in size as it did so, producing dark grey smoke. The smoke pulled itself together and became the upper half of a blood-red dragon. The eyes opened and it spun until it located Zeira. Those eyes narrowed to slits as Zeira timidly approached. Reaching the image of her king, Zeira bowed.

"My Lord."

"I don't even know your name," a gravelly voice hissed out. "Who am I addressing?"

"I am Zeira, of the Phoenix caste."

"Phoenix? I know everyone who claims they're from that caste, but you?"

"My mother is Gynnyth, if that helps."

"I've heard of her, but not of you. Perhaps you just … wait. I remember now. There was one offspring she was quick to hide from me. Something about …"

"Oh, don't say it," Zeira groaned aloud.

"… a dragonlet whose fire only appeared on the wrong end. That's you? Judging by your reaction, it clearly is so. By what right do you aggravate the human Thunder King and threaten the peace we've had for so long? Our borders are under attack. What excuse have you?"

"I, er, don't, My Lord."

"You've thrown Blaze and all the surrounding areas

into chaos. Attacks are up, our borders are threatened, and everyone who has something to say has crawled up my arse waiting for me to do something. Now that I have found the youngling responsible, what say I simply banish you instead? It would solve many of my problems, Zeira."

Skellig appeared by her side, with Gocri again taking the right.

"Go ahead," Skellig urged. "Banish her. She would be welcomed in Gale."

"Gale," the Fire Lord scoffed. "Why am I not surprised? And you. What are you? Ice?"

"Glacier," Gocri rumbled. "And Bliss would take Miss Zeira as well, if Blaze is foolish enough to let her go."

"You're insinuating I'm a fool?" the Fire Lord snapped.

Gocri shrugged. "You're the one who suggested banishing one of your own. Yes, if you do something like that, then I would say you are as foolish as they come. You have no idea what we've been able to accomplish together."

Jerica stepped forward.

"What's this? Another one of your fans, Zeira? Who is this?"

"Why don't you ask her?" Skellig challenged.

"Very well. You, human. Who are you and what are you doing here?"

"My name is Jerica, and I'm here because I'm Zeira's kai."

"What?! Zeira has found a rider?"

Jerica made a sweeping motion with her hand. "They all have. I'm a kai to all of them."

"Impossible. Dragons don't share kais, unless …?"

Jerica nodded. "That's right. I can bond with any of them, from any region. And, let me tell you, we've been having some fun playing with everyone's powers. Mix a Terran with fire, and the ability to fling an object over an extended distance and what do you get?"

"Don't make me say it," Zeira grumbled.

"I will," Skellig said. "Flaming poo boulders. That one is one of my favorites, too."

"This isn't possible," the fire lord insisted. "You're telling me you're a … a … *kairie*?"

Jerica unbuckled her bracer and held up the arm displaying the mark she was becoming more and more fond of.

"I know of such things," Zeira's king reported, his tone softening. "It is a full dragon. You *are* a kairie. And … you've chosen one of my dragons?"

"That all depends," Jerica said, fixing the leader of the fire dragons with a steely glare. "Is Zeira still a member of Blaze? Are you going to stop your efforts to drive her out?"

Skellig's eyes widened as he watched the fire lord lower his head and—with extreme reluctance—nod.

"Good. Now, Zeira? Is there anything you need to ask him?"

Zeira stared at Jerica and fought to tamp down a rising taste of bile in her mouth. "I don't believe so."

"Good, then in that case, you can …"

A shadow fell over Jerica, who automatically looked up.

"Well, well, if it isn't Darazok Aeogan," came a familiar voice.

The Fire Lord's head rotated and tilted upward in order to make eye contact. When he did, Skellig watched Zeira's king swallow nervously. For the first time, the fire lord gasped with surprise and, possibly, trembled a little.

"You."

"Me."

"Aren't you supposed to be sleeping?"

"Aren't you supposed to be leading?" Othos was quick to return. "You were always a pain, Darazok. Grow up. Stop acting like a youngling and look to those who depend on you for their very existence."

"Othos, do you know him?" Zeira timidly asked.

"I've known him since he hatched," Othos answered. "Sadly, his demeanor really hasn't changed."

"Othos," Darazok finally said, bowing his head. "I did not know you were involved."

"And why wouldn't I be?" Othos questioned. "These commendable dragons have banded together to save this world. They're risking their lives for complete strangers. Zeira, it would seem, single-handedly freed Skellig from his ice prison and Gocri from a crystal prison. Together, they've rescued the human, learned they can all bond with her, and realized they're a very formidable team."

"I *am* proud," Darazok finally admitted. "I thought for certain that the inclusion of a Blaze citizen would have been detrimental, but I am surprised to see I'm wrong. Well done, Zeira. Trust me when I say it's a name I won't be forgetting any time soon."

"That's quite a reversal for you," Skellig observed, nodding. "Good for you ... My Lord."

"I heard the hesitation in there, but you said it anyway," the Fire Lord observed. "I appreciate you looking out for her."

"We all do," Sif added.

"You should know, Zeira," Darazok continued, "that I've been in touch with the other kings and queens. We are all preparing for war."

Zeira's head hung once more. "It was not my intent to force anyone to ..."

"Just a moment," Darazok interrupted. "I said we are preparing for war. We have been for quite some time. Everyone can sense something is wrong. Only the bravest have had the insight to do something about it."

"I don't know what to say to that," Zeira admitted.

"You honor us, Zeira. All of you do. All dragons are preparing to go to battle."

Zeira nodded. "That's good, I guess."

"No, Zeira. You're still not hearing me. I said *all dragons*."

Zeira's eyes widened with shock, as did everyone else's.

"All dragons, everywhere? United against the Thunder King?"

"Yes. Where's Othos? Is he still here?"

Skellig turned to look for the sol dragon, but could see he was no longer there.

"I do believe he's vanished again," Sif reported.

Zeira lifted her head. "Let me ask you something, My Lord. You and Othos obviously know one another. How is it he keeps disappearing? You seem to be familiar with his behavior."

"Othos is a celestial, a genesian," Darazok reported. "That

class of dragons have abilities you could only dream about, including his omniscient sight," the Fire Lord grumbled. "It's something he's lorded over me for centuries. The ability to watch any item you want, from anywhere in the world. It's an ability craved by many."

"We figured that out a little earlier today," Zeira admitted.

"I take my leave. I will inform your mother you are safe."

"Th-thank you."

The Fire Lord's smoky apparition puffed out, as if a gust of wind had caught it. Zeira groaned and sank to the ground.

"I have never, *ever* talked to directly to my king. I'll be thinking about this day for quite some time."

"I think we all will," Skellig reported. He took a step forward but immediately yanked his foot back and reached down to pick up one of Othos' fallen scales. He handed it to Jerica. "We need to dispose of these, like we did last time."

"I couldn't agree more," Jerica said. "If there's a way to make them work to his advantage, Doolan will find it. We must be sure he *never* gets his hands on them."

"*Who* doesn't get their hands on *what*?" a new voice asked. The owner was wearing bright red robes tied with a blue sash. "Pardon the intrusion, but I couldn't help but give in to my curiosity. You've located your sixth dragon, so I have to ask: have you procured what I asked for?"

Chapter 14 — Goblet

That was our agreement. The scales for my services in creating this enchanted goblet of yours. Look, let me make this simple for you. No scales, no goblet. Understand?"

Jerica tromped back to the village, with Doolan following along. She stepped inside her father's foundry, followed closely by human-sized Sif and Jerica's family. The others elected to remain at Kinzler's Point, although they were all watching — and listening — through Jerica's shared mental connection.

Just let me eat him, Gocri implored. *He might be old, and taste terrible, but it's a risk I'm willing to take. I'll swallow him whole. No one will know.*

It's so very tempting, Jerica confessed. *But, Doolan has a point. That was the arrangement. I just haven't figured out how to break that arrangement without compromising my own principles.*

She felt a tap on her shoulder. Turning, she saw her father, giving her a questioning glance. She tapped the side of her head, looked pointedly at Sif, and nodded. Understanding, Hallis nodded as well and guided the group deeper into his shop, stopping at his private workspace in the far corner. He made eye contact with one of his laborers, who immediately nodded and brought stools and chairs.

"It's rather loud in here," Doolan complained, as the incessant clanging from various workers hammering away at their stations echoed mercilessly throughout the confines of the shop. "Isn't there somewhere else we could go?"

"This place be safe," Hallis said, shaking his head. "We be jus' fine 'ere."

"Aren't you worried about what your servants will think we're doing?" Doolan asked.

"Servants?" Hallis sputtered angrily. "These be my workers, loyal through an' through. They be my friends, and I trust all o' 'em wit' my life. No, we be stayin' 'ere."

"As you wish." The mage turned to Jerica. "As I was saying earlier, you know what our arrangement is. I gave you an option to avoid spending any personal time with me. Honestly, you have no idea what you're missing out on, but let's put that aside for now. If you don't have the scales, I can only assume you prefer to give me one night?"

Jerica was quick to jump to her feet and lay a restraining hand on her father's shoulder. On top of which, she felt the growl from every single dragon currently sharing her senses. Even Sif, in the guise of a young girl, had started growling, drawing curious looks from Theresa and Vyler.

"I've got this, Dad. Guys, let me handle this. Doolan, as I said before, there's no way I'm spending any amount of time alone with you. I know full well what your *private time* entails. Yes, I have the scales, but no, you're not getting them until the goblet has been enchanted *and* I know it works."

"You have four scales from an actual sol dragon?" Doolan scoffed. "I'm going to need proof."

Tell him who you got the scales from, Skellig urged. *If this satisfies your mage, then we'll know he already knows about the powers the scales contain.*

And if he doesn't care? Jerica asked.

Then, he must have some other motive for wanting them, Zeira said. *I agree with Skellig. I think this will help us determine what his intentions are.*

I know his intentions, Jerica argued, *and they're not good.*

"Doolan, these scales come from Othos. We found him, asleep, on a deserted island. When we woke him, he was almost the same size as the island. And that's all I'm going to tell you."

Doolan nodded. "That will suffice, my dear. I'm so very pleased to hear you found him. Very well. I will return in a few hours. Have your goblet ready, and I will enchant it when I return."

"It'll be ready," Jerica promised.

"I thought you weren't going to give him the scales!" Vyler protested, once Doolan had departed. "Aren't you a little concerned with what he has in mind for them?"

"Of course I am! That's why he's not going to get his hands on them. I just have to figure out a way to make that happen without violating my own morals."

"You're a better person than me," her sister told her. "If I were you, then I would be looking for some way to use this goblet against him. I mean, if it becomes enchanted, there must be a way."

We're all working on it, Skellig announced.

"My, er, friends are on it," Jerica relayed.

Theresa nodded. "Good. So, what happens next?"

"Next," Jerica explained, "we have to actually make the goblet. I would imagine any type would do. So, who's best at making something like that? Dad, can you do it?"

"Not nearly as well as ye could, girl."

"What? Oh no. I defer to someone who has more experience than me."

Their little group fell silent. Everyone was staring at Jerica.

"Knives!" Jerica exclaimed, pulling one from a leather scabbard on her belt. "Dirks, blades, and the like. That's what I make. I've never made a goblet before."

"No time like the present," her father told her. "Ye can use my station, J. What tools will ye need?"

Jerica looked from face to face. Did they really expect

her to be the one to make this weapon to be used against the Thunder King? Shouldn't that be left for someone with more experience?

"Believe in yerself," her father urged, lowering his voice. "Ye can do this, J. I know ye can! Think about the task. What do ye need to do?"

She took several calming breaths. "Well, the metal is in the shape of a small bar. It'll need to be melted." Jerica tied her hair into a high ponytail and reached for her father's apron, hanging from a hook on the wall. "Vyler? Do you have the bar?"

"I do," Vyler confirmed. He reached into his jacket and produced the small bar of jhorium. He peeled back the cloth concealing it and presented it to Jerica. "I'll be honest and say I won't be sorry to see this gone. It made me nervous carrying it around."

"Why?" Theresa asked. "Was it heavy?"

"No, it's *wanted*," Vyler corrected. "From what everyone tells me, a certain someone would stop at nothing to get his hands on it."

Hallis handed her a medium-sized crucible. "Use this 'ere. The forges are lit. Ye know what ye have to do, J."

Nodding, Jerica set the bar of jhorium inside the heavily scarred melting pot and placed it on the grated vent. Making sure everyone was well away from her, she opened the vent fully and watched as the crucible started glowing red. In a matter of moments, the pot was red hot, with every square inch glowing from the intense heat blasting forth from the vent. However, the jhorium remained unchanged.

"It's not melting," Jerica reported, as she felt around the crucible's insides with a poker. "It doesn't even feel soft. What do we do now?"

"It ain't meltin'?" Hallis asked, thunderstruck. "What deviltry be this? Why won' it melt?"

"Not hot enough," Jerica decided. "It melted last time, didn't it? When it was processed? I mean, it'd have to. You got it into the shape of a bar."

"I had the pot burnin' hot fer hours," Hallis said. "That's the difference."

It's not hot enough, Skellig and Gocri echoed, at the same time.

"Yeah, we figured that out," Jerica said, to no one in particular. "If we give it enough time on the vent, we'll be able to get it to melt, but I don't think we have the time. We need to make it hotter, quicker, only no one knows how. Do you guys have any ideas?"

Dragonfire would do it, Skellig said.

I don't have dragonfire here, do I? Jerica replied.

True. I am sorry for suggesting it. I'm just giving out ideas.

No, I'm the one who should be sorry, Skellig. I shouldn't have snapped at you.

What about you, Miss Jerica?

What's that, Gocri? What do you want me to do?

I think he's suggesting you *might be able to accomplish this*, Skellig said. *You and your magic, that is.*

Oh. Hmm, I don't know of anyone who is a fire thrower. Vyler's here. He might know of someone. Thanks, guys.

"Vyler, do you know of anyone in Cael who can start a fire with magic?"

"Let me think. No, the only one I can think of moved away a few years ago."

"Did he move somewhere close?" Hallis asked.

"Maribou," Vyler proclaimed, after falling silent for a few moments. "He moved to Maribou."

"On the other side of Terra. That won't work."

What about me? Zeira asked. *After all,* I *am a fire dragon.*

Umm, wouldn't that mean I'd have to expel fire in the same manner as you? That would mean … it would mean … you want me to use my bum?

Your what? Skellig asked, confused.

Her posterior, Sif translated, smiling. *And wouldn't that be something to see?*

It's not something I'd ever show!

"What's goin' on, J? Ye be blushin' more than a bride on her own weddin' day."

"My friends are giving me suggestions," Jerica explained. "And it's not going to happen."

Haven't you used my power before? Zeira asked. *You didn't have any problems then, so why would you now?*

"I guess I can try. But, if I feel my, er, bum heating up, then I am definitely stopping."

Acknowledged.

Jerica sat on the closest stool and closed her eyes. What could she use? Nuri had her echolocation, but she didn't see how that could be relevant here. Skellig had his lightning. Again, terribly useful, only the Spark dragon didn't produce flames. Then, there was Gocri with his frost breath, and Sif with her smoke. Useful?

Jerica shook her head. No, the only way this was going to work was if she concentrated on Zeira's fire. She'd have to see if she could possibly enhance, or *alter*, the ability in some fashion. So, first things first. She would use Zeira's fire, being careful to exclude the delivery method, and then she'd have to come up with a suitable method for expelling the flames. Her mouth? She shook her head. How unusual would that look? As much as she loved dragons, the last thing she wanted to do was to spit fire as they did. Well, most of them.

She sighed and rubbed her temples. But, in doing so, she caught sight of her hand. Hands! Would that work? Could she use one of her hands as a means of producing flames?

Focusing on her right hand, and imagining it producing fire at will, using Zeira's as a source, she felt something. Her hand! It was tingling! Not only that, but it was now a strange reddish color. Did that mean it was working? Could she produce fire from her hand?

"I need everyone behind me," Jerica said, as she rose to her feet and approached the open vent. The crucible was still glowing red, and it looked as though it would melt at any moment. However, the strange thing was, now she couldn't feel the heat. It was almost as if …

"Jerica!" her father scolded. "What are ye doin', girl? Don' touch that! Ye want to be scarred fer life? Put on a glove that … what are ye …? How the blazes are ye doin' that?"

Jerica had gingerly poked a finger at the crucible, and still feeling no heat whatsoever, had rested her entire palm on the scorching hot surface. Looking up at the ceiling, she smiled.

Thanks, Z.

What are you thanking me for? You're the one wielding the magic here.

Yes, but your magic is allowing me to handle fire. Can you see what I'm currently doing? I'll try and melt the jhorium now, just as soon as I see about finding some type of mold.

Mold? Skellig repeated. *Why would you want that? I realize we are different species, but I have yet to encounter anyone who thinks mold is a good thing.*

Mold, as in what you pour liquid metal into in order to obtain a predetermined shape.

Ah. Thank you for clarifying.

"Dad? I don't suppose you happen to have a mold of a plain goblet, do you?"

"Blast, girl. I hadn' thought o' that. Lemme look."

Hallis hurried over to his shelves and started pulling out bins.

"Cutlery, tools, spaulders, gauntlets. I don' see no … wait. Wait! Wha' 'bout this? Will it work?"

Jerica took the proffered mold and studied the design. It wasn't necessarily a goblet, but it was close. In fact, it looked like it could be a …?

"I've seen these types of cups before. Is it a chalice?"

"Aye. Made it fer Doolan earlier this year. He wanted … better not tell ye what it was fer. Forget I said anythin'."

Using the mold would result in a finished product that was just over eight inches tall, with a circular base of nearly four inches. The mouth of the cup measured in at fourteen inches at its widest point, while the bowl could hold at least sixteen ounces. It wasn't what she had envisioned, but someone could drink from it, so it would have to do.

"It'll work, thanks, Dad. Now, would all of you stand right there? In a semi-circle. I'd rather not show the others what I'm about to do."

"What *are* you going to do?" her mother nervously asked.

"I'm going to melt that bar," Jerica stated. At the same time, her hand became engulfed in flames.

Her mother cried out in alarm and rushed to help, but Hallis held her back.

"Look at her. J be wieldin' magic better than Doolan

'imself. That's our girl, love. Now, step back 'ere. I see what J wants. We need to block 'er line o' sight. J, we be ready."

Jerica nodded. Looking down at the strange green bar in the bottom of the melting pot, she envisioned a jet of fire blasting from her hand. Taking a deep breath, she angled herself so that any excess flames would be safely removed by one of the ceiling vents. Clenching her hand in a tight fist, she held it over the pot and opened it. A red-hot blast of flames slammed down into the pot. Flames poured out in all directions eliciting cries of alarm. Jerica repositioned herself, directing the fire away from the group and making it disappear harmlessly up the chimney vents.

The jhorium rippled once, then, without preamble, the bar melted into a small puddle of hot, molten metal.

"It's ready," Jerica declared, as she stepped away from the bowl, but frowned as soon as she noticed no one else was near. "Dad? Do you have the tongs? Can you move it closer to me, or … what's the matter?

"What do ye need tongs for, J? Can' ye just pick it up?"

Jerica's face sobered. "I forgot about that. Just a moment. Let me see. Good, it's not heavy. All right, Dad, can you tip the mold up? Clamps in place? Here we go."

"Nice an' easy, girl. Nice an' easy."

"Look at that! It's almost a perfect fit!" The amount of metal was just enough to fill the entire mold. "The base might be a little asymmetrical, but that's all right. This will do."

You're doing great, Jerica, Zeira praised. *What's the next step?*

"The mold has to cool," Jerica answered. "We can either let it cool on its own, or we could dunk it in a vat of water. Dad, what do you think?"

"Water has my vote."

Water hissed and steam collected around the ceiling as the mold cooled. Giving the metal a full ten minutes, switching vats several times, the mold was then pulled and placed on the floor. Hallis leaned down to unfasten the clamps holding both halves of the mold together.

"Well, wouldja look at that. Turned out purty, J."

"*It* turned out *pretty*, and you're right. It did."

Hallis was holding a sparkling, emerald-green cup that

could have been used at the most elegant of dinner settings. Jerica took the cup from her father and carried it over to the polishing wheel. Applying a liberal amount of polish, she pumped the pedal a few times, and buffed out the manufacturing marks left by the mold.

"Ooo, it's pretty," Theresa decided.

"And this is what you-know-who wants?"

"You shouldn't be afraid to say their names," Jerica scolded her brother-in-law. "He's just a man who has too much power at his fingertips. I'm going to start calling him by his name, and not his title."

"He has a name?" Theresa asked.

"Of course he does," Jerica replied. "Dinty. I forget which region he's king of, but ..."

"Spark," her father interrupted.

"Thanks, I knew that. What I meant was, we don't know which Spark region he's from."

"There's more than one?" Vyler asked, amazed.

Jerica shook her head. "We'll go into that later. For now, we have the goblet. Now, it's up to Doolan." It wasn't exactly like the one Zeira had described from her mystical vision, but with any luck it would do the job.

What about the scales? Skellig asked. *I know you don't want to give him any, but if you don't, he might not enchant the cup to do what we need it to do.*

I think I know what I need to do. I came up with a plan when I was standing over the melting pot. It could very well work.

Can you share it with us?

The human wizard approaches.

"What? Already?"

Her father looked her way. "Problem?"

"Doolan is on his way back."

Hallis immediately selected a hammer from a nearby rack. "Ready."

Jerica laughed, swatted her father on his arm, and placed the chalice on a nearby counter. Moments later, they heard the activity in the workshop come to a halt. One of the workers poked his head into their area.

"The mage is back."

Hallis nodded. "Thanks, mate. Send 'im back, would ye?"

"Why, hello, everyone," Doolan crooned, as he practically danced into the room. "How is everyone this fine day?"

"Someone be in a good mood."

"Someone *is* in a good mood, but not for long," Jerica muttered, under her breath. "Doolan. The cup is ready for you."

"Where is it? Oh, is that it? It's a pretty thing, isn't it? And this is using the metal the esteemed Thunder King desires so much?"

"It is, and ye can keep that to yerself," Hallis ordered.

Doolan waved a dismissive hand. "Where are my scales?"

Jerica shook her head. "First, the cup."

"That was not the agreement, young Jerica. Before I will perform any work, you *must* show me the scales."

"What are you going to use them for?" Jerica demanded. "Why would you risk helping us and incur the Thunder King's wrath unless it was something you truly wanted?"

"It is my business, and not yours," Doolan coolly informed her.

Jerica pretended to think for a few moments. "Do you know what? I think I've changed my mind. I know what your plans are for the scales."

"I highly doubt that, child."

"At first," Jerica continued, ignoring the mage, "I thought you wanted them so you could render yourself invisible, thus allowing you to live out your wildest desires with *whomever you want*. And honestly, I think that's what you originally planned to do."

Doolan had started to sweat. Beads of perspiration trickled down his wrinkled brow. "N-now, l-let's not be hasty. You don't …"

"Upon further examination of the scales, and after interrogating their owner, we learned about another aspect of their power: Othos' impressive visual abilities. He can actually single out every single person on this world and watch what they're doing, if he so chooses. Now, think what that kind of power would do in *your* hands. No, it cannot be allowed. I'll find another mage."

"There are none as powerful as I," Doolan feebly declared.

"In the rest of this region? Probably not. But, I'm not limited to this region anymore, am I? So, I'm sorry to have wasted your time, but the answer is going to be no. You can go now."

Doolan didn't budge.

"What if ... what if I enchanted your goblet without payment?"

"And why would ye do that, mage?" Hallis demanded. Jerica noticed the hammer was raised, as though he was planning on throwing it should the need arise. She gently pushed his arm down. "Ye've already made yer intentions clear. Ye won' be touchin' my girl, and ye won' be touchin' any other girl, either, is that clear?"

"Crystal, my dear Hallis. To prove my intentions are pure, let me do this for you. Hand me the cup. See? I can feel it brimming with power. That's the, er, jhorium, or raw power of the metal. Give this cup a simple task and ye will have the most sought after cup ever created." Doolan reached into a pocket.

Watch him closely, Gocri ordered. *I trust him not. One false move, just one, and he becomes lunch. I don't care what anyone says, he goes down the hatch.*

Jerica giggled, drawing a concerned look from her father.

The mage's eyes were closed, and he was clutching an object in one of his hands, but everyone could still see those arthritic hands tremble with fear. Clearly, Doolan didn't care for dragons at all.

Soft chanting filled the air. Doolan's hand opened, revealing a small, brightly colored sphere. An orb as blue as the outdoor sky pulsed in Doolan's hand, while his other was placed over the mouth of the goblet. For nearly ten minutes, the mage chanted. The orb flashed a final time and then vanished. Doolan turned triumphantly to Jerica and held the cup aloft.

"There we have it. A cup with the power to ... *suggest* a course of action, whether favorable or unfavorable. This cup has become a powerful talisman, and in doing so, needs to be registered with the Guild of Mages."

"Except, it's not, is it?" Jerica asked, in an innocent tone. "You have no intention of it. I certainly don't. Why bother saying that, then?"

"Am I that transparent?" Doolan finally asked, annoyed. "How is it you know so much?"

"Because, you *are* that transparent. Now, give me the cup."

"We need to test it first," Doolan insisted. "In case we need to change anything, we need to try it out."

Hallis pointed at a bucket of clean water on the counter where the chalice was originally sitting.

"There be water. Go ahead. You try it out first. We will give ye somethin' to do."

Doolan strode over to the bucket, ladled a spoonful of water into the chalice, and then held it out to Jerica.

"I invite you to be the first."

"Why? So you can get me to do something I typically wouldn't do?"

"Always so defensive," Doolan tsked. "Tell you what, I have an idea."

"I'm not going to like this, am I?" Jerica asked.

"Yes and no," Doolan said, shrugging. "I will hereby give this cup to you, free of charge of any service I have performed."

"In exchange fer …?" Hallis suspiciously asked.

"That Jerica will be the first to confirm — or deny — that the cup works."

Hallis pointed at the cup. "Hand it over. Ye won' be the one makin' my daughter do anythin', got it?"

"I imbued it with my power, so it should be me who gets to administer the questions, but since I'm trying to make amends, I will allow it."

Hallis looked at Jerica. "What do ye say?"

"If you're holding it, then I say we're fine," Jerica said. "Let's do it."

A smile formed on the mage's face. "Most excellent. If you will hand the cup to your lovely daughter, we can begin."

Hallis sniffed the contents, and when nothing could be detected, the blacksmith shrugged and passed the goblet to his daughter.

"Be careful, J. I still don' trust him."

Jerica took the cup and placed the brim to her lips, allowing a tiny trickle of water to enter her mouth. Swallowing carefully, she was about to put the cup down when she noticed the water inside had started bubbling. Doolan laughed, more like a cackle.

"Oh, I do hope you forgive me some day, my dear child. You may have deduced my plans for the scales, but you clearly never imagined what my true purpose was: this cup. With this chalice, I can command kings, assume the mantle of Guild Master of all Mages. I can …"

"I shoulda known not to trust ye, ye daft …"

"Drop that hammer and sit on the ground," Doolan ordered, his voice becoming stern. "In fact, all of you will do just that: have a seat on the floor."

Everyone dropped to the floor.

"What be this? Why can' I move? I'll clobber ye so hard, ye weasley imbecile, that I …"

"Shut up!" Doolan barked.

What's going on? Skellig demanded. *What is the wizard doing?*

I think he did something to the cup, Jerica said. *Vyler, my sister, and my parents are all doing everything he tells them to do.*

Which means the chalice is working, Zeira said. *We're on our way. Let's see that old fool try and enchant a dragon.*

"It's safe to say the cup works," Jerica said, using a surprisingly emotionless tone in her voice. "For that, I do thank you."

"And you, my dear, lovely Jerica. Why don't we start with … what's this? Why aren't you sitting with the others? No matter. You can start by removing that dress of yours. Perhaps I should send your parents away? I don't think they want to watch."

"Ye'll be nuthin' more than a bloody mess by the time I be done with ye," Hallis was saying. "This enchantment will wear off at some point, mage. When it does, so help me, ye will want …"

"You will not say another word," Doolan ordered. "None of you will."

Her father's mouth closed, and no matter how hard he tried, would not open again. Tears streamed out of her mother's eyes. As for Vyler, his were shooting daggers at the mage, but he, too, couldn't speak, no matter how much he frantically pawed at his mouth.

Doolan was about to smile and take a seat on the nearest stool when he noticed Jerica was still standing, with her arms folded across her chest.

"You will sit down."

Jerica ignored him and looked at Sif, who was, unfortunately, sitting on the ground. "Can't move?"

Sif shook her head.

Jerica calmly walked over to the counter, picked up the chalice, and up-ended it on the ground. Wiping the inside clean, she then dipped a second ladleful of water into the cup. She looked at Doolan and gave him the cup.

"I do believe it's your turn."

"And I do believe I said for you to sit down."

Jerica walked to a row of polished swords, hanging neatly on the wall, selected one, and resumed standing in front of Doolan once more. She hefted the sword and glared at the mage. Holding the sword up, as though she was going to decapitate him, Jerica took a single step.

"Why won't you sit?" Doolan cried. "Drop that sword! Sit down! Do as I say!"

Jerica unsnapped the bracer she wore on her right arm and held it up.

"I figured this mark might make me immune to most magic. Thankfully, I was right. Kairies are more powerful than I would have imagined. Now, you will take a sip from that cup, or so help me, your days of leering at young girls will be over. Indefinitely. In fact, it already is, but it'll be hard to ogle a person when you don't have your head, won't it?"

Doolan's eyes widened with fright. He frantically started rummaging through his robes. Taking two steps, Jerica placed the tip of her sword against his chest.

"Last chance."

"All right! Here, look, I'm taking a sip! How did you know I spiked the water?"

"Because I know *you*. Now, release my family and friends."

"Get up," Doolan automatically ordered. "You're no longer under my power."

"How do I know you still don't have some type of hold over them?"

Doolan tried to keep his mouth closed, but it refused to obey. "Oh, that's because I do. Until I break the spell, they will remain under my power."

It was Jerica's turn to pull a stool over and sit down.

"This is fun. Tell me, mage, how would you break the spell?"

"I simply say the trigger word and knock three times."

"Do it."

His eyes were livid with rage, but Doolan had no choice but to obey. He reached over to the counter and knocked three times.

"Corsets."

"Will they fall back under your spell?" Jerica asked.

"No, not unless I can plant another spell inside that goblet, like I did the first time."

"What were you planning on doing with the scales?"

Beads of sweat were now pouring down the mage's face as he struggled to fight the enchantment. "To watch girls undress."

Vyler squawked with outrage, as did Hallis and Nyssa.

"You disgusting piece of filth!" Theresa cried.

"Does the Thunder King know we have the jhorium?" Jerica asked.

"Yes."

"How?"

"I told him."

"What did he say?"

"I didn't talk to him personally. I only sent a message. What are you going to do with me?"

Make him suffer, Skellig ordered.

Tell him to jump into the jaws of the white dragon, Gocri said.

Send him off in a boat, Nuri added.

"Here's what's going to happen, Doolan," Jerica began. "Beginning now, if you so much as *think* about doing something unsavory to an unwilling female, your testicles are going to burn with the fiery passion of a thousand suns. The only way you will get them to stop burning will be to jump into the nearest body of water and stay there, for a minimum of an hour. Each consecutive violation will add an hour to that time, is that understood?"

Doolan closed his eyes and seethed.

"Favor me with a response."

"I ... understand."

"Now, this is where you really need to pay attention. You *were* a lousy mage, a blight on our village. Now, you're not. Should you act against anyone who requests your help, or disrespect them in any fashion, you will promptly seek out the closest dragon and throw yourself into their mouth. Is that understood?"

"Y-y-yes."

"What'll happen if you charge too much for powder?"

"I w-will get eaten by dragons."

"And if you ignore a villager's request for help?"

"I will get eaten by a dragon."

"And if you try to take advantage of a young girl?"

"Then, my t-t-t-testicles will burn and I will have to j-jump into a large body of w-water."

"Good."

"Can I go now?"

"Not yet. There's one last thing I need from you."

Doolan sighed heavily. "What do you want me to do?"

"You will forget we have this cup."

Nice, Skellig chuckled.

Clever, Zeira agreed.

"The only thing you will remember is that the jhorium was taken from Cael, and that there's absolutely no point to bringing another Cerebus here. Understand?"

Doolan was seething so hard that little flecks of spit collected on his upper lip, as if he was foaming at the mouth.

"Let's just make sure this sinks in." She presented the goblet to Doolan. "Take another sip for me."

His eyes flashed fire, and his lips peeled back in a snarl, but he was powerless to resist. Once he had taken his second sip, and handed the cup back, Jerica smiled.

"What's going to happen once you leave this shop?"

"I will … forget about the cup."

"Who has the jhorium?"

"I won't remember."

"If the Thunder King asks whether or not a second Cerebus should be shipped out here?"

"I will advise against it," Doolan sullenly answered.

"Who destroyed Cerebus?" Vyler asked.

Doolan didn't answer.

"Who destroyed Cerebus?" Jerica repeated.

"I … I don't know."

Jerica turned to her family. "I think we're done here."

Chapter 15 — Kai

Spirits were high the following day. The chalice had been deemed a brilliant success, especially since it had been tested on none other than Doolan himself. Vyler reported the mage had gone straight to his private workshop after leaving Hallis' forge yesterday, where he proceeded to have a full-blown temper tantrum, resulting in many smashed items and the frequent use of foul language. However, when the village militia appeared and demanded to know what he was doing, Doolan was unable to tell them anything other than he was having a bad day.

Jerica, her sister and brother-in-law, her parents, and all five dragons—Othos was mysteriously absent once again—gathered one last time at Kinzler's Point, in preparation for their departure.

Jerica's parents were giving her last-minute instructions, with an occasional directive toward one—or all—of the dragons.

"What are ye gonna do when ye get there?" Hallis was asking. "No, wait. Don' tell me. I don' wanna know. Jus' know that we got yer backs here, in Cael."

"You *have* our backs," Jerica corrected, giving her father a tender smile. "And it means the world. Do you think Doolan will find some way to wreak havoc against you?"

"Let 'im try. I've always wanted t' thunk that there bastard good."

"I'm not going to even try with that one," Jerica giggled. "Mom, it's up to you to keep an eye on him."

"Oh, I will," Nyssa vowed.

Her sister stepped forward and embraced her in a fierce hug.

"You have no idea what we went through when we saw you disappear from that terrible altar. I've half a mind to tell Vyler it needs to be torn down. No more sacrifices."

"You needn't worry about that," a voice said, overhearing the comment.

Theresa, Jerica, and their mother, Nyssa, collectively turned to see who had spoken. Nuri was shaking her head.

"Once I realized the true nature of that device, and the fact that there was but one purpose for it, I decided to get rid of it."

"You destroyed it!" Jerica exclaimed.

"Every last piece of it," Nuri confirmed. "There will be no more deaths. But, if the humans take it upon themselves to construct another, I will be there to destroy it."

"Good for you," Skellig said, nodding. "Now, let's see. Goblet?"

"Check," Jerica confirmed.

"Programmed?" Sif added.

"Confirmed," Jerica said, smiling.

"Kai?"

"Present and accounted for! All right, my turn. Is everyone here? Zeira?"

"I'm here."

"Skellig?"

"I am ready."

"Nuri?"

"I'm ready."

"Gocri?"

"Ready, Miss Jerica."

"Sif?"

"Always."

"Othos? Oh, just kidding. I know you're not here."

"I am here," Othos' voice stated, drawing gasps of surprise from humans.

"Where have you been this time?" Jerica good-naturedly asked, not really expecting an answer.

"Determining that your next course of action, should you choose to act upon it, will be your last."

Suddenly, it was so quiet that only the lapping of waves could be heard. One by one, everyone turned to Othos, who was standing, motionless, in the sea.

Zeira found her voice first. She stepped forward and stared.

"I don't suppose you'd care to elaborate?"

When Othos didn't volunteer any additional details, Skellig cleared his throat. When the sun dragon turned to make eye contact, Skellig sat back on his haunches and put his hands on his hips, in a very uncharacteristic human pose.

"I do believe you need to clarify. We have everything we need. The jhorium has been found. I even think we've managed to convince the Thunder King to dig elsewhere."

"The cup has been made," Zeira continued, "and has been enchanted to make others do as they're told. What are we missing?"

"A viable plan," Othos said, raising his voice. "Should the lot of you head out now, you will be doomed from the start."

"How so?" Zeira asked.

"Am I to understand that your group believes it's ready to confront the Thunder King?" Othos asked, as he looked at each member of their group. "You all need a great many more preparations before you have a chance at becoming victorious. Meeting up with him now would end up ... that is to say, you would end up ..."

"... getting massacred," Skellig guessed. "Fine, if this is so blatantly obvious, why didn't you tell us before?"

"It's because I just found out," Othos answered.

"*How* did you find out?" Jerica wanted to know.

Othos took several steps forward and then lowered himself to the ground. "Because I was given some reputable advice."

A very familiar face appeared. He was grinning, covered with wrinkles, and his hair was long and stringy, tied back in ponytail. His face was clean-shaven and he was wearing traveling clothes consisting of a dark blue tunic and black trousers. Various daggers and tools were strapped to his belt. Belying his age, the white-haired rider nimbly leapt off Othos' back and landed on the ground. He turned to Jerica and bowed.

"Zebulon!" Jerica cried, shocked. "What …? How …? Were you on his back? Oh! Are you a kai?"

"I am, indeed, young Jerica. How nice it is to see you all again! Sif, you're looking fantastic. No problems with your shapeshifting?"

Sif smiled at the ancient human. "None whatsoever. I have you to thank for that."

"J? Who be this?" Hallis inquired.

Zebulon turned to Hallis and bowed again. "Ah, you'd be Jerica's father, wouldn't you? And, of course, this lovely lady must be her mother, Nyssa. A pleasure to meet you both. Who else do we have here?"

Jerica introduced her family to the seer she'd met in Ponotoa.

Vyler grasped the seer's forearm and gave it a shake. "You are welcome here, Zebulon. And Ponotoa, isn't that the name of the city where …?"

"Yes, Cerebus visited it not that long ago and left utter destruction in its wake."

Zeb nodded, and let out a heavy sigh. "Too true, my dear girl, too true. Heard the beast paid Cael a visit, too, and you had better luck preventing the destruction than I did. I can only imagine you and your fine companions had something to do with it?"

We did, Skellig confirmed.

"Hello, Skellig," Zeb said, as he looked over at the Spark

dragon. "And Gocri, and Nuri, and Zeira. Your group has made tremendous strides, haven't you? And you, Miss Jerica. You've no doubt discovered, by now, your powers are growing?"

"You knew they would?" Jerica countered. "Why didn't you say something?"

"Oh, dear child, don't you remember how timid you were? How do you think you would have responded had I said your magic would soon be stronger than a mage's?"

"It's stronger than a mage's?" Jerica repeated, amazed.

"Ye melted that bar," Hallis reminded her. "I watched as yer blessed hand burned, J, and ye didn' have so much as a scratch on ye. *That* be power, girl."

"Your father is right," Zeb said, nodding. "Be that as it may, as powerful as you are, or as powerful as all of you are together, you're still not ready to face your adversary. There are things you simply don't know. Yet."

"Like what?" Skellig asked, growing uneasy.

"New alliances are being forged," Zebulon said, sighing. "King Dinty has realized his attempts to kill you have failed, so he's rushing to protect himself the only way he knows how: with threats and intimidation. One of you will definitely not like what I'm about to say, but I'm sorry, it has to be said. Dinty has assumed control of the valthans."

"What?" Nuri exclaimed. "How could he … why would he want to .. how did this happen?"

"We don't know, my dear valthan. Othos and I have spent the last two days in trying to determine what leverage Dinty has over them."

"Two days," Jerica said, nodding. "Is that when you and Othos found each other again?"

Zebulon nodded. "It is. I can't thank you enough for awakening Othos for me. I have been looking for him for so long that I was starting to worry he had vanished."

"In a way, I had," Othos said. "I fell asleep and turned into a mountain, remember?"

"Imagine my surprise," Zeb continued, "when, two days ago, I felt my old companion's presence in my mind once more. My dear Othos had returned! After so many centuries had passed, we were together again. It was like the old times once more."

"Several centuries?" Vyler asked, amazed. "H-how old are you?"

"Excessively older than you, my dear boy," Zeb said, with a cryptic smile. "Now, back to business. Dinty has the valthans under his thumb. I don't know how, but I guarantee you Othos and I will not let the matter drop. We *must* find whatever leverage he has and remove it."

"I couldn't agree more," Nuri said. "I cannot let my fellow valthans suffer under his rule."

"How many valthans are there?" Skellig curiously asked.

"We number in the thousands," Nuri reported. "Over four, I believe."

"Four thousand?" Skellig repeated, thunderstruck. "As in, four thousand of you swimming around in the open seas? I never imagined."

"My element is the most prolific," Nuri reminded everyone. "There is more room for us, and there is plenty to eat in the sea. It really isn't any surprise there are so many of us."

"I'm more concerned if the valthans are now doing the Thunder King's bidding," Zeira groaned.

"Has your queen become bewitched?" Gocri asked.

"There's more than one queen," Nuri announced.

"One for each city."

"City?" Jerica repeated. "The valthans have cities?"

"Four of them," Nuri confirmed. "Like with any species, not all of us choose to live in such close proximity to others, but many do."

"Do you?" Skellig wanted to know.

"No. Maybe. I don't know."

"Is this really what's important right now?" Vyler asked. "Thunder King is marshalling his forces. We need to have a plan."

Jerica looked up. "Zeira, I know I have no business suggesting a course of action, but I think what we need to do is obvious."

"Deal with the enslaved valthans."

"Exactly. If we're going to take on Thunder King, er, King Dinty, we need to strip him of any excess powers."

Zebulon's eyes widened with alarm. "We have a new problem, I'm afraid."

"What is it?" Vyler asked. "Do I need to alert the militia?"

"This foe is more than a match for you, baron, and any other human foolish enough to stand in his way. Skellig, be prepared, my good Spark dragon. Your sire will be here in less than ten seconds."

"Again? Blast it all to the heavens and back. How many are with him this time?"

"It's only him," the seer reported.

Jerica looked relieved. "Oh, then that shouldn't be too bad. We were able to hold him off last time."

"He returns without any support?" Skellig was saying. "There is something we do not know. I trust this not."

"Good for you, Skellig," Zebulon praised, "and you shouldn't. Dym is far craftier than anyone believes. I don't trust this, either."

Skellig spread his wings and launched himself into the air.

I'll deal with this, Skellig said, not bothering to hide the urgency in his voice.

"I'm right there with you," Gocri promised.

Othos, you see no one else but Dym?

Correct, Skellig.

What is he playing at? Skellig growled. *We defeated him before. He must know that, together, we're formidable and quite capable of defeating him again. Something has changed.*

"Your instincts serve you well," Zebulon said, nodding. "He's here."

A load roar ripped through the air. Villagers were screaming out calls for the militia. Doors slammed as people sought cover indoors. Hallis gathered Jerica's group together and herded them toward his shop. Once inside, Hallis snapped his fingers to get his workers' attention.

"Lads? We jus' closed. See to the windows. Secure 'em up tight! I wan' no unwanted intruders in here."

There were grunts of acknowledgements. Sturdy wood shutters were swung into place and bolted down. The main shop entrance was closed, and a second, heavier door was pushed into place. Once it, too, was securely locked into position, Hallis looked at his wife and pointed deeper into the shop.

"I wan' the four of ye in the cellar, now. No arguments, jus' go!"

Dym must have passed over their area once more, because another roar sounded, followed by a score of screams and shouts.

"I have to get outside!" Jerica insisted. "I need to see if I can help Skellig!"

"Ye'll do no such thing, girl," Hallis declared, as he pushed Theresa, Vyler, and his wife toward the vent Jerica had used earlier when she tried to melt the jhorium bar. Stomping down on an unmarked floorboard, Hallis grabbed the corner and pulled, revealing a narrow staircase leading down. "Stay down there until I say ev'rythin' is safe. Understand? Jerica, what the blazes are ye doin', girl? Get back here!"

Jerica had turned the moment her father had his back to her, signaled for two of the workers to open the door, and dashed out the moment it was opened.

Hallis singled out Sif and pointed at the door. "Don' just stand there, dragon. Git on out there! Protect her!"

Sif nodded and hurried out. Within moments, the vapor dragon assumed her natural form and took to the air in an attempt to locate their kai.

"What do you want, Dym?" Skellig asked, as he circled high above Cael in a lazy circle. "I know you've come alone. Foolish, but intelligence is not something you're known for, is it?"

"I should've ripped your throat out when I had the chance," a loud, angry voice hissed.

"You won't get the opportunity ever again," Skellig said, raising his own voice. "What do you want?"

"Call off your ice pet, or …"

"His name is Gocri, and you would do well to remember it."

"Fine. Send Gocri away. I just want to talk."

"I'm not going anywhere," Gocri's gravelly voice responded.

"You will if you want to take down the Thunder King," Dym argued.

"Why should I listen to you?" Skellig asked. He had just dipped his left wing to circle about the village once more when he caught sight of his sire's long green tail, disappearing into a cloud bank. "Do you expect me to believe you want to help?"

"I never said I wanted to help you," Dym snarled, "but I do have information you will want to sink your talons into. If you want it, you have to come to me. Alone."

"Don't even think about this," Gocri said. "He's clearly trying to trick you."

I know he is, Skellig told his friend, switching to their mental connection, to keep their conversation private. *Can we afford not to investigate any and all leads? Return to Zeira. I can handle this.*

I trust this not, Gocri insisted.

I know, my friend. Nor do I. Just stay as close as you can.

Will do.

Gocri banked left and disappeared from sight.

"Where's the other one?" Dym growled. "Where's fire?"

"She's safe. She's protecting our kai. Now, speak. What do you want?"

"I propose an exchange."

"An exchange? With you? Not interested."

"Hear me out. Thunder King wants information about your kai. You will want the information I have, so I propose we settle this the honorable way."

"You wouldn't know honor if it came up and bit you on your tail," Skellig scoffed.

"A contest," Dym continued. "To see who the better dragon is. The winner will be given the information the loser possesses. Now, do we have a deal?"

Absolutely not, Zeira stated. *There's no way you can trust him.*

Agreed, Gocri added. *Until his motives are known, we cannot place Jerica, or any information about her, in peril.*

"What kind of contest?" Skellig suspiciously asked.

Don't ignore us, Zeira implored. *We don't trust this!*

"A simple set of challenges, to see which of us is the

better dragon. It's time to step up … *underling*. You've always said you're better than me. Prove it. Let's see if you can outfly me."

"And how would that be determined?" Skellig wanted to know.

Do not do this! This is undoubtedly a trick!

"Less than an hour north is a series of rock formations rising out of the sea," Dym said, as he automatically turned north. "They have peculiar shapes, with some nearly a hundred feet tall. This would be the perfect setting to see how well you fare under duress."

"Are you suggesting that, once one of us is flying through this … this course, that the other will be trying to hit them?"

"We have to make it challenging somehow," Dym said. His voice lowered to a delighted hiss. "You're scared, aren't you? You're afraid you'll be bested, admit it!"

Jerica, do you know of the formations he's talking about?

Yes! We call them the Tentacles of Tyrrus. You'll see how they got their name, trust me. We figure they were made by underwater volcanic vents years and years ago. Dym is right. They have some very unusual shapes and can get very tall.

Is it safe to fly?

Absolutely not! You shouldn't even think about trying your luck, Skellig. Promise me you won't.

"So, if I fly through these formations, and manage to avoid being hit, what are you proposing to offer as an enticement?"

Skellig… Don't ignore us! We're worried about you!

"How does revealing the source of Thunder King's powers sound to you?"

"Now, why would you do that?" Skellig asked. "Won't your human master take offense to you divulging his secrets?"

"What he doesn't know, can't bite him later. Do we have a deal or not?"

"How do I know whether your information is valid?"

"You're just going to have to trust me."

"And you're going to have to do better than that," Skellig sneered. "In all of our history together, at what point in time would I ever trust you?"

"Because you can't resist a good challenge," Dym noted. His green form suddenly appeared next to Skellig and, together, they flew northward, as if each knew that's where they were going to end up. "Are you telling me you'd pass up the chance to see if you're better than me? Come on, Skellig. Let's test your skills. Let's see if you have what it takes to beat me."

I'm telling you, Zeira was saying, *this is a poor idea.*

Agreed, Gocri said.

He's playing you, Sif added.

We have more pressing matters to attend to, Nuri implored. *He's taunting you. Don't fall for it!*

"Very well," Skellig hissed. His lips had curled back in a snarl and his fangs were bared. "We will settle this once and for all. When you lose, you will remove yourself from my life *after* you've told me everything you know about the human who calls himself Thunder King. You will disclose the nature of his power, what the source is, and how to defeat him."

"And you," Dym hissed back, "after you lose, you will tell me all about your precious kai. Who she is, what she can do, and the secret to her power. Are we agreed?"

"Agreed. After you."

"You may go first."

"With you on my tail? Not a chance. You will remain out front where I can see you at all times."

"So be it."

Are we going to allow this? Nuri's voice asked.

This is between Skellig and his sire, Othos interjected. *There is bad blood between them. It would be best to let them resolve this on their own.*

We will still be nearby, Zeira vowed. *When Dym cheats, and we all know he will,* we *will be there to support Skellig.*

This isn't necessary, Skellig's voice said. *I'll be perfectly fine.*

You're taking unnecessary risks, Zeira scolded. *Your sire is playing with you, and he's winning.*

Not for long, he isn't.

Nearly an hour later, Skellig was flying over the strange formations he'd soon be flying *through.* Below him, stretching out of the sea was a series of long black shapes, comprised of igneous rock. The rock *tentacles* stretched out, up, away, and even back into the sea. Rising to heights of one hundred-fifty feet, the formations spread out over five square miles.

"Whenever you're ready," Dym said, throwing enough of a sneer into his voice to warrant a low growl from Skellig.

Skellig shook his head. "First, the ground rules. There will be no ambushing. No hiding behind a larger formation, or approaching from the opposite direction. Second, the pursuer will maintain an altitude of at least three hundred feet at all times. Next, if a strike is made, the pursuer will wait until given permission to proceed. And finally, there will be no targeting of the rocks themselves. The pursuer agrees to not use the formations as weapons. Violation of any of these terms will immediately cause the pursuer to forfeit. Is that understood?"

"So many rules," Dym taunted. "Does it make you feel any better when you specify an escape avenue should things go poorly for you? Let's face it, you know they will."

"I don't think I've ever noticed that about you before."

Dym turned to look at him. "What?"

"I don't remember you being so afraid. Who's done that to you? This human king?"

"I am *not* afraid."

"Good, let's hope not. I wouldn't want to spoil the fun by ending your run too soon."

Stop baiting him, Zeira pleaded. *Just finish this and be done with him.*

"Are you ready?" Dym asked again. His wing talons sparked with anticipation.

"The contest begins once I pass those two pillars. After that, it'll be finished when I fly out the opposite side."

"Agreed."

Skellig ... Jerica sobbed.

I'll be fine, Jerica. Trust me.

Skellig flew low, out over the open water. Circling about, he targeted the two towering pillars directly in his path and started flapping his wings. Casting his eyes skyward, he saw his sire maintaining the pace directly above him.

The moment he banked and flew *sideways* through the two

pillars, time seemed to stand still. Righting himself and then executing a hard left turn, he zipped under a formation with a low opening no higher than thirty feet above the surface. Skellig skimmed through and made another sharp turn, just as a jagged bolt of lightning slammed into the water barely ten feet from his wing.

Twisting and turning, zigzagging from one formation to the next, Skellig managed to stay one step ahead of Dym for the entire duration of the exercise. Every time Dym fired a blast, and it would inevitably miss, he'd roar with frustration. At the end, the green Spark dragon had to admit he had yet to score a hit.

"I didn't think you had it in you. However, it doesn't mean you won. You've yet to land a strike on me, and you had better believe it'll stay that way."

"After you. You do realize that all I have to do to win this wager is tag you once, don't you?"

"It'll never happen, underling."

"Let's find out."

From the moment Dym began his run, Skellig knew that landing a shot was inevitable. His sire's boasts were nothing but empty threats. He wasn't moving as fast, his speed was nowhere close to his own, and he simply wasn't able to anticipate which direction to move after dodging one of his offspring's lightning strikes.

The end of the course was nearing. Dym furiously flapped his wings as he strained his body to reach the end. Flying overhead, Skellig saw the three pillars in his path and instinctively knew how his sire was going to navigate the obstacle, probably before even Dym did. Charging up one of his talons — Skellig figured he'd only need the one — he waited until Dym had cleared the first before he predicted where Dym would be next, and fired off a shot.

The bolt of lightning struck Dym square on the back, eliciting a roar of disbelief. While Skellig was sure the strike probably stung, it was nothing compared to the blow to his sire's ego, to be outdone and outmaneuvered by his own offspring.

Dym exited the formations and, breathing heavily,

adjusted his course so that he was flying toward Skellig.

Skellig! Othos' concerned voice shouted. *Get clear! He's about to …*

Skellig's eyes widened. Leaving no time to react, Dym collided with Skellig in midair. A brilliant flash of light, an ear-shattering explosion. When the light finally died down, both Skellig and Dym were gone.

What happened to him? Zeira sounded worried.

I don't see him anywhere, Othos sullenly reported.

What were you trying to warn him about? Gocri asked.

All three dragons emerged from their hiding places among the clouds; Gocri dipped low and inspected the rock formations as he flew over.

"Are these things made of a reactive mineral?"

"To answer your question, they're made of ice," Othos said. "It's clear that Dym planned the collision to trigger a spell. My friends, Skellig has been taken!"

Don't miss the exciting conclusion in

Crash the Thunder
(Dragons of Andela #3)

AUTHOR'S NOTE

Now, that's more like it. A story that doesn't take me nearly two years to finish. This one went—as expected—a lot faster, and you'll be pleased to know I've already started jotting down ideas for the next one, namely *Crash the Thunder*.

Next up for me is a return to Pomme Valley, for Zack and the dogs' next adventure, *Case of the Rusty Sword*. Then, it's time for yet another return trip when we go back to Lentari in *Blast from the Past* (Tales of Lentari #10). I'm really looking forward to getting that one done. And finally, rounding out the year, will be CCF#17, *Case of the Unlucky Emperor*. When will I get to Dragons of Andela #3? I'm hoping to squeeze it in this fall, so stay tuned to the blog. I'll keep you guys posted.

If you like audiobooks, and are willing to leave a (hopefully good) review, feel free to reach out to me and see if I have any promo codes. Audible gives me a certain number, with the stipulation that whomever uses the code leaves a review, so let me know. I'll see if I can hook you up.

As always, any news about me or the books can be found on my official blog, or will be sent out through my newsletter. Haven't signed up yet? Scan the QR code to go to the signup page.

Finally, if you enjoyed the book, I would encourage you to leave a review wherever you purchased it. The more positive reviews, the easier other readers can find me in all the major online retailers. That's all for now! Until next time, happy reading!

J.
March, 2022

FAN SUBMISSIONS

Thanks to the help of some fans & readers, several characters in this book have some unique names!

Vanze — Vance Schollmeyer
Skellig — Kate Craven
Doolan — Elizabeth Davis
Gocri — Robert Allen Chalk
Zeira — Caryl Nantze
Akainu, Dym — Andrew Dyer
Sifula, Hamish — Carol Minot
Nuri — Nicki Jones
Myrdaynth — Justin Morgan
Darazok Aeogan — Kimberley Richardson
Brenin Draig — Claire Jones
Zebulon — Jennifer Salmon
Aldebrand — Mechelle Salyers
Konungr — Yuliya Mulvaney
Brakkis — Justin Morgan
Ligeia — Julie Granger

ABOUT THE AUTHOR

Jeffrey M. Poole lived in picturesque southern Oregon with his wife Giliane, and their dog, Kinsey the corgi. He is the best-selling author of cozy mystery series Corgi Case Files and of fantasy series Bakkian Chronicles, Tales of Lentari, and the Dragons of Andela. Jeffrey's interests include astronomy, archaeology, archery, scuba diving, collecting movies, playing retro video games, and tinkering with any electronic gadget he can get his hands on.

He is also a member of SFWA, the Science Fiction & Fantasy Writers of America, and MWA, Mystery Writers of America. Scan the QR code to sign up for his free newsletter..

Books by Jeffrey Poole

Epic Fantasy
BAKKIAN CHRONICLES
The Prophecy
Insurrection
Amulet of Aria
Disneyland Debacle (short story)
Winter Wonderland (short story)

TALES OF LENTARI
Lost City
Something Wyverian This Way Comes
A Portal for Your Thoughts
Thoughts for A Portal
Wizard in the Woods
Close Encounters of the Magical Kind
The Hunt for Red Oskorlisk (short story)
May the Fang Be With You (Pirates trilogy #1)
The Hammer is Strong with This One (Pirates #2)
These are Not the Stones You're Looking For (Pirates #3)
Blast from the Past

DRAGONS OF ANDELA

Harness the Fire
Strike the Spark
Crash the Thunder

Mystery
CORGI CASE FILES

Case of the One-Eyed Tiger
Case of the Fleet-Footed Mummy
Case of the Holiday Hijinks
Case of the Pilfered Pooches
Case of the Muffin Murders
Case of the Chatty Roadrunner
Case of the Highland House Haunting
Case of the Ostentatious Otters
Case of the Dysfunctional Daredevils
Case of the Abandoned Bones
Case of the Great Cranberry Caper
Case of the Shady Shamrock
Case of the Ragin' Cajun
Case of the Missing Marine
Case of the Stuttering Parrot
Case of the Rusty Sword
Case of the Secret Staircase (short story)
Case of the Unlucky Emperor
Case of the Ice Cream Crime
Case of the Hobbit Heist

www.ingramcontent.com/pod-product-compliance
Lightning Source LLC
Chambersburg PA
CBHW020602110726
47899CB00002B/335